P9-DDX-455

Vincent pulled the front door open.

"Vincent Argeneau?" the woman asked.

When he nodded, she stuck out her hand. "I'm Jackie Morrisey and this is Tiny McGraw. I believe Bastien called you about us?"

Vincent stared at her hand but—rather than take it—pushed the door closed and lifted the phone back to his ear as he turned away. "Bastien, she's *mortal!*"

"Did you just slam the door in Jackie's face?" Bastien asked with amazement. "I heard the slam, Vincent. Don't be so damned rude."

"*Hello!*" he said impatiently. "She's *mortal.* Bad enough she's female, but I need someone who knows about our 'special situation' to deal with this problem. She—"

"Jackie *does* know," Bastien said dryly. "Do you think I'd send you an uninitiated mortal? Have a little faith." A sigh traveled down the phone line. "She has a bit of an attitude when it comes to our kind, but is the best in the business. Now open the door for the woman."

"But she's mortal and . . . a girl!"

By Lynsay Sands

A BITE TO REMEMBER
A QUICK BITE

LYNSAY SANDS

A Bite To Remember

AVON BOOKS
An Imprint of HarperCollinsPublishers

AVON BOOKS
An Imprint of HarperCollins*Publishers*
10 East 53rd Street
New York, New York 10022-5299

Copyright © 2006 by Lynsay Sands
The Care and Feeding of Unmarried Men copyright © 2006 by Christie Ridgway; *Her Officer and Gentleman* copyright © 2006 by Karen Hawkins; *A Bite to Remember* copyright © 2006 by Lynsay Sands; *Never A Lady* copyright © 2006 by Jacquie D' Alessandro
ISBN-13: 978-0-06-077407-3
ISBN-10: 0-06-077407-X
www.avonromance.com

First Avon Books paperback printing: July 2006

Avon Trademark Reg. U.S. Pat. Off. and in Other Countries, Marca Registrada, Hecho en U.S.A.
HarperCollins® is a registered trademark of HarperCollins Publishers Inc.

Printed in the U.S.A.

10 9 8 7 6 5 4 3 2 1

One

"Vincent? Are you there? If you're there, pick up the phone."

Vincent Argeneau forced one eyelid upward and peered around the dark room. His home office, he saw, managing to make out the shape of his desk by the sliver of light coming through the door cracked open to the hallway. He'd fallen asleep on the couch in his office.

"Vincent?"

"Yeah?" He sat up and glanced around for the owner of that voice, then realized it was coming through his answering machine on the desk. Giving his head a shake, Vincent got to his feet and stumbled across the room. He snatched up the cordless phone, dropped into his desk chair, and growled, "Bastien?"

"Vincent? Sorry to wake you, cousin. I waited as late as I could before calling."

Vincent grunted and leaned back in the chair, running his free hand over his face. "What time is it?"

"Five P.M. here in New York. I guess that makes it about two there in L.A.," Bastien said apologetically.

"Two," Vincent muttered. No wonder he was exhausted. He'd been up until 9 A.M. dealing with phone calls, then had drawn the blackout curtains in the room and lain down on the couch here rather than go to his bed. He hadn't wanted to miss Bastien's call.

"Are you awake?"

"Yeah." Vincent scrubbed his hand over his face again, then reached out to turn on his desk lamp. Blinking in the increased light, he said, "I'm up. Were you able to get a hold of that private detective company you said was so good?"

"That's why I couldn't call any later than this. They're on their way. In fact, their plane was scheduled to land at LAX fifteen minutes ago."

"Jesus!" Vincent sat up abruptly in his seat. "That was fast."

"Jackie doesn't waste time. I explained the situation to her and she booked a flight right away. Fortunately for you, she'd just finished a big job for me and was able to put off and delegate whatever else she had on the roster."

"Wow," Vincent murmured, then frowned as he realized what Bastien had said. "She? The detective's a woman?"

"Yes, and she's good. Really good. She'll track down your saboteur and have this whole thing cleaned up in no time."

"If you say so," Vincent said quietly. "Thanks, Bastien. I appreciate it."

"Not a problem. Happy to help."

2

Vincent opened his mouth to speak, then paused as he heard a woman's muffled voice in the background. He began to grin. "Is that Terri?"

"Yes. She says hello, and says to warn you—" He paused to clear his throat. "Er . . . Vincent, mother is on her way out there too."

"What?" Vincent stood abruptly. The news was rather shocking. Aunt Marguerite hadn't visited his home in decades. Usually, he visited her in Canada. She'd chosen the worst possible time to decide to visit sunny California. "Why?"

"Er . . . well, that's a funny thing really." Bastien gave a nervous laugh. "It seems she's come to the conclusion that you may be lonely and depressed."

"What!" Vincent gaped at the phone.

"Yeah. She thinks your being here in New York and witnessing Terri and I getting together—as well as seeing my siblings with their life mates—may have upset you, your still being single and all. She seems to think you may need cheering up or maybe some help seeing to the situation."

"Dear God," Vincent muttered, raking one hand through his hair.

"Yeah, I thought you might feel that way," Bastien said sympathetically. "I did try to dissuade her from going, but . . . You know how my mother is once she gets an idea into her head."

"Dear God," Vincent repeated.

"She's on a later flight," Bastien informed him. "She won't arrive until six o'clock your time and she's arranged for a car rental so you won't have to pick her up."

3

"Does she know about what's going on here?"

"No," Bastien said. "And unless you want her interfering, I suggest you not tell her."

Vincent gave a bark of laughter. Interfere was an understatement. If Marguerite Argeneau knew someone was sabotaging her nephew's business, she'd be determined to track them down and sort it out. She was very protective of those she loved and he was fortunate enough to count himself in that category.

"Dear God," he said unhappily.

"Just stick her in a guest room, give her a bunch of tourist pamphlets, and let her entertain herself," Bastien suggested. "She'll get bored and move on eventually."

Vincent grimaced, thinking nothing was ever that easy. "I'm guessing I wasn't expected to pick up this Jackie and . . ." He paused, trying to recall the second name Bastien had mentioned.

"Tiny," he supplied. "No, they'll have a rental too. Otherwise I'd have called sooner."

"Right." Vincent sighed.

"I'm guessing you probably have about half an hour before they get there. I figured that was enough time to get ready."

"Yeah," Vincent agreed.

"Okay. I guess I'll let you go wake yourself up before they arrive."

"Yeah, okay. Hey, tell Terri—" Vincent paused and glanced toward the hallway as a knock sounded at his front door. Frowning, he stood and headed out of the office, taking the cordless phone with him. "Hang on. There's someone at the door."

"That's probably the package I sent out for Mom," Bastien said. "If so, you'll have to get it in the refrigerator right away."

"Must be nice having your meals prepared and delivered," Vincent said dryly as he walked up the hall.

"We'll eventually sort that out too, cousin," Bastien said quietly, and Vincent felt guilty for bellyaching. Bastien had set his scientists to work on finding a cure for his problem years ago. If there wasn't one yet, it wasn't for lack of trying.

"Is it the blood?" Bastien asked as Vincent pulled the front door open.

"Umm . . . no," he answered, his gaze running over the duo on the marble step before him. He'd never set eyes on such an unlikely pair. The woman was blond, the man a brunette. She was extremely short and curvy, he was a great behemoth of a man who stood well over six feet. She was dressed in a black business suit with a crisp white blouse underneath, he wore casual cords and a sweater in pale cream. They were a study in contrasts.

"Vincent Argeneau?" the woman asked.

When he nodded, she stuck out her hand. "I'm Jackie Morrisey and this is Tiny McGraw. I believe Bastien called you about us?"

Vincent stared at her hand, but—rather than take it—pushed the door closed and lifted the phone back to his ear as he turned away. "Bastien, she's *mortal*!"

"Did you just slam the door in Jackie's face?" Bastien asked with amazement. "I heard the slam, Vincent. Jesus! Don't be so damned rude."

"Hello!" he said impatiently. "She's *mortal.* Bad enough she's female, but I need someone who knows about our special situation to deal with this problem. She—"

"Jackie *does* know," Bastien said dryly. "Did you think I'd send you an uninitiated mortal? Have a little faith." A sigh traveled down the phone line. "Look, her father started the Morrisey Detective Agency and did lots of work for us. She's known about us since she was in her late teens and has always kept the secret. Jackie has run the company since her father's death. She has a bit of an attitude when it comes to our kind, but is the best in the business. Now, open the goddamned door for the woman."

"But she's mortal and . . . a girl," Vincent pointed out again, still not happy with the situation.

"I'm hanging up, Vincent." Bastien hung up.

Vincent scowled at the phone and almost dialed him back, but then thought better of it and returned to the door. He needed help tracking down the saboteur out to ruin him. He'd give Ms. Morrisey and her giant a chance. If they sorted out the mess for him, fine. If not, he could hold it over Bastien's head for centuries.

Grinning at the idea, Vincent reached for the doorknob.

"The nerve of the man!" Jackie scowled at the door that had just slammed shut in her face. She was exhausted after their long flight and this was the last welcome she'd expected after dropping everything to fly out here to help Vincent Argeneau.

"It isn't the warmest reception we've had," Tiny agreed, his voice as deep and powerful as mountains shifting.

Jackie snorted at the understatement, then glanced at the big man curiously as he moved sideways on the wide marble stoop under the portico at the entrance of the two-story mansion. She raised an eyebrow in question as he peered through one of the narrow windows on either side of the entrance, but was then distracted by the low murmur of a voice coming from the other side of the dark oak door.

Frowning, Jackie leaned forward and pressed an ear to the wood, trying to make out what Vincent Argeneau was saying. Her eyes narrowed and she began to fume on hearing the protest that she was mortal *and* a girl.

The door suddenly opened again and Jackie straightened abruptly. A blush tried to make its way up her face at being caught with her ear to the door and that just made her angrier. It put her on the offensive. Before he could say a word, she spat out the facts from the file she'd studied on the plane.

"You were born in 1592 to Victor and Marion Argeneau, both vampires—or immortals as you prefer to be called. Marion was good friends with her sister-in-law Marguerite Argeneau and you were, in fact, born two months behind Marguerite's son Bastien. The two of you spent a good deal of time together growing up and are as close as brothers. Your mother died in 1695, burnt at the stake while pregnant with what would have been your sibling. Your father has been reclusive since then, spending his time acting as an enforcer for the council. You see very little of him.

"You decided to become an actor when you met Shakespeare at ten. You've traveled the world, staying no more than ten years in each place before moving across the globe and starting again. You've been in California eight years, ten years in England before that, and before that, Russia, Spain, and France. You have shares in Argeneau Enterprises, but also own V.A. Inc., which has fingers in several pies. One of those pies is your own production company, which presently isn't producing anything because a series of events you think are sabotage has forced you to shut down any and all productions."

Jackie fell silent and took great satisfaction in the expression on Vincent Argeneau's face. He looked staggered. It served him right. She was only here as a favor to Bastien. She had other cases she'd rather be working, but did this guy consider that? No, he slams the door in her face, then has the nerve to protest to Bastien about her being *mortal* and a *girl*. Jackie was used to people judging her on her sex and size. It annoyed her sometimes, but she could deal with it. However, she'd be damned if she was going to put up with prejudice against her species. She was human and proud of it. Some of these night feeders were too darned smug in her opinion. They slept all day, drank bagged blood at night, then acted all superior because they couldn't catch the common cold and had perfect health.

That thought reminded Jackie of a point she'd left out.

"You inherited your father's genetic disposition, which won't allow you to feed off bagged blood like the rest of your kind. On a strict diet of bagged blood, you'd starve to death. You're forced to hunt your meals and feed off living donors." She arched her eyebrows and added, "Tiny and I aren't on the menu. If you bite either of us, we're on the next plane back to New York. Understood?"

Jackie didn't wait for a response. Deciding she'd spent long enough on the doorstep, she moved past him into the house, aware that Tiny stayed directly on her heels.

"Your security here is nonexistent," Jackie announced, glancing into each room she passed on her way up the hall. "Your front gate was wide open. We drove straight in. Anyone can."

"My home security isn't in question." Vincent Argeneau sounded irritated, she noted, but otherwise, appeared recovered from his shock at her bulletlike recitation of his life to date.

"It should be," Jackie informed him, then pointed out, "Now that you've closed down your productions, your saboteur has lost his original target. He'll be looking for another, and your home is the first place that comes to *my* mind."

Jackie glanced back as she reached the end of the hall and wasn't terribly surprised to see him peering worriedly toward the front door. She hadn't heard the lock click into place when he'd closed it a moment ago. He moved back to lock it now and she smiled to herself as she pushed through the door into the kitchen.

Tiny waited just inside the room as Jackie walked around, opening and closing cupboards while she waited for Vincent to catch up. She was peering into his empty refrigerator when he hurried into the room.

"You have a lot of glass in this house," she commented. "French doors, sliding glass doors and windows deluxe. Do you, at least, have a functioning security system on those?"

His hesitation was answer enough.

"What are you looking for?" Vincent asked instead of admitting he didn't have an alarm system.

Jackie shrugged. "If Tiny and I are going to be staying here, I need to know what we need. As expected, you have nothing in the way of food in this house, not to mention dishes, silverware, or appliances," she added dryly.

Closing the refrigerator door, she glanced at her assistant. "You'd better start making a list, Tiny. Just write *everything* on it."

"You're staying *here*?" Vincent asked with horror.

"If you hadn't closed down your productions, we would be renting somewhere and taking on positions on one of your plays as our cover while we nosed around. Since you *have* shut down all your plays and made yourself and your home the only available targets, we'll have to stay here and choose a different cover." She turned to peer at him. "I understand you don't have a personal assistant?"

"No," Vincent answered reluctantly.

"You do now," Jackie informed him. She gestured to Tiny as she added, "You also have a cook/housekeeper."

Vincent stared at her and then glanced to Tiny, who nodded solemnly.

Leaving him to absorb the changes that were about to overtake his life, Jackie headed for the kitchen door. "I'm going to make a few calls. I presume I can use the phone in your office?"

"Yes, of course." The words sounded almost automatic, he was looking bemused by all that was taking place.

"Do you want me to unload the luggage?" Tiny asked as she reached his side.

"Yes, please. And I'll need my briefcase from the car, as well. After I make the phone calls, I'm going to go through the second-floor rooms. If I'm not in the office, you'll find me upstairs."

"Okay, boss," Tiny murmured as he trailed her from the kitchen.

Vincent didn't follow this time and Jackie let her shoulders relax a little as she walked back up the hall.

"You were kind of tough on him," Tiny commented as they reached the door she'd spied the office through on the way in.

Jackie shrugged. "He needs a wakeup call. They get to a certain age and think they're invulnerable. This place is a burglar's dream. It's luck alone that he hasn't been robbed blind, or attacked . . . And now he has someone out to get him. We don't have time to handle him with kid gloves. We have to secure this place quickly so we can concentrate on tracking down his saboteur."

"And he was rude slamming the door in our face," Tiny added dryly, bringing a smile to her lips. The giant rarely let her get away with lying to herself.

"Yeah," Jackie admitted. "He was rude. And he doubted I can handle the job, and my pride was hurt, and I made sure he rethought that opinion."

"You think he's rethinking?" Tiny asked.

"I think he's wishing he'd never called Bastien and asked for aid finding someone to help deal with this matter," she said with a pleased grin.

"If he's miserable then our work here is done," Tiny said solemnly.

"I wish," Jackie drawled, but was chuckling softly as Tiny left to go out to the car and she headed into the office. The giant man's ability to jolly her out of any mood was priceless and she'd thanked God for it many times. Jackie suspected she was going to need it many, many times before this job was through.

Sighing, she dropped into the desk chair and stared at the phone. It was cordless, and now that she was here staring at the empty receiver, Jackie recalled that Vincent had been talking on the phone when he'd answered the door. He still had that phone.

Shaking her head, she stood again and started around the desk, pausing when Vincent Argeneau suddenly appeared, the cordless held up in his hand. After a hesitation, Jackie continued forward and reached for the phone, but he held onto it when she would have taken it.

"I apologize for my rudeness in slamming the door in your face. I'm afraid I'd just woken up and wasn't on the ball, and—from the information Bastien had given me—I wasn't expecting you for another half an hour."

"Our flight caught a good tailwind. We landed early," Jackie explained.

Vincent Argeneau nodded. "Well, I was startled to find you on the step, then even more startled that you were mortal. Bastien hadn't warned me that it would be otherwise and I just assumed that it would be one of our own dealing with the situation."

Jackie hesitated, then felt her shoulders relax and nodded slowly. "Apology accepted."

"Good. Then perhaps we can start again." He released the

phone and held out his hand with a conciliatory smile. "Hello, my name is Vincent Argeneau. You must be the amazing Jackie Morrisey that my cousin Bastien has sent to save my bacon. It's a pleasure to meet you. I'd appreciate any help you can give me in this matter. Welcome to my home."

Jackie automatically placed her hand in his, then blinked at the little frisson of awareness the contact caused. Startled, she quickly pulled her hand free. Her words came out fast and sharp as she said, "I'd like to have someone come out and set up a proper security system. It will run you a lot of money. If you have a problem with that . . ." Her voice trailed away as he nodded.

"If you think it's necessary, by all means, arrange it. With that out of the way, perhaps you can concentrate on my saboteur. I realize now I've been lax about such things. I suppose I'm lucky I haven't been robbed blind, or attacked. Thank you for the wakeup call."

Jackie stiffened as she recognized her own words to Tiny moments ago, and suddenly recalled that Vincent's kind had exceptional hearing. They could also read minds, she reminded herself grimly. She'd have to be careful around him and try to keep her thoughts blank when he was near. It was a trick she'd learned years ago. His people could read minds, but—hopefully—only if you were thinking something. Keep your thoughts blank, or recite some silly children's rhyme over and over, and they were somewhat hampered. She'd have to remember that around this man.

"I'll leave you to your phone calls and go shower and dress."

His words drew Jackie's attention to his bare chest and

she blinked in surprise, wondering how she'd missed that earlier. The man was standing there, his dark hair sleep-tousled and wearing nothing but a pair of dark blue pajama bottoms. It left the wide, pale expanse of his chest on view. Jackie had been so angry with his behavior on answering the door, she hadn't even noticed his state of undress. Or how handsome his chiseled face and silver-blue eyes were. Amazing, she thought with disbelief.

"Once you're finished with the security people, I'll take you and Tiny shopping for the things you'll need in the kitchen during your stay," he announced. "Now, if you'll excuse me . . ."

Turning on his heel, Vincent Argeneau left the room. Jackie moved to the door and stared after him. Her gaze slid with interest over his muscular bare back and his behind in the pajama bottoms as he walked back to the stairs. Realizing what she was doing, she shook her head and turned away to move quickly back to the desk.

"Do not even go there," Jackie reprimanded herself as she searched for a phone book to look up the numbers of local security firms. "The last thing you need is to start falling for a vamp. Been there, done that, and have the scars to prove it."

"Talking to yourself already. That's always a bad sign on a job."

Jackie gave a start at Tiny's words and glanced up to find him standing in the doorway, a large box in his hands. "What's that?"

"A delivery from A.B.B. The delivery truck pulled up as I walked out to the car."

"A.B.B.?" Jackie grimaced, knowing it would be blood

14

Bastien had sent from the Argeneau Blood Bank for his mother to feed on while here. He'd warned her that Marguerite Argeneau was flying out to tend to Vincent, whom she was sure was lonely and depressed as he contemplated his single status in comparison to his cousins, who were each finding their life mates. Jackie didn't think he seemed depressed, but then she hardly knew the man.

Tiny shifted, drawing her gaze back to the burden he held. She stared at the box that no doubt held a cooler full of bagged blood and decided this job was probably going to be a trial. They didn't normally have to live in such close proximity to immortals and have their feeding habits in their faces. She didn't think she'd like it.

Sighing, Jackie found the listing of a security agency in the book, and began to dial the number on the cordless. "Put it in the kitchen and let him know it's here. He'll want to put it away."

Nodding, Tiny left the room as she waited for her call to be answered.

Two hours later, Allen Richmond of Richmond Security was rattling off all the improvements that had to be made, and the items that had to be installed, to make Vincent Argeneau's house secure. With each point he mentioned, Jackie put a mental check mark beside each item on the list in her head. This was the third man who'd looked over the house in the last two hours, but the first who hadn't missed anything. This was the company she would deal with.

"Can you do it today?" she asked when he finished.

"It'll cost you," the older man warned, running a hand over his short gray hair. "I'll have to bump another job, use equipment from another job as well. My men will have to work overtime and . . ." He paused to do some figures on the pad he'd been making notes on as they'd toured the house and property, then mentioned a figure that would have made most people pale. However, it was no more than she'd expected and Jackie glanced at Vincent, who had joined them for the end of the tour.

"Can you afford it?" she asked bluntly.

Vincent scowled as if offended, then growled, "Do it."

Jackie turned to Allen and nodded. "Do it."

"I'll call the office and have the men and equipment out here within the hour." Allen Richmond walked away toward his car, pulling a cell phone from his pocket as he went.

"Well . . ." Vincent frowned. "I guess that puts a spanner in the shopping plan."

"I can keep an eye on the house while you and Jackie shop," Tiny rumbled as he joined them under the portico.

Jackie frowned at the suggestion. The last thing she wanted to do was go shopping with Vincent Argeneau. Unfortunately, it was after four o'clock and heading for dinner time. They'd need food . . . and coffee. She lived off the black liquid and couldn't go all night without. Giving in with a sigh, she said, "I'll get my purse."

"I should warn you, Jackie hates shopping," Tiny informed Vincent as she headed into the house.

Jackie rolled her eyes at the understatement, but didn't get the chance to comment. The telephone was ringing as she opened the door.

"I'll get it." Vincent was suddenly rushing past her toward the office.

Jackie followed him and grabbed her purse off the desk as he picked up the receiver and said hello. She'd turned to leave the office when he said, "What?" with such distress that she paused and turned back with concern.

The man looked both stunned and horrified.

Two

"So the call was from your production assistant, telling you that the lead in the play who was supposed to open tonight has quit and the play can't open?"

"Yes," Vincent answered wearily, his gaze on the road ahead. Jackie was driving, but he was supposed to be directing her to somewhere to buy kitchen appliances. He didn't have a clue where people bought such things. He hadn't told her that, however, but was hoping to spot a likely store before she realized it.

"I was under the impression you'd permanently closed down all of your plays until you sorted out the matter of who is sabotaging them?"

"No, not exactly," Vincent murmured and wondered what Bastien had told her before sending her out here.

Before he could voice the question, Jackie answered it by saying, "Bastien wasn't very specific about details. He just said that someone was sabotaging your plays. I was hoping both Tiny and I could sit down with you later this evening to go over the particulars, but wanted to get the urgent matters out of the way first."

"The urgent matters being securing my home and seeing to the shopping," Vincent murmured, a faint smile curving his lips as he glanced her way.

"You may be able to live and function without food, but we can't," Jackie said defensively. "And I positively cannot function without coffee."

"Of course not. I wouldn't expect you to," he assured her quickly. "It's common sense to see to the basics first. A safe roof over your head and food are basic needs."

"Not for you. At least not the food," Jackie pointed out. Before he could comment, she suddenly braked and swerved into the driveway of a mall.

"Sorry, I guess I got distracted," he muttered, glancing over the large complex.

"No problem," Jackie said as she parked. "I almost missed it myself and I *was* paying attention."

Vincent merely grunted and slid out of the car to follow her inside. He really expected the next little while to be boring and possibly even annoying, but soon learned differently. As he concentrated on selecting items to go in the kitchen, Vincent found his frustration slipping away.

"I don't know why you don't like shopping." Vincent commented as he snatched the cheap white plastic coffeepot away from Jackie and set it back on the shelf. He then picked up the more expensive chrome and black model and dropped it in the cart.

Not sure what would be needed in the kitchen, Vincent had simply been picking up one of everything; one blender, one mixer, one crockpot, one juicer, and so on. He'd have asked Jackie what she thought he needed, but Tiny hadn't been kidding when he said she hated shopping. She'd been snapping and growling since they'd arrived. He thought it was kind of cute. Jackie was like a little snarling Chihuahua . . . but much cuter.

"Please do not tell me you are one of *those* people."

Jackie sounded disgusted and it made him hesitate warily. "What people?"

"People who believe in retail therapy," she said dryly, picking up a toaster.

"I don't know. It does seem to be relaxing me though," Vincent admitted. He took the toaster from her and switched it for another.

"What was wrong with that one?" she asked sharply.

"This one is better," Vincent said with a shrug as he set his substitution in the cart. "It's chrome and black and will match the rest of the appliances."

"So was the first one," she pointed out impatiently.

"But this one is a cool shape and it will toast *four* slices," Vincent pointed out.

Jackie rolled her eyes. "There are only two of us. We don't *need* a four-slice toaster."

"There will be four of us. You forgot my aunt and myself," Vincent reminded her.

"You don't eat," she said with exasperation.

"I do," Vincent corrected. Not often, he acknowledged to himself, but he would start eating more while she was here.

His gaze landed on the next appliance in the aisle and he brightened. "Oh, look, a waffle maker. I've had waffles. They were good."

Vincent pushed the cart further along the aisle to look at the contraption.

"What do you mean you *eat*?" The question burst from Jackie as she trailed after him. Some of her annoyance appeared to have eased, replaced with confusion by his claim. "Your kind don't eat, you suck blood."

Vincent smiled at an older woman pushing a cart past them in the aisle. Jackie's words had made her stiffen and glance their way with shock.

"We're practicing our lines for a play," he lied with a charming smile. The woman relaxed and smiled uncertainly back, then began moving again. Vincent waited until she'd left the aisle before turning an arched eyebrow on Jackie. He needn't have bothered, she was already bright red with embarrassment over her slip.

"Sorry," she muttered, taking the waffle maker from him and placing it in the cart. She insisted, "But you *don't* eat. None of you eat . . . Except for Bastien. He used to eat in business meetings, just to be polite I think. He's started to eat just lately, but I gather that has something to do with Terri."

"Well, I eat," Vincent informed her.

"Then why is your kitchen completely empty of food?" Jackie asked archly.

"I eat out a lot," Vincent muttered, and—leaving her to chew on that—he moved further up the aisle to the next contraption, an ice cream maker. "Do you like ice cream?"

Vincent glanced at Jackie and found her grumpy expression briefly gone. She was eyeing the ice cream maker with something close to lust.

Realizing he was watching her, she schooled her expression into one of indifference and shrugged. "Ice cream is okay."

He wasn't fooled. Smiling to himself, Vincent set the ice cream maker in the cart.

"I think we have everything. We should go. We still have groceries to get," Jackie reminded him.

"There's one more aisle. We should—"

"Trust me, Vincent, I think you have almost everything they sell. You couldn't possibly need anything else," she said impatiently. Jackie paused and frowned when she saw the way he'd stopped and was smiling at her. Her voice was wary when she asked, "What?"

"I like the way you say my name. So sharp, so concise—"

"So annoyed," Jackie said with exasperation. She added, "We *do* have *everything*. You've picked up one of every appliance in the store."

"I suppose you're right," Vincent conceded, taking pity on her beleaguered expression. "I guess we can check out."

He pushed the heaped cart to the front of the store and then paused, his gaze moving over the checkouts until he spotted the beaming manager waving him to an end aisle where their other two carts were already unloaded onto the checkout belt. Vincent was really quite impressed with this store. Once the first cart had been full of table linen, dishes, and silverware, he'd gone in search of somewhere he could leave it while he filled a second one. The manager had taken the cart for him and sent someone to watch at a discreet distance while they'd filled the second cart. The moment it was full, the store worker had appeared with another empty cart and switched with him.

"Excellent service," Vincent complimented as the manager and clerk began to help him unload.

"New house?" the manager asked with a smile.

"Good guess," Vincent complimented, which could be taken as agreement or not as the man liked.

"Not much of a guess." The manager chuckled. "It has to be a new house. About the only thing you haven't got here is a microwave."

Vincent stilled and turned accusingly on Jackie. Sighing, she threw her hands up in the air and turned to head back to the housewares section.

Half an hour later, Jackie watched impatiently as the last of their items were rung through . . . including a black and chrome microwave. "We won't have room in the car for all this," she pointed out. "And we still have to get the actual groceries."

"I'd be happy to have one of the boys deliver your purchases for you," the manager said accommodatingly.

"Oh great!" Vincent beamed and Jackie just managed not to roll her eyes. It would just figure that he actually seemed to enjoy shopping. The man had been relaxed and cheerful through the entire grueling two hours in this store. She'd have been happy to grab a coffeepot and paper plates, but not Vincent. *If they were doing it, they were doing it right*, he'd said, and proceeded to take his time over choosing the dish patterns, as well as the style of drinking glasses, and then had insisted on color-coordinating all the appliances.

Jackie shook her head. Who cared if the teapot was white plastic, the cappuccino machine was chrome, or the vegetable steamer was blue? Vincent did. He wanted everything black and chrome to match.

Sighing impatiently, she shifted her feet as Vincent handed over his credit card.

"The man at the house is called Tiny. If the gate is closed and locked and you have to buzz, just tell him it's a delivery authorized by Jackie," Vincent instructed.

"I'll call him to warn him it's on the way," Jackie said impatiently. "Can we go now?"

"Don't mind her," Vincent advised the manager. "She just flew in from New York. You know how New Yorkers can be."

"Oh . . . Yes." The manager nodded solemnly, looking— for all the world—as if he wanted to offer Vincent his sympathies for having to deal with her.

Finding the whole matter beyond exasperating, Jackie turned on her heel and headed for the automatic doors.

"Come again!" the manager called cheerfully as Vincent followed.

"We are not doing this at the grocery store," Jackie said grimly as she started the engine of the rental car. "We are not going to buy out the grocery store. You're a *vampire,* you're not *supposed* to eat."

"And you're a woman. You're *supposed* to like shopping," he responded mildly. "I guess things aren't always what they seem, are they?"

In her impatience, Jackie managed to stall the car. Feeling her face go red with embarrassment, she ground her teeth together and restarted the engine. Pausing then, she took a deep steadying breath.

"Must be jet lag," she muttered under her breath as she pulled out of the parking spot.

"No doubt," Vincent said agreeably.

"Are you always this damned cheerful?" she asked with irritation.

"Mostly always," he assured her with a grin.

Jackie blew her breath out on a sigh. "You're nothing like Bastien. He's . . ."

"Serious? Sober? Solemn? And all those other *S*'s?" Vincent suggested with amusement.

"Grown up," she said dryly.

"He's a businessman. I'm an actor," Vincent pointed out as if that said it all.

Jackie frowned. She'd forgotten, but he was also a businessman, with his own company. It made her wonder how much of his cheerful, easygoing behavior was for show.

"Do you have Tiny's list?" Vincent asked as they walked into the grocery store ten minutes later.

Jackie reached into her pocket and pulled out the scrap of paper Tiny had handed her on the way out the door. She unfolded it, read the single word at the top, blinked and then burst out laughing.

Curious, Vincent took the list from her. He smiled faintly. "Well, you did tell him to write *everything* on it."

"Yes," Jackie agreed with a sigh, acknowledging to herself that they weren't going to get in and out quickly here either. They did need everything; Vincent's home didn't even have the staples, like salt and pepper.

Lynsay Sands

"Here." Vincent reached into his pocket and pulled out some money. Handing it to her, he gestured to the end of the store. "Why don't you go pick up a couple of drinks for us and I'll start the shopping?"

Jackie followed his gesture to the coffee shop sign at the end of the store and nodded with relief. A dose of caffeine would make it all bearable. "How do you take your coffee?"

Vincent blinked at the question. "Regular?"

Jackie arched her eyebrows. His answer told her that he didn't normally drink coffee. However, since he was giving her a reprieve from shopping, she let it go and merely headed for the coffee shop.

Ten minutes later she'd downed half her cappuccino and felt about a hundred times better. She didn't even mind that Vincent seemed to want to look at everything on the shelves. The man was practically salivating as he looked at the pictures of the food on the cans and boxes. His reactions made her think she had to be right and he didn't normally eat as she'd suspected.

Unfortunately, when she said as much, Vincent just shrugged and said the restaurants he went to didn't serve things like this. Jackie was sufficiently mellowed by her caffeine boost to let the matter go for now, but she still was sure he didn't eat.

The kitchen purchases had arrived at the house and Tiny had put most of them away by the time they returned. That still left the groceries. Jackie and Vincent helped the giant put them away before she fetched her briefcase and set it on the table.

Retrieving a notepad and pen, she closed and set the

briefcase on the floor, then sat down and glanced toward the two men. Vincent and Tiny were trying to figure out how to work the ice cream maker . . . without bothering to read the instructions, Jackie noticed, and bit back a smile. It was so typically male one could almost forget the man was a vampire.

The thought made her frown. The last thing Jackie wanted to do was forget that. He was attractive and charming and . . . a vampire. She had to keep the last part in mind and ignore the rest. It was for her own good.

Mouth tightening, Jackie watched the two men for another minute, then said, "Vincent?"

"Yes?" He glanced over in question.

"Bastien gave me a very brief rundown of what was happening here, but as you know, it wasn't much." She was too tired to bother to hide her dissatisfaction. "Tiny and I need to go over it with you to learn everything."

"Work time," Tiny said with regret, setting the ice cream machine aside. "You two go on. I'll make coffee and start dinner. I can listen while I work. Jackie will feel better once she's eaten. She's always grouchy when her sugar's low."

Jackie set her teeth at the comment. She wasn't being grouchy. All things considered, she thought she was reacting remarkably well. It was after seven o'clock at night, for heaven's sake. She'd spent the better part of the day in airports and planes, eating rotten food and drinking worse coffee, then arrived here to go shopping. She . . . Okay, so supper would be good.

"I'll make something quick." Tiny moved to the refrigerator.

Smiling, Vincent moved to join her, his gaze moving curiously from the pen she held to the notepad on the table.

Jackie resisted the urge to cover her notes and cleared her throat. "As I mentioned, from what Bastien said, I understood that you had decided to close down the plays because of the sabotage attempts."

"Yes and no. None of them are running right now, and I did sort of close them down, at least temporarily, but it wasn't all at once, and it certainly wasn't my choice," he muttered unhappily as he took the seat across from her, then explained, "One by one I had to *delay* the openings of each play scheduled to begin, and *temporarily* shut down plays that were already open."

"Why? Bastien mentioned accidents and minor catastrophes."

"Yes." Vincent ran a hand wearily through his hair as he thought of the events that had taken place over the last several weeks. "We've had two plays suffer minor fires, an accident where paint got spilled over every single costume for another play—"

"Slow down, slow down," Jackie said with a frown. She'd started to try to take notes as he spoke, but he was going too quickly and she couldn't keep up. "Perhaps we should go over the events one at a time and in order. What was the first incident that you think is tied into all this?"

"That was here in L.A. A can of paint got knocked off a shelf in the costume department and splashed over every costume in the room." His mouth tightened. "No one knows how the paint got there, or why the lid was off, or who knocked it over."

Jackie considered the matter, thinking that it could have been an accident.

"The next accident was a fire in one of the theatres in Canada," Vincent continued. "It was a small fire. The theatre itself didn't sustain much damage, but our stage set was ruined. It, too, seemed to be an accident at the time, a cigarette in a garbage can. It wasn't until the other stuff started happening that I thought perhaps those two incidents hadn't just been random accidents."

When Jackie merely nodded, he continued, "Next, there was another fire, this one here in Los Angeles. It was a bigger fire than the one in Canada."

Jackie arched an eyebrow. "Was anyone hurt?"

"No, fortunately the building was empty at the time, but the fire destroyed the theatre entirely, taking our costumes and sets with it," Vincent said grimly.

Jackie made another note on her notepad.

"The next event was at the second play in Canada. I was told a cable broke loose and a part of the stage set fell on the female lead." Vincent grimaced. "She broke her arm. I had to replace her."

Jackie frowned and made another note, then put an asterisk beside it.

"Then the male lead of another play here in Los Angeles fell down a set of stairs and broke his leg. I was still thinking it was just a run of bad luck," Vincent admitted with a grimace and shook his head. "Dan Henson, the actor, *claimed* someone had pushed him, but I didn't believe him until later."

"Why?" she asked.

"He was a drinker and drunk at the time." Vincent shrugged. "I thought it was just—"

"An accident," Jackie finished for him dryly. "When did you start to realize these accidents might not be accidents?"

"When the cast of the New York play I was in started dropping out sick one right after the other with contagious anemia."

Jackie stared at him with disbelief. "Contagious anemia?"

"Yes." He gave a short laugh. "I think my family thought I'd fed myself out of a show."

"Did you?" Jackie asked.

Vincent stiffened, then turned a cold look her way. "No. I don't feed off my cast and crew. In fact, I don't feed off people I know or employees. Usually," he added dryly, as if he might be willing to make an exception in her case.

Jackie shrugged. She'd had to ask. "So, your cast started falling ill with anemia and you shut down the show and flew back here to California."

"I didn't have a choice. You need a cast to have a play." Vincent shrugged and then added with regret, "I hated to do it, though. It would have been a big hit."

Jackie stared at him doubtfully. "I believe Bastien said the play in New York was called *Dracula, The Musical*?"

"Yeah." He sighed. "It was good. The next *Rocky Horror Picture Show*."

"Right," Jackie didn't bother to hide her doubt. "What happened to make you close down all the plays? Was it just the combination of accidents?"

Vincent grimaced, then reluctantly admitted, "I'm ashamed to say it, but no. I've been in the business a long time, these things happen. Not usually one right after the other or anything, but I know how to deal with these sorts of events and we handled each emergency as it arose."

"Then what made you close them all down?"

Vincent frowned, and began to fiddle with the corner of her notepad. "The actors and actresses made me close them down. In each play at least one, or sometimes two, actors or actresses and their understudies have suddenly quit, or walked off stage. They've all been leads. We had to scramble to replace them and delay openings, or temporarily close shows to allow the replacements to learn their roles."

Jackie considered this briefly and then asked, "How many plays have been affected by actors or actresses walking off?"

"All of them. Two in New York. Two here in California. And two in Canada."

"Six," she said with a frown. "And the lead actor or actress has suddenly quit from each of them?"

"Yes."

"Are they under contract?"

"Yes."

Jackie's frown deepened. "I presume these contracts have some sort of legal provisos, or recourse, to prevent their just walking out?"

"Oh yes," he said with a harsh laugh. "I could sue every one of them into poverty for the rest of their lives, but none of them seems to care. Not that it matters, suing them doesn't help me get the plays up and running in the meantime."

"And now one of the replacements—as well as her understudy—have walked as well?" Jackie murmured, thinking of the phone call he'd received earlier.

"Yes. It was one of the two here in California and was the first of the six that was scheduled to reopen. The replacement actress and her understudy quit this morning," he said grimly.

"Hmm . . . I don't suppose it could be a coincidence?"

"No," Vincent hissed the word through gritted teeth and then added, "I've been in the business for four hundred years. Having one play close down because an actor and understudy have walked out is rare enough, but having six at once?" He shook his head. "Definitely not a coincidence. Someone is out to ruin me."

Jackie bit her lip, watching her hand doodle nonsense on the pad as she thought. Finally, she glanced up and said, "I gather you've tried to read their minds? To see what was making them drop out?"

"Their minds were blank on the subject. They just knew they had to quit."

"They were wiped, you mean," she said dryly. "Which means your saboteur is another vamp . . . or at least someone with a vampire for backup. Although I suppose the contagious anemia made that obvious."

Vincent nodded grimly. Somehow, the fact that one of his own kind was behind the sabotage made it seem that much worse than it would have been were it a mortal.

Jackie sat back in her seat with a sigh. She considered the escalation in events. Accidents to property, then arson, then accidents to people, then outright feeding on people, and now controlling them and making them quit. It sounded as though the incidents were quickly picking up speed and momentum.

"How much time was there between the fire and the stage set accident where your actress broke her arm?"

"A week," Vincent answered, his expression curious.

"And between the stage set accident and the male second lead being pushed down the stairs?"

He paused to consider. "About five days."

"And then between that and the first person falling ill with this anemia?"

"Three or four days, maybe, but then they started dropping like flies, one after the other."

Jackie nodded and made another note.

"They got closer together as each incident occurred," Vincent realized.

Jackie met his gaze. "And more serious."

"From property, to injury," Vincent realized, following her thinking.

"Yes." Jackie agreed, then stood and walked out of the kitchen. She sensed rather than heard Vincent follow her. The man moved as quietly as a shadow.

She found Allen Richmond in the living room, overseeing the work being done on the windows and doors there.

"How long until you'll be done?" Jackie asked abruptly as she paused at the security man's side.

"Most of it will be finished tonight. The ground floor anyway. We'll have to come back tomorrow to finish the upper floor," he answered promptly.

Jackie nodded. "And the gate?"

"Already done," he assured her.

"Is it closed and locked?"

Allen Richmond paused, his eyes narrowing on her face,

obviously picking up on the fact that these weren't just idle questions. "I had it left open so the men could come and go. I'll have it closed at once."

Satisfied, Jackie turned and led Vincent out of the room just as Tiny opened the kitchen door and peered at them.

"Supper's ready," the giant announced.

Nodding, Jackie managed not to run up the hall. She was absolutely famished and was terribly glad Tiny could cook. He'd started working for her father the same summer she had and her dad had put the two of them together from the start. Most people thought Tiny's size had been the deciding factor and Ted Morrisey had hoped the giant would keep his daughter safe. But Jackie knew that wasn't true. Tiny's personality had made the decision. Tiny, for all his size, or perhaps because of it, was the most laid back, calm individual on the planet. A stark contrast to Jackie's almost hyper, impatient, let's-get-things-done-now, need-to-prove-herself attitude. He was her rock, calming her when she lost patience, and gentling her when she was moved to be hard. They were friends, and while she was now his boss rather than just his co-worker, he still let her know when she was being a little Napoleon. It was something Jackie knew she needed.

"Oh Tiny, this looks wonderful," Vincent praised as he followed Jackie into the kitchen to see the food on the table.

"It's just a black bean stir-fry," Tiny said modestly. "It was fast and easy."

"Hmm." Vincent pulled out a chair for Jackie. "Well, it smells delicious."

Jackie eyed him suspiciously as she sank into the seat

Vincent was so gallantly holding out. She still didn't believe the vamp normally ate food. The man hadn't even had a teaspoon in his kitchen, but it looked to her as if he was going to eat now.

Vincent seated himself across from her as she dished up a good portion of stir-fried vegetables and beef onto her plate. She then offered him the serving bowl as Tiny set glasses of water by each of their three settings.

Vincent took the food and served himself before passing it on to Tiny as the giant joined them at the table. Both Tiny and Jackie watched as Vincent scooped up the first forkful of food and lifted it to his mouth. Her expression was cynical, Tiny's was expectant.

Surprise was Vincent's first reaction as he closed his lips around the mouthful of food. The emotion flickered across his face and then gave way to pleasure. "This is good."

Tiny relaxed in his seat, Jackie just shook her head. The man didn't normally eat at all. She'd stake her life on it, but didn't comment and merely concentrated on eating. It really was good.

Jackie finished eating first, rushing through her food as she rushed through life, always hurrying to get to the next task. Tiny, of course, ate like he lived, savoring each moment and calmly enjoying it. Vincent was somewhere in the middle, gobbling it up at first, then slowing as he no doubt grew full. If he hadn't eaten for decades as she suspected, his stomach surely would have shrunk, Jackie thought, but again didn't say anything. He was the one insisting he ate, he could live with the consequences.

Jackie thanked Tiny for the meal as she stood, then

carried her plate over and rinsed it off before setting it in the dishwasher. Her gaze then moved to the coffee pot and she brightened on seeing the full pot of black liquid.

"Oh Tiny, you're a dream," Jackie said with a smile as she found one of the new mugs and poured herself a cup of the black gold. "Does anyone else want one?"

"I'll have one please," Tiny said as he finished his dinner and stood. "I made ice cream for dessert."

"Really?" she asked with interest, peering around for the ice cream maker.

"I'll get it," Tiny insisted, moving to the sink to rinse his own plate. "Take the coffees to the table."

Leaving him to it, Jackie carried the coffees over. Vincent hadn't asked for one, so she hadn't poured him one.

"Here you are." Tiny placed a small dish of ice cream before her, and announced, "Chocolate with cherries."

Jackie picked up the spoon and scooped up a bite, moaning with pleasure as it hit her taste buds.

"Good?" Vincent asked with interest.

Jackie nodded and swallowed, then taunted, "No dessert until you finish your dinner."

Honestly, the man looked as crestfallen as a child at her words and continued determinedly with his meal.

"He doesn't have to finish his supper. He took too much." Tiny whisked Vincent's half-finished plate of stir-fry away, replacing it with ice cream. "Eat up."

Vincent beamed at the man and set to work on the ice cream.

Jackie made a face as he sighed with pleasure.

"Ms. Morrisey?"

A Bite to Remember

She shifted in her seat and glanced over her shoulder at Allen Richmond as he poked his head into the room.

"A car followed one of the men through the gate as he returned from his break. There's a woman out here looking for Mr. Argeneau."

37

Three

Jackie stood to investigate the woman looking for Vincent, only to pause as a tall, curvaceous, brunette urged Allen Richmond out of the way and stepped into the kitchen. Jackie stared. The woman was beautiful. She also looked extremely familiar. However, Jackie didn't understand *why* until Vincent moved forward saying, "Aunt Marguerite!"

This was Marguerite Argeneau, Bastien's mother and Vincent's aunt. There was a painting of her in the living room of the apartment in New York where Bastien stayed when in the city. Jackie had met him there a time or two over the years and always found the woman in the portrait fascinating with her medieval gown and faraway look. She was even more beautiful in real life and—despite knowing as much as she did about immortals—Jackie still found it difficult to accept that the woman was over seven hundred years old.

While Marguerite Argeneau was older than Vincent, she

was still very young as far as immortals went. Their history went back before the beginning of written history, to the existence of Atlantis and—according to her father's files—there were at least a handful of immortals who had actually fled the fall of Atlantis.

It seemed the mythical land truly had existed, and it *had* been technologically advanced as some people suggested. So much advanced, in fact, they'd been able to combine nano technology with bio-engineering to create specialized nanos. These nanos, when introduced to a body, used the blood of the host to repair damaged tissue and fight disease as well as to reproduce and regenerate themselves.

They had been programmed to shut down and disintegrate once finished with their work. However, the human body was constantly under attack from sunlight, the environment, or simple aging. There were always repairs to be done and so the nanos didn't shut down, but continued to regenerate and reproduce themselves to keep their host at peak condition. Those nanos were the equivalent of drinking from the fountain of youth.

Unfortunately, there were some drawbacks. The nanos used more blood than the human body could produce, and so the nanos altered their hosts to allow them to get the blood they needed. They made their hosts the perfect predator, giving them increased strength, speed, and fangs to gain the needed blood. And because sunlight dehydrated the body and increased the need for immortals to feed, it had also given them amazing night vision so that they could live and hunt at night to avoid the damaging rays of the sun, in effect, making them vampires.

"Thank you, Allen," Jackie murmured as Vincent greeted his aunt.

Nodding, the man backed out of the kitchen, allowing the door to close behind him.

"How was your flight?" Vincent asked as the two broke apart.

"Fine, fine. We had a two-hour delay, though, which is why I'm late getting in."

"Oh, yes. Bastien said your plane was landing at six," he murmured.

Jackie glanced at her wrist watch. It was now well past eight. Obviously, they'd both forgotten about his aunt. The fact that Bastien's mother was flying out to California had slipped her mind entirely. She wished it had slipped the woman's mind. Jackie hadn't considered her visit a problem until Bastien had suggested she not mention what was happening here unless she wanted Marguerite's interference.

Jackie wasn't keen on interference from anyone, but would never be rude to Bastien's mother. Not telling her anything seemed the smartest move. She just hoped Vincent had the sense to keep his mouth shut on the matter too.

"And who is this?"

Jackie let go of her thoughts and forced a smile as Marguerite turned bright, curious eyes toward her and Tiny.

"Oh." Vincent's smile was stiff as he introduced them. "This is Jackie, my P.I.—"

"P.A.," Jackie corrected quickly, giving him a meaningful stare. She then smiled brightly and held out her hand. "It's nice to meet you, Mrs. Argeneau."

"Thank you, dear. It's nice to meet you too," she said, taking her hand. "Call me Marguerite."

Jackie's smile froze as she felt a ruffling sensation in her mind. Her defenses immediately kicked in and she thought of a brick wall, then started to recite "Itsy Bitsy Spider" in her head for good measure in an effort to keep the woman out of her thoughts.

Marguerite's eyes widened briefly, then narrowed, but Jackie just forced a wider smile. If the woman felt rebuffed, it was too bad. In her opinion, it was rather rude to intrude on people's thoughts. Not that most people would even have realized she was doing it.

Marguerite fluttered at the edges of her mind for another moment, then released her hand and turned to Tiny.

"And this is my . . . er . . . cook, Tiny," Vincent added with a pained expression.

Jackie watched Tiny, relaxing when she saw his lips begin to move as he shook Marguerite's hand. He was reciting "Little Bo Beep." At least that was what he'd once told her he did when he thought a vampire was trying to rifle through his thoughts.

Their efforts might have kept Marguerite out of their heads; Jackie couldn't be sure. Unfortunately, the very fact that they'd tried had the added side effect of making Vincent's aunt suspicious. Jackie could see the emotion flicker in her expression as she glanced from one to the other. After a moment of tense silence, the vampire turned suddenly to Vincent.

"Did Bastien send a package on ahead as promised?"

"Yes, it arrived this afternoon," he assured her. Then he realized, "Oh, of course. You must be hungry after your flight."

Vincent moved across the room to the refrigerator and opened it, revealing bagged blood stacked up neatly in amongst the cheese and veggies. "One or two bags?"

Marguerite stiffened at the sight of the blood in plain sight. Her gaze slid to Jackie and Tiny, taking in their inscrutable expressions before she answered.

"Two, please. I'll have them in my room," she added, apparently uncomfortable with the idea of feeding in front of them.

Vincent grabbed a couple bags, then ushered her out of the room.

"She's pretty," Tiny commented as he sat back down at the table to pick up his spoon and dig into his ice cream again.

"She's *old*," Jackie responded dryly. "Super old. About seven hundred years too old for you."

"Yeah." He sighed. "She probably thinks of me as a punk kid."

"Probably," Jackie agreed, then blinked and suddenly wondered if that was how Vincent and other vampires saw *her* . . . as a punk kid. She didn't like the idea, but supposed it would explain the arrogance she sometimes sensed from them. Perhaps it was more condescension; the amused patience of the aged with exuberant youth. On the other hand, she thought, while they may think of her as a punk kid, they still called her when they had a problem.

"So who are Jackie and Tiny?" Marguerite asked as she followed Vincent into one of the remaining guest rooms.

"My P.A. and cook," he answered quickly, but had to turn away to hide his expression as he set her suitcase on the bed. Aunt Marguerite had always been able to tell when he told a lie.

"Uh-huh." She didn't sound convinced. "And when did you start eating?"

Vincent didn't even try to claim that he'd always eaten. While Jackie and Tiny didn't know him and couldn't be sure he hadn't always done so, Marguerite did know him. He'd stayed at her apartment while in New York and hadn't eaten a thing the whole time he was there. That thought reminded him of a conversation he'd had with Marguerite's son, Lucern, at the man's wedding to his editor Kate a couple weeks ago and he brightened.

"Lucern was telling me that he finds eating helps him build his own blood so that he has to feed less. I thought I'd give it a try." It wasn't a lie. Lucern *had* told him that this was why he ate when the rest of them didn't. It helped him keep his body mass as well as build blood. Vincent had actually considered eating as well as feeding to see if it reduced the number of times he had to feed in a day, but with one thing and another, he hadn't actually set out to try it. Until now.

"And how do your cook and P.A. know about us?" Marguerite asked, pausing by the bed and turning to spear him with her eyes.

"How do *your* housekeeper and her husband know?" He gave a shrug. "They were told. It saves me having to spend my time pretending when I'm at home."

Marguerite's mouth compressed. "And these men crawling all over the house?"

"They're installing a security system. Crime is rife here. You can't be too careful." Vincent waited for her next question. It was obvious his aunt didn't believe a thing he was saying and Vincent really wished he could just tell her what was what, but the last thing he needed was his aunt sticking her nose into this business.

"Have you tried to read her yet?"

Vincent's eyebrows rose with surprise. The question was not one he'd expected.

"No," he admitted. Vincent didn't often read the humans around him. To him, it seemed like an intrusion and he didn't care to intrude on the thoughts of his friends. As for non-friends, ambition and drive could color everyone's choices and both of those were high in the world of theatre. After the hundredth time of finding out the pretty lady flirting with you so charmingly was really only interested in what you could do for her career . . . Well, it just seemed better not to bother reading them anymore. Not that this was a concern with Jackie. Still, he'd had no reason to read her, so hadn't bothered.

Marguerite merely nodded. "I think I'll unpack and take a shower. Between waiting in the airport and the recycled air on the plane, I always feel gritty after travel."

"Okay. Come downstairs when you're ready and I'll give you a proper tour of the house," Vincent said, leaving her alone.

Jackie and Tiny were still in the kitchen when he went in. Vincent sat down in his seat, picked up his spoon, then frowned at the melted puddle in his bowl.

"I'll get you fresh." Tiny took his bowl and stood to carry it to the sink.

Vincent couldn't help noticing that Jackie frowned after

the man and supposed she didn't like Tiny serving him. The title cook/housekeeper was just his cover after all. She didn't say anything to the large man, however, but turned to Vincent and asked, "So what did you do to piss off one of your own kind?"

He blinked at the question. "What do you mean?"

"Well, you must have done something. There's a reason they're sabotaging you like this."

"It doesn't have to be an immortal," Vincent said resentfully.

Jackie arched one eyebrow. "No, of course it doesn't. Maybe it was a coincidence that the entire cast of your play suddenly went anemic. Although, as far as I know, there really is no such thing as *contagious* anemia."

Vincent's shoulders sagged. "Yes. That seems to suggest one of my kind is behind it," he acknowledged with a sigh. Then he admitted, "I was hoping though that it was a mortal who either hired, or got some help, from an immortal."

"Does it really matter?" she asked quietly. "Either way, an immortal is involved and surely they don't normally side with mortals against immortals?"

"No," he agreed. "And I *have* tried to think of who might be behind it, or even involved, but I really can't think of anyone."

"Hmm." Jackie sat back, a frown pulling at her mouth as Tiny returned to set a bowl of ice cream before Vincent. "Well, think about it some more. If you come up with anyone, let me know."

Vincent nodded, then asked, "So, what are we going to do first?"

Jackie's eyes narrowed. "*We* aren't doing anything. *You're* going to go about your business. The saboteur is a problem for Tiny and me." She pushed back her chair and stood. "I'll go check on how the men are doing with the security system."

Vincent watched her leave, his gaze fixed with interest on her pert little behind.

"Jackie's right. You're better to leave the detecting to the detectives," Tiny said, drawing his attention. "And we'll leave the acting to you."

Vincent grunted and took a spoonful of ice cream, savoring the cold, sweet treat and wondering why he'd stopped eating all those centuries ago. Had he really just got bored with it? It didn't seem boring now.

"So," Vincent said after a minute. "Tell me about Jackie."

Tiny raised his eyebrows, then shrugged. "She's smart, sharp, and somewhat cynical. She's also my boss."

The last was added as a warning that he'd be loyal and Vincent nodded to let him know he respected that. "Bastien said her father started the company?"

"Ted," Tiny agreed. "He was a real hard-noser. He expected a lot out of everyone . . . including his daughter. And Jackie never disappointed him."

"Never?"

"Never in the ten years I've known her," Tiny said solemnly.

Vincent considered that briefly, then said, "Her father's dead?"

"Yes. Cancer," Tiny said grimly. "Two years ago."

"So she's been running the company for two years?"

46

"Three," he corrected. "Ted was pretty sick the last year. Jackie pretty much took over. He was just a figurehead."

Vincent nodded. "It must have been hard. I mean when it comes to detectives, one just always assumes it will be a man in charge. I suppose most men would want a male detective."

Tiny smiled faintly. "Not so much nowadays. Women are in every field and in charge more often now. Actually," he added with amusement, "more often than not, the only ones who give her a hard time are your kind."

Vincent raised his eyebrows in surprise and Tiny shrugged. "A lot of immortals are older; from a time when women weren't in power positions. They aren't always comfortable with her being in charge. Like you weren't when you slammed the door in her face. Jackie often works twice as hard to earn their respect."

Vincent frowned, ashamed now that he'd given her a hard time.

"Not Bastien, though," Tiny went on. "He treats her with the same respect he gave Ted. And he will intercede if one of your kind gives her too hard a time . . . or he tries, anyway. Jackie often won't allow his help."

Vincent could believe that. Jackie seemed the stubborn, hard-headed sort, determined to do it on her own. He supposed she'd had to be. Despite what Tiny said, he knew there was still sexism in the business world today and not just among his kind.

Vincent dipped his spoon into his bowl, and found it empty. He'd finished off the ice cream. "This was good, Tiny. Thank you."

47

Standing, he carried the bowl to the sink and rinsed it before setting it in the dishwasher as he'd seen Jackie and Tiny do. Vincent headed for the kitchen door. "I have to go out."

"Out? By yourself?" Tiny scowled, obviously not pleased.

"Out," Vincent repeated firmly. "By myself."

"Do you think you should? If the saboteur has turned his attention to you . . . Maybe you should tell Jackie—"

"Jackie said I was to go about my business. Unfortunately, I need to feed two or three times a day. So, I'm going about my business," he said simply.

Tiny hesitated, then nodded and asked, "What do I tell your aunt if she comes looking for you?"

Vincent paused with his hand on the door, then seemed to come to a decision. "I suppose I'd best go see if she wants to go with me. It would be rude to just abandon her on her first night here. I'll take her to a couple of clubs, show her the night life. We shouldn't be too late."

"I'll tell Jackie. Have fun," Tiny murmured as Vincent pushed out of the kitchen.

"It's four minutes after ten," Tiny announced. "Two minutes later than it was when you last checked the time."

Jackie forced her eyes away from the clock and scowled at her friend and co-worker. To look at him, one would have thought Tiny was completely absorbed in whatever he was doing on the portable computer on the kitchen table. Apparently, they would be wrong. At least, Tiny wasn't so absorbed he hadn't noticed the way her eyes kept wandering to the clock to check the time.

48

"He's fine," Tiny assured her, then stood and walked over to begin opening and closing cupboard doors. He added, "The saboteur hasn't struck out at him personally in any of the previous attacks."

"The saboteur was targeting his business then. Vincent has taken those targets away by closing his plays. He and his home are the only targets left to the saboteur," Jackie pointed out. "Besides, I'm not *worried* about him, I'm just . . . concerned." She frowned at the admission, then asked with irritation, "What are you looking for?"

"I'm checking to see what ingredients we have. There's a recipe I want to try."

Jackie rolled her eyes and began to tap her nails on the table, then realized what she was doing and folded her hand closed to end the telling action. After a moment, she stood abruptly. "I'm going to bed."

"It's just after ten," Tiny pointed out with surprise. Jackie never went to bed before eleven o'clock at night.

"It's just after ten here," she agreed. "But in New York—where we got up this morning—it's just after one."

"Oh, right." He nodded and turned back to close the cupboard door. "Well, I'm not tired yet, I'm going to bake some muffins for breakfast. It should only take an hour, then I'll probably go to bed too."

Jackie paused at the door and glanced back to find him donning the pink *"I'm the cook!"* apron Vincent had insisted on purchasing that day. The sight of him in the ridiculous thing made her irritation deepen.

"You don't have to cook, Tiny. It's your cover, not your job."

49

"I know," he responded calmly. "I like to cook. It relaxes me."

"Right," Jackie murmured and knew it was true. Tiny had taken a gourmet cooking course years ago and she'd often caught him leafing through women's magazines over the years, looking at recipes. She suspected Tiny was a very small woman in a large man's body, which was probably why they got along so well. Her father had always claimed she was a big, tough guy in a little woman's body.

"What a pair," Jackie muttered under her breath as she walked down the hall, then winced at how loud her voice sounded in the silent house. The security men had finished with the ground floor and left a little less than an hour ago. Allen Richmond had promised to have them back first thing in the morning to start work on the second floor. Jackie had been pleased with his assurance at the time, but now realized that might not be too convenient. Marguerite and Vincent were vampires. They slept during the day and wouldn't be up "first thing" for the men to work in their rooms.

Frowning over the problem, she walked upstairs and glanced along the hall, silently counting rooms, the master bedroom, her room, Marguerite's room, Tiny's room, and two more guest rooms presently unused. With her and Tiny up, she supposed that would give the men four rooms to work on until Marguerite and Vincent got up. She'd have to warn them to work quietly so they didn't wake up Vincent and his aunt.

It was the professional thing to do, but part of her resented the need for it. Jackie was never quite comfortable working with vampires. Bastien teased her that she had a bad attitude when it came to his kind, and he wasn't wrong. Fortunately, Bastien Argeneau knew the source of her attitude and was understanding enough to overlook it. Jackie wondered now if Vincent would be as understanding. She suspected he would. He seemed intelligent, nice, good-humored . . . he also seem to get along great with Tiny, whose judgment she'd always trusted. He was also drop-dead gorgeous with a nice smile and sexy silver-blue eyes.

He's a *vampire,* Jackie reminded herself. It was something she couldn't forget . . . mustn't forget. She feared the moment that happened, she might be foolish enough to start to like the guy in more than a professional manner, and she *so* wasn't going there again. Jackie had learned her lesson young and learned it well with Cassius.

Her teeth set at the very thought of the vampire she'd been involved with at nineteen. An image of him rose in her mind: six feet, four inches tall, with shoulder-length gold hair. The man had been as beautiful as a Greek god.

Jackie instinctively started to push him from her mind, then stopped herself and let the memories play. Not so much as a punishment, but in the hopes reliving the memory would save her from doing something foolish now, eleven years later. Jackie suspected it would be a good thing to reflect on the lesson she'd learned, especially in lieu of the fact that she was living in the home of a vampire that she found very attractive.

"There! You've admitted it," Jackie said on a small sigh as she entered her room and closed the door. "You find Vincent Argeneau attractive."

It was a scary admission for Jackie and immediately made her feel vulnerable. She hadn't felt anything but mild disdain and anger toward a vampire since Cassius.

Jackie had been a good student and a dutiful daughter until the summer she met Cassius. She'd been a naïve and foolish child . . . but had thought herself a woman. She'd met the vampire when he came to her home to see her father about a case he was working for him. He'd been a pale, blond god in her eyes, Adonis as he'd surely been meant to look.

Awestruck by his beauty when he'd come calling, Jackie had worshipped him with her eyes as she'd stammered out that her father wasn't yet home. She could still recall the amused smile that had curved his lips at the time. Jackie hadn't understood it then, but did now. The man had been silently laughing at her shy adoration.

Jackie had hardly been able to believe her luck when he'd asked if he might wait for her father. Blushing and smiling and chattering away, she'd seated him in the living room, then excused herself to make tea, too nervous and overset to recall that vampires didn't drink tea. Something she'd known since she was eighteen and had started to work in her father's company.

Ted Morrissey had been excited and eager when he'd got the first call from Bastien Argeneau with a job he wanted looked after. His company had been small then and the referral from another client to the head of such a large multinational company had been like winning the lottery. However, it was soon after that her father had stopped talking about his cases, at least ones involving the Argeneaus or anyone connected to them. Jackie hadn't understood why until her first day of work for her father when he'd taken her into his office, sat her down, and said what he was about to tell her could never be revealed to anyone . . . Vampires *did* exist.

Young and eager to believe in the unbelievable, she'd gotten over the shock quickly, and then had spent the first couple weeks of her apprenticeship going through every file her father had on each of the immortals. By the time she was nineteen and faced with the handsome Cassius, she'd considered herself something of an expert on the immortals.

Oh, the arrogance of youth, Jackie thought sadly. She'd been fussing over the tea tray in the kitchen when Cassius had joined her there. He'd told her she shouldn't trouble herself, then had pressed a hand gently to her cheek and stared into her eyes. Jackie's breath had caught in the back of her throat at the action, her mouth suddenly dry. She could still recall the trembling that had started in her body, leaving her shaky and weak so she'd had to lean back against the kitchen counter to stay on her feet.

When he'd kissed her, her mind had filled with passions she'd never dreamed of; a wave of want and need that had seemed to consume her. Jackie had been lost.

Cassius had broken the kiss when they heard the front door open. By the time her father found them in the kitchen, Jackie was nervously finishing with the tea tray, and Cassius was seated at the table, but Ted Morrisey had eyed them both with a concern that told her he suspected something had been going on. He didn't say anything, however, not right then. He told Jackie to forget about the tea and ushered Cassius into his office.

Jackie had sagged against the counter once alone, her hand pressed to her heart. It had felt like it would beat its way right out of her chest. She was sure she'd met the man of her dreams and had been horrified when he left and her father came to her and said she was to stay away from Cassius. It was for her own good.

Jackie's obedience had ended there. When Cassius called to invite her out, she lied and snuck about to see him, resenting her father for not understanding young love. Somehow, the lies and sneaking just made it all that bit more exciting, if it were possible.

Cassius had taken her to fine restaurants and plays. Jackie had felt terribly sophisticated on his arm, and while she'd at first been nervous and anxious when he'd started to make love to her in the limo on the way home, that had soon given way to mindless passion. By the time she'd gotten out of that limo, Jackie was sure she was in love.

Cassius had appeared equally enamored of her. Seeming unable to keep his hands off her, he'd started things in the most inappropriate places; kissing her and running his hands up under her skirt in restaurants with only the table to hide what he was doing, pulling her into alleys and making love to her against the wall of the building with only the cover night offered, and finally making love to her in his private box at the theatre where anyone might look over and see. Jackie was always reticent when he first initiated these encounters, but soon found herself overwhelmed by passion and eager to do whatever pleased him. He was like a drug and she a junkie who couldn't get enough.

Her father soon learned she was seeing Cassius behind

his back. How could he not? While she was lying and sneaking out, their dates were always in public and someone eventually mentioned it to him. Jackie came home from what would be their last date to be confronted by her father. They had a terrible row, ending with Jackie yelling that she hated him and would see Cassius if she wanted and there was nothing he could do about it. She'd then run out and taken a taxi straight to Cassius's apartment. She'd buzzed his apartment and the door was immediately released for her, but when she'd reached the apartment she'd found it full of strangers. Cassius was having a party, anyone could have buzzed her in, he probably didn't even know she was there.

Forcing a smile, she'd greeted everyone as if she'd known about the party and been invited as she wound her way through the crowded rooms, looking for Cassius. His office was the last place Jackie looked, and it too had appeared empty at first. Confused and desperate to find him, she was backing out when a laugh made her pause and glance back. It was only then Jackie noticed that the door leading onto the balcony was cracked open. Realizing he must be there, she'd crossed the room to the door, then paused when she saw he wasn't alone. Jackie hadn't recognized the two men with him, but the shine of their eyes in the night told her they were immortals like Cassius.

Jackie had reached for the door to slide it further open to let him know she was there, but one of the men had said something that made her pause.

"You seem to be seeing a lot of that little Jackie."

"Hmm. I was," Cassius had allowed, then shrugged. "But

55

I'm growing bored. She's too unsophisticated. Her adoration was amusing at first, but is becoming annoying." He smiled faintly. "I do like making her do things she doesn't want to do though. Her mind is as malleable as clay and so easily controlled. I barely have to exert myself to get into her thoughts and convince her that yes, she really does want me to screw her in my theatre box where anyone might see."

"You surprise me, Cassius," one of the men had commented. "From what you were telling me you had grown tired of sex and—"

"This isn't about sex," he'd said impatiently. "Although it's a lot more interesting when you know you're making her do things that are against her morals." He'd shrugged. "But I'm growing bored with the game and am thinking to end it soon. I just need to decide how I want to end it. Something magnificent. Perhaps bursting in on one of Ted Morrissey's business meetings and screwing her on the boardroom table in front of important clients. Imagine his humiliation as she squeals like a bitch in heat."

"Jesus, Cassius, I knew you didn't like Ted, but this is just—"

"He doesn't show me the proper respect," Cassius snapped, displaying an anger Jackie had never witnessed from him. "He acts as though he's as good as us and he isn't. None of them are. They're all simple-minded children that we feed from and can control as we wish and he needs to understand that."

Numb with shock, and suddenly terribly, terribly frightened of being discovered there, Jackie had eased away from the door and hurried out of the room. She'd glanced anxiously over her shoulder every half second as she'd made her escape, knowing that if Cassius saw her before she got out, there would be trouble. He'd read her mind and know she'd heard everything . . . He wouldn't have let Jackie leave, knowing what she knew. He would have taken control of her mind, as he'd apparently been doing, and kept her with him until he'd made her do something that would publicly humiliate herself and her father.

Jackie's fear had eased once she was in a taxi on the way home, but it hadn't gone completely. Cassius had been controlling her and would do so again if given the chance. It had seemed to her to be in her best interests to be sure he couldn't. A much humbler Jackie had approached her father on returning home. She'd told him everything, and as she'd hoped, he'd known what to do. He'd called Bastien Argeneau at once and the vampire had come to their home to talk over the matter.

Jackie had been terribly embarrassed at the time, but looking back, Bastien had been extremely kind. He'd assured her that all of his kind did not look down on mortals as Cassius did, and that she hadn't been foolish or stupid, that Cassius had used his abilities to control her behavior and she shouldn't now feel embarrassed at anything she may have done. Then he'd assured her she needn't fear Cassius getting the chance to control her again. They would send her away for a while to keep her safe while he dealt with the matter.

Jackie had found herself on a plane to Europe the next morning. She'd gone to University at Oxford for a year before returning to take a job at her father's company again. She'd never asked what had been done about Cassius. From what Jackie had pieced together over the years, she knew he'd suddenly found it desirous to move out of New York. She also knew he'd been warned off of ever bothering her and her father again.

Jackie dropped onto her bed with a sigh. The memory of those few short weeks in her life no longer caused the pain it once had. She'd been crushed at the time, heart sore and humiliated as she tried to sort out what—if any—of her feelings and passions had been her own and which had been planted by Cassius. She was pretty sure her initial attraction to him had been real. Even now she could acknowledge that Cassius was a handsome man. But his words had made her doubt everything else she'd experienced. Had any of the overwhelming passion been hers? Or had he placed it in her mind, controlling her with it?

To this day, Jackie didn't know the answer to that question. All she knew was that vampires were a dangerous lot, able to subvert a mortal's will. And she'd spent years struggling to strengthen her mind against their abilities to read her thoughts, knowing the entire time that in the end, if they really wanted to, they would easily break down her defenses and not only read but control her mind. That knowledge made her instinctively fear them. Which, in turn, made her angry.

Bastien Argeneau was the only vampire Jackie had even come close to trusting since then. But then, he'd always treated her with gentle respect, and he was even now engaged to a mortal. Jackie really believed that he didn't look down on her people. She was less sure about the rest of his kind, however, so stayed on the defensive with them all. It just seemed the safest way to deal with things.

And, Jackie decided, she would continue to handle it thusly. She had to keep her defenses up, especially now that she was living in the same home as Vincent. She was not going to risk another humiliation like the one Cassius had visited on her. Jackie had to harden her heart against Vincent. It was a simple matter of self-preservation.

Four

Vincent rolled over, opened his eyes and peered at the bedside clock, a frown drawing his eyebrows together as he saw the digital reading. Eleven forty-eight. Dear God, it wasn't even noon. He usually slept until six or later to avoid as much sunlight as possible.

Eleven forty-nine. Vincent glowered at the changing digital reading. Something had obviously woken him. His sleepy mind was just trying to sort out what that might be when the sound of voices came muffled through his bedroom door. Frowning, he turned to peer toward it. It was two men's voices, growing louder as the speakers drew nearer. He tensed as they reached his door, then they apparently continued on down the hall because the voices began to fade again.

"What the hell?" Tossing his blankets and sheets aside, Vincent slid his feet out of bed and got up. He didn't bother dressing, but moved to the door and pulled it open to peer out, eyes widening at the sight of all the men moving in and out of the half dozen open doors off the hallway.

Leaving his room, Vincent started forward, glancing through each open door he passed. There was only one door on the upper floor that was still closed, the door to the room where his aunt Marguerite slept. Wondering how she could possibly sleep through all this racket, Vincent took the stairs, his thoughts scattering as he reached the main floor and found it flooded with light. Every window in the house was covered with a heavy protective curtain that kept the light out and made it safe for him to move around when necessary during the day. Presently, every one of those curtains appeared to have been pulled open to allow sunlight to spill across the hardwood floors.

Growling, Vincent headed for the kitchen, expecting to find Tiny there, but the man was conspicuous in his absence. Turning away from the empty kitchen, he started back up the hall, glancing in each room he passed, searching for Jackie and an explanation for the small army of men who had taken over his home. Vincent found both Jackie and Tiny in his office.

"Morning," Tiny rumbled on spotting him, then turned back to watch Jackie who was on the phone.

"I've already explained who I am. I'm Mr. Argeneau's new personal assistant and he asked me to call and have you send over this information. Just pull the files and fax the list to me." Jackie sounded impatient, apparently not appreciating the resistance she was getting from whomever she was talking to. Vincent watched her expression tighten as she listened for another moment, then Jackie clucked with irritation and snapped, "He's just walked into the office. Hold one moment, please."

Leaning forward, she pressed the button to put the call on hold and scowled at Vincent.

"Your production assistant is being difficult. Please tell her to fax over the list of employees on the New York production," she snapped, then pressed the hold button again and handed him the phone.

Vincent hesitated, not used to being ordered about, but then sighed and took the phone. "Lily?"

"Oh, Mr. Argeneau, that woman claims she's—"

"Yes, yes," Vincent interrupted, then tried for a more pleasant tone as he said, "Yes, Lily. Jackie is my new personal assistant and I did ask her to contact you. Just send over whatever she's asked for and anything else she calls you about in future. Okay? Thanks."

Vincent handed the phone back to Jackie without waiting for agreement, then listened impatiently as she repeated orders she'd obviously already given several times. Once finished, Jackie hung up. "Thank you."

When Vincent's mouth tightened, Tiny considered his exhausted face and then announced, "I think I'll go check on lunch."

Jackie watched the giant go and then said, "Really, thank you. Your Lily was being a pain."

Vincent had intended on blasting her for the noise the men were making, but curiosity got the better of him and, instead, he asked, "How did you find her number?"

"It wasn't hard; you put her under *P* for production assistant in your Rolodex," Jackie pointed out with amusement.

"Finding her wasn't the problem, getting a hold of her was. When I called her office, the switchboard gave me her home phone number. I must have called twenty times before she finally answered."

"She didn't have to answer at all," Vincent muttered. "Lily doesn't normally start work until I do."

"Which reminds me, what are you doing up so early?" she asked with a frown. "I expected you to sleep at least until dinner."

Her question reminded him that he was annoyed and Vincent scowled. "What are all these men doing in my house?"

Jackie appeared surprised at the question. "You know very well what these men are doing here. They're the security team. They're finishing the installation of the alarm system and cameras on the windows and doors upstairs."

Yes, he did know that, but . . . "Couldn't they have come later in the day? They woke me up."

Jackie sat back with a sigh. "The sooner everything's in place and fully operational the better."

Vincent scowled, but he was unable to fault her reasoning. Unfortunately.

"I did ask them to try to keep the noise down," she added apologetically. "I'll talk to them again so that you can get some more sleep."

"No, no. I'm awake now." Vincent shifted impatiently on his feet, his gaze looking over Jackie, noting she wore another business suit, this one gray with a red blouse under it. Very sharp, very nice on her, he thought, his gaze slipping to the wide expanse of neck left bare by the open top two buttons. He found himself staring at the creamy white flesh with fascination. To him, it was tantamount to waving a pizza under the nose of a starving man. Without even thinking about it, Vincent found himself taking a step closer, pausing only when his thighs bumped against the edge of the desk.

"For heaven's sake, stop looking at me like lunch!" Jackie said irritably as she stood up. "And, do you always have to wander around here shirtless?"

Vincent blinked and glanced down at himself, only now becoming aware that he was wearing only a pair of soft cotton pajama pants. Apparently, she found his state of undress distressing, he noted, and glanced up to catch Jackie staring at his chest. Her eyes slid down over his pecs to his flat stomach in a caress he almost felt. Vincent found himself with the sudden urge to stretch and flex some of those muscles she was eyeing with such interest, but before he could, Jackie blinked as if waking from sleep and jerked her eyes up to his face.

She blushed bright pink at being caught gawking, then he saw her mouth tighten and spoke quickly to prevent her grouching at him again. "So what's all this then?"

Jackie hesitated, then glanced down at the stacks of paper on his desk. Sighing, she pushed one hand through her golden hair and visibly relaxed. "This is your mail, Mr. Argeneau."

"Hmm. Mail." Vincent ignored the return of the formal address and nodded as he glanced over the piles. He never opened his mail. He just stacked it up on the table in his hallway until the table couldn't hold it anymore, then dumped it all in a box.

"You had three months worth of mail in your hall," she informed him dryly.

"Yes, well—"

"I opened and sorted it all, stacking it in order by date with the oldest on top," Jackie went on, ignoring his efforts to explain himself. "This first pile is just bill receipts. I gather you have direct debit for all your bills?"

"Yes," Vincent answered absently, his gaze slipping from the stack in question, to the creamy flesh of her throat and lingering there before he forced it away.

Jackie nodded. "I'll file them later today if you'll tell me where your files are kept."

"I usually just toss them in a box and throw them in that closet," Vincent admitted, gesturing to a door to their right.

Jackie's eyes widened incredulously at this news. "What about when tax time rolls around? Don't you—"

"I send the boxes to my personal accountant," Vincent answered. "Most of it isn't stuff he needs, but I let him sort it out."

"That's—that—" Jackie paused, cleared her throat and then said, "Accountants charge by the hour to *sort* out such things."

Vincent shrugged, not terribly concerned. Money wasn't a big issue for him. Between his shares in Argeneau Enterprises, along with his own company interests and investments made over the last four hundred years, he wasn't stinking rich, but he was rich enough.

"Whatever," she said finally with a shrug. "I'll put them in the box."

"Sure." His gaze slid to her throat again and away. He really had to move this along and see about feeding. "What is the rest of this?"

Jackie pointed to the next stack. "This is all nice fan mail. It's pretty obvious you don't answer your fans."

He could hear the disapproval in her voice and propelled the conversation along again by gesturing at the last two piles. "What are these then?"

"This stack is all business letters," Jackie answered, pointing to the larger pile. "Letters from your agent, play directors, etc."

She paused then and he suspected Jackie was biting her lip on commenting on the fact that he hadn't bothered to open such important mail. Clearing her throat, she gestured to the last pile. "This pile is the important one. It's what I was looking for when I opened your mail in the first place."

"What are they?" Vincent asked, picking up the top letter.

"They're unusual fan letters and nasty letters from angry employees who were fired, and upset actors and actresses who were passed over for roles. They're possible suspects."

Vincent grunted and read the letter he'd picked up. It was only a couple of lines long. He read it, paused, then reread it, his hunger suddenly forgotten.

I know who you are. I know what you are.

Frowning, he glanced at the envelope Jackie had stapled to it. The postal cancellation was local and dated little more than two months old, the return address was his own. He shifted the letter and envelope to the bottom of the pack and read the next, and the next. The first several were all the same. Short. Simple.

I know who you are. I know what you are.

Then one read:

Oops, someone had an accident.

Vincent stiffened and glanced at the envelope. It was dated the day after the stage set accident where the actress had broken her arm. Frowning, he set it aside and looked at the next. It read:

Oops, someone stumbled.

Vincent knew what he would find before he even looked at the envelope, but he checked anyway and his mouth flattened out with anger as he saw it had been posted the day after Dan Henson broke his leg.

"These are from him?" Vincent said, shifting that letter to the bottom to reveal the next.

Someone was thirsty.

He wasn't surprised to find the cancellation was New York and was dated in the midst of his cast members coming down with their contagious anemia.

"Yes, it would seem so," Jackie said, taking them from him. "But they might not be. They're creepy, but don't make any threats. And they're all posted the day after the events. It could just be someone with a sick sense of humor."

When Vincent snorted at the possibility, she shrugged. "I

don't want to jump to conclusions. Any of these other letters might be from him. Tiny and I will look into them all."

Vincent nodded and then asked, "Why did you want the list of employees?"

"I'll have to check into everyone working for you, but I want to start with the play you were rehearsing in New York."

"Why especially that one?"

"Four of the plays were already open when the actresses or actors walked and anyone who went to them could see who was the lead and so on. But that isn't the case with two of them, one in Canada and the one in New York. You hadn't yet publicized who was in *Dracula, the Musical,* had you?" she asked.

"No. We were still in rehearsal and preparing promotion, but hadn't released any information yet," he admitted.

Jackie nodded. "The attacks in New York would have to have been carried out by someone with access to the sets and actors. To have been biting your cast, they had to first know who was *in* your cast. I presume the rehearsals weren't open to just anyone who felt like wandering in off the street?"

"No." Vincent sighed. "There were security guards on the doors at the theatre we were using in New York to be sure no one came in."

Jackie pointed out, "Of course, one of your kind could have controlled the minds of the security guards to allow them to get in. If that's the case, the lists won't help. We'll just have to hope he took a job on set to assist in gaining access. Otherwise, we'll have trouble tracking him down."

When Vincent frowned, she added, "We'll worry about

that after we go through the people on the list, which we'll do the minute your production assistant faxes them over." She pursed her lips. "That could be a while. This Lily has to actually go to the office and then find the files."

Picking up the first stack of letters, Jackie moved around the desk, passing Vincent on her way to the closet. He inhaled as she went by, eyes closing briefly at the scent of spices and her own skin. God, she smelled good. And he was so hungry. Vincent was always hungry when he first got up, but this went beyond that. The more he stood about looking at and smelling Jackie, the hungrier he got, to the point that he was now almost unbearably ravenous. If he didn't leave soon he might be moved to do something rash, which was never a good thing. His kind learned at a young age that rash behavior could be deadly behavior.

Forcing his eyes open, Vincent saw that Jackie was framed in the door of the closet. She was muttering to herself and shaking her head as she bent to rifle briefly through the large box of mail on the floor. His gaze trailed over her pert bottom as her gray skirt pulled tight over her behind and he found himself licking his lips as he imagined walking over, running his hands over those sweet curves, then letting his hands slide up and around her waist as she straightened in surprise before him.

Vincent could almost hear her little murmur of surprise as he'd urge her bottom back against his groin. Cuddling her there, he'd then let his fingers slide up over her stomach, urging her jacket open so that he could cup her full breasts through the silk material of her red top. He'd hold them as she arched into the caress, then urge her long blond hair to the side, baring her neck. He'd press kisses to her neck and then—

Vincent stopped his thoughts abruptly as he felt his teeth slide out. He then blinked in surprise as he realized it wasn't the only part of his body that had responded to his imaginings. He was sporting a very healthy erection that was making a tent out of his cotton pajama bottoms. Even more surprising, as Vincent had imagined what he would do, his feet had carried him over to stand behind Jackie. He was close enough to smell her sweet perfume and it was a sort of torture that only increased his hunger, both of them.

Giving himself a mental shake, Vincent backed a step away and then turned on his heel and moved to the door. He had to feed. *Now.*

He glanced back toward Jackie as he opened the door, but she was still busy in the closet. Leaving her to it, Vincent slid silently out of the room.

Jackie stared at the heaping box of mail in the office closet and shook her head. How the man made any money was beyond her. He didn't answer his fan mail, didn't even look at his business letters, and his accountant must be charging him through the roof for sorting through the mess in his closet.

"You seriously do need a P.A., Argeneau. It's just an incredible waste of money having your accountant wade through this junk and—"

Jackie paused and scowled as she turned to find the office empty. The man had slid out as silently as a thief while her back was turned. Frowning, she moved to the door and opened it to peer into the hall just in time to see Vincent stop one of the security guys as he came down the stairs. She watched narrow-eyed as he spoke to the man, then he suddenly herded the worker into a side door further down the hall. And herding was the only word for it. Jackie pictured the poor man as a sheep being led to the slaughter. Not that she thought Vincent would kill him. He was just going to feed on him, she was sure.

Jackie slipped out of the office and moved quickly down the hall to pause outside the door the two men had disappeared through. She glanced quickly around to be sure no one was in the hall to see, then pressed an ear to the wood and held her breath as she listened.

Not a sound came from the room. Not a word. Not a murmur. Nothing.

After another hesitation, her mouth flattened out grimly and Jackie opened the door and slid inside to peer around. She spotted Vincent and the worker almost at once. The security man stood across the room, staring out of the window. Vincent stood behind him, his teeth sunk into the man's neck.

"Ah-ha!" Jackie cried as she slammed the door closed behind her.

Vincent stiffened and then whirled to face her, guilt on his face and a drop of blood by the corner of his mouth. The worker didn't react at all.

"I thought you said you didn't feed on your employees!" Jackie snapped, hands on hips.

Vincent's mouth curled down with displeasure. "I don't. He's not *my* employee."

"Oh, that's just semantics," she protested. "He's in the

71

employ of a company in your employ. That makes him your employee, if only indirectly."

Vincent opened his mouth to respond, then paused and turned back to his dinner. The worker immediately began to move. His face utterly blank, he turned around and crossed the room.

Knowing that Vincent controlled him and was probably sending him from the room and back to where he belonged, Jackie opened the door and held it for him to exit, but turned to raise an eyebrow in Vincent's direction before closing it. The vampire ignored her look of enquiry for another moment, his attention wholly on the laborer. She knew he was rearranging the man's memories and thoughts, so waited patiently until he glanced her way and nodded.

Jackie immediately closed the door as soundlessly as possible and then waited for Vincent to speak. He didn't keep her waiting long.

"I was hungry."

"That's it?" she asked with disbelief. "That's all you have to say for yourself?"

Vincent shrugged. "I was hungry so I fed. What do you do when you're hungry?"

"It's hardly the same thing," Jackie growled.

"Why? Because you feed on fluffy little baby cows and chickens and I feed on mortals?"

Jackie could only glare in response.

"At least my feedings do not necessitate the death of my chosen meal," Vincent pointed out dryly.

Jackie found herself blinking several times in response to this comment. She was at a loss for words. Not a single argument was coming to her aid here and for a moment frustration reared within her, but then she realized there simply was no argument to that. She and her kind— mortals—did kill to eat. His kind didn't have to kill to survive. In effect, immortals did much less harm to their chosen meal than mortals did, she realized, and suddenly felt on uneven ground as most of her outrage slipped away like smoke.

Before Jackie could rally her defenses, he started forward, continuing, "I was hungry. I always wake up hungry, and you smelled as delicious as Tiny's homemade cookies. However, you and Tiny are off limits for biting, so I bit one of the workers from the security company." He shrugged. "As you saw for yourself, he walked out of here. He was not unduly harmed, and will not remember the occasion. I am sated for now and no harm was done except perhaps to your delicate sensibilities."

Jackie had to force herself not to take a step back when he paused directly in front of her. Vincent was close enough that she could smell him, close enough she could feel the heat from his naked chest, close enough she could touch him if she chose to and part of her really, really wanted to. Instead, Jackie barked, "My delicate sensibilities?"

Managing to tear her eyes away from his very close, very wide chest she scowled at Vincent. "Is that some kind of insult?"

Vincent raised his eyebrows, looking every bit as arrogant and condescending as his kind could get. "Not at all. I am simply surprised that someone who knows so well what we are, and has worked with us for so long, would be so shocked and outraged when she sees us doing what it is in our nature to do."

"Doing what it is in your nature to do," Jackie echoed grimly. For some reason the words reminded her of the old fable about the scorpion and the frog. The scorpion convinced a frog to give it a ride across a river, but stung it halfway across. As the frog began to sink under the river's surface, taking the scorpion with it, he asked why, and the scorpion said it was "in his nature."

It was a good reminder to her, Jackie supposed. She mustn't ever forget that Vincent was an immortal, a vampire with a vampire's nature and attitudes. She and Tiny—and every other mortal he encountered—were probably nothing more than walking dinner to him.

Still, his irritation with her upset urged her to remind him, "The others of your kind drink blood from a cup, or even straight from the bag, but you're the only one who actually bites people."

"Hardly the only one," Vincent said with a shrug that drew her attention back to his bare chest. "Simply the only one you've met."

Jackie knew that was true, but she was finding it terribly difficult to think with the man standing so close.

"Besides," he pointed out. "You wouldn't have seen it at all if you'd simply minded your own business, rather than followed me in here."

That, unfortunately, was also true. She'd followed him in here expecting to catch him in the act, had even *wanted* to, but this was his home and it really was none of her business. Unfortunately, Jackie was very curious about his feeding.

Tilting her head to the side, she gave in to that curiosity.

"Do you prefer men or women?" she asked and then—when he stiffened—added hastily, "To bite."

Vincent relaxed and shrugged. "Do you prefer meat from a male or female cow?"

"There isn't a difference," she said with confusion. "Steak is steak."

"And so it is with me. When I'm hungry, I don't care. Whichever is handiest or easiest to get to; it's all blood whether from a male or female."

"Oh." While she could understand that blood was blood, Jackie still found it surprising that—to him—feeding was just feeding. None of the files had got this in depth into their feeding habits. Most had been filled with data about the history of their people, each person's individual history, and so on.

The only thing any of the files had said about their feeding habits was that they could survive on blood without food, but not food without blood. That they were now restricted by their council to feeding off bagged blood rather than off living hosts except in cases of emergency, or necessity such as in Vincent and his father, Victor's, case. And the only exception was love bites as they were called, bites between an immortal and a consenting mortal or immortal lover. Jackie had some experience with the last rule. She'd consented to let Cassius bite her while they were dating and it had always been an incredibly erotic experience. In fact, it made it hard for her to imagine that feeding might not be that mind-blowing, sexy, whole-body rush of pleasure that she'd known.

She wasn't willing to discuss Cassius with Vincent,

however, so simply said, "I guess I've been influenced by books and movies over the years. They always portray it as much more—well, it appears somewhat . . . intimate and sensual, yet you make it sound like sitting down to a sandwich."

"It can be both," Vincent acknowledged. "Though more often than not it is like sitting down to a sandwich. I am hungry, so I feed."

"Do you always bite from behind?" she asked.

"I prefer to approach men from behind; it makes it easier to alter their memory. They can look at television or at the scenery and I can put the memory in their mind that while they continued to watch T.V. or to look out at the yard, I was chattering on with some horribly boring diatribe."

When Jackie looked confused, he explained, "Men are more visual by nature and rarely listen to conversation they find boring. Their minds drift and they focus on something else, usually what they're seeing. They learn to simply respond in a way that seems appropriate to tonal changes."

Jackie's lips twitched, knowing that—unless you were discussing work, or sports, or something they found interesting—men did "zone out" and just respond with nods or affirmative murmurs when your voice became questioning.

"And women?" Jackie asked, curious about his take on the female sex.

"Women pay more attention to conversation. Communication is more important to them, so—while men will be satisfied with a vague memory of my blathering on with some boring subject—women would fret over not recalling what it was about. It's easier to approach them face to face and embrace them as you bite, then give them the vague memory of a passionate moment."

While Jackie could agree that men were less verbal than women, the idea that women were less likely to remember the actual physical activity seemed odd to her. "I can believe that women find conversation more important, but surely when it comes to passion, if it's just a *vague* memory, they will fret over that too?"

"Oddly enough, no. Most women seem less concerned with the intimate details of where they were touched and so on and tend simply to recall how they felt and the passion they enjoyed."

Jackie wanted to argue the point, but as she tried to think back to her last boyfriend and recall his kisses and caresses, it was all rather blurry. She had a vague recollection of standing in her kitchen and his urging her back against the counter as he kissed her, but other than that it became a blurry memory of sensations and her body's responses. Now it made her wonder if men remembered it more clearly, like a play-by-play in a football game. While she was curious about that, Jackie didn't have the nerve to ask Vincent and soothed herself with the promise to maybe ask Tiny sometime . . . maybe.

Blinking her thoughts away, she found herself staring at Vincent's chest. Her gaze slid over him, taking in the pearly white flesh that had rarely, if ever, seen sunlight. In this day and age of sun worship and tanning salons, it should have appeared unhealthy and even unattractive to her. It wasn't. Instead, he was beautiful, almost like a marble statue come to life. Her eyes traced the breadth of him and then trav-

Lynsay Sands

eled down over pecs and an admirably flat abdomen toward the waist of his cotton pajama bottoms. They were loose and comfortable, but there was no missing that he definitely had a healthy package. This was when another question occurred to her.

"You said you give them a memory of . . . er . . . passionate moments. Does that mean you don't actually make love to them every—?" Jackie paused abruptly as the slight bulge in his pajama bottoms became more noticeable and she realized that not only was she staring rudely, but what she was asking was incredibly rude and nosy as well.

Dragging her eyes from his lower body, Jackie glanced toward his face to see that Vincent had arched an eyebrow at her impertinence. She immediately began to backpedal as she felt her face suffuse with a blush. "I just mean, surely— while you obviously wouldn't *every* time—sometimes you might be moved to . . . ?"

He continued to stare at her in silence and Jackie shifted her feet, angry at herself for being so stupid. After a moment, however, she came to the conclusion that it was his fault. He was the one standing about half-naked, giving her these ideas. Shifting impatiently, she turned abruptly away and headed for the door.

"Where are you going now?" Vincent asked, following her out into the hall.

"Lunch," Jackie answered sharply. "Tiny put on chili this morning and promised it would be ready for lunch."

"Chili?" he asked with interest, keeping pace with her when all she wanted was to get away from him and the over-

78

whelming effect he was having on her normally sensible thoughts.

Jackie glanced at him out of the corner of her eye, then shook her head. "I don't mean to be rude, Argeneau, but if you're joining us for lunch, you can just go put on some clothes. I can't think of anything less appetizing than your sad, white chest staring at me across the table."

Vincent scowled and stopped walking. Leaving him glaring after her, she stepped into the kitchen and let the door swing shut between them.

Vincent remained standing there for several minutes, scowling after her, then he recalled the way her eyes had slid over his chest when he'd first entered the office. His tension immediately began to ease.

Jackie may claim his "sad, white chest" was unappetizing, but her eyes had been saying something entirely different earlier . . . which meant she didn't want him half-naked at the table for another reason, like maybe she found it too attractive and distracting.

Well, Vincent decided, she'd just have to suffer his sad, white chest staring at her across the table today. In fact, he might just walk around shirtless more often. All the time, even. Smiling to himself, he continued on to the kitchen. Vincent suddenly had an appetite for chili.

Five

Jackie stared down at her chili and ground her teeth together. She'd been so sure she'd convinced Vincent to go put on some clothes when he'd stopped dead in the hall at her insults. It would appear she'd been wrong. The man had followed her into the room a moment later, cheerful as could be . . . and still half-naked.

Damned man, she thought irritably. Vincent was gorgeous and knew it. He'd been stretching and flexing his pecs through the entire lunch, making it difficult for her to concentrate on what she was eating. It could have been sawdust for all she knew.

"Jackie, is that one of the cups we bought?"

She glanced up to see Vincent pointing toward a lone cup on the counter. Jackie peered at it blankly and then back to him as she answered, "Yes, of course it is."

"Oh. I guess it just looks different in this light." Vincent slowly drew his hand back and gave a shrug, drawing her gaze to his chest as it moved. Jackie stared at the shifting muscles and then realized what she was doing and jerked her eyes up to Vincent's beaming face.

The irritating vamp knew exactly what effect he had on her, she realized. Her eyes narrowed coldly, but before she could say something they might both regret, the kitchen door swung open and Marguerite sailed into the room.

"Good afternoon!" she sang.

She was smiling and cheerful, but Jackie still frowned and offered, "I'm sorry, Marguerite. Did the men wake you? I meant to warn them to work more quietly but—"

"No, no," she interrupted. "No one woke me, I set my alarm for noon. I wanted to be up early to help you."

"To help me?" Jackie asked, alarm bells ringing.

"Yes. The early bird catches the saboteur, you know."

Jackie's head jerked toward Vincent, accusation sharp on her face.

"She read my mind last night while we were out," he muttered apologetically.

"Vincent never could lie to me," Marguerite announced with a small smile.

Jackie ground her teeth together and forced herself to count to ten. Her first instinct was to protest most vehemently. Unfortunately, Marguerite was Bastien Argeneau's mother, and—for that reason alone—Jackie would never take the chance of offending the woman. She had to handle this delicately. Her mind raced briefly and then suddenly hit on a plan to keep both of the immortals out of the way while she and Tiny worked.

"Well, this works out nicely," she announced and couldn't help noting that Marguerite's eyes had suddenly narrowed and Vincent's face had turned suspicious.

Ignoring their reactions, she said, "I was thinking this morning that it might be good if Vincent went out and talked to the actress who walked out on the play yesterday, just on the off chance that the saboteur had neglected to clear her mind as efficiently as the others. However, I didn't want him to go by himself in case the saboteur really has turned his attention his way. I thought I'd have to go with him and put off going through the letter writers to eliminate as many as I could. This way, though, you can go with him and Tiny and I can stay here and get through the letters."

"Lovely." Marguerite beamed and Jackie was just beginning to relax, when she added, "However, as you say, the saboteur may turn his attention to him now that the plays are no longer a target and if that's the case, perhaps he should stay here and go through the letters with you while Tiny accompanies me."

Jackie's eyes widened in dismay. She'd hoped to get rid of both of them, not be stuck with Vincent. Alone. "Oh, I—"

"Besides, the more sunlight he avoids the better. I can just slap a bag of blood on my teeth. Vincent can't," Marguerite pointed out and Jackie felt her shoulders droop in defeat. Apparently recognizing victory when she saw it, the woman moved to slip a hand through Tiny's arm. "Come along, Tiny. I rented the cutest little sports car. You can drive it if you like."

Tiny glanced toward Jackie in question, but relaxed and

allowed Marguerite to lead him out of the room when she nodded grimly.

"Nice try, but Aunt Marguerite always gets what she wants. Or mostly always," Vincent said dryly as they watched the door close behind the pair.

Jackie scowled at the man. "If you hadn't told her—"

"I stuck to the cover story," Vincent interrupted to assure her. "She read my mind last night while we were out."

"Well, couldn't you keep her from doing that?" she asked with exasperation. "Surely immortals can keep other immortals out of their thoughts?"

"Yes, if we concentrate on guarding our thoughts we can keep other immortals from reading them," Vincent admitted, but before Jackie could use that against him, he added, "However, no one can be on guard all the time. She knew I was lying and the minute I let my guard slip, she was in there routing away at my thoughts."

Jackie shook her head with disgust. "It sounds an uncomfortable way to live if you constantly have to be on guard against others reading your thoughts."

"It is," he acknowledged. "Which is why many of us are more solitary by nature until we find our life mates. Once we reach adulthood, most move to their own homes to have a place to relax after work and not constantly be on guard."

Jackie glanced at him curiously. "After work? Do you work mostly with immortals then?"

"Most of the actors and actresses are mortals, but a lot of the production people and office workers at the production company are immortal," he answered.

Jackie frowned. This news meant there were a lot more suspects than she'd hoped. Sighing, she carried her bowl to the sink to rinse it. Vincent stood to follow suit and Jackie's mouth tightened as he joined her at the sink and she caught a whiff of him. He smelled good and it wasn't cologne. The man hadn't showered or dressed yet. What she was smelling was him . . . And she liked it.

Moving away from him as quickly as she could, Jackie headed for the door. "I'll be in the office."

"I'll shower and dress and be right with you," Vincent said as he rinsed his own bowl.

"You don't really need to help me with the letters," Jackie said quickly, pausing at the door. "I can handle it on my own."

"I'm sure you can, but it will go quicker with two of us," Vincent argued easily as he turned off the water and set his bowl aside.

Jackie's gaze dipped down over his body as he neared and then she turned swiftly away and slid from the room. She was almost running as she moved up the hall and was slipping into the office before the kitchen door opened behind her.

Jackie closed the door with relief and peered around the office. It was a good-sized room but the idea of being stuck in here alone for hours with Vincent made it shrink in her mind.

Crossing the floor, she scowled at the stacks of letters on the desk, then snatched up the rest that didn't have to do with the case and filed them in the box in the closet. She then settled at the desk and turned her attention to the letters she'd decided were possible suspects. They had to look into each person and start eliminating suspects. Of course, the eight or so from the anonymous writer who just kept saying *I know who you are. I know what you are,* would be difficult to eliminate. They had neither a signature, nor a return address, but she could at least start eliminating the others. Her father had always said, round up all the suspects, eliminate all you can, and who you're left with is probably the culprit. Of course, that was assuming you could eliminate everyone but the culprit, which wasn't always the case.

Sighing, she set to work and was well into it when Vincent entered. She had to pause then to tell him what to do and then returned to work, managing to almost ignore his presence . . . Almost. It was like trying to ignore an elephant on your chest, but she did her best.

They worked on the letters through the afternoon and managed to get enough information on half of the letter writers to eliminate them as possible saboteurs. It was close to five when Vincent announced he was going to get a drink and slipped from the room. Jackie continued to work for another couple of minutes before a case of the yawns made her stop.

This kind of work was the boring side of being a private investigator. Hoping a little fresh air would revive her, Jackie stood and opened one of the French doors. Her gaze moved over the driveway as a car came into view. Jackie stared at the vehicle, sure she hadn't heard the buzzer announcing a car at the gate.

She watched the car park behind Allen Richmond's SUV. The doors immediately opened to allow two women to spill out and move toward the house. They were both tall and blond, but one had a full, curvaceous body, while the other had the thin, gawky body of a youth.

"I don't know why you wouldn't just let me fax them over here, Sharon. She told me to *fax* them," the slender girl said and Jackie realized she must be the production assistant, Lily. Dear God, the child didn't look old enough to be out of high school.

"Because if you'd faxed them, we wouldn't have had an excuse to come over and check out this Jackie person," said the woman Lily had addressed as Sharon.

"Who cares?" Lily snorted. "I don't want to meet her."

"Well, I do," Sharon countered. "As Vincent's secretary, I should keep abreast of these things. Besides, if you really didn't care and didn't want to meet her you could have given me the papers to bring over myself," she pointed out, and Jackie found herself examining the woman from head to toe. Sharon looked to be in her late twenties to early thirties. She was pretty and dressed smartly in a short, straight black skirt and white blouse.

"*I* was the one told to send them to her. If they're coming over, I'm doing it myself to make sure it gets done," Lily said grimly. In contrast to the other woman, Lily wore jeans and a Planet Hollywood t-shirt. Production assistant chic, Jackie supposed.

The pair passed by, so busy nattering at each other that neither woman noticed the open French doors, or Jackie standing half behind the closed one. Leaving her spot by the door, she moved out into the hall and opened the front door just as Sharon reached out to press the doorbell. Both women stilled and gaped, so taken by surprise that neither seemed sure what to say at first.

"Sharon and Lily." Jackie's greeting just seemed to surprise them even more. The two women looked at each other, then back to her in silence.

Jackie immediately felt a ruffling at the edge of her mind. Instantly on the alert, she projected a brick wall in her mind and began to silently recite "Little Jack Horner." She also peered more closely at the women. Lily had pretty but plain hazel eyes. She wasn't the vampire then. Every immortal had a metallic shine to their eyes, either silver or bronze. It had something to do with increased night vision and was their most telling feature.

Her gaze slid to Sharon and Jackie's eyes narrowed. The secretary had silvery green eyes, definitely a vampire . . . and the one presently trying to rifle through her thoughts. Continuing with her silent recitation, Jackie held her hand out toward Lily, smiling as she said, "This would be the list of employees I called you about?"

Lily nodded.

"Lily had to wait for me to come into the office to find out where I'd filed them," Sharon excused their tardiness. "And then she doesn't drive, so I brought her over."

"Hmm." Though she'd overheard the reason they were really here, Jackie didn't comment. She simply waited patiently with her hand extended for the papers Lily held.

"I didn't know Vincent was hiring a P.A.," Sharon said as the silence drew out.

"Neither did I until he hired me," Jackie said pleasantly.

Sharon frowned. "He usually has me call the agencies to send people out when he wants to hire someone. It's how Lily and Meredith and everyone has been hired."

"How interesting," Jackie said mildly, but ground her teeth

together as the ruffling continued on the edge of her thoughts. She was beginning to find the woman's persistence irritating.

Finding no satisfaction in that line of questioning, Sharon tried a new one. "I don't know why Vincent would possibly want the list of employees. I thought he'd closed this play for good. Is he thinking of starting it up again?"

"I have no idea," Jackie lied easily. "But it's not my place to wonder. I just do what I'm told," she added pointedly, then glanced at the younger girl. "Can I have the lists, Lily?"

"Oh, yes. Sorry." Lily handed them over and then glanced at Sharon.

Jackie got the feeling the girl was silently begging to leave now. If so, Sharon's answer was a resounding no as she turned and said, "Well, Meredith—Meredith in accounting, she handles payroll," she explained. "Meredith hasn't heard of you either."

"I'm sure Mr. Argeneau will take care of that eventually," Jackie said calmly, but made a note to herself about such slip-ups. Covers only worked if they were credible.

"Well, you'd better be sure he fixes it if you want a check on payday." Sharon was turning out to be an annoying woman. She was curious and determined to have her curiosity satisfied.

"I'll make a note of mentioning it to him," Jackie murmured.

"Make a note about what?" Vincent asked suddenly from behind her and Jackie nearly jumped out of her skin in surprise.

Turning, she grimaced and said, "Sharon was just informing me that I haven't been put on payroll yet."

Vincent's eyes widened and then he forced a smile. "That's because you'll be paid out of the household account. Like Tiny."

"Who's Tiny?" Sharon asked curiously.

"My new housekeeper," Vincent answered.

Jackie's eyebrows rose as she noted he'd left out the cook part of the title.

Ignoring her look, Vincent said, "Thank you for bringing the files over, ladies."

He'd apparently decided to send them on their way, but Jackie had one more thing she needed to know. "Did someone buzz you in at the gate? I didn't hear the buzzer."

"I have a remote," Sharon announced.

"Sharon often has to drop things off and it's just easier with her having a remote," Vincent said into the silence that followed her words.

"Of course." Jackie smiled pleasantly. "If you'll excuse me?"

Leaving Vincent to handle the women, Jackie turned away and walked straight upstairs to find Allen Richmond. She discovered him in Vincent's room, overseeing the work being done there. While waiting for him to finish instructing one of the men, Jackie ran her gaze over the room. She'd taken a quick peek the day before as she'd toured the upstairs, now she took a more thorough look around. Vincent Argeneau had a taste for the decadent. The room was huge and decorated in tans accented with deep reds. There was a large entertainment system with a huge television as well as stereo equipment, but the king-size bed was the central focus. It was an ocean of red sheets that had a sheen to them, suggesting they were some blend of satin. Sateen perhaps.

"Miss Morrisey? Can I help you?"

Jackie turned from her examination of Vincent's room to peer at Allen Richmond as he approached. She got right to the point. "When you fixed the gate, you didn't change the sensor or code, did you?"

"No. You didn't request it."

Jackie nodded. "Can you change them?"

He raised his eyebrows in surprise. "Yes. Is there a problem?"

"I'm afraid someone has a remote who shouldn't," Jackie explained.

"It would be cheaper to ask for the remote back and just have to change the code," Allen pointed out.

"I knew you'd be up here," Vincent said dryly as he entered the room. "There's no need to change the gate code and sensor."

"Can you get the remote back?" Jackie asked, turning to him.

"I could," he said slowly, obviously not pleased with the idea.

"Would you *be willing* to?" Jackie asked, getting to the point.

When Vincent winced at the idea, she nodded and turned back to Allen. "Change both the code and sensor and get Vincent a new one."

"But Sharon might be offended that—" Vincent began in protest.

"Sharon will never know until she tries to use the remote again, and then you'll simply tell her you had your entire security system overhauled and forgot to mention it," she said reasonably.

Sighing, he nodded at Allen Richmond. "Do it."

"No problem. Whatever the customer wants," Allen said with amusement and headed out of the room.

Jackie was quick to follow. She was uncomfortable in the lush room now that Vincent was there.

"Tiny and Aunt Marguerite are back," Vincent announced as he followed her. "And the coffee I put on should be ready."

Jackie recalled that he'd gone in search of a drink before the women had arrived and supposed that he'd been making the coffee then.

"I'm surprised you didn't insist I get the remote back from Sharon," Vincent admitted suddenly as they started downstairs.

"Sharon doesn't seem the most understanding of women," Jackie said mildly. "And there's nothing likely to cause more havoc than a secretary pissed at her boss. The last thing we need at this juncture is havoc. Changing the sensor and code are the easiest solution all around."

"Good thinking," he murmured. "Sharon can get a bit testy."

"Why do you keep her on then?"

Vincent hesitated, then sighed. "She was the wife of a friend of mine. When he died, she was left with nothing and had to start over." He shrugged. "She needed a job and I needed a secretary. I couldn't possibly fire her."

Jackie glanced quickly away from his handsome face and sighed. The man was too damned nice by half. Unfortunately, the last thing she wanted him to be was nice. It made it difficult not to like him. Jackie scowled and reminded herself of Cassius as they reached the bottom of the stairs and started up the hall.

She forced a smile as she pushed through the door to the kitchen and found Tiny and Marguerite there. As Vincent had said, they were back. Tiny was transferring something from the refrigerator to the oven and Marguerite looked as if she'd just been leaving the room, but paused now as they entered.

"Oh, there you are. I was just coming to look for you."

"We were upstairs talking to Allen," Jackie explained, and then asked, "Did you find out anything?"

"Nothing," Tiny answered with a grimace as he straightened from the oven. "The woman's brain was an empty slate."

"In more ways than one," Marguerite added dryly.

Jackie smiled faintly. "Well, we had a little better luck. We eliminated at least half of the letter writers from the list of suspects, and the assistant brought the employee lists by."

"She *brought* it?" Tiny asked with interest.

"Yes. *Brought* rather than *fax* it as I requested," she said dryly. "Vincent's secretary wanted to check me out."

"No, she didn't," Vincent countered with amusement. "After you left, Sharon explained that the fax machine was down. Lily doesn't drive and so Sharon offered to bring her over. It was good of her to go to the trouble."

"Is that what she told you?" Jackie asked dryly. "Well, I hate to ruin your illusions where your secretary is concerned, but I heard them talking as they walked by the office and clearly heard Sharon say the reason she'd brought

Lily over rather than let her fax the information was because she wanted to check me out."

When Vincent looked stunned at this information, Jackie commented, "I'm surprised she lied to you when you could just read her and know she's lying."

"I told you, we can only read another immortal if they aren't guarding their thoughts," Vincent muttered with a frown. "And I don't go around reading my employees anyway. I don't read anyone. It's rude and intrusive."

"Vincent's still young," Marguerite said almost apologetically. "After another couple hundred years, he'll find it easier to use the skills he has. Reading minds cuts through a lot of misunderstandings."

Jackie bit her lip as she realized that here she'd been thinking Marguerite was rude in trying to read her mind, yet was advocating Vincent's reading Sharon's mind, as well as Marguerite's reading the actress's. It seemed she had some double-standard issues.

"This secretary, Sharon, is an immortal?" Tiny asked curiously.

"Yes," Jackie said, glad for the distraction and then added, "And a barracuda."

"No, she isn't," Vincent said with surprise. "She's fine."

"She's pushy, nosy and rude," Jackie said irritably. Double standard or not, if Sharon had tried to read her mind one more time, she'd have plowed her.

Vincent was frowning. "That doesn't sound like the Sharon I know at all."

"This is Hollywood. Everyone's an actor out here," Jackie said with a shrug. The comment was directed as much to herself as him. It was a reminder. She had to stop thinking Vincent was nice. He was an immortal by birth like Cassius, and an actor by chosen trade. She mustn't forget either fact.

But neither detail changes the fact that he's nice by nature. Vincent's a good man.

Jackie glanced sharply toward Marguerite as those words drifted through her mind. The woman had projected them into her thoughts. She'd read her mind and silently sent her answer so the men wouldn't hear. Jackie wanted to be angry, but instead was afraid. Marguerite seemed to be encouraging her to like Vincent and the last thing she needed was encouragement. She was having trouble fighting it as it was.

Why fight it then?

Jackie ground her teeth together as the question floated through her head.

"What was the production assistant like?" Tiny asked suddenly and Jackie turned to him, relieved to have something to occupy her mind besides Marguerite's words.

"Lily seemed all right," she said. "She's young though, looks like a teenager."

"Lily's older than she looks," Vincent said.

"That's good to know, because she looks about twelve. You do know about our child labor laws, don't you?"

"Lily is well over eighteen, hardly a child," Vincent assured her, sounding annoyed.

"Hmm," Jackie murmured doubtfully. "I can't wait to meet the rest of your staff."

"The rest of them?" Vincent looked startled. "Why would you need to meet my staff?"

A Bite to Remember

"Anyone in your company could have accessed these employee lists," Jackie pointed out, gesturing to the papers she'd taken from Lily and still held.

"So?"

"So, that means anyone in your company could find out who was in your New York cast. It makes them suspects."

"My people wouldn't—"

"Vincent," she interrupted patiently. "Someone's angry enough with you to be causing these problems. They seem to be trying to ruin you."

He didn't look pleased, but said, "Yes, but I've never deliberately hurt anyone in my life."

"You're over four hundred years old, you may have slighted someone, or broken the heart of someone on your staff two or three hundred years ago and not remember."

"I hardly think this is about slighting someone two or three hundred years ago," he said stiffly. "And I've never broken anyone's heart. It can't be about that."

"Then what *is* it about?" Jackie asked sharply.

Vincent shook his head, frustration plain on his face. "I don't know."

"So, it's something you've forgotten because of its insignificance to you," she said pointedly.

His mouth tightened. "I'm not an asshole, Jackie. I'd hardly forget something that hurt someone enough they'd do this."

Jackie shrugged. "Asshole. Immortal. Whatever."

"Dinner's ready!" Tiny stepped between their glares and placed a serving dish of chicken on the table.

Jackie blinked at the food. "When did you have time to cook a meal?"

"I wasn't sure of our schedule so I cooked it this morning while the chili was simmering. I put it in to warm when we walked in," he explained, then added firmly, "It's warm. Eat."

Jackie bit her lip as she took in his grim expression. Tiny obviously felt she'd overstepped and been rude. He wanted her to stick a piece of chicken in her mouth and shut up. Aware that she *had* been rude with that last crack about immortals and assholes, Jackie sighed and settled into a chair at the table, her mind searching for the words to apologize without making a big deal out of it. She never got the chance though. While Vincent's nose had quivered over the delicious aroma of the roasted meat, he said, "Thank you, Tiny. It looks delicious. However, I'm afraid I'm not hungry."

Tiny sighed as the vampire left the room, then turned on Jackie. "He isn't Cassius."

She jerked back in shock. "How . . . ? You . . ."

"Your father told me about Cassius during that last year while he was sick," Tiny admitted quietly. "He feared the prejudice it caused in you against immortals might someday become a problem, that you might misjudge a case, or something similar. He thought if I knew about it, I could help keep that from happening."

"I see," Jackie said stiffly, her emotions in chaos. She was angry that her father had told Tiny, as well as embarrassed that her friend knew how she'd been controlled and used by Cassius. "Are you saying you think I'm allowing my past

SABLE

SABLAS

Ⓢ Blueline ®

Sample S.O.S.
New Product

Échantillon S.O.S.
Nouveau produit

NEW!
NOUVEAU!

To Order: D1651BT
Pour commander D1651BT

experience to make me misjudge this case? You don't think it's a vampire sabotaging Vincent?"

"Oh, I think you're right about the saboteur being an immortal," he assured her.

"Then what—?"

"But I think you're misjudging Vincent," he added solemnly.

"I—"

"That asshole remark was bitchy," Tiny said bluntly. "And that isn't like you. Even when you absolutely detest someone, you're coolly polite and professional. But you aren't with Vincent. I think it's because you're attracted to him and it scares you because of your experience with Cassius. And, I think you're being unpleasant in an effort to make him keep his distance."

Jackie stared, feeling exposed and vulnerable. Before she could even come up with something to say, movement out of the corner of her eye drew her attention to the door as it closed behind Marguerite.

Jackie groaned inwardly as she realized the woman had heard everything and probably read the rest in her thoughts. She hadn't exactly been guarding them. This just wasn't her day and this case was one she now wished she'd never taken on. One way or another, Jackie was sure she was going to end up hurt.

"I'm afraid I'm not hungry either, Tiny," Jackie said wearily. "I think I'll go shower and change into something more comfortable, then do some work."

Tiny sighed as he peered at the meal he'd prepared, but didn't say anything to dissuade her as she left the kitchen.

Lynsay Sands

✝ ✝ ✝

Vincent was pacing the length of the living room, his mind in an uproar when Marguerite found him. She eyed his stiff stature, then asked, "Have you tried to read Jackie yet?"

Vincent waved the question away with irritation. "No. As I said in the kitchen, I don't like to read people's thoughts."

"Well, you shall have to try to overcome your reticence and read Jackie's," Marguerite said firmly. "There's something in her past that causes her distrust of immortals and I think it would help if you knew what."

Vincent stiffened. "She doesn't trust us?"

"She doesn't trust anyone with immortal blood in their veins," Marguerite said quietly. "Except perhaps for Bastien and even he she only trusts so far."

Vincent frowned. "Why?"

"Try to read her mind and you might find out," Marguerite suggested. "Otherwise you'll have to read Tiny."

"*Try* to read her mind?" he asked and then his eyes widened as Vincent recalled Bastien saying Marguerite was coming out here because she thought he was lonely and might need help cheering up, or even seeing to the situation.

"Oh, no," he said grimly. "No, no, no, no. Do not even go there."

"Go where?" she asked innocently.

"Do not start playing matchmaker. I could read Jackie if I tried, I just haven't tried. She is not my life mate."

"I don't know Vincent. I've seen it four times now in the last couple years. There's a certain chemistry between life mates and you two seem to have it."

"Aunt Marguerite," he said in warning.

"So, prove me wrong. Try to read her," she challenged.

Vincent's mind raced. Part of him was excited at the idea that Jackie might be his life mate. The other part was absolutely terrified. He'd lived more than four hundred years on his own. Four hundred years was a long time to wander the earth in search of a mate, and that's what he'd been doing.

Vincent wanted a life mate. He wanted someone to share his hopes and dreams and even his sorrows with. His parents' relationship had been full of love and support and caring. They'd been true life mates, bonded and inseparable until his mother's death. He wanted that. He wanted someone to laugh with and cry with and to hold close in the dark of night and the harsh light of day. It was why he'd traveled so far and wide during his life. Vincent had been actively seeking his life mate.

During the first three hundred years, Vincent had gained a reputation as a ladies' man because he went out of his way to meet as many women as he could. It was only the last fifty years or so that he'd grown tired of the hunt and begun to fear he might never find her. Not all immortals did.

Now, his aunt was holding out that hope to him and he was afraid. Oddly enough, he wasn't just afraid that he might be able to read Jackie, which would mean she wasn't his life mate, but he also feared not being able to read her, a sure sign that she was his life mate.

Vincent liked Jackie, he found her intelligent, and funny and sexy and he even enjoyed her strength and her slightly hard edge. His own mother had been a strong woman and he wanted that kind of woman for himself. But . . .

"Go try to read her," Marguerite said quietly. "If you can

read her, there's nothing to worry about or fear. If you can't . . ." She shrugged. "Then you can begin to consider the possibilities."

Vincent nodded slowly, then turned and made his way back to the kitchen. He'd try to read Jackie. If he could, nothing had changed. If he couldn't . . . Everything had.

Six

Vincent was disappointed when he returned to the kitchen to find Jackie had already left. His disappointment was balanced by relief, however. He had a little time to adjust to the possibility that she might be his mate. It was time he could use.

"Oh, hey," Tiny smiled and got to his feet as he entered. "If you're hungry, there's lots of chicken left."

Vincent opened his mouth to say "no thanks," but then caught himself. Actually, he *was* hungry. He hadn't felt hunger for anything other than blood for a long time, but now he was experiencing actual hunger pangs at the thought of the delicious smelling chicken Tiny had brought out earlier.

Reading Vincent's expression correctly, Tiny moved to the refrigerator to pull out the chicken.

"Thanks, Tiny," Vincent murmured as Tiny filled a plate with chicken and then added some coleslaw. Taking the plate from him, he led the way back to the table and settled across from the other man to eat.

Vincent bit into the first piece of chicken and sighed as the robust flavor hit his tongue. "Mmmm. If you ever decide to give up detective work to start your own restaurant, let me know and I'll bankroll you."

Tiny merely smiled at the compliment as he ate his own food. The two of them ate in silence for a while, then Vincent said, "So, if I were to ask you what Jackie's problem is with immortals, I don't suppose you'd tell me?"

Tiny was silent so long, Vincent had begun to think he wouldn't answer, then he asked, "What do you think of Jackie so far?"

Vincent considered the question before admitting, "I think she's beautiful, intelligent and interesting. She appears tough as nails, but I suspect isn't as hard-boiled as she appears." He hesitated, debating revealing that Marguerite thought Jackie might be his life mate, but in the end just said, "And for the first time in a very long time I've met a woman I'd like to get to know better."

Tiny nodded, but remained silent for several more moments. He finished off his own food before finally saying, "She *is* beautiful, intelligent, and interesting. And she *isn't* as hard-boiled as she'd have everyone believe she is. Of course, there's a reason for her hard attitude, but I couldn't possibly tell you. That would be betraying a friend, and I couldn't betray her like that . . . even if it was for her own good."

Disappointment was just claiming Vincent when the man added, "I like you. I think you're a good man. I think you're the kind of man who could make Jackie happy."

Vincent raised his eyebrows, but remained silent, waiting. His patience was rewarded when Tiny added, "When we first meet immortals, Jackie and I are always on the alert for the possibility that they'll try to read our minds. Jackie stays that way because of an experience I couldn't possibly divulge without betraying her trust. I, however, tend to relax my guard if I come to like the immortal . . . as I do you."

Vincent blinked, wondering if Tiny was suggesting what he thought he was.

"Of course, if you were to read my thoughts and learn about Jackie that way, I wouldn't be betraying our friendship," he said mildly. "However, if you were to do that, I would expect that you'd never ever admit such a thing to me, because then I might have to feel bad about not guarding my thoughts properly."

Vincent felt a smile tugging at his lips at the man's cleverness.

"Now, you just sit there and eat quietly. I'm just going to spend a few moments pondering the reason Jackie has a hard-on for immortals and how sad it is that she does."

Vincent prevented himself from laughing by biting into a fresh piece of chicken. As he chewed, he cleared his mind and began to probe the thoughts Tiny was offering up.

"I'm surprised you didn't have Allen Richmond install a higher wall and put electric wire along the top," Tiny teased as they walked along the perimeter of the yard, following the high brick wall that ran around Vincent's property.

Jackie smiled, but seriously considered the possibility. It

wouldn't be a bad idea now that they knew the saboteur had definitely turned their attention Vincent's way.

A frown claimed her lips as she thought of the letter that had arrived today. Jackie had found it on returning downstairs from taking a shower and changing. She'd spotted the small stack of fresh mail on the hall table as she was passing it. Realizing Tiny and Marguerite must have collected the mail on returning, she'd picked up the small stack and leafed through the envelopes as she walked into the office. There had been two bank statements, a credit card statement, an electric bill, and a new letter from the writer they suspected was the saboteur.

Jackie had stiffened as she saw the telltale return address. It was the same as the delivery address. She'd quickly opened it and read:

Ready to play?

The hair on the back of her neck had suddenly stood on end and adrenaline had shot through her like a cold bullet. Clutching the note, Jackie had whirled toward the door and hurried to the kitchen, only to find Tiny there alone. Vincent and Marguerite had left ten minutes earlier to make the rounds of the clubs.

Jackie had spent quite a while discussing the implications of this letter with Tiny. It was a change in pattern. The previous letters had all been dated the day after each event took place, taunting Vincent after each occurrence. This one seemed to imply a threat of something to come. It had Jackie worried and she knew Tiny was worried too, but they didn't know what they should be worried about. They had no idea what the saboteur's plans were.

After discussing it for quite a while, Tiny had suggested a walk around the perimeter of Vincent's estate. Jackie knew it was just an excuse to work off a little of the tension and anxiety the letter had caused in them both. She didn't really expect to find anything of interest as they followed the high brick wall that ran around Vincent's property.

"I doubt a higher fence or electric wire would do much good," she said now. "Immortals can jump higher than us, but who knows how much higher?"

"Hmm." Tiny eyed the wall with consideration. "And no doubt they can climb trees too. There are lots of those on both sides of the wall."

Jackie nodded. "The real security is the motion sensor cameras and alarms on the house itself. Hopefully those will help."

Tiny grunted agreement and they fell silent. When he spoke again it was to change the subject. "Marguerite is an interesting woman. She cares about Vincent a lot."

"Oh?"

"She seems to thinks he's lonely," Tiny added and Jackie glanced at him with a start of surprise.

"Lonely?"

"Yes. Marguerite thinks he's losing interest in life. He takes on acting roles less and less often, and she thinks he's spending more time at home. Marguerite says she doesn't think he's been feeding enough either, that she'd noticed he'd lost weight when she saw him in New York."

Jackie had spent enough time around immortals to know

that boredom was their worst enemy. When they lost the passion for life and fed less and became reclusive, it could lead to indifference and depression, then self-destructive behavior. She didn't like the idea that Vincent might be sinking into depression.

Her thoughts scattered as Tiny suddenly took her arm to turn her to the left. Jackie glanced around to find they'd reached the gate at the driveway and he was urging her up toward the house.

The lights on the ground floor were shining brightly, but Vincent and Marguerite hadn't yet returned. Jackie wasn't pleased that he was away from the safety of the house just now, she had a feeling things were going to start happening soon.

"You've got that hinky feeling," Tiny commented.

Jackie smiled faintly at the term they'd coined for her sense that something was about to happen. "It's showing, is it?"

"You're about ready to crawl out of your own skin with tension. That's usually a good sign that you've got that hinky feeling."

She nodded and blew her breath out on a sigh. "I do and the walk hasn't helped ease it much."

"Why don't you go for a swim?" Tiny suggested.

"Maybe I will," Jackie murmured.

"In the pool or ocean?" he asked. While the house was on prime oceanfront property, there was also a heated outdoor pool. Excess in Hollywood.

"The pool," she decided. Excess or not, Jackie had seen *Jaws* on television at an impressionable age. She wouldn't be able to relax in the ocean if she was scanning the horizon for shark fins and jumping every time some poor fish brushed against her.

"If you're swimming in the pool, I'll join you."

"You saw *Jaws* as a kid too, huh?" Jackie asked with amusement.

"Oh yeah. Wouldn't go in the local pool for a week afterwards."

They chuckled together as they entered the house, then parted to go to their rooms and change, agreeing to meet at the pool. Jackie made quick work of stripping her clothes and donning her red one-piece swimsuit. She returned downstairs and went into the kitchen to find she'd beat Tiny back.

Pausing at the security panel, Jackie punched in the code to release the kitchen door so that their opening it wouldn't set off the alarms. She then stepped out onto the patio only to hesitate.

The air was still warm from the day's heat, but it was dark night outside and she briefly debated whether to turn the pool lights on. In the end, Jackie decided the light shining from the kitchen windows lit up the area well enough. It wasn't as bright as daylight, but light enough they wouldn't swim head first into the side of the pool, which was good enough for her.

The patio tiles were cool under her bare feet. Jackie dropped the towel she'd brought with her onto one of the iron chairs around the patio table, then walked over to sit on the edge of the pool. She dangled her feet in the water and leaned back to peer up at the star-studded sky, her thoughts wandering briefly. After a moment, Jackie glanced impatiently back toward the house, wondering what was taking Tiny so long.

She was about to go look for him when the kitchen door opened and Tiny walked out in baggy swim trunks with Sylvester the cat on them. Jackie grinned with amusement and shook her head. The man's size scared most people silly, but no one would be scared if they knew the real man.

Or perhaps they would, Jackie decided. Tiny had as much courage as common sense and was stronger than your average bear.

"What are you waiting for?" Tiny asked as he crossed the patio. "You're dying to dive in. Go on."

Chuckling softly, Jackie pushed off, gasping as the water enveloped her. Heated it might be, but the water was still cooler than her body temperature. She quickly dove under the surface to wet herself everywhere and speed up her body's adjustment to the temperature. When she broke the surface again and glanced around, Tiny was in the water, swimming laps. Jackie relaxed for a while, just paddling her feet, then she too began to swim laps.

It was a good twenty minutes later when she noticed movement at the side of the pool. Stopping abruptly, Jackie peered about, relaxing when she saw it was Tiny. He'd got out and was now drying himself off at the poolside.

"Are you done?" Jackie asked.

"I'm here. Go on and keep swimming," Tiny assured her as he sat down with the towel wrapped around his shoulders.

Nodding, Jackie continued with her laps. When next she

stopped, Tiny was no longer in the chair and Jackie glanced around sharply to see where he'd got to. She then saw the shape moving toward her through the water and gave a little laugh.

A heartbeat later, her amusement gave way to confusion and even fear as she realized the figure moving through the water was too small to be Tiny. Just as Jackie was about to strike out for the pool's edge, the swimmer surfaced in front of her and she blinked as Vincent's head and shoulders popped out of the water.

"You're home." As greetings went it was pretty lame, but it was the first thought that popped into Jackie's head.

Vincent chuckled at her surprise. "We got home a couple minutes ago. When I realized you two were out here swimming, I changed and came to join you."

Jackie nodded and glanced toward the house. "Where did Tiny go?"

"He headed in to change and dry off now that you wouldn't be left alone."

"Oh." Jackie shifted in the water. While she hadn't been ready to get out when Tiny was there, now that Vincent was there instead, all she could think of was getting out. It suddenly felt dangerous being there, like she'd suddenly discovered she was swimming with a shark.

Jackie headed for the ladder, but then recalled Tiny's words earlier, about her fear and Vincent not being Cassius. Tiny liked Vincent and Jackie trusted her co-worker's judgment. She decided to stick it out and try to be pleasant despite her fears and anxieties. She could handle it, Jackie assured herself, and determinedly ignored the defense mechanisms screaming at her to flee, or insult him, or do whatever was necessary to get herself out of his sphere of influence.

As if sensing her discomfort, Vincent began to backstroke away from her, giving her space. Jackie watched, finding herself admiring his efficient stroke.

"I'm surprised you chose to swim in the pool rather than the ocean," he commented.

Jackie's gaze flickered to his face, then she eased into a side crawl as she said, "I like to see what's in the water with me."

Vincent chuckled softly.

"I take it you like to swim in the ocean at night?" she asked.

"Yes. I rarely use the pool." They fell silent for a minute, then he asked, "Is the ocean cold to swim in during the day?" Before she could answer, he said, "I suppose it would be, wouldn't it?"

"You've never swum during daylight?" Jackie asked.

"No, never," Vincent answered. "Is it nicer than swimming at night?"

Jackie frowned as she considered. "Not nicer, just different," she decided. "Do you miss the freedom to go out in sunlight when you wish?"

"You can't miss what you've never known," he said simply.

His answer made her wonder what else Vincent didn't miss because he'd never known it. She tried to think of things that were strictly daytime activities, but found she couldn't come up with anything. Jackie worked days and there wasn't much she did on her days off that couldn't just as easily be done at night. Swimming, fishing, barbecuing . . . all of them could be done at night. She supposed sunbathing with a book would be out, but then the specialists claimed the sun caused skin cancer anyway.

"What's it like to live so long?" Jackie asked suddenly.

Vincent stopped swimming and moved to the side of the pool to hold on to the rim while he considered her question. After a moment, he shook his head. "I don't know what to say. It's all I know, I have no way to compare it to *not* living long."

He glanced thoughtfully off into the distance, and Jackie thought that would be the end of his answer, but then Vincent spoke again. "At first, it was great fun and I felt sorry for mortals who saw their youth and beauty wither away with each passing year while I stayed young and healthy."

When he paused, Jackie found herself saying, "It must be incredible though. Traveling the world, seeing the different ages, meeting great people like Shakespeare."

Vincent smiled faintly. "If only you *knew* they were great when you met them."

She raised her eyebrows. "What do you mean?"

"Well, *now,* four hundred years later, Shakespeare is 'the bard,' but back then he was just another playwright, a successful one, but still just a playwright. When I met him, I had no idea I was in the presence of someone who would be so important historically." Vincent grinned. "Had I known, I might have treated him with more respect."

"You were a child when you met him," Jackie pointed out.

"I was a spoiled brat," Vincent corrected, and shook his head.

"The file my father's company had compiled on you says meeting Shakespeare convinced you to become an actor." There were files on quite a few of the immortals in the agency's cabinets, all holding bits of information gleaned over the years.

Vincent laughed. "Then the file is wrong. It wasn't meeting *him* so much as seeing all the pretty ladies that haunted the theatre and admired the actors. It also helped that the church was up in arms over the theatres then, calling them immoral and indecent. That just made it more attractive."

"Rebellious youth," Jackie said with amusement.

"Perhaps," he allowed. "But I've always backed the underdog and without the support of royalty and the nobles, theatre would have been crushed by the church."

Vincent leaned back against the pool edge and allowed his feet to float just under the surface, gently paddling them in the water. "The theater was special back then, so much energy and excitement."

"And now?" she asked.

"Now." He frowned. "Now it's a lot of cold ambition and the pursuit of the almighty dollar. Very little seems new and creative anymore, especially in Hollywood where—rather than create brilliant new scripts and shows—they just repeat old money makers or bring video games to screen."

Jackie frowned. Vincent did sound tired and cynical and she wondered if Marguerite's fears weren't justified after all.

"If you think so little of Hollywood, why do you live out here? Why not live closer to your family?"

"I've been wondering that myself, lately," he admitted, then gave a laugh. "To tell you the truth, I half suspect I *have* been rebelling."

"Really?" she asked with surprise.

"Well, you know, fathers want their sons to follow in their footsteps."

"And sons often rebel," Jackie said with a faint smile, but her smile faded as she added, "Your father is an enforcer for the council."

Vincent raised an eyebrow and she knew that some of her anger had shown in her voice. The council was the governing body for immortals, and the enforcers were the equivalent of their police. Jackie had always resented that immortals saw themselves as above human laws and felt they had a right to their own laws and enforcers.

On the other hand, she knew mortal police couldn't enforce mortal laws on them. The idea was laughable. Should Vincent, or another immortal, be pulled over for speeding, all he need do was slip into the officer's thoughts and convince him that he hadn't been speeding, and, in fact, that the officer had never seen him. It was pretty much the same for every law. Having experienced having her mind controlled and what they could make mortals do against their will, Jackie knew how scary their abilities were. One of their kind could probably kill someone in front of a room full of witnesses and make every last person forget what they'd seen. Their enforcers were necessary.

As for their own set of laws, while Jackie wished they had to follow *all* mortal laws, she understood that immortals were so spread out that the enforcers couldn't possibly keep up with making them follow every law. So, they'd decided on the laws that were important to them such as restricting them to bagged blood and not feeding off mortals except in emergencies and in cases of medical issues that required live donors. Most of the rest of their laws seemed to simply be meant to prevent the possibility of overpopulating the earth; restricting them to having only one child every hundred years, and allowing each to turn only one mortal in their lifetime.

Jackie knew these laws were enforced with death, and not a very pleasant one either. According to her father's files, the last immortal to try to turn more than his allotted one, had been hunted down here in California. He'd been staked out in the sun all day, then beheaded at sunset. The beheading had probably been the kinder action. Leaving him out in the sun all day, so he dehydrated and his nanos began to eat his organs in search of needed blood was apparently the true punishment. According to Bastien, there was no worse torture for one of their kind and the man would have been grateful for the beheading when it came.

"How many enforcers are there?" Jackie asked suddenly. It was a subject she'd always wondered about.

"I'm not sure," Vincent admitted. He guessed, "Perhaps a dozen or so here in North America."

"How many of your people are here?"

He shook his head. "To tell you the truth, I'm not sure about that either. I'd guess there are about five hundred here in North America."

"And Europe?"

"More," he said solemnly.

Jackie nodded. She knew that the European immortals

were ruled by a different council than the North American council and that there had been friction between the two for centuries. It went back to when some of the immortals had first moved to the Americas, scared out of Europe by the witch hunts. The European council had felt the immigrants should still have to answer to them, but the immigrating families had different issues, and felt the European council was out of touch with their needs. They'd wanted to rule and police themselves.

According to Bastien, the battle that had ensued had paralleled the American battle for independence in a way, but on a much smaller scale. In the end, the European council had just washed their hands of their people in the new world. They hadn't really had a choice. They weren't in the Americas to enforce their control.

Jackie steered the topic away from the councils and asked something she'd wondered about since arriving in California. "How much blood do you need a day?"

Vincent hesitated, then said, "Most go through three or four bags a day. Some need more. It varies."

"And you?" she asked. "How many people do you bite a day?"

"Only one or two a day now."

"Why do you need less blood?"

"It's not that I need less, but . . ." He shrugged indifferently. "I only feed enough to get by."

"Enough to get by," Jackie echoed, recalling Tiny saying Marguerite thought Vincent had lost weight when she'd seen him in New York. Obviously, feeding "enough to get by" wasn't enough. "Why?"

Vincent didn't pretend not to understand what she was asking, but avoided her gaze as he said, "I'm beginning to find the hunt a terrible bother."

"A bother?" Jackie asked with concern, positive this was bad.

"Everything seems to be a bother these days," he admitted with dissatisfaction. "You were right. I didn't eat before you and Tiny got here. I stopped eating about three hundred years ago. I shouldn't have, because it helps in building my own blood and reduces the amount I need to feed, but having to eat food as well as hunt became a bother. Food became boring, and hardly worth the trouble."

"Food became *boring*?" Jackie goggled at him, sure he was joking. She'd never imagined boredom was the reason vampires didn't eat, and had difficulty believing it. How could anyone think food was boring?

Vincent chuckled at her reaction. "Yes."

"So you all stop eating eventually because of *boredom*?"

He hesitated, then said, "Some stop eating and some don't. My cousin Lucern was born two hundred years before me, during a time when size and strength were important. He was a warrior, large and muscular. It takes a lot to keep his muscle mass. He has always eaten as well as fed, and when he tires of eating, he continues to do so out of necessity, to keep his mass. On the other hand, my cousin Lissianna, as a woman, has no such concerns. When she tired of eating, she simply stopped . . . though, she has started eating again since meeting Gregory."

"And you weren't concerned about body mass?" Jackie asked.

116

Vincent grinned and held out his arms. "By the time I was born, skill was more important than strength in any battle one engaged in. We dueled with épées, or used pistols. I didn't need the same muscle mass Lucern did to wield his great sword and have never desired to have it. So, when I grew tired of food, I simply stopped eating."

Jackie tilted her head and eyed him. He made it sound like he was a skinny little guy, but he wasn't. He wasn't as muscle-bound as Schwarzenegger, but he had nice wide shoulders and a muscular physique all the same.

She shook her head. "I still find it hard to believe you could find food boring."

Vincent chuckled at her expression. "Lots of things become boring after a couple hundred years."

"Like what?"

Vincent raised his eyebrows. "What do you mean?"

"What else has become boring to you? What else have you stopped doing because it seems more trouble than it's worth?" she explained.

"Sex."

The answer startled her and Jackie felt herself blush in the darkness.

"Cat got your tongue?" Vincent teased when she remained silent.

"I don't know what to say," she admitted. "I guess I find that as surprising as that food could be boring."

"Yeah." He sighed. "I was pretty surprised myself. I used to enjoy sex a lot. I was good at it too."

Jackie *really* didn't know what to say to that. Vincent said it so nonchalantly, not bragging, just stating a fact like someone

117

else might say they were good at crosswords. It was hard not to believe it was true. On the other hand, she supposed all men thought they were good at sex, whether they were or not.

Growing tired from treading water, Jackie gave up her position in the center of the pool and swam to the edge a little way down from him. She held on to the side of the pool like he was doing to give her arms and legs a rest as they talked.

"Enough about me," Vincent said suddenly. "I know your father started the detective agency. What about your mother? What did she do?"

"Mother died when I was four," Jackie admitted. "I don't recall much about her. She was a secretary in my father's company before and after I was born."

"So your father raised you?" When she nodded, Vincent asked, "So, were you a tomboy, or a girlie girl?"

Jackie smiled with amusement at the question, then blinked in surprise when he said, "I bet you were a tomboy."

"Why?" she asked warily.

Vincent shrugged. "You were an only child, raised by your father and probably eager for his attention. That usually leads the girl to try to be the son he never had to gain his approval."

Jackie scowled. She *had* been a tomboy, and she supposed she *had* tried to be the son he never had to gain her father's attention and approval. Perhaps she was still doing so despite his being dead, trying to be the son he would have wanted.

"Come." Vincent suddenly propelled himself up and out onto the tiles around the pool. Standing, he then bent to offer her a hand. "You're starting to shiver; time to get out of the water."

Jackie realized with surprise that he was right, she *was* shivering. Still, she almost refused his hand, but then sighed and reached up. Vincent caught her fingers and suddenly she was standing dripping wet on the patio tiles. He'd lifted her out one-handed and with no effort whatsoever. Almost before that realization had struck, he'd collected her towel and wrapped it around her.

Jackie shouldn't have been surprised, but always found it startling how strong and quick immortals really were. She'd decided long ago that most of the time these beings moved at what must seem a sluggish rate for them, probably in an effort to appear normal to the mortals around them.

Her thoughts on their speed and strength scattered as Vincent used the ends of the towel he'd wrapped around her to brush the drops of water from her face. It started out as an almost maternal action, but then his hands slowed and softened and she became aware that his eyes had settled on her mouth and stayed there. His expression stilled, becoming serious. It was an expression Jackie was not used to from Vincent Argeneau. He generally wore good humor and amusement like a uniform, but neither of those masks was on his face now. His expression was solemn, his eyes beginning to glow silver-blue with a hunger she didn't think had anything to do with blood.

Jackie found herself holding her breath. His body was a whisper away from her own and if she swayed just the teensiest bit forward, her breasts would brush his chest. The idea made a shiver of anticipation ripple down her back and that made Vincent blink and frown.

"Come, it's chilly tonight and you're cold." Vincent

released her towel and took her arm to urge her toward the kitchen door. "Inside to warm up."

Jackie nodded and led the way, telling herself she was relieved he hadn't kissed her. All in all, this encounter had been relatively painless, nice even. She hadn't sensed his trying to read her thoughts, and he hadn't taken control of her and made her do anything she didn't want to do. Perhaps she *had* allowed her old fears to make her treat him unfairly. Maybe he was just as nice as Bastien. And perhaps all immortals *didn't* look down on mortals and set out to use and hurt them as Cassius had done. This was a huge admission for Jackie to make; it shook the foundations of a belief system she'd lived by for years.

Seven

"Perfect timing," Tiny announced as Jackie and Vincent stepped into the light and warmth of the kitchen. "I'm just taking out the first batch of cookies. By the time you change into dry clothes, they should be cool enough to eat."

Jackie smiled at Tiny and shook her head as he pulled a sheet of cookies out of the oven. The man had changed into cream-colored joggers and maroon slippers and was wearing the *I'm the cook!* apron again. He was six feet, seven inches and two hundred and eighty pounds of domesticity running about the kitchen in a pink apron and flowered oven mitts.

And he was her best friend in the world, Jackie reminded herself as the scent of freshly baked chocolate chip cookies hit her.

"Tiny, you're going to make me gain ten pounds on this job if you keep cooking like this," she complained, drawing her towel tighter around her.

"It's your fault," Tiny said with a shrug. "Your hinky feeling made me nervous and—"

"Cooking relaxes you," Jackie finished with amusement.

"What hinky feeling is that, dear?" Marguerite asked, drawing Jackie's gaze to where the woman sat leafing through one of Tiny's women's magazines full of recipes. Seated at the table, she was a knockout in the short black dress she'd worn to go out with Vincent earlier and didn't look a day over twenty-nine or thirty. Damn, Jackie thought, there were some real benefits to being an immortal.

"Jackie sometimes gets these feelings," Tiny explained as he carried his tray of cookies to the cooling rack. "A sort of tension and anxiety just before something happens on a case. She had it earlier tonight."

"Before something happens?" Marguerite asked with interest.

"Usually something bad," Tiny muttered as he used a spatula to slide the cookies from the tray to the cooling rack before they began to stick.

"How bad?" Vincent asked with a frown of concern.

Tiny grimaced. "She had it the time I got shot."

"Shot?" Marguerite asked with alarm.

Tiny nodded. "We were working for Bastien. He suspected someone was sneaking out paperwork and samples of some of the different miracle medicines his scientists were working on."

Jackie grimaced as she recalled the occasion Tiny was talking about. Argeneau Enterprises was heavily into medical research. It could be a very lucrative field, especially if you saved on expenses by stealing someone else's ideas and research. That had been happening at Argeneau's and the Morrisey agency had been called in to look into it. This was at the start of her father's illness, when he'd started delegating more important cases to Jackie. She and Tiny had been on the job.

"Well," Tiny continued. "We had narrowed it down to two suspects and were following one of them after he'd left work when Jackie got her hinky feeling. He parked in a big public lot and left on foot, and we parked and followed. He led us down this alley and Jackie really started getting itchy, but the man was way ahead of us so I was sure it would be all right." He shook his head. "Then, all of a sudden, two guys jumped out from behind these bins and took a couple of shots at us."

Tiny scowled. "The bastard knew we were following and used his cell phone to call his buddies and set us up before leading us to the parking lot."

"Were you badly hurt?" Vincent asked with a frown, but Jackie noticed his gaze had moved to her and was sliding over her as if looking for possible bullet wounds.

"Nah, I was just winged," Tiny assured them. "But ever since then, when Jackie starts getting her hinky feeling, I get nervous."

"Has she ever been wrong?" Marguerite asked.

"Never," Tiny answered solemnly as he finished with the baked cookies and moved to start plopping little balls of batter on the now empty tray.

"Oh." Marguerite considered that and then frowned as she saw Jackie shiver. "You're turning blue, child. You'd best hurry upstairs and change."

"She's right," Vincent said, urging her toward the door. "Go change."

Jackie didn't need much urging. She was cold and ready to get out of her wet swimsuit. Casting a grateful smile Vincent's way, she hurried up the hall, then jogged up to her room.

With the thought of freshly baked cookies spurring her on, Jackie made a quick job of changing and running a brush through her still-damp hair. Vincent was in the office when she returned below. She could hear him talking on the phone as she reached the ground floor. Despite the lure of the cookies, she detoured that way to see what was going on. He was hanging up as she reached the doorway.

"That was Bastien." Vincent stood and she saw that—as fast as she'd been, he'd been faster—he wore tight jeans and a chest-hugging T-shirt.

Jackie nodded. "Is everything all right?"

"Fine. He was just checking on how things were going with Aunt Marguerite here." Vincent walked around the desk, moving toward her. "I offered to call her to the phone, but he was just heading to bed so asked me to say hello to her for him."

Jackie smiled at the amusement on his face, guessing that he suspected the going to bed tale was just an excuse for the man to avoid his mother. Bastien had made comments over the years that suggested she could be a bit interfering when it came to her children's lives. Having lost her own mother when she was young, Jackie wouldn't have minded some of that interfering herself, but supposed the grass was always greener.

She opened her mouth to ask if there had been any messages from her firm that she needed to know about, but paused as her gaze ran over the spotless desktop.

"What is it?" Vincent asked, noting her sudden stillness.

"Did you move the papers that were on the desk?" she asked, stepping past him.

"No. There were no papers on the desk when I came in," he said, following her.

"I'm sure I left the employee list on the desk this evening. I planned to work on them tomorrow morn—" Jackie froze again as her gaze landed on the French doors. One wasn't quite closed. She whirled on Vincent. "Did you turn the alarm off when you came home?"

"No, of course not," he assured her, then added, "It wasn't on."

"What?" she asked with amazement.

"I thought you'd turned it off while you were out at the pool," Vincent said with a frown.

"No. I only released the kitchen door." Jackie turned back toward the hallway to shout for Tiny, then hurried over to close and lock the French doors.

"What's wrong?" Tiny hurried into the room with Marguerite on his heels.

"The French doors were open and the employee list is missing," Jackie said tersely as she began to quickly search the desk, checking the drawers to be sure she hadn't put it in one of them without thinking, then checking the floor in case the papers had simply fallen off. She knew even as she searched that it was a waste of time. Jackie distinctly recalled setting the papers in the center of the desk so that they would be the first thing she saw in the morning.

"Why didn't the alarm go off?" Tiny asked with a frown, pausing beside Vincent on the opposite side of the desk. Marguerite remained by the door, a concerned expression on her face.

"That's what I want to know." Jackie straightened from searching the floor under the desk. "Vincent said the alarm was off when he and Marguerite came back."

"Impossible," Tiny said firmly. "It was on when we came back from our walk."

"Yes, it was," she said grimly. "And apparently one of us turned it off between when we came back and when Vincent and Marguerite returned."

"One of *us*?" Tiny asked with amazement. "Impossible. Neither of us would turn it off."

"Not on our own, no," she agreed. "But we could have been controlled and our memory of it wiped."

Jackie was acutely aware of how her comment affected everyone. All three people stilled. Marguerite's eyebrows flew up in surprise, Vincent looked as if he'd turned to stone, and Tiny just looked disbelieving.

Giving up on finding the papers, she moved around the desk and out into the hall to the panel by the front door. Tiny followed, peering over her shoulder at the alarm.

"It's not just off, the entire system is shut down," he said with dismay.

"What does that mean?" Vincent crowded up next to them in front of the panel.

"It means it has to be reset," Jackie muttered and set to work doing so.

126

Vincent watched for a minute, then glanced toward Marguerite. The woman had followed, but was staying well out of the way. "Bastien called. He said hello."

"Thank you," Marguerite murmured.

Finished with the alarm, Jackie turned to move back into the office.

"What are you doing now?" Vincent asked, trailing her.

"Calling the security company. They monitor the cameras. Our best hope is that the motion-sensitive cameras caught our saboteur on film as they approached the house," she explained, picking up the phone.

Jackie hung up ten minutes later, the apologies of the night manager still ringing in her ears.

"No tapes?" Vincent guessed grimly as she sat back in the desk chair with a sigh. He, Tiny and Marguerite had heard her end of the conversation, of course, and managed to piece together enough to understand that much.

"No tapes," she affirmed. "The manager thinks they somehow *forgot* to put discs into the machines."

Tiny made a face at the possibility and asked, "The saboteur?"

Jackie nodded. "We were too slow. After leaving here, he must have paid them a visit, removed the discs, and any computer copies, then wiped the memories of the men."

They were all silent for a minute, then Jackie stood. "Those cookies ought to be cooled by now, Tiny. Is there any coffee to go with them?"

Tiny nodded silently, then straightened abruptly, his face covered with horror. "The second batch!" he cried and rushed from the room.

Jackie, Vincent, and Marguerite followed more slowly. They arrived in the kitchen to find Tiny dumping a tray of blackened cookies into the sink and waving his big oven mitt-covered hands around to dispel the smoke in the air.

While Marguerite hurried over to soothe the distraught giant, Vincent rushed to open the door to let the smoke out. Jackie had started to follow Marguerite to Tiny's side, but froze as the alarm suddenly went off in response to Vincent's opening the door. The house was filled with a shrieking wail.

"Well, at least we know it works!" Vincent shouted as Jackie whirled on her heel to hurry back up the hall to the security panel.

"What now?" Tiny asked when they finally all settled at the table. Jackie, Tiny, and Vincent had cookies and coffee. Marguerite had passed on the cookie and was drinking blood rather than coffee. She claimed the caffeine hit immortals harder than mortals. The warning hadn't deterred Vincent.

Jackie took a sip of coffee, sighing as her muscles finally began to relax. The last few minutes had been a bit stressful as she tried to concentrate on recalling the security code with the alarms blaring in her ears and the phone ringing. Vincent had answered the phone to find the security company calling to be sure everything was all right, and requesting the code word that proved it was really him and that everything was okay, but Vincent hadn't been able to hear them over the alarm. Once Jackie had finally got the alarm shut off, it had taken a few tense moments for their muddled minds to recall the code word Allen Richmond had given them. They'd recalled it at the same moment, Vincent barking it into the phone even as Jackie said it at his side.

Relieved, they'd hung up and had reset the alarm yet again before returning to the kitchen where Tiny had removed the evidence of his burnt cookies. He'd poured coffee and set a plate full of the first batch of cookies on the table. Now, they were seated around it, all four of them looking glum.

"Now, you and I each recount what happened from after we returned from walking the perimeter, to when Vincent came out to the pool," Jackie announced.

"Why?" Tiny rumbled.

"To see if our memories match events," Jackie said. "Either one of us—or both of us—lost some time somewhere for however long it took the saboteur to make us shut off the alarm so he could come in, get the papers, and leave."

Tiny shook his head, obviously still not believing either of them could have been controlled like that. Jackie understood. As humans, they tended to depend on their minds, counting on their perceptions and calculations day in and day out. The concept of the mind letting you down was difficult to accept.

"I'll start," she announced, hoping to make it easier for him. "Okay, what I recall is that we were talking about *Jaws* the movie when we came back. I unlocked the door and punched in the code to keep the alarm from going off while you locked the door."

Tiny nodded, but Jackie simply continued running through the details of changing and so on, then returning below. She recounted every minute she could recall until she stopped swimming to find Vincent in the pool. She then stopped and took a sip of coffee, frowning over the spots where there might be time missing.

"Your memory seems intact," Marguerite commented, but Jackie shook her head.

"There were several places where my memories could be false," she said with a sigh and then glanced at Tiny. "Your turn."

"My memories are pretty close to yours," Tiny said with a frown. "I remember telling you about not swimming in the local pool after seeing *Jaws* . . ."

Jackie frowned as Tiny continued recounting what he recalled. She was listening closely, but thinking this was useless. They might never know which of them had turned off the alarm and it didn't really matter who had done it anyway. The fact was it had been done, and now the employee list was missing.

"Wait a minute," she said suddenly, stopping Tiny's recounting. "Say that again."

When Tiny stared at her uncertainly, Jackie prompted. "You came downstairs . . ."

"I came downstairs and walked through the kitchen and outside and you were—"

"Back up," Jackie interrupted again. "I want you to go slowly and say exactly what you remember. You came out of your room, and closed your door, and walked downstairs . . ."

"I came out of my room," Tiny repeated slowly. "I closed my door, then turned and walked to the stairs. I came down the stairs and walked through the kitchen and outside—"

"How did you get to the kitchen?" Jackie asked.

Tiny stared at her blankly.

"Do you remember walking from the stairs to the kitchen door?" she said more specifically. "You keep skipping that."

The giant sat back slowly, a frown beginning to pull at his face. "I remember walking downstairs . . ." Tiny's voice faded as he struggled to recall getting from the bottom of the stairs to the door to the kitchen.

After a moment where his hands clenched and he started to look upset, Jackie reached out and covered one of his hands with hers. "It's okay."

"I don't remember walking from the stairs to the door," Tiny said with shock.

"It's okay, Tiny," Jackie said quietly.

"I let him in," the giant said with horror that for those few minutes he'd had no control over himself or his actions. Jackie understood that horror. It was what she'd felt when she'd realized what Cassius had done to her.

"I didn't even catch that he didn't mention walking from the stairs to the door," Vincent said with quiet admiration.

"No, neither did I," Marguerite admitted.

Jackie shrugged. Despite her distracted thoughts, she'd been envisioning the walk while Tiny had spoken, reliving it as she'd experienced it. In her mind she'd reached the bottom of the stairs then Tiny was saying he was walking through the kitchen. It had been like a movie skipping a scene in her mind.

"I let him in. I turned off the alarm." Tiny peered at Jackie. "I'm sorry, Jackie. I don't know—"

"There's nothing to be sorry for, Tiny," she assured him

quietly. "Believe me I *know*." She emphasized the last word, her gaze steady on his, then she simply said, "Cassius."

Tiny sat back in his seat, slowly nodding his head. He understood. She'd been there. He sighed. "So, I guess this tells us that the saboteur's name must have been on the employee list."

Jackie was silent, her thoughts moving over what the missing papers could mean.

"Doesn't it?" Tiny asked when she didn't immediately agree.

"Maybe," she acknowledged.

Vincent frowned from one to the other. "The name *must* be on the list. Why else would he take it?"

"To send us in that direction," Jackie murmured thoughtfully.

"What?" Marguerite sat up. "I don't understand."

"The list is easily replaced," she pointed out. "We simply have to have Lily fax us another copy in the morning. So, if the saboteur took the list because his name was on it, it was a waste of time and barely slows us down. But there's another issue here."

"What issue?" Vincent asked.

"How did he know the list was here?" Jackie asked.

Tiny straightened in his seat. "It's someone in the office."

"What?" Vincent frowned.

"There are only two possibilities here," she pointed out. "The only people who could possibly know that Sharon and Lily brought over the list of employees today are the people in your office. Either the saboteur is someone from your office, or the saboteur broke in for another reason and just happened to see the employee list there with his name on it and took the opportunity to steal it."

Jackie pursed her lips, then said, "The second option is possible, but doubtful. It calls for a lot of chance and luck on the saboteur's behalf."

"I suppose this means we should go through the house and make sure nothing else is missing, or has been disturbed," Tiny suggested reluctantly.

"Yes," Jackie agreed with a sigh, her gaze sliding to the clock on the wall. It was nearly one o'clock in the morning. By the time they finished searching the house . . . She didn't even want to speculate on how late it would be.

"I'll search the house," Vincent said, having caught her glance at the clock. "You and Tiny just check your rooms, then go to bed. I'll check the rest of the house. I'm probably the only one here who knows what belongs where anyway."

"Vincent's right," Marguerite agreed. "It's late for you. I can help him check the house."

When Jackie hesitated, Vincent assured her, "I'll wake you if we find anything wrong."

Jackie felt like she was shirking a responsibility, but nodded and stood. "Then I'll go check my room and go to bed."

Tiny hesitated, then stood as well. "Same here, I guess."

Murmuring goodnight, the two of them slipped from the kitchen and started upstairs.

"Jackie?" Tiny said as they walked upstairs.

"Hmmm?" she asked.

"I'm sorry."

"I told you, it's not your fault, Tiny," she said firmly. "I know. I've been there. Cassius controlled me the same way."

"I know. And I'm not sorry for turning off the alarm. Well, I am," Tiny corrected himself dryly. "But when I said sorry it wasn't about that. I'm sorry for what I said earlier today, about Cassius and Vincent and stuff. I didn't realize what it must have been like. I've thought many times over the years that—well, you weren't in control, so shouldn't let what Cassius made you do upset you so much. I didn't understand how *not* being in control could be the most damaging part. It's like your own mind betrayed you. Like it let you down. Anything could have happened between my memory of coming down the stairs and walking through the kitchen. I don't even know how much time is missing. It really *is* scary."

Jackie was silent as they finished mounting the stairs, then turned to him as they reached the upper landing. "Yes, it is scary. But you weren't wrong when you said what you did today. I was judging every immortal by Cassius, and that's wrong. You did me a favor giving me hell today. Vincent isn't Cassius and I *was* being rude and mean and bitchy to him. I was punishing him for what Cassius did. And he didn't deserve it. You were right about Vincent too, I think he *is* a nice guy. And I *am* attracted to him and I was scared by that and reacting badly."

Stepping forward, Jackie gave Tiny a hug. "They have skills and abilities we don't and in some ways that leaves us at a disadvantage if they use them against us. But just because they have them doesn't mean they're all going to use them against us. My believing that is like my assuming because you're bigger and physically stronger than me, you're going to use it against me. I should know better than making blanket judgments like that."

Tiny nodded thoughtfully. "So, you're cautioning me not to be afraid of them now like you've always been?"

"Basically, yes." Jackie chuckled and turned away to head to her room. "Sleep well, Tiny, I want you rested for tomorrow. We're going to Vincent's company to catch us a saboteur."

Eight

"Where's Jackie?" Vincent asked the question between bites of the blueberry muffin that Tiny had set before him with coffee when he'd entered the kitchen moments ago. It was only a little after three, early for him to be awake, but awake he was, and feeling well rested and cheerful for all that he wasn't used to being up at this hour.

"Asleep on the couch in the office," Tiny answered as he settled across the table from Vincent with his own muffin and coffee.

Vincent stopped chewing and stared blankly at the man. The answer sounded so unlike the professional and hard-working woman he'd come to know, he could hardly believe it.

"Asleep?" Vincent asked, just to be sure he hadn't misheard.

Tiny grinned and admitted, "I found it rather shocking

myself, but I don't think she slept well last night. She got up at her usual time this morning with huge rings under her eyes and with that 'I haven't had enough sleep' grouchy look I've learned to tiptoe around."

"How do you handle her when she has that look?" Vincent asked with amusement.

"Place a coffee and a muffin in front of her and keep my mouth shut until she's either got some more rest, or woken up properly and made her way past it," he said with a shrug. "Which is exactly what I did, and then I told her you'd left her a note in the office and she went to the office."

Tiny took a sip of his coffee before telling him, "Jackie was on the phone most of the morning. We had lunch and then she settled on the couch in the office this afternoon to go through the last of the letters, but when I went in to see if she needed any help, she'd fallen asleep there. She looked like she needed it, so I turned out the light and left her sleeping. Besides, it isn't like we're working normal hours here, is it? I didn't see any reason to disturb her."

Vincent nodded. His own hours alone insured they worked past a normal workday. He had no problem with Jackie sleeping, it just surprised him that she was.

"I'll wake her up once you're done with your muffin and are ready to go," Tiny announced. "The three of us are supposed to go to your production company today."

Vincent popped the last of his muffin into his mouth and stood. "I'll go shower and get dressed, then have another muffin afterward while you wake her."

Leaving the kitchen, Vincent headed for the stairs, but found himself veering off toward the office at the last moment. He just had to see for himself that the so businesslike Ms. Morrisey was snoozing in the middle of the day.

Reaching the office, he eased the door open and slid inside, then pushed it silently closed again even as his eyes sought out the couch. The curtains were all closed, blocking out the midday sun. It left the room in darkness, but Vincent had the exceptional night vision his kind enjoyed and had no problem crossing the dark room without bumping into anything.

At the side of the couch, he paused and peered down on Jackie's sleeping figure. She was wearing another dark outfit though he couldn't tell what color it was in this light, but the blouse she wore appeared to him to be white. His eyes traveled over her again and he almost sighed aloud. No one should look this sexy in sleep.

Jackie's face was soft in slumber, her defenses down. She was positioned on her back, one arm above her head, the other lying out to the side and hanging off the couch. Her blouse was pulled tight across her breasts in this position and had allowed one more button than usual to slip through its button hole, leaving a generous expanse of creamy flesh on display. He could even see the lace of her bra peeking up from under the silk of her blouse. It was a sight to put ideas in a man's head and Vincent found himself wondering what it would be like to run his tongue along the line of that lace and dip it between the generous curves of her breasts. He could imagine how soft and warm her skin would be if he tugged her top open and slid the lace down so that he could replace it with his hands. She would be full and ripe in his palms, the nipples hard little pebbles, eager for him to lick and suckle.

Jackie sighed and shifted in her sleep and Vincent forced his gaze away from that tempting area to let his eyes move further down her body. One of her legs was lying straight out along the couch, the other was half-bent at the knee and her skirt was twisted enticingly high around her thighs, revealing the tops of her stockings and more creamy white flesh above them.

Vincent swallowed thickly, fascinated by the sight. He had a sudden urge to drop to his knees and bend forward to run his tongue across the smooth skin along the top of her stocking. He could almost taste her salty flesh on his tongue and imagine the ripple that would go through her muscles were he to urge her legs apart and run his tongue further up her thigh . . .

Before he'd grown bored with sex, Vincent used to like to feed on the vein in the thighs of his women. He'd like to now. He'd like to kiss and caress Jackie. He'd like to drop to push her skirt up over her hips and duck his head between her legs. He'd enjoy pleasuring her as the blood sang in the veins next to his ears, rushing toward the spot he was lavishing with attention. Then, as she cried out with her pleasure, he'd turn his head and sink his teeth deep, plunging them into the vein and pouring his pleasure into her mind even as he took from her.

Jackie cried out and arched on the couch and Vincent blinked his fantasies away to peer down at her. Her breath was coming in little excited pants, her chest rising and falling quickly, her hands now curled into the cloth of the couch. More than that though, her legs were spread as if he had indeed knelt between them, urging them apart, and her body was bowing in sleep as if he was really doing the things he'd imagined.

Vincent blinked in surprise and began to back away from the couch as her breathing began to slow and her body to relax. He knew exactly what had happened. Damn. Her mind had been open in sleep and his thoughts had somehow slipped through into her dream world. She'd experienced it all as if he'd actually done it. Hell, his own body had reacted as if it had really happened. He had the mother of all erections poking his pajama bottoms out like a tent. It was a state he hadn't enjoyed for a very long time. All of it was something he'd never experienced before. He'd put thoughts and memories in people's minds of course, but never without intending to, never connecting to them in their sleep.

A little bewildered and befuddled, Vincent slipped from the room and headed upstairs. His shower would be a cold one, he decided.

"I don't think Tiny's too pleased to be left behind."

Jackie glanced at Vincent and then followed his gaze out the window as she started the rental car. Tiny stood framed in the light spilling out of the front door of Vincent's house in the growing dusk. With the light coming from behind, his face was cast in shadow and it was impossible to see his expression, but Jackie didn't have to see it to know what it was. His stiff stance in the doorway told her he was unhappy.

Shaking her head, she shifted the car into gear and steered up the driveway. "Yes, I know, and at first I planned on his coming, but then I realized Sharon and Lily had already been told he was your housekeeper. There's no reason you would bring your housekeeper to the office at the production agency. Your production assistant? Yes. Marguerite? Her too. But not your cook."

"I realize that," Vincent acknowledged. "I think he does too, but he's still not happy with it."

"Tiny's a worrier," she said with a shrug. "He'll worry until we get back. He always does."

"He cares about you," Marguerite commented from the backseat.

"Yes." Jackie smiled faintly as she brought the car to a halt to wait while the security gates at the roadside opened. She and Tiny had been partners for a long time and were good friends. More than that, he was the closest thing to family she had since her father's death.

Vincent shifted in the seat next to her and Jackie glanced over to see him looking relaxed and at ease in the passenger seat. She let her gaze wander over him briefly, then— recalling that Marguerite was behind her and could see her checking out her nephew—she turned her attention forward again as the gates to his driveway finished opening.

A small silence folded around the three of them as she pulled out onto the street and Jackie was content to let it be as she drove.

As she'd expected, Vincent and Marguerite had not found anything missing or out of place in the house during their search last night. Vincent had left her a note to that effect on the desk in his office so she wouldn't be left to wonder until he awoke. In truth, Jackie had forgotten all about the search until she'd read the note. She'd had trouble getting to sleep the night before. Her mind had been busy going over everything that had been said and done since she'd met Vincent Argeneau. And not for business purposes. Now that she'd acknowledged he was nice and not like Cassius, her defenses had been badly weakened. She couldn't seem to think of much besides the man and how handsome he was.

In the end, Jackie had only managed a bare four hours of rest before her alarm had gone off this morning. Feeling like death, she'd stumbled to the bathroom and tried to shower herself awake.

Much to Jackie's irritation, when she'd finally made her way downstairs it was to find Tiny in the kitchen, wide awake and cheerful as hell as he'd placed a cup of coffee and muffin on the table in front of her. She'd gulped the coffee, but passed on the muffin. Jackie always felt slightly nauseous when she hadn't had enough sleep and this morning had been no exception.

Tiny—recognizing the rings under her eyes and used to her moods when she hadn't slept enough—had kept conversation to a minimum, merely telling her there was a note for her in the office. Grunting what she considered to be a thank you, Jackie had poured herself another coffee and wandered off to the office to find the note.

She hadn't been surprised that the search had proven that nothing else in the house had been disturbed or taken last night. It was what she'd expected. The list of employees had been the target then . . . or had become the target when their saboteur had seen it lying there. It made her eager to get to the production office and get her hands on another copy of it. Unfortunately, she'd had to wait for Vincent to wake up to do that.

Jackie had spent part of the morning on the phone with the office in New York, getting updates on the cases underway there, then had settled on the couch with some paperwork and promptly fallen asleep. If falling asleep on the job weren't bad enough, she'd then proceeded to have wet dreams about Vincent Argeneau. Just recalling them was enough to make her flesh tingle.

"So what excuse do I give everyone for coming into the office today?"

Vincent's question drew Jackie's thoughts from her heated memories of the passionate dream she'd enjoyed that afternoon. Remonstrating with herself to keep her thoughts on the job at hand, she glanced his way as she parked the car in the lot of the large white building that housed V.A. Productions.

"What do you mean what excuse do you give?" she asked with surprise. "It's your company. Surely you come here?"

"Well, yes," he said, managing to sound doubtful. "But why am I bringing *you* and Marguerite here?"

"I'm your personal assistant and you want to familiarize me with all aspects of your business," Jackie answered promptly, reminding him of her own cover in this case. "And Marguerite asked to come along because she's never seen your company." She met the woman's eyes in the rearview mirror. "You haven't, have you?"

"No," Marguerite assured her. "This will be my first visit."

"Good," Jackie opened her car door and got out, then walked around the car to meet Vincent and his aunt as they disembarked on the other side. They walked in together, Vincent between the two women.

Jackie had known that Vincent had money. That had been obvious from his house: big, beautiful and expensively decorated, it was also on some prime real estate. Everyone wanted to live on the water out here. Still, she supposed she'd just assumed that he was your average level of wealthy and had, perhaps, purchased his home years ago, when the land was worth less. Three steps inside the doors of the big white building that housed his production company, however, told her that the man wasn't just wealthy, he was loaded.

Jackie had expected the building to house several other companies aside from his own. It didn't. The entire building housed V.A. Productions and nothing else. The entry led into a large lobby with two receptionists and an armed guard. All three were mortal, she saw, glancing from face to face and noting their eyes. And all three glanced toward them with polite enquiry when Vincent ushered the women through the front door. Their expressions were quick to change to shock, however, as they recognized the V.A. in V.A. Productions. The shock was still on their faces as he led Jackie and Marguerite past the desk and into the elevator.

"Why do I get the feeling that you don't come here often?" Jackie asked dryly as Vincent pushed the button for the top floor and the elevator doors closed on the three stunned faces.

"They recognized me, didn't they?" Vincent said with a shrug.

Jackie lifted an eyebrow at the comment, but Vincent didn't notice. His attention was fixed on the elevator panel over the doors, watching the floors light up as he added, "Besides, I've never been here this early and the guards are on a different shift than our other workers. They switch shifts at seven P.M. rather than six like the rest of the building. Security suggested it so that they wouldn't be changing guards as everyone was arriving or leaving."

"Smart," Jackie commented with approval, then forgot all about it as the elevator gave a ding and the doors began to open.

This was obviously the executive floor, she saw as they stepped out into a world of plush carpet and muted music.

Another reception desk awaited them here, this one also sporting two receptionists and an armed male guard. As in the entry, the receptionists were both a male and a female and both were human.

And, as with the ones below, these three people looked shocked to see Vincent Argeneau entering, but none of them did more than nod in greeting as he passed.

Jackie waited until they were started down a long hallway before moving closer to Vincent to ask, "Are your night security here human as well?"

"No. Immortal," Vincent assured her.

"I'm surprised immortals would take the position," Jackie commented. Among humans, security guards were among the least respected and lowest paying jobs. She didn't understand why, herself. After all, security were basically on the front line should anything happen. They were also responsible for the safety and security of everyone in the building, but still the job was considered the lowest of the low. And, in her experience, immortals were far too arrogant to take on what was considered to be no better than a grunt job by most people.

"We pay well," Vincent explained. "Still, the position is usually filled with the young borns and the newly turned."

Jackie nodded absently, but asked, "So you have three shifts for security, seven P.M. to three A.M., three A.M. to eleven A.M., and eleven A.M. to seven P.M., right?"

"Yes."

"And the guards are human from eleven A.M. to seven P.M., but immortal from seven P.M. to three A.M. What about the three A.M. to eleven A.M. shift?"

"Human."

Jackie nodded. She'd expected as much. "We'll need to talk to your security chief. They need to change things."

"Why?" Vincent asked with surprise.

"Because while it's smart to stagger the shifts so that security isn't changing while the other workers are, the shifts need to be rearranged," Jackie murmured, working it through quickly in her head. "The security shifts need to change an hour before the others rather than an hour after. The three shifts should be five P.M. to one A.M., one A.M. to nine A.M. and nine A.M. to five P.M. And you need to put immortals on both the five P.M. to one A.M. shift and the one A.M. to nine A.M. shift, or split up the groups so that each has an immortal and a human on it. The way it stands, an immortal would have no trouble slipping in before the seven P.M. to three A.M. immortal shift starts and any time after it ends."

"You're right," Vincent said with a sigh. "We've never really been concerned about immortals breaking in here. The security is to keep mortal thieves out, or to handle upset mortals who didn't get roles or jobs and keep them from causing trouble, not to defend against immortals. There's never been a reason to fear immortals causing trouble."

"There is now," Jackie pointed out.

"Yes," he acknowledged with a small sigh that spoke of his unhappiness with the knowledge that his saboteur was one of his own. Jackie cast him a sympathetic glance, but didn't say anything as he suddenly took both her arm and Marguerite's to turn them into the last door at the end of the hall.

"Vincent!" Sharon nearly leapt out of her seat as they entered what was obviously her office. You would have thought the woman had been shocked with a cattle prod, she got up so swiftly.

"Hi Sharon. You remember Jackie. And this is my aunt, Marguerite Argeneau," Vincent greeted as he paused before the woman's desk.

"Oh, Mrs. Argeneau, hello," Sharon gushed, hurrying around the desk to offer her hand. Jackie couldn't help noticing that her presence was completely ignored.

Vincent seemed to notice too, however. At least, she thought the tightening around his mouth might be because of the rude exclusion of her presence. He didn't comment, but he did immediately begin to herd her and Marguerite toward the inner door and away from the woman's fawning over his aunt.

"Is there any coffee around here?" he asked as he walked and then added pointedly. "Jackie might like a coffee. So would I. What about you, Aunt Marguerite?"

"No, thank you," Marguerite murmured as he ushered them into his office.

Sharon wasn't given time to respond to his comments as by the time he'd finished making them, Vincent was closing the door to the office.

147

Jackie glanced around the large, luxurious office as she and Marguerite followed him to the desk. Pausing in front of the two chairs before his desk, she then turned slowly, her gaze drifting over everything in the room. All she could think as she took in the huge marble desk and opulent décor of the room was that the man had expensive taste. Or perhaps it was his decorator who did, Jackie decided as she took in the stark black and white interior. The office was nothing like his home, where the neutral base colors were all offset by colorful accessories such as throw rugs, pillows, candles, and paintings in rich, vibrant colors.

"I take it you really don't come in here often?" Jackie asked with amusement as Vincent walked around the desk to drop into the chair behind it.

"What makes you think that?" he asked, expression wary.

"Oh, I don't know," she said with amusement. "Perhaps it's everyone's apparent shock at your being here now . . . and the dust on your desktop," Jackie added to prevent his coming out with the "I've never been here this early," comment again.

"She's right, dear," Marguerite commented. "It is rather dusty. I think you need a new cleaning service."

Vincent just grimaced and said, "I fear I prefer acting to the business end of things . . . or I used to." He acknowledged his growing boredom with what used to be his passion for acting with an unhappy expression. "I tend to travel a lot with the acting too, so I have a vice president who takes care of the boring business stuff."

"Human or immortal?" Jackie asked curiously.

"Both," Vincent answered. "I actually have two vice presidents. One human for daytime matters, and one immortal who manages everything at night. Neil and Stephano Notte pretty much take care of everything between the two of them and just check in with me on occasion to be sure we're all in agreement on things."

"Ah yes, the Notte brothers," Marguerite murmured, settling in the chair beside the one Jackie stood in front of. "Bastien has mentioned them. He says you made a wise choice employing them."

Jackie raised her eyebrows at this comment, then said, "Let me guess: Stephano is the immortal and Neil the mortal."

"Why would you say that?" Vincent asked.

"Because Neil is a nice, normal, mortal-type name, and all you immortals seem to have exotic -ien, -ius, or -o-type names," she answered dryly.

"Exotic -ien names?" Vincent asked with bewilderment.

"Yes, you know, like Bastien. Exotic names rather than normal pedestrian names like everyone else has today," she explained.

"Actually, Bastien was a common name when I gave it to him," Marguerite murmured with amusement.

"Yes, and so was mine," Vincent added.

Jackie grimaced. "Yes, well, that's my point. Older vampires have older names that are no longer in common usage. Like Stephano."

"Actually, I believe Neil is the immortal and Stephano the human," Marguerite announced with amusement, then raised an eyebrow at Vincent. "Am I not right?"

Vincent nodded and Jackie's eyes widened with surprise. "You're kidding?"

"No."

She considered that briefly, then sighed and dropped into her chair. Just when she thought she had these guys figured out, they pulled a fast one on her. Immortals usually had strange or exotic names and metallic eyes. It looked as if the metallic eyes part was the only thing she could count on.

"So . . ." Vincent raised an eyebrow. "What do we do first? Meet everyone here to give them the once over? Or get the list of employees from *Dracula, the Musical*?"

"Both," Jackie decided. "Sharon can round up the list while you introduce me around, then we'll take the list home with us so Tiny can help go over it."

Vincent nodded at the suggestion and had started to push his chair back when the office door suddenly swung open, making them all glance toward it. Sharon entered carrying a tray with two coffees, cream, and sugar on it.

"Oh, Sharon, thank you," Vincent said, getting to his feet.

The secretary set the tray on the desk and explained, "I don't know how to make coffee. Fortunately, there was some left over from the day shift."

"That's fine," Vincent assured her, then glanced to Jackie before adding, "I brought Jackie in today to meet everyone and familiarize her with the business. Aunt Marguerite wished to come along since she'd never been here."

Jackie bit her lip to keep back her amusement as he repeated almost word for word what she'd suggested. It did the trick. Sharon relaxed and smiled as she said, "Of course. Is there anything I can help with?"

Vincent's glance slid to Jackie, then he said, "Actually, yes there is. We're going to need another copy of the employee list you and Lily brought over yesterday."

"Another copy?" She frowned, but said, "Of course. I'll round up the paperwork again and photocopy it."

"Thank you," Vincent said as she left, then stood and leaned over the desk to peer at the coffee tray. Jackie stood as well and they both moved to fix a cup each. Vincent reached for the sugar and Jackie the cream, but both of them paused and grimaced as Jackie poured the cream into the nearest cup and the liquid turned a dark gray. This coffee was terribly old and unbearably strong. There was no doubt it was undrinkable.

"There's a cafeteria downstairs," Vincent announced, setting the sugar back on the tray. "We can stop in there and grab a cup on our introduction tour."

"Good thinking." Jackie set the creamer on the tray and straightened as he walked around the desk. It seemed they were leaving right away, which was fine with her. Jackie and Marguerite followed him to the door. When he opened it for them, they stepped into Sharon's office, then paused at the sound of slightly raised voices coming from an open door behind Sharon's desk.

"What do you mean they were the originals?" Sharon's voice sounded shocked.

"I told you that when you insisted on driving me over," Lily's voice answered with exasperation. "I was supposed to fax over copies, but you insisted on taking them over in person and I said I'd make copies and you said no, we'd just take the ones I had. Well, those were the originals, *our* copies. We don't have any more of them."

"Well, I didn't realize they were the *originals*," Sharon said shortly.

"You had to, Sharon. You took them out of the drawer

yourself and insisted we take them." Lily sounded completely bewildered by the other woman's words.

Jackie's glance slid to Vincent as he moved past her to approach the open door.

"Is there a problem, ladies?" he asked as Jackie and Marguerite followed and peered over his shoulders into a small file room.

"I'm afraid we brought the original copies of the employee list to you yesterday," Sharon announced with a glance in the hapless Lily's direction. "We don't have backups. I hope it's not too important?"

Jackie's gaze narrowed on the woman. The secretary didn't look terribly sorry to have to make the announcement. In fact, there was a satisfied gleam in her eye as she peered in Jackie's direction.

Vincent glanced back toward Jackie with concern, but before he could say anything, Lily spoke up. "We still have it on computer, Sharon. We can just pull up the file and print it again."

"Oh . . . Yes." Not looking terribly pleased with the idea of the extra work, Sharon slid past them all and moved to her desk. Settling into her seat, she turned on her computer. The secretary glanced up to smile a bit stiffly at the four of them as Vincent, Jackie, Marguerite, and Lily moved around her desk to wait. She then ignored them and began to click away with her mouse as the computer finished going through its startup cycle. She clicked several times, then stopped suddenly and began to frown.

"Is there something wrong?" Vincent asked, his gaze narrowing.

"No, no," she assured him, but the secretary was frowning as she added, "It doesn't appear to be where I thought it was. I must have saved it in a different folder."

Jackie felt concern tighten in her stomach. She was beginning to suspect the files had been removed. It made perfect sense that the saboteur might have made his way here after getting the papers from the house. That should have occurred to her last night. If it had, they could have headed straight here and perhaps got to the files before the saboteur had . . . Unless the saboteur had hit the office first. She wasn't at all surprised when Sharon glanced up with obvious frustration and admitted that the file appeared to be missing.

Lily and Sharon turned wide questioning eyes to Vincent then, but he and Marguerite had turned to Jackie. She didn't at first respond, but was busy considering matters. Owning her own company as she did, she knew that there would be other departments that might have the information. Costuming would have had to have a list of at least the actors along with their sizes to dress them. Security might have a list of who had been used in security. Each department would be a source for who was hired in each area, but there was one department that should have the information on everyone in the production. Anyone who had worked on that play should have earned a check for the time they worked on it, which meant that accounting should have a list of all the individuals.

"Accounting should have a copy," Lily blurted suddenly, the production assistant's mind obviously having run along the same lines as Jackie's. She moved forward now, saying, "I'll go ask Phillip if he'll—"

153

"Phillip is on vacation," Sharon pointed out.

"Oh," Lily paused and hesitated, then said, "Well, his secretary, Meredith, should be able to pull it up for us."

"You're right, Lily," Vincent smiled at the production assistant.

"Shall I go ask her if she would—?"

"No, no." Vincent patted her shoulder. "I wanted to introduce Jackie around anyway. We'll stop in there first and ask Meredith to pull it up. Good thinking though. Thank you."

When Jackie added her smile of approval to Vincent's and the girl smiled shyly back, she found herself shaking her head as she turned to lead the way out of the office. Honestly, the girl didn't look more than twelve or fourteen when she smiled like that. Jackie almost expected to see braces sparkling out at her. However, the girl was smart and at least trying to be helpful, unlike Sharon.

"Do you want to head right to accounting, or meet people along the way?" Vincent asked as he led her along the hall.

"Either way," she answered. "It doesn't really matter."

Vincent turned a questioning gaze to Marguerite then, but she just shook her head. "I'm just here to tag along. However you like it, Vincent."

Nodding, he paused at the first door they came to and ushered them inside.

"Mr. Argeneau." The blonde behind the desk hid her surprise behind a smile of welcome as she stood up. "Mr. Notte didn't warn me that you'd be coming in today."

"Stephano didn't know, Amelia," Vincent assured her as he ushered Jackie and Marguerite across the office. "Is he in? I want to introduce him to my aunt and Jackie."

"No, I'm afraid not."

Vincent paused halfway to the inner door and turned to her with obvious surprise. "He isn't? But he's always in here late. He stays to brief Neil when he comes in."

"Well, he is here somewhere, but he stepped out for a minute," the woman explained, then frowned as she added, "He should be back soon. In fact, I was just wondering what was holding him up when you came in. He has tickets to a show tonight and planned to leave early."

"Oh. Well, I'm sure he'll return shortly, then," he said and added, "We'll keep an eye out for him on our tour, but if he should stop back here without meeting us, tell him not to worry about it. We can catch him another time, there's no need to delay leaving."

Amelia nodded, looking relieved that he wasn't upset. "If he returns, I'll tell him you were here."

"Thank you," Vincent said as he led them out.

They didn't go far, just to the next door up the hall.

"This is Phillip's office," he explained as he led the way inside.

"The accountant who's on vacation," Jackie murmured as they paused in front of the empty desk in the outer office. "Is his secretary off while he's away?"

"I don't think so. Sharon would have mentioned if Meredith were away too," Vincent said, then glanced toward the door to the inner office.

Following his gaze, Jackie spotted the cracked open door and raised her eyebrows. "Perhaps she's in there."

Vincent moved to the door and pushed it open. He glanced inside, then went terribly stiff. It was as if someone had shoved a pole up his back. She wasn't the only one to notice.

"What is it?" Marguerite asked with concern as Jackie moved to join him in the doorway.

At first glance everything seemed in order . . . until Jackie noted the legs sticking out behind the desk, a man's legs in trousers and dress shoes. Those legs weren't moving.

Slipping past Vincent, Jackie crossed the room and moved around the desk, stopping short the moment she was able to see the whole man. She knew it wasn't Phillip, the accountant. He was on vacation. Whoever it was, however, was dressed like an accountant, full business suit, nice tie, expensive dress shoes . . . In fact, the only thing that ruined the image of the wealthy, successful businessman was the knife in his chest.

Nine

"I'm guessing this is Stephano Notte?" Jackie asked, unable to look away from the pale, prone man. The mortal vice president of the company who had been missing from his office.

"Yes." Vincent's voice was almost a whisper and she peered his way. On first glance, one could be forgiven for thinking he wasn't affected. His face was a cool mask of indifference, but not his eyes. They were glowing silver-blue and swirling with a mix of pain and fury and what she thought might be guilt. Jackie suspected he feared the saboteur was behind this and was blaming himself for it. She'd like to tell him that it probably wasn't the case, but the plain envelope sticking out of the breast pocket of the man's jacket belied that. The return address was all that was showing, but it was enough; it was Vincent's address.

"He's alive."

Jackie tore her eyes away from the lifeless figure and glanced at Marguerite with surprise. "What?"

"He's alive," she repeated, staying by the door, but pushing it closed after a nervous glance out into the outer office. "I can hear his heart beat."

Jackie turned back to the man and knelt to check for a pulse. She was sure she wouldn't find one, it looked like he'd been stabbed through the heart. Surely he hadn't survived that?

"They must have missed the heart," Marguerite said, apparently reading her mind. "I can hear it beating. It's slow and not very strong, but it's beating."

"I can hear it too." Vincent knelt abruptly at the other side just as Jackie found his pulse. It was thready, but there, she realized with amazement. Stephano Notte wasn't dead. Yet.

"We need to call an ambulance," Jackie said urgently, straightening and moving toward the desk.

"He won't survive long enough for that," Vincent announced. "He's dying as we speak."

"We have to try," she said grimly as she picked up the phone.

"Vincent, what are you doing?"

Marguerite's sharp question made Jackie pause and turn back to see Vincent rolling up his sleeve.

"When I say *now,* take the knife out," Vincent ordered as he opened Stephano Notte's mouth.

"No, you can't!" Marguerite protested, rushing forward. "Let me."

Jackie frowned, her hand clenching the phone as she

tried to sort out what was happening. Marguerite rushed to Vincent's side, but wasn't fast enough to stop him from biting into his own wrist. It was a deep bite and must have been painful, but he didn't even wince. He merely shifted the gushing wound over Stephano's open mouth and let the blood pour in just as his aunt reached his side.

Marguerite had reached out to catch his shoulder as if to physically stop him from what he was doing, but now sagged in defeat at his side.

Legs suddenly weak as she grasped what was happening, Jackie slumped against the desk, the phone still clasped in her hand. She watched fascinated as Vincent slid his free hand under the man's neck and lifted him slightly to facilitate the liquid going down.

"Oh, Vincent," Marguerite moaned the words, sadness heavy in her eyes as she—for some reason—peered from him, to Jackie, and then back and shook her head.

Disturbed by the woman's reaction, but not understanding it, Jackie set the phone back and moved shakily to stand on Stephano's other side as Vincent turned him. At least, she thought that was what he was doing.

"Take out the knife." Vincent's words were hissed through gritted teeth.

Glancing at his pale face with concern, Jackie automatically knelt to do his bidding. She didn't really think, she just did it, her hand closing around the metal handle and pulling upward. It wasn't until she met resistance that her mind realized that she was pulling a knife out of a man's chest. A shudder of revulsion rushed through her, followed by a wince of sympathy as the knife finally came free and slid from the wound.

The moment the metal weapon was clear of Stephano's flesh, Vincent took his wrist away from the prone man's mouth and allowed the last of the blood dripping from his wrist to drop into the open wound on Stephano's chest.

"Will it work?" she asked as Vincent's wound stopped bleeding and he set the man back flat on the ground.

"I don't know. We might have been too late," he said unhappily.

Marguerite removed a handkerchief from her purse and handed it to him, and Vincent quickly wrapped it around his wrist. He tucked the end under the binding to keep it in place, then bent forward again to lift Stephano's eyelids and peer into his eyes.

"It will work," Marguerite said and the regret in her voice made Jackie glance her way sharply. It took a moment for her to sort out why the immortal was so upset by this turn of events, however, then Jackie recalled the rule about only turning one mortal in a lifetime. Most immortals saved that turn for their life mate. Vincent had just used it to save his vice president. If he found his life mate, he wouldn't be able to turn her.

Her eyes returned slowly to Vincent. His expression was grim, his face pale as he watched over the man who he'd just sacrificed so much for, and she felt tears sting the back of her eyes. Had she really thought all immortals were selfish, arrogant beings who only saw mortals as walking dinner? Dear God, the man had just given up the opportunity of ever having anyone to share his very long life with to save a mortal.

"What's done, is done," Marguerite murmured fatalistically,

drawing Jackie's blurred vision back. She asked, "What do we do now?"

Jackie stared, not a single idea forming in her head. It was Vincent who said, "He'll need blood and lots of it. But we need to get him out of here without anyone realizing he survived."

Blinking her inertia away, Jackie took a moment to sort out why he thought no one should know Stephano had survived the attack, but then she realized he'd been stabbed head on; he must have seen his attacker. If the saboteur knew he'd survived, he'd make another attempt to kill him to keep him from revealing who he was.

She was impressed that Vincent had picked up on that right away. His thoughts were working much more quickly than her own at the moment. However, now that it was faced with a problem, her own brain started to function once more.

"Why stab him?" she asked suddenly. When Vincent peered at her blankly, she explained, "Stephano is a mortal. If the saboteur is an immortal as we're assuming, why didn't he just wipe his memory? Why stab him?"

"Stephano's mother was mortal when she had him," Vincent explained. "As was his father. She was widowed when he was still quite young and became the life mate of an immortal. Of course, Mrs. Notte became an immortal herself, had her son Neil who is also an immortal. She wanted to turn Stephano too, but he wouldn't allow it."

"Stephano grew up the only mortal in a family of immortals," Jackie realized.

"In instances like this, the mortal often learns to block

some of our abilities," Marguerite said. "Like you have. It's simple self-defense."

"So, the saboteur couldn't completely control him?"

"It's possible. Or perhaps, couldn't wipe his memory fully," Marguerite suggested. "And rather than take the chance he'd remember, killed him. Or thought he did."

Nodding, Jackie reached forward to grab the letter sticking out of Stephano's breast pocket, only to pause as she saw the knife still clutched in her hand. It was actually a letter opener, not a knife. Grimacing, she set it on the carpet beside her, then snatched the letter from his pocket and opened it. All it said was:

A friend of yours? I'm afraid he got in the way.
The next one will be someone you chose.

"What does it say?" Vincent asked.

Jackie silently handed the letter over, her thoughts occupied with what the words meant. The first part was obvious. Stephano must have interrupted the saboteur while he was in here doing something and only been killed because he got in the way. The last sentence was the one that troubled her.

"The next one will be someone you chose," Vincent read aloud. "What the hell does that mean?"

"I'm guessing it means that now that he's moved on to murder, he intends to continue in that vein," Jackie murmured, her gaze dropping to the man on the floor. Stephano Notte might still die, and even if he didn't, it would only be because he'd been turned. The saboteur had intended for him to die and was working on the premise that he had.

"Yes, but what does he mean by it will be someone I choose?" Vincent asked with distress.

"Chose. Past tense," Jackie corrected with a frown and shook her head. "I'm not sure what he means by that."

Although she had some ideas, Jackie acknowledged to herself. None of them were good though and she really would rather they didn't come to pass.

"How long until we know if he's going to survive the turning?" she asked.

"He'll survive," Marguerite assured her. "I've seen people in worse shape survive it."

"Okay," she said slowly, her gaze sliding back to the man on the floor. He was pale and unmoving and she wouldn't have found it hard to believe he was already dead, except that the wound on his chest appeared smaller to her than it had been when she'd first pulled the letter opener free.

"How long does a turning take?" she asked. That was one thing there was very little information on in the agency files.

"The worst of it is usually done in the first twenty-four to forty-eight hours, though it can take a little longer depending on the extent of the injuries or illnesses they have," Marguerite answered. "He'll wake up after that, but the turning won't be completely finished for weeks afterward."

Jackie nodded. It was the waking up part she was interested in. The moment Stephano woke up, they could get the name of the saboteur from him, round the man up, and prevent anyone else from getting hurt or dying. She frowned. A lot could happen in twenty-four to forty-eight hours.

"All right." Vincent stood abruptly. "We need to get him out of here and back to the house to start giving him blood."

"And we need to do it without anyone knowing he survived," Jackie added, standing as well.

"An ambulance is the best bet," Marguerite announced. When Jackie and Vincent glanced her way, she shrugged. "Stephano was mortal. An ambulance would be called in. And the police. They would take the body away."

Jackie nodded. If they just snuck him out of the building, the saboteur might suspect he didn't die. But . . . "How do we handle the EMTs?"

"Either Aunt Marguerite or myself could control the ambulance attendants," Vincent suggested. "Travel with them and have Stephano delivered to my house, and then wipe the memories of the EMTs."

"I'll do that," Marguerite offered. "That way, you can stay here and handle the police when they come, then see if the saboteur managed to get the information we were looking for or not."

"Thank you, Aunt Marguerite," Vincent murmured as Jackie moved to the phone to place the call to emergency services. She kept her call vague, saying only that they needed an ambulance and the police at V.A. Productions. She didn't want to say anything that might be questioned later. Marguerite could put the idea in the attendant's heads that it was just a minor injury to one of the workers and Vincent could do the same with the police, but not if she called saying someone had been stabbed.

"They're on their way," Jackie announced as she hung up.

Vincent nodded and then glanced at his aunt. "How much blood do you have at the house?"

"Enough to see him through a day or so, at least," Marguerite said.

"I'll arrange for more," he murmured and then the three of them turned sharply toward the door as it suddenly opened and a man filled the doorway.

Tall, slender, in a dark suit and with jet-black hair, the man smiled at them in greeting. "I thought I heard voices in here."

"Neil." Vincent sounded shocked and Jackie supposed, like herself, he'd forgotten all about Stephano's brother and the fact that he should be arriving soon.

"I just got in," Neil Notte admitted, still smiling. "Amelia told me you were here with your aunt and another lady. She said you were looking for Stephano. Have you found—?"

His mouth froze open as his gaze found the man on the floor. He paled and alarm immediately filled his face, then he rushed forward. Jackie moved to close the door he'd left open, then turned to see him kneeling beside Stephano. Vincent knelt beside him, speaking in quiet tones, but there was confusion on Neil's face and he kept saying, "What?" over and over, making Vincent repeat himself. Jackie watched silently for a moment, then shifted uncomfortably and turned to the door.

"I'm going to go wait for the ambulance and police to bring them here. Try not to let anyone else in."

Without waiting for a response, she slipped out of the room and crossed the secretary's office to the hall.

* * *

It was nearly dawn when Jackie led Vincent into the kitchen of his home. Tiny and Marguerite sat at the table playing poker, but stopped their game and began to gather the cards together when they entered. Apparently, the pair had simply been trying to pass the time until their return.

"You took a lot longer than I expected. I was starting to worry," Tiny said in a deep rumbling voice as he got to his feet. "Are you hungry?"

Jackie shook her head. "I ate in the cafeteria at the office."

Tiny nodded. "Coffee?"

"Yes, please," Jackie murmured as Vincent pulled a chair out for her.

"I'll make fresh," Tiny said and moved to the counter to match action to words.

"Did you also eat, Vincent?" Marguerite asked, eyeing his pale face with concern as he took the seat next to Jackie.

"I grabbed a bite at the office," Vincent answered brusquely.

Jackie ignored the look he cast her way and ran a hand through her hair. Vincent hadn't had a chance to go out and feed before they'd headed for his production company, something Jackie hadn't even thought of before they'd headed out. She hadn't thought of it until halfway through the evening when she'd noticed that not only was he frightfully pale, but his jaw was tight-clenched and there were lines of pain by his eyes.

Realizing he needed to feed, and knowing Vincent wouldn't leave what was happening at the company to take care of the matter, it was Jackie who'd suggested he feed on one of his human employees. She didn't know which of them had been more shocked at her suggestion, but after closing his gaping mouth, Vincent had refused the suggestion, reminding her that he didn't feed on his employees. However, once she'd made the suggestion, Jackie had recognized the practicality of it. She needed Vincent to be at full strength and thinking clearly at the moment, which meant he needed to feed. So she'd persisted until he'd given in. That didn't mean he was happy with doing so, and from the looks he was casting her way, Vincent seemed to be blaming her for what he'd done.

"You need more." Marguerite's tone was uncompromising. "The cramping from dehydration has already started."

Jackie glanced at Vincent sharply and frowned. While he seemed pale, she didn't see the lines of pain around his eyes that she'd noted earlier, but Marguerite sounded so certain Jackie couldn't doubt her. She supposed that meant he'd *really* been suffering by the time she'd noticed his need today.

"I'll go out later." Vincent waved her concern away, then endeavored to change the subject by asking, "How is Stephano?"

"Neil is with him," Marguerite answered. "I've told him several times that I'd sit with Stephano to give him a break, but he won't leave his side."

Vincent nodded at this news, apparently not surprised. "Did you have any problems with the EMTs?"

"No. That all went smoothly. Neil handled one, while I took the other."

"Good, good." Vincent ran one hand wearily through his hair, then asked, "Has everything else been all right here today? There were no problems?"

Marguerite hesitated and then heaved a deep sigh when Tiny sent her a meaningful glance as he turned on the coffeepot and approached the table. Without saying anything, the older vampire reached to the side, picked up a newspaper, unfolded it, and laid it on the table.

Vincent raised his eyebrows, but peered down at the open front page. A headshot of a woman filled a quarter of the front page and he frowned at the grainy picture of the pretty young blonde for several moments before speaking.

"She looks familiar," Vincent commented, his eyebrows drawn together and Jackie leaned closer to read the byline under the photo. *Body of beautiful young actress found in the hills.*

"She was at the club you took me to the night I arrived," Marguerite said quietly.

Vincent's eyes widened with recognition. "I fed on her."

Marguerite nodded.

Frowning, Jackie pulled the paper closer and quickly read the article. It seemed the woman had gone missing early last evening while she and Vincent had been handling the police at V.A. Productions. Her body, mutilated and drained of blood, had been found in the hills at around ten o'clock. Jackie was surprised the story had made the morning paper. They must've scrambled to get it in, though there wasn't really much information; just the picture and a paragraph with the bare bones of the story.

"The next one will be someone you chose," Vincent

murmured the words that were presently running through Jackie's own mind.

"That was what I first thought of too," Marguerite admitted.

They were all silent. This was bad. This woman was someone Vincent had chosen to feed on. It meant the saboteur had to have followed him that night . . . and still may be doing so. Now that the saboteur had stepped up the game to murder, anyone Vincent fed on . . . he might be marking them for death.

Jackie glanced at Vincent. She saw the recognition of this in the horror on his face and frowned. He looked even paler than he had. In that moment, she knew without a doubt that he'd refuse to go out and feed on anyone else until this was resolved . . . but he *had* to feed. He would die horribly and painfully if he didn't.

"Tiny, order a pizza," she said grimly.

"I thought you weren't hungry," the giant said with surprise. "I can make some—"

"Pizza," Jackie said firmly. "Order it to be delivered."

The moment Tiny nodded and moved to pick up the phone, Jackie took the paper away from Vincent and set it aside. "Don't worry about this. This is done. There is nothing you can do about this."

"Jackie's right," Tiny said as he finished his phone call to the pizza place and hung up. "There's nothing you can do about that now, let's concentrate on what we can do. Had the saboteur removed the list from the accountant's office?"

"From the accounting office and every other office in the building. The entire play—along with its employees—has been erased from the computer files at the company. From every department. So have all hard copy files," she announced glumly, as she watched the giant retrieve three coffee cups and move toward the pot as it spat out the last bit of coffee.

After seeing Stephano, Marguerite, and Neil out with the ambulance attendants, Vincent had handled the police. He'd taken them into Phillip's office to control their minds and put the least damaging story in their thoughts before sending them on their way too. The two of them had then made a complete tour of the building, stopping at his office first to tell Sharon that Stephano had been murdered.

Leaving her to spread the news, they'd then gone on to check every file room and computer in the building for information on the play *Dracula, the Musical*. They'd come up with nothing. The saboteur had gotten there first . . . again.

Tiny's mouth tightened as he poured the coffees. "So, the saboteur did come in after the papers that night . . . He's very thorough."

"Yes," Jackie said unhappily. Criminals were sometimes stupid, but even the intelligent ones often slipped up, leaving some trail to follow. This man was neither stupid, nor making mistakes. At least, none she'd found yet.

"What do we do now?" Vincent asked.

Jackie frowned. "There's a possibility Stephano won't be able to tell us who attacked him. From what Marguerite said earlier, he might be harder to read or wipe, but the saboteur may have managed it. He just might not have been sure the memory wiping took and stabbed him to be certain he couldn't tell anyone who he was."

Vincent frowned at the possibility.

"So, we should really proceed as if he can't tell us."

"How? What do we do?"

Jackie opened her mouth to speak, then paused as the buzzer sounded, announcing someone at the gate. Tiny stood and moved to the panel by the door that led into the garage. He turned on the monitor and Jackie wasn't surprised when it turned out to be the pizza delivery. She watched the giant push the button to open the gate, then reached into her pocket and withdrew a twenty-dollar bill, which she handed to Vincent.

"What's that for?" he asked with a scowl.

"For you to pay the pizza boy," she said mildly.

"Why would I pay the pizza boy?" he asked with surprise.

"Because it isn't for me, it's for you," Jackie explained patiently. When he stared at her blankly, she heaved a sigh and turned to Marguerite to comment, "Bastien once told me that your daughter was a hemaphobic."

"Yes, but she's cured now," Marguerite assured her, obviously pleased to make the announcement.

Jackie nodded. "Yes, he told me that too. But I gather that she could only feed herself by biting and that there were occasions when you would order pizza so that she could feed off the delivery person?"

"Ah." Marguerite smiled with surprised pleasure. "Smart girl."

They both turned to peer at Vincent as realization dawned on his expression. For a moment, there was a struggle on his face, then he tightened his mouth and shook his head. "I can't feed on him. If the saboteur—"

"Have you ever ordered pizza to feed your hunger on the pizza deliverer?" she asked patiently. When he shook his head, Jackie nodded her satisfaction. She'd suspected not. "Then the saboteur will think the pizza is for your human houseguests, won't he? Which leaves the delivery boy safe from being marked for death by your saboteur." I hope, she added silently, her gaze sliding to the kitchen door as the front doorbell sounded.

Vincent's gaze swiveled toward the kitchen door, but he made no move to get up.

"Vincent, you need to feed," she said quietly. "This is the safest meal I can offer you. Please go collect the pizza."

When he continued to hesitate, Marguerite stood and headed for the door. "I shall let the boy in and take him to the office."

Jackie watched her go, then turned to Vincent. "Go. Feed off him and tip him well for your conscience if you must, but feed. And do it quickly. If he's in and out quickly, there's less chance the saboteur will even consider the possibility that you fed off him."

Vincent's eyes widened abruptly and he got to his feet. Waving away the money she held out to him, he reached for his own wallet as he hurried out of the room.

Jackie sat back in her seat with a sigh of relief. The problem of feeding him had been handled . . . at least for tonight.

"That takes care of tonight, but what will we do about his need to feed tomorrow?" Tiny asked in an unhappy rumble, his thoughts running along the same line as hers. "I don't think he'll go out and feed if it might mean marking someone for the saboteur to target. He needs to feed."

"I know," Jackie said unhappily and pushed one weary hand through her hair. "I'll have to think of something."

Tiny nodded and then changed the subject. "Neil is grateful for what Vincent did by turning Stephano, but doesn't seem to think his brother will be."

Jackie glanced at him with surprise. "Why?"

"He says that when his mother married her husband and became immortal, she offered to use her right to turn one immortal on Stephano, so that he would be immortal like the rest of the family, but he refused. He said he'd take the hand fate had dealt him."

Jackie considered that, wondering how she'd feel if she was turned without her permission. It was considered a no-no to turn someone without their consent, unless it was an emergency and their consent couldn't be gained. As had been the case with Stephano.

"You know Vincent can't turn a life mate now," Tiny said quietly.

"Yes, it was very selfless of him to turn Stephano as he did," Jackie said on a sigh as Marguerite returned. Vincent was presumably still with the delivery boy. "We'll have to hope his selflessness is rewarded and his life mate, when he meets her, is already an immortal."

"He already has, and she isn't," Marguerite said grimly and Jackie glanced around at her with surprise.

"He has?" Jackie asked and for some reason this news sent pain shooting through her chest. Recognizing the feeling as jealousy, she ignored it, telling herself that it was for the best. She would have no illusions now and wouldn't be foolish enough to allow herself to fall for the guy any harder than she already had.

"Yes, he has," Marguerite announced, but before she could say any more, Vincent entered the room. He looked better than he had when he'd left. He wasn't quite so pale, but he still looked tired and worn out by the day's events.

"You should get some rest," she said with concern. "We all should. We'll start on this first thing in the morning."

"I want to go check on Stephano first," Vincent murmured. "Then I'll head to bed."

Murmuring goodnight, he left the kitchen again and Jackie found herself frowning as she watched him go and realized the implications of what he'd done by saving Stephano's life.

Vincent would have to watch his life mate age and die and then would have to continue on without her. If he even got the chance to do that, Jackie thought. She knew, if it were her, she wouldn't want that. She wouldn't want to love and be with a man who would continue to look twenty-five to thirty years old while she aged, and wrinkled, and her hair turned white.

It would be fine for a while, until she hit about forty and then she'd look like the older woman with the young stud. By fifty or so, people would start to mistake her for his mother, then at seventy as his grandmother. She supposed they could avoid that by not going out in public much, but there was still the fact that while his body stayed young and beautiful, her own would age. She knew life mates bonded, but was there enough bonding that he would still find her attractive when her body began to sag and wrinkle? Or would the woman have the courage to let him see her so? Jackie didn't think she could. She'd be more likely to set him free and hope he found another. She wouldn't want him to watch her body and health disintegrate and the last breath leave her body. She couldn't be that selfish.

Ten

Jackie pushed the button to open the driveway gate, moved to the front door, tugged it open, and waited impatiently. A scowl pulled at her lips as she watched a little white hatchback careen up the driveway, and her irritation only intensified as the car squealed to a halt in front of the house.

"You're early," she snapped, glaring at the young man in the drugstore uniform as he sauntered up to the door. "I told the girl not to send the order until two-thirty P.M. It's only one-thirty P.M."

The guy wasn't a day over twenty and had longish hair that he now brushed back in an affected manner as he offered her a charming smile. His nametag read Darryl. "I was passing, so thought I'd stop and see if you were in early. You are. So here I am."

Darryl held up the small drugstore bag, his expression

expectant, but Jackie continued to scowl as her mind raced over what she should do. She'd spent most of the night pondering ways to bring a meal to Vincent. Just before she'd dropped off to sleep, she'd come up with this one.

Jackie had a prescription for birth control that she hadn't bothered stopping after breaking up with her last boyfriend. It was near needing renewal. She'd decided to have her drugstore fax the prescription to the nearest neighborhood drugstore, then call and ask for it to be delivered . . . at two-thirty P.M.

Vincent usually got up between three and four, but Jackie had intended to wake him just a bit early to see him fed. She was hoping the saboteur had been watching long enough to know that three was the earliest Vincent usually woke up. If so, he might not be watching when this delivery was made. If he was already out there somewhere watching, she hoped he'd just think it was a plain old delivery for her. Jackie could see Vincent fed and save anyone from being marked for death at the same time. Brilliant. Or it would be if Darryl, the delivery guy, hadn't decided to deliver early. Now she wasn't sure what to do. Did she wake Vincent up to feed? Or did she send the guy on his way and find some other way to feed him later?

Jackie debated the issue briefly, but there seemed little to debate. If she didn't wake up Vincent then a perfectly good opportunity to feed would be wasted.

"Come in," she sighed with irritation and turned to lead the way up the hall. "I need to get my purse. Follow me."

There was a moment of silence, but then she heard the shuffle of feet and the door closed.

"Do you want me to wait here?" Darryl asked uncertainly as she started up the stairs.

Jackie scowled at him over her shoulder. "I said follow me, didn't I? So follow."

"Right." Darryl rushed forward, the bag swinging from his fingers as he hurried to catch up to her.

Muttering under her breath, Jackie shook her head and continued upstairs, knowing Tiny wouldn't come out of the kitchen to see what was up. He already knew. She'd talked to him about it before making the necessary calls to set the matter in motion. Jackie had needed to know his opinion on the matter, wanting to be sure he didn't think it was disgusting that she was dragging unsuspecting fellow mortals to the house to be fed on by a vampire. She herself could hardly believe she was doing it.

Fortunately, for her conscience, Tiny had merely shrugged and rumbled, "He has to feed. Think of it like they're making unknowing donations to the blood bank."

Sensible Tiny, Jackie thought and felt some of her tension and irritation slip from her as she recalled his words. She'd needed him to say exactly that to make it all right.

"So, let me guess, your purse is in your bedroom, right?"

Jackie glanced over her shoulder at the knowing comment from Darryl and caught him ogling her behind as he followed her up the stairs.

Great! Jackie thought with disgust. Now the guy had the completely wrong idea. Still, she decided that idea would make things easier, so played along, forcing a smile to her face when he finally deigned to glance up and saying, "As a matter of fact, it is. You don't mind, do you?"

She'd tried to instill a sexy purr into her voice, but suspected it sounded more like a growl. Jackie wasn't the sort to play games, especially when she didn't mean it. It was a flaw of her character that could hamper her at work at times.

"No baby, I don't mind," Darryl assured her with a leer. "Lead the way to your boudoir of love."

Jackie managed not to roll her eyes until her face was forward again, then she let the eye rolling rip. *Men,* she decided, especially young men, could be the most egotistical idiots on the planet when they thought they smelled the possibility of sex. Honestly.

Pausing at Vincent's bedroom door, Jackie turned to glance back toward the delivery guy and froze. Her mouth—which she'd opened to speak—stayed there, hanging loosely as she saw that Darryl had started to strip. The drugstore package now sat on the hall table at the top of the stairs. His shirt lay in a heap several feet past that, and he was already working on the zipper of his jeans.

Snapping her mouth closed as the zipper went down, Jackie turned sharply and opened Vincent's door without knocking. She was desperate to get Darryl to Vincent before the idiot was completely nude.

The room was in complete darkness which took her by surprise. Jackie wasn't sure what she'd expected, but she hadn't expected pitch black. Moving cautiously, she hissed Vincent's name in a bare whisper and moved in the direction she remembered his bed was in from the day she'd come in search of Allen Richmond and found him in Vincent's room. Jackie immediately stilled as the bit of light coming from the hallway disappeared when Darryl stepped into the door frame, cutting it off.

"Wow, you like it dark, huh?"

"Vincent?" Jackie hissed, ignoring the man as she felt the edge of the bed bump her knee.

"No babe, my name's Darryl. You can call me Vincent if you like though," he added quickly as if afraid she might change her mind if he didn't play the game.

Jackie's slightly panicked mind had just registered the fact that Darryl's voice had grown closer, when he suddenly stumbled into her back, plunging them both forward onto the bed.

"Whoa, babe. There you are." Darryl chuckled and squirmed on her back as Jackie quickly struggled to get out from under him. She managed to do so, rolling to the side and onto her back beside him, only to have him lunge on top of her again so that they were now face to face.

Jackie froze as she felt his naked legs rub across hers. She then reached out to push at his stomach, misjudged her aim and found herself with a handful of Darryl's jewels. They were nothing to write home about.

"Dear God, you're completely naked!" she squealed, wondering how he'd been so quick. Jesus. He had to be some sort of quick-change artist, but then, perhaps most horny young guys were.

Releasing Darryl's dangly bits, Jackie threw her hand out to the side and thumped at the bed. "Dammit Vincent! Wake up!"

Much to her relief her hand hit something hard. A knee or hip bone was her guess as a grunt sounded from the top of the bed.

"Trust me, baby. I'm awake."

Jackie screeched with frustration as Darryl's hands began roaming over her body. Reaching out, she thumped her fist at the mound in the bed she'd hit moments ago. This time, instead of a grunt, there was a sleepy "Hey!" then the lights went on.

Jackie blinked in the sudden brightness and found herself staring at Vincent, who was now sitting up in bed and blinking right back. He stared with incomprehension at Darryl, who had his hands closed over her breasts, then his gaze dropped to her face with incomprehension and Jackie closed her eyes briefly, and said through gritted teeth, "Will you control him please?"

"What?" Vincent asked blankly, apparently still not quite sure what was going on.

"Control him!" Jackie snapped. She took advantage of Darryl's confusion to shove him off and roll quickly closer to Vincent to hiss, "Slip into his mind and blank it out."

"Hey, you know, I'm not into threesomes with other guys," Darryl said with a frown. "Maybe if your friend here was a girl . . . we could talk, but I'm not into the gay scene. I have—"

Jackie sagged on the bed as the young man suddenly went still and his face went blank.

"What's going on?" Vincent asked with confusion. "Why is he naked?"

"He thought I was luring him up here for sex and stripped on the way upstairs," Jackie explained wearily as she got to her feet beside the bed.

"Were you?"

To give him his due, Vincent obviously wasn't quite awake yet. Still, Jackie found herself stiffening with offense. Turning, she glared and snapped, "Feed."

"Feed?" Vincent seemed no less confused by the instruction than anything else happening in that moment.

"Yes, feed," Jackie repeated succinctly. "Feed, then wipe his memory, have him dress and send him on his way."

She started for the door, then paused abruptly and turned back. "I almost forgot. Here."

"What's this?" Vincent asked as she moved back to hand him money.

"It's for the prescription," she explained. "With a big tip. Give it to him when you're done."

Jackie turned away again and started past Darryl, then paused to kick him in the leg.

"That's for groping me. I know I let you think it's what I wanted, that's the only reason I'm not really hurting you," Jackie told the blank-faced young man and then stomped out of the room, weaving around Marguerite, who had appeared in the doorway.

Vincent stared after Jackie, a slow smile easing across his face as his befogged mind finally grasped what was happening. Jackie was feeding him. She'd brought the drugstore delivery guy up here for him to feed on just as she'd had Tiny order a pizza last night for him to be able to feed. She was taking care of him . . . which must mean she cared about him . . . at least a little. The idea made him feel all warm inside.

"It took you long enough to wake up."

Vincent glanced toward his aunt as she crossed the room to set what he suspected must be the delivery guy's clothes on the foot of the bed. Marguerite arched an eyebrow at the bewilderment on Vincent's face and shrugged.

"I couldn't believe you slept through that racket. I woke up when they were halfway up the stairs. I was beginning to think I'd have to step in myself when she finally thumped you one."

"I had trouble getting to sleep this morning," Vincent explained with a grimace. It was something of an understatement. He'd gone to talk to Neil, discussed the saboteur situation with him, then come to bed, but had lain awake fretting over the attack that day and worrying over the fact that if he went out and tried to feed, he might be marking whomever he chose to feed on for death . . . Something he wouldn't do.

It had been after noon when he'd finally drifted off to sleep, which was why he'd been so slow to wake up.

"After noon," Marguerite murmured, obviously reading his mind. She shook her head. "Which explains why you still look so groggy."

Vincent nodded.

"Feed," Marguerite suggested. "After you have finished I shall wipe his memory for you and see him out."

Vincent almost protested at his aunt taking care of him, but then gave in. He *was* tired, and while he should have too much pride to allow two women to take care of him, it felt so good he was reluctant to pass it up. No one had cared much for him since his mother's death three hundred years ago, he thought, then acknowledged that this wasn't really true. Aunt Marguerite and his cousins had always cared for him, or would have if he hadn't avoided them as much as he had over the years. Vincent had found it painful to be around them and see the close, loving family unit they were when his own relationship with his father had fallen apart with his mother's death. He hadn't even been able to cope with his aunt caring until now.

However, with Jackie trying to look after him too, it seemed different. It made him feel good instead of sad. It made him feel cared for in a special way rather than like the poor, pitied orphan cousin.

"You were never the poor, pitied, orphan cousin, Vincent," Marguerite said quietly. "You were family. Now, feed."

Vincent shifted off the bed and walked to the delivery boy.

He made quick work of his meal, then left Darryl to his aunt's tender mercies and went into his *en suite* bathroom to shower. He was in an exceptionally good mood and even found himself whistling show tunes in the shower.

Were anyone to ask him what had him in such good cheer, his answer would have been one word. Jackie.

Truthfully, Vincent shouldn't be as happy as he was. A saboteur was out to ruin him, people around him were getting hurt and even killed, and now he feared feeding and endangering whomever he fed on.

In effect, Vincent should be miserable. And he probably would be, if it weren't for one thing . . . Jackie.

As far as he could tell, Bastien had been right on the money in sending Jackie to him. Vincent had every confidence in her ability to quickly clear up the problem of the saboteur. But that wasn't why he found himself smiling as he shampooed his head and sang, "I'm gonna wash that saboteur right out of my hair," taking liberty with the lyrics as he went. Vincent was smiling because of what Jackie had just done. And last night, she had ordered the pizza with the specific intention of seeing him fed. He knew that went against her very nature and beliefs. This was the woman who had been offended on catching him snacking on one of the laborers, yet when his aunt had commented that he needed to feed, she'd immediately turned to Tiny and asked him to order a pizza.

He was rather amazed that Jackie was allowing herself to care for him at all, having been warned by Bastien that she had some attitude toward immortals, and learning about Cassius from reading Tiny's mind. But he was glad she did. The more he knew her, the more he liked her, and the more he found himself attracted to her.

After showering and pulling on jeans and a t-shirt, Vincent jogged downstairs and into the kitchen on a natural high.

"Good afternoon!" he said brightly to the trio seated at the table as he made a beeline for the coffeepot. One sniff of the air told him it was fresh coffee and he sighed with pleasure. Vincent suspected he was becoming addicted to the drink and didn't care. Carrying the coffee back to the table, he settled in the seat across from Jackie, smiled at her widely, then managed a more solemn expression as he said, "So? Did anything happen while I was sleeping? And what are we going to do today?"

Jackie opened her mouth to speak, but before she got out even a word, Vincent added, "Thank you for my breakfast, by the way. That was really sweet. No one's ever brought me a meal before. I've always hunted my own. Well, except when I was a kid of course, we had nursemaids then, but no

185

one's brought me a meal since I started to hunt for myself and this was even more special, you bringing me breakfast in bed like that."

Jackie blinked at his words, then started to blush and Vincent grinned.

She cleared her throat, then said, "I'm sorry about waking you up. I asked the drugstore to send the delivery at 2:30. He arrived early. I wasn't sure what to do when he got here, then decided it would be better for you to feed while he was here. You could always go back to sleep afterward."

"Oh no, no sleeping. I'm up now and wide awake. I've had enough sleep," he assured her, eliciting something of a snort from his aunt. Fortunately, Jackie didn't appear to hear it.

Smiling and in a much better mood than she'd been in after grappling with the delivery guy in his room, she nodded. "Good."

"So what are we doing now?" Vincent asked, standing as he spotted the muffins on the kitchen counter. Tiny had made blueberry muffins. God, he loved the big guy. Such a good cook and he always made the tastiest stuff. Moving to the counter, Vincent fetched a muffin then glanced back toward the table to ask, "Anyone else want one while I'm up?"

He waited until everyone had said, "No, thank you," then moved back to the table.

"That kid wasn't high or something, was he?" Jackie asked as Vincent sat down and began to take the paper baking cup off the bottom.

Vincent blinked in surprise. "No. Why would you think that?"

"You seem rather . . . er . . . cheerful," she said finally.

Vincent opened his mouth to say that yes, he was, then recalled that he really shouldn't be. He'd had to close plays. People were dying. Stephano, a good friend and excellent vice president, had been attacked. The fact that he liked Jackie and thought she might like him back shouldn't nullify all that, he lectured himself. And it didn't, he realized. Thinking about Stephano and the poor dead girl he'd fed on managed to dampen some of his good cheer.

Frowning, he glanced toward the door and commented, "I should go check on Stephano. Is Neil still here?"

"Yes. He's working from Stephano's room. He had his portable brought over and moved the fax machine and printer up from your office," Jackie announced. "Stephano hasn't woken up yet."

Vincent frowned at this news, but wasn't really surprised. It hadn't even been twenty-four hours since the start of the turning, and Stephano had been badly injured.

"You go check on Stephano and talk with Neil," Jackie suggested. "I want to grab a notepad and pen. I had an idea while we were waiting for you to come down."

Vincent considered asking what the idea was, but decided he'd find out soon enough, and simply stood to leave the room.

It was a short visit. Stephano wasn't awake yet and Neil wasn't in a mood for chat. His voice was brusque as he announced that he hadn't been able to contact his mother in Europe, and Vincent knew he was worried that she would hear the news that her son was dead before he could contact her and explain the true situation. However, Neil didn't want to leave such news on an answering machine, so had simply left a message for her to call him back at Vincent's home.

Neil then took him by surprise, by asking if he should be arranging a funeral. When Vincent simply stared at him nonplussed, he pointed out that if Stephano were really dead they would be having a funeral for him, and as they wanted the saboteur to think he *was* dead, shouldn't they be arranging a fake one? Neil had nearly lost his brother once, and wasn't willing to risk him again. He would do whatever it took to keep the saboteur from hunting Stephano down and finishing the job.

Vincent had agreed that this would probably be a good idea, but said he'd talk to Jackie about it first. If she agreed, they'd start making phone calls to arrange it. Vincent would, of course, cover the costs. He then frowned, and added that he'd talk to Jackie about Neil at least seeming to interview replacements for Stephano as the daytime vice president as well. This, too, would be something they'd have done if he was dead.

It was as he was about to leave to return downstairs that Neil had suddenly blurted, "Thank you, Vincent."

Surprised, he paused by the door he'd been about to open and glanced back. "For what?"

"For saving Stephano." His expression was solemn. "I realize what you gave up by turning him."

Vincent stilled as Neil's words sank in. *I realize what you gave up by turning him.* It was only at that moment that Vincent realized just what he'd done. It had been instinct. Stephano had been dying, attacked by a saboteur who was trying to hurt Vincent. It was his fault. He'd done what he had to do to save him . . . without considering for a moment the ramifications.

He could turn only one.

He'd turned Stephano.

"Vincent?" Frowning, Neil moved to his side and grabbed his arm as if he thought he might need steadying. "Are you all right?"

"Yes," he said weakly, but wasn't at all sure it was true. Vincent didn't regret what he'd done and would do it again in a heartbeat, but it was still heart wrenchingly painful to accept what his actions meant for him . . . and for his future. Whether he could read Jackie or not, whether she was his life mate or not, he could never turn her. He may have finally found the woman he was meant to live out his life with and she was now forever beyond his reach. Or, at least, she would be there for only a heartbeat of time in the many centuries that his life was likely to last.

Vincent turned to the door and pulled it open.

"I . . . er . . . I have to go," he muttered and hurried from the room, desperate to be on his own.

Neil didn't try to stop him and Vincent stumbled out of the room, then along the hall to the top of the stairs where he paused and closed his eyes. His mind was whirling. A great, huge ball had lodged itself painfully in his throat, his chest was aching, and he felt nauseous.

All Vincent had ever wanted his whole life was a life mate of his own and now he could never really have one.

"Vincent?"

Blinking his eyes open, he stared down at the foot of the stairs. Jackie had apparently returned from retrieving her notepad and pen from the office and spotted him at the top of the stairs. She was now staring up at him with concern.

"Are you all right?"

Vincent forced a smile and started downstairs. "Yes. I was just thinking."

"They must have been pretty grim thoughts. You looked upset," she commented as he reached her side. "Is Stephano all right?"

"Yes," he answered and felt a little of his distress ease. Stephano was alive. He was alive. Jackie was alive. And where there was life, there was hope.

His smile becoming a little less forced, he took her arm to lead her to the kitchen where Tiny and Marguerite waited. Vincent quickly told them about Neil's suggestion about the funeral and putting out feelers for a vice president to replace the supposedly dead Stephano and as he did, the pain in his throat began to ease. The one in his chest didn't, however. He suspected it never would.

"He's right," Jackie said slowly when he finished. "Neil should at least seem to be arranging a funeral until Stephano wakes up and we know if he recalls who attacked him. And you're right about his putting out the word that a new daytime vice president will be needed. Both of those are things that would be done if Stephano were really dead."

She tapped her pen on the notepad she'd fetched while he was upstairs, then nodded. "We'll have to at least start the arrangements of the funeral. If Stephano can't name his attacker, it may even be a good idea to carry it out. The attacker will surely be one of the people who attend."

"Why are you so sure he would attend?" Marguerite asked curiously.

"Because of the letters. He seems to be enjoying taunting Vincent with what he's doing. I think he'll want to see how much he's upset him by killing Stephano."

Vincent frowned, once again searching his mind for someone, anyone, he might have hurt in any way, even unintentionally. But there was no one he could think of who could possibly want to harm him this way. Pushing these frustrating thoughts aside, he glanced at the notepad lying on the table. "What are we doing now?"

Jackie drew the notepad closer and said, "I called the computer whiz I usually use in New York about retrieving the files the saboteur erased. Unfortunately, he can't fly out until the day after tomorrow. But, I was thinking, while we can't access the computer files, we can still get started on the list another way."

"The list of employees on the Dracula play?" Vincent asked.

"Yes."

Marguerite frowned. "But we won't need the list if Stephano can tell us who his attacker was."

"If he can," Jackie agreed. "But there is no guarantee that he'll be able to, and I'd rather not waste time just sitting around waiting for him to wake up, then find out that he can't."

Vincent nodded in understanding. He had no desire to sit around waiting either. Having something to do would make the time pass more quickly. "How can we work on the list?"

"You name off all the people you remember being in the

play and then we go to them and see who they remember and so on. We might actually have the list made up before my computer whiz gets here."

"Maybe you should call and cancel having him come out here then," Tiny suggested. "He can be pretty pricey."

Jackie shook her head. "No. I want to be sure we have everyone listed. Besides, Vincent will need the files for work anyway, so he has to have them pulled up."

"You're right," Vincent agreed. "We will need those files back, but this list is a good idea."

Jackie smiled slightly, then picked up her pen and began to make columns on the page. "So, let's see. I guess we can start by listing the departments. Security, production, actors . . ." She stopped writing and glanced up at him. "Shall we start with security?"

Vincent nodded. "Max Kunstler headed security."

"Max Kunstler? The security chief at V.A Productions?" Jackie asked with surprise. She'd met the man the day before while going from department to department with Vincent in search of files the saboteur might have missed.

Vincent nodded again. "Uh-huh. Unless there's a problem, there isn't really much to do around the production company most of the time. Max schedules the security guys, and so on, but other than that . . ." He shrugged. "Max doesn't like to just sit around twiddling his thumbs, so he often oversees the setup of security for the plays. He goes to the theatre, decides what needs doing and how many men should be on site, hangs around for a couple weeks to be sure everything's running smoothly, then returns to the company to take up the reigns there again."

"Oh." Jackie wrote his name down, then glanced at Vincent and said, "So he knew about the sabotage attempts before we spoke to him?"

"He knew, but he didn't believe they were sabotage."

Jackie's eyebrows rose. "Why?"

"The same reasons I didn't. The male actor who broke his leg was a drunk, the actress injured when the set fell on her just seemed bad luck at the time, the fires seemed accidental . . ." He shrugged.

"And when the 'contagious anemia' cropped up?" Jackie asked, arching one eyebrow. "He didn't wonder then if it might be more than an accident?"

"Oh yes," Vincent said dryly. "He knew that wasn't an accident. He thought that was me."

"Well, surely you explained to him that it wasn't you, that you hadn't been biting them," she asked with a frown.

"Yes, of course I did," he assured her. He added, "That doesn't mean he believed me."

Jackie began to rub her fingers over her forehead, then shook her head. "I didn't like Max much. Until you got firm with him, he seemed . . ."

"Arrogant? Patronizing? Disrespectful?" Marguerite suggested.

"That about covers it," Jackie's voice sounded dry. "Met him before, have you?"

"No. I've never met Max or anyone else who works for Vincent." Marguerite glanced toward her nephew briefly and when he didn't protest explained, "However, I've seen that attitude in others. I fear Vincent's condition makes some of our kind feel superior to him."

"Superior?" Jackie asked slowly.

Marguerite nodded. "Immortals like to think of themselves as perfect. Perfect health, peak strength, peak intellectual abilities . . ." She shrugged. "And some mistakenly believe that the genetic anomaly that prevents Vincent's feeding off bagged blood—like the rest of us—suggests he isn't quite perfect."

Jackie was silent for a minute, then shook her head. "But this anomaly wouldn't have shown itself until about fifty years ago or so when everyone switched to bagged blood."

"Yes," Marguerite agreed.

"So, up to that point, everyone accepted him as fine, immortal, equal?" she asked.

"Yes."

"Then, when you all switched to bagged blood and he and his father found they couldn't feed that way, some of the others . . ."

"Began to look down on them and consider them inferior," Marguerite finished.

Vincent heard the anger in his aunt's voice, but he was used to it. It bothered her more than it did him. Vincent had enough confidence in himself he didn't much care how others thought of him.

Except Jackie, he acknowledged to himself now. Vincent was very interested in her reaction. Had she turned a pitying look his way, he would have been upset. Instead, she looked merely bewildered as she turned to him to ask, "Why would you keep someone like that working for you then?"

Vincent felt himself relax. Smiling faintly, he shrugged, "If I refused to hire anyone with that attitude, I wouldn't have any immortals working for me. It's pretty common. Besides, Max is good at his job, and he never pushes too hard with me."

Jackie nodded a slow acknowledgment to that. She'd noticed that while Max had shown a hint of arrogance, and seemed a touch patronizing and just that bit disrespectful, he hadn't been foolish enough to make any of these attitudes terribly obvious. On the other hand, she'd also noticed that some of Vincent's natural good humor and easygoing attitude had been missing at the office, replaced with a cool steel she hadn't seen in him before.

"Okay," she said finally. "So, Max was there. Who else was in security?"

"There was a Bob, a Tony, a John, and a Francis."

Jackie bit her lip as she wrote the names down and then asked, "I don't suppose you caught their last names?"

"No, sorry." He grimaced. "I didn't need to know their last names."

Jackie waved his apology aside. "We can get a list of the other security people from Max. Let's move on to production. I imagine you took Lily, she—"

"No." Vincent shook his head.

"No?" she asked with surprise. "But she's your production assistant."

"Yes, but she was on vacation at the time," he explained, "So I took Sharon instead."

Jackie blinked. "But Sharon's a secretary, why would you take her as a production assistant?"

"I didn't really need a production assistant. I was the lead actor, so we had a different producer on the play. What I really needed was more of a personal assistant and Sharon could handle that easily enough."

"I see," she murmured, crossing out Lily's name and putting Sharon's in place instead. Jackie then raised her head and said, "Why don't you just start listing off everyone you can think of and I'll write them down. Then we'll pick the brains of those people to see who they recall."

Eleven

The nightclub was loud, hot, dark, and crowded.

Jackie fiddled absently with the straw sticking out of her Diet Coke, her gaze moving slowly over the people sitting, milling, and dancing around them. Jackie was having that hinky feeling again. She was sure the saboteur was somewhere in the crowd; watching them . . . and awaiting an opportunity to make his next move. Now that the saboteur had stepped up the game, moving it to murder, whatever was coming couldn't be good.

"Relax, Jackie. He's not going to strike in the middle of a dance club." Vincent spoke close to her ear, and still he had to shout to be heard over the cacophony of sounds around them.

Forcing a smile, she gave up her survey of their surroundings and glanced around the table, noting that while Tiny looked as tense and alert as she, both Vincent and Marguerite appeared relaxed. It just went to prove that Marguerite was as talented an actor as Vincent, because Jackie knew the two immortals weren't as relaxed as they appeared. Or, at least, she didn't think they could be.

It was two days since Jackie had awakened Vincent with his drugstore Darryl breakfast. They'd spent the time since then collecting their list of names of employees on the play *Dracula, the Musical*. First, they'd put down everyone Vincent recalled, then they'd gone to interview Max and Sharon—the only people in the company that were on the list—to see who they recalled.

Max had been busy, questioning everyone in V. A. Productions about what they'd seen or heard at the time of Stephano's attack—or murder, as they were all led to believe it was. However, he'd taken time out to aid them in the list and been very helpful, recalling even more names than Vincent.

Sharon, on the other hand, hadn't been very helpful at all. The secretary hadn't been openly difficult, she'd merely claimed to have a bad memory, at least when it came to mortals. While she'd been able to name the immortals working on the play easily enough, when it came to mortals, Sharon recalled them only as some "little blond mortal" or "some rude little mortal."

Jackie had been interviewing the woman alone and suspected that if Vincent had been with her, the woman would have been more helpful. However, there had been at least a dozen people at the company in a panic to talk to him after the events of the day before, and she'd suggested he deal with them while she spoke to Sharon.

Some of the people on the list they'd managed to compile had worked for the company before, or were working for them now in some capacity or other and so were on file. Jackie had pulled those, and made copies of everything before they'd headed back to Vincent's home. Leaving Tiny to begin investigating the people so far on the list, she and Vincent had then continued compiling it, going to each person listed to see if any more names could be added.

That had taken the better part of the last two days. Which might have seemed a waste of time since her computer whiz was supposed to arrive today, but as it happened, his appendix burst. He was laid up in a hospital in New York and would not be any use to them.

The moment she'd received the news this morning, Jackie had immediately started putting out feelers for a computer expert here in California to help them with the matter. In the meantime, however, they had their own list to work with. They'd worked that list every spare moment of the last two days, stopping only to eat.

The first night, they'd had Chinese takeout; Vincent snacking on the delivery guy before sending him on his way and joining Jackie and Tiny to gorge on the delivered food itself. The next day, Jackie had arranged for Vincent's pool to be cleaned and he'd breakfasted on the pool cleaner on awaking at 4 P.M. They'd ordered pizza that night. All of them were busy with the list, too busy to take time out to cook. Besides, feeding off the delivery drivers was the safest way for Vincent to feed at the moment.

Today, Jackie had called in a cleaning service to clean the windows. Vincent had breakfasted. She'd been trying to come up with another way for him to feed when Tiny had pointed out that the saboteur would soon realize Vincent must be feeding off the delivery guys and others if he didn't soon hit a nightclub, his usual hunting ground.

In a panic at the idea of someone being marked for death because she'd brought them to the house, Jackie had decided they should go out to a club tonight. A decision that was aided by the fact that Stephano Notte still hadn't woken up. Both Vincent and Marguerite were growing concerned at this turn of events. It seemed that this was unheard of, at least neither of them had heard of it, nor Neil apparently. The turning was normally a painful event that the turnee screamed and thrashed their way through, but this wasn't the case with Stephano. He had lain silent and still throughout, and he wasn't waking up as they'd expected. All three immortals were concerned and that concern had spread to Jackie and Tiny. The house had become a dark, depressing place to be.

That being the case, Vincent had easily agreed to Jackie's suggestion of visiting the clubs, but had warned her that he had no intention of feeding. Jackie understood. She was even glad he wouldn't. However, she was hoping if they made it difficult enough to keep up with them, the saboteur would simply think Vincent had fed and he'd missed it. To that end, they'd been club hopping for the last several hours. They'd driven to the first club, stayed half an hour, walked out, hopped in one of the taxis waiting in front of the club and had it take them to another club, where they'd stayed another half an hour before grabbing another taxi.

They were now at their fourth club, and Jackie found herself scanning the faces around them, hoping to recognize someone either from one of the other clubs they'd hit tonight, or from the people who were on the list of employees of the New York play. They'd spoken to almost everyone on the list so far. At least, everyone living here in Los Angeles. Although, so far, they'd only concentrated on making the list, not really questioning them about what they'd seen or heard that might help them figure out who the saboteur/killer was.

Jackie hadn't recognized anyone in the clubs yet, so she was beginning to hope the saboteur hadn't been able to keep up and had either lost them at some point, or would think that while he'd been scrambling to catch up, Vincent had slipped away to feed.

"Come on. A little dancing will help you relax," Vincent shouted by her ear, then caught her hand and stood to tug her out onto the dance floor.

Jackie started to protest, but gave it up since Vincent wasn't listening anyway. Besides, she could see a lot more people from the dance floor than at the table.

"Did I mention you look lovely in that dress?"

Jackie stumbled over her own feet as Vincent murmured that compliment by her ear. Her hands immediately dug into his shoulder and hand in an effort to keep her balance, then she glanced sharply up to his face.

"No, huh?" Vincent asked with amusement as he took in her startled expression. "That was truly remiss of me."

"Oh." Jackie cleared her throat, but couldn't seem to come up with anything brighter than that to say as his hand moved on her back, urging her closer.

"You look incredible in red," Vincent added, apparently not finished with his compliments.

"Uh." Jackie swallowed, terribly aware of his hand moving

lower on her back. Where his hand moved, a trail of fire followed, leaving tingling flesh in its wake.

"I have to thank you for the last few days, Jackie," he said solemnly, ducking his head to speak by her ear. "Without you, I would have been in a horrible state. It's no fun going hungry, but for one of my kind, it can be torture."

"Oh, well, it's my job," she muttered with embarrassment.

Jackie tried to duck her head away to avoid his gaze when he pulled back, but he stopped her with a hand to her chin. Forcing her face up to meet his solemn gaze, Vincent shook his head and said firmly, "No, it isn't. We both know that. And I know about your attitude to my kind too, which makes it even more special. Thank you."

Jackie managed to pull her face free and glance away only because he let her. She found out why when his lips brushed butterfly light across her ear as he whispered, "Thank you." Then they fluttered to her cheek as he murmured, "thank you" again, and finally, they hovered over her own lips and he breathed, "thank you" once more before he kissed her. This time it was no soft butterfly of sensation; Vincent's mouth was firm on hers as he showed her just how grateful he was.

Jackie—ever the consummate professional—immediately pulled away . . . or would have if her body were cooperating. Unfortunately, her body overrode her mind's orders and, instead, she melted against him like chocolate on a hot sidewalk. A small sigh of defeat acknowledged her body's defection as her mouth opened beneath his to allow his tongue to sweep in. A moan slid up her throat as desire awoke in her belly and Jackie let her arms creep up around his neck, suddenly a firm believer in the old saying "If you can't beat 'em, join 'em."

"Oh sorry."

Jackie and Vincent pulled apart as they were jostled by another dancer. She turned and glanced around to see who it had been, but whoever it was had already moved away and disappeared into the crowd.

Sighing, she glanced back to Vincent, shaking her head when he moved to take her back into his arms.

"Ladies room," she said as an excuse for her defection, then turned and made her way quickly off the dance floor, headed for the bathrooms. Jackie glanced back once she'd reached the hall leading out of the main area, just to be sure Vincent had returned to the safety of their table. Spotting him reclaiming his seat, she relaxed and moved up the hall, firmly lecturing herself on her business ethics.

"One does not go around kissing their clients," she reprimanded herself. "A good private detective never allows themselves to become involved with—and therefore distracted from their prime purpose of protecting—the client. God, he's a good kisser."

Recognizing that last part as her mind's efforts to derail her good intentioned self-recriminations, Jackie sighed as she pushed through the bathroom door.

Vincent was a vampire, she reminded herself, pulling out what should have been the big guns. Unfortunately, her mind was less than impressed, reminding her that while Vincent was an immortal, he was nothing like Cassius and perhaps all vampires weren't bad. If not, then Vincent definitely fit into the "not a bad vamp" category.

The thought that finally made her regain some control of her wayward desires was her recollection of Marguerite telling her Vincent had found his life mate and she wasn't an immortal.

Stopping in front of the sink, Jackie stared into the mirror and saw the confusion on the face reflected back. If Vincent had found his life mate, why was he kissing her? The reflection didn't have an answer, but her mind began to work the problem.

Marguerite had said Vincent's life mate was not an immortal and she began to list all the mortal women she knew in Vincent's life. There was Lily . . . and herself.

Jackie blinked at her reflection. Lily was sweet and young, but while she'd seen the two together and wouldn't be surprised to learn the young production assistant had a crush on Vincent, she didn't think he was interested in the girl. At least, she'd never seen any sign of interest on his part . . . not like his kissing her just now.

Jackie's eyes dropped to her own mouth in the mirror. Her lipstick was missing, but her lips were still red and slightly swollen from his kisses. While she'd been kissed many times before, it had never been with the heat and raw desire that had exploded between her and Vincent . . . even Cassius's kisses with his use of the immortal telepathic ability to put desire into another's mind hadn't been as hot. If they hadn't been jostled by someone, she might very well have climbed Vincent like a bean pole right there on the dance floor.

"No," she said the word softly, denying the conclusion her mind seemed to be heading toward. She could not be Vincent's life mate. Surely, fate couldn't be so cruel?

A stall door opened behind her, and Jackie quickly turned on the taps of the sink before her and began to splash water on her face in the hopes of clearing her mind. She saw the tall, young brunette come out and join her at the row of sinks, but paid her little attention other than to note that she was slim, with short brown hair. It wasn't until she turned off the taps, and the brunette moved to her side to extend one of the little brown paper towels, that Jackie noted the way the woman was looking at her.

The brunette's eyes were moving slowly over Jackie's body in the short red cocktail dress she'd donned for to-night's excursion. She murmured thank you as she accepted the towel, shifted uncomfortably, then did her best to ignore the woman as she patted her face dry.

"You have an amazing body."

Jackie blinked at their reflections in the mirror, her gaze traveling over her own figure next to the taller, slimmer woman. In truth, Jackie didn't think there was anything amazing about her body. She was short and no matter how often she worked out or how healthily she ate, couldn't seem to get rid of the extra fifteen to twenty pounds she was sure she'd look better without. At the ripe old age of thirty, how-ever, she'd come to the conclusion she might as well get used to it. It was probably here to stay.

Unsure what else to say, Jackie murmured "Thank you," and crumpled up the paper towel she'd used to dry her face, but the woman wasn't done. As Jackie moved to throw the paper towel in the garbage, the girl added, "I'd like to lick every inch of it."

Nothing on God's green earth could have stopped her

from whirling to face the girl with a look of abject horror and disbelief. Jackie even almost blurted, *Do I look gay to you?* before catching herself back, but it was her first thought. A stupid one, she acknowledged. You couldn't tell someone's sexual preference by their looks.

Jackie opened her mouth to politely tell the woman that she didn't swing that way, but paused and stiffened as the brunette stepped closer and ran one hand lightly down her arm as she added, "Why don't we go someplace else and party?"

Jackie opened and closed her mouth several times, but nothing was coming out. Her brain appeared to have temporarily disengaged. This was one of those situations she had absolutely no experience dealing with. It was the first time she'd ever been hit on by another woman.

Apparently, taking her silence as a good sign, the girl suddenly caught her hand and began to tug her to the door. "I know a spot where we can . . ."

The rest was lost on Jackie as the brunette pushed the bathroom door open. Loud music immediately rang in her ears, drowning out the rest of what she was saying. The only reason Jackie didn't pull her hand free and urge the brunette back to the bathroom where she could explain she wasn't interested was because the girl took her by surprise, turning right toward the back of the club, rather than left to head back into the dance and seating area.

Jackie's brain immediately began churning along different lines. Vincent needed to feed. He'd only fed once today. He claimed he'd be fine missing one meal, and maybe he wouldn't die from it, but she knew it would cause him pain.

And what if they weren't able to come up with a way to feed him tomorrow?

The girl kept talking the whole time as she dragged Jackie into the bowels of the building. At least the brunette's mouth was moving every time she glanced back. Reassured by her very human green eyes, Jackie decided to wait and see where she'd lead her, hoping that they might be able to use this somehow to help Vincent. It might be an opportunity they could use. At least she hoped so.

The brunette rushed her down one hall, turned down another, then hurried through a door and into a kitchen. The room was large, spotless and presently empty. It was late enough that food was no longer offered.

"—never done this before, really. Always fantasized about it, but I—" The girl's nervous chatter was suddenly clearly heard as the door closed behind them, reducing the deafening music to a murmur barely heard through the door.

"Hang on," Jackie said quickly. Now that the girl would be able to hear her, she tugged on her hand, trying to pull free, but the woman was stronger than she'd realized and merely tightened her grip, saying, "It's right here. Just through this door."

Jackie started to tug on her hand again, but paused as they sailed through yet another door. They were now in a small storeroom lined with shelves bearing industrial-sized cans and jars of food: pickles, sauces, ketchup, soups . . . Jackie moved further into the room and turned back toward the door, her gaze moving around the shelves with surprise until she'd made a full circuit and reached the brunette again. The confidence she'd appeared shrouded in as she'd propositioned

Jackie in the bathroom was definitely missing now. In fact, the girl looked nervous, then she took a deep breath, as if gathering her courage. A determined look entering her eyes, she took a step toward Jackie, one hand reaching toward her.

"Okay, wait." Jackie took a step back, one hand rising to hold her off while she tried to think if she could use this or not. If the saboteur were watching Vincent and she went and brought him here to feed on the girl, then pretended to lock the door from the outside while the girl really locked it from the inside . . . She could have Vincent instruct the girl to lock it and wait there for at least half an hour, or even more maybe, before slipping out. There was a good chance the saboteur would never know the brunette was here. He might even think Vincent had fed off Jackie herself if they entered alone and left alone. The girl should be safe . . .

She peered at the brunette, considering the matter, then felt her conscience twinge as she noted the girl's uncertain expression. In this light, she could see the brunette wasn't as old as she'd first thought. Jackie would guess she was maybe nineteen or twenty, a kid really. What on earth was this child doing propositioning women in bathrooms and dragging them off here to a storeroom? She'd caught the girl's words about this being a fantasy and something she'd never done before, but geez . . .

"I—" Jackie stiffened and whirled as she felt a hand brush lightly down the back of her hair. She found herself staring at a tall, sandy-haired man in his forties. He wore tight jeans and a shirt left open almost to his navel to reveal a gold chain around his neck. He was also leering.

Sleazeball, Jackie pegged him right away. Sleazeball trying

to stave off his midlife crisis by dressing too young, wearing lots of gold on his fingers, wrist and neck, and sporting a girl-friend who was young enough to be his daughter.

On the other hand, Jackie thought. She'd just been kissed by a four-hundred-year-old on the dance floor. Who was she to criticize people's choices?

"Trevor!" the brunette sounded distressed. "You were supposed to wait until we were into it and then—"

"Shut up, Shell," he said, sounding almost bored. "You weren't going to get into it. She's obviously got cold feet. I just thought I'd let her know I was part of the package too. See if maybe she'd be interested after all."

Jackie's attempts to be charitable died the moment she heard how Trevor addressed Shell. She was young, obvi-ously looked up to the big greaseball, and she "shut up" as instructed, an unhappy look on her face. Jackie suddenly started to rethink things.

"Where did you come from?" she asked, taking a wary step back from Trevor. He hadn't been in here when she'd done her first survey of the small room.

Trevor smiled faintly, then moved around the standing shelf at the back of the room, gesturing for her to follow. Jackie did, staying an arm's length away from him and watch-ing as he moved up to the wall. It was wood, a rough panel-ing and at first she had no idea what he wanted her to see, then he pushed on a panel and it slid open. A door was hid-den in the paneling, although that may not have been delib-erate. Between the poor light and the fact that the door was the same wood as the wall, the door was invisible at first glance.

"My office," Trevor announced with a smile as he gestured to the room beyond. "I'm the manager here."

Jackie peered at the expensive décor, her mind racing. This was perfect. This was almost foolproof.

She turned and walked back around the shelf into the storage room, her thoughts lining themselves up in her head. Her gaze landed on Shell and she smiled. "Trevor was wrong, I wasn't getting cold feet."

Shell didn't look all that happy about this news at first, then she suddenly beamed a smile that looked decidedly forced. A glance over her shoulder showed Jackie that Trevor was coming back around the shelf and she suddenly thought she understood. This was no fantasy, at least not Shell's, this was all about keeping Trevor happy. He wanted a threesome, so Shell—desperate to keep him happy—agreed to a threesome.

"So you *are* interested?" Trevor paused behind her, his hand sliding around her waist and moving up her stomach toward her breasts.

Jackie caught his hand, bringing his roaming to an abrupt halt. Ignoring him, she told Shell, "I stopped you because I need to go give my friends an excuse for my disappearance, otherwise they'll freak out. That girl who was found in the hills was a friend of ours and it's made us all jumpy."

"I heard about that," Shell said with a shudder. "She was a friend of yours?"

"Yeah," Jackie lied, moving toward the door. "Give me five minutes to tell them I'm catching a ride home so they don't worry. Then we'll have all the time in the world."

"She isn't coming back." Trevor's voice was unpleasant and sneering.

Jackie paused at the door and glanced back. "Yes, I am."

He shook his head. "You're bailing on us."

Jackie frowned. If he really believed she was bailing, he might take Shell and leave here while she was gone. Hesitating, she glanced over herself, trying to think what she could leave behind to convince him. Her purse was at the table, all she had was what she was wearing. Blowing a breath out, Jackie stepped out of her shoes and kicked them into the center of the small room, then cocked one eyebrow. "Believe me now?"

Trevor nodded, his lips parting in a smile that was all teeth. "See you soon."

Jackie tugged the door open and slipped out of the room. She managed to find her way back to the hallway outside the ladies room, then continued on to the table.

"I was starting to worry," Vincent shouted by her ear, having stood as she hurried up to the table.

Jackie saw a frown crest his face as he straightened from yelling in her ear, and guessed he'd noticed the difference in height when his gaze slid down to her feet. His eyebrows immediately drew together. "What happened to your shoes?"

"Never mind that," Jackie instructed. She leaned over the table, saying to Marguerite and Tiny, "We'll be right back. Wait here."

Marguerite's eyes narrowed and Jackie knew she was concerned and trying to read her thoughts. She didn't try to block her, but let Vincent's aunt read what was happening,

211

figuring it would be faster than explaining verbally. When Marguerite relaxed and sat back with a nod, Jackie straightened. Tiny still looked concerned, but Jackie knew Marguerite would explain everything, so she merely turned to catch Vincent's hand and started to lead him back the way she'd come.

"Where are we going?"

Jackie heard his question as she led him around the dance floor, but almost didn't answer. Then she realized she couldn't take him in there cold, with no knowledge at all of what was going on. Stopping in the center of the dance floor, Jackie turned into his arms, urging him to dance as she leaned up and said, "Read my thoughts."

Vincent stared at her solemnly, and she thought there was a sadness in his eyes, then his gaze focused on her forehead. They both stood still and Jackie waited for the ruffling that would tell her he was reading her mind, but it never came.

"I can't," he spoke so softly that she couldn't hear him, but she could read the two words on his lips and saw the pain the acknowledgment caused him.

Jackie stared back blankly. Bastien had once told her that not being able to read someone was the sign of a true life mate. The confusion she'd experienced in the washroom tried to reclaim her, but she pushed it ruthlessly aside. Later, she could consider the ramifications of everything and the mess they appeared to be in, for now she had to see him fed.

"While I was in the ladies room a girl hit on me," she said abruptly, and Vincent jerked back with surprise.

"No! A woman?" A disbelieving smile tugged at the corners of his lips, removing some of his sadness.

Jackie nodded, then leaned up to continue. "Yeah, then she dragged me to this storage room."

Vincent made a choking sound and Jackie paused and pulled back to peer at him again. He looked as if he'd swallowed his own tongue.

"Nothing happened!" she said quickly, then went on to explain the rest, before adding, "You could feed safely. If the saboteur is watching, all he'd see is us entering and leaving. And, afterward, you could have Trevor and Shell slip through the door into his office, lock it from that side and leave from there so that even if the saboteur does check the storage room, they won't find anyone there." She paused and raised her eyebrows at his smile. "What?"

"I like your brain," Vincent said with a grin. "You see an opportunity and you use it. A definite survivor. You'd do well as one of our kind."

They both stilled at his words and she saw the pain that suddenly cut at her chest, reflected in his eyes along with the recognition that she could never be one of his kind now.

"Jackie, I—" he began with regret, but she shook her head.

"No. Not now." Pulling out of his arms, she caught his hand and led him to the hall that led to the bathrooms.

"So, she really hit on you?" Vincent asked by her ear, his chest rubbing against her back as he did. Apparently, he was willing to let the other matter drop for now and pretend everything was fine. Or try to. For an actor, he was having trouble disguising the sadness he was experiencing. He gave it a good try though. "What did she do?"

"She said I had a good body," Jackie paused to yell by his ear.

"You do," Vincent assured her quickly. "But that's just a compliment. It's hardly hitting—"

"And offered to lick every inch of it," she added dryly.

"Ohhhhhhh." Vincent was silent for a moment, then groaned aloud, drawing her eyes back to his face. One look was all it took for her to know he was picturing that one in his head . . . and liking it.

"Men," she muttered with disgust as she headed off again. Why did the idea of two women together always seem such a turn-on to them?

"Jackie, we might have a problem," Vincent yelled, his chest brushing against her back again as she turned down another hall.

She paused and glanced past him to be sure no one was following, then asked, "What kind of problem?"

"I might have trouble controlling two of them at once," Vincent admitted as she turned to lead him into the kitchen.

"What?" Jackie stopped dead and turned to face him. "But I've seen Bastien control more than one human at a time."

"Well, yes, he wouldn't have a problem. The older we are, the better we are at everything and Bastien is over four hundred."

"So are you," Jackie pointed out, lowering her voice so they wouldn't be overheard by the couple in the storeroom ahead.

"Yes, but it's been a while since I tried to control more than one. It's like any skill, the more you practice it, the better you are and I don't—" He paused and frowned at her alarmed expression, then patted her soothingly and said, "I'm not saying I *can't* do it, just that it may be a bit tricky.

Can you distract one while I get control of the other? Once the one is under, I'll slip into the mind of the second one as well."

"Oh." Jackie hesitated, uncertain how she would do that, but finally just nodded. "Yes, fine. I'll distract the girl. Trevor's a jerk, put him under first. Come on."

Jackie led him to the storeroom door.

Twelve

The storeroom was empty when Jackie opened the door, and for one horrible moment she feared the couple had left, then she heard voices and realized they'd merely moved into the office.

Turning back, she whispered to Vincent to lock the storage room door. The last thing they needed was the saboteur perhaps trying to follow them in and discovering what she'd set up. Despite her dislike of Trevor, she didn't want him dead.

Leaving Vincent to follow when he finished with the door, Jackie scooped up her shoes from where she'd left them and walked around the shelf to enter the office.

"I thought you'd given up on me," Jackie said lightly as she entered. Trevor was seated in his desk chair to her right and Shell was seated on a large leather couch against the wall on her left in the black and gray office.

"No, we just thought this room would be more comfortable," Trevor announced, his eyes traveling over her.

Nodding, Jackie moved past Shell on the couch, sitting on her side furthest from the door to draw her attention away from the storage area. As she'd hoped, Shell shifted on the couch, turning slightly so that they faced each other with her back to the door.

"Well." Jackie forced a smile, her eyes skating from Shell to the doorway and back. Vincent was just approaching, easing carefully forward, his eyes seeking out everyone in the room.

Jackie started wracking her brain, trying to think of something to say that would distract Shell when Trevor stood up. "What are you waiting for, Shell? You—"

When he went suddenly silent, Jackie glanced his way, noting his blank face with relief, then she was distracted by Shell, who hadn't noticed Trevor's sudden silence and had taken his first question as instruction. She'd moved up on her knees and was bending toward Jackie as if to lay a kiss on her. That was a little more distraction than she was willing to give. Her panicked eyes shot to Vincent for help just as he glanced their way.

His eyebrows shot up as Shell closed in, then his gaze narrowed on the girl. Jackie turned her attention back to the brunette at the exact same moment as Shell suddenly collapsed forward, against her chest.

Jackie released a slow breath, then glanced from Trevor standing stiff and still behind his desk, to Shell, who lay limp against her. "What did you do to her?"

"Nothing. I just slipped into her mind and blanked it," Vincent said with a shrug.

"Why is she so—" Jackie nodded toward the seemingly unconscious girl. "Trevor isn't and neither was the laborer."

"She's easy," Vincent said simply.

"Ha-ha," Jackie said dryly and he bit his lip, probably to keep back a laugh.

"I told you it's been a while. I just used a bit more oomph than needed," he explained, moving further into the room. "She'll be fine."

"Oh, well, good," Jackie said with a sigh. "So go on and bite her."

Vincent caught the limp girl's arm and raised her off Jackie to lean her back against the couch. His gaze skated over her blank face. "She really hit on you, huh?"

"Just feed, Argeneau," Jackie said dryly.

"Hmm. I know I'm in trouble when you start calling me Argeneau." He sounded more amused than worried, but then he hesitated and said, "I can't with you watching."

"What?" she asked with surprise.

"I'm not used to an audience," he explained in pained tones. "Turn your back."

Jackie shook her head, but stood and moved to the door to the storage room. She leaned against the door jamb with her back to the room, slipping her shoes back on as she waited. After a moment of silence, Vincent said, "Make noise."

"What?" She glanced over her shoulder with amazement.

"Hum," he instructed. "I don't want you to hear."

"Oh, for heaven's sake! You're like a woman embarrassed to take a pee with people on the other side of the stall listening. Honestly." She glared at him, but it had no effect. He just waited patiently. Sighing, Jackie turned her back and began to hum, then feeling stupid, she stopped and said, "I'm going to go see if anyone is in the kitchen. Join me after you've finished here."

Slipping into the storage room, she pulled the door mostly closed, then walked around the shelf and crossed to the door leading into the kitchen. She pressed an ear to the door and listened. When she didn't hear any sound from the kitchen, Jackie hesitated, then unlocked the door and eased it open a crack so she could peek out.

The kitchen appeared empty, though she couldn't see all of it. Jackie considered stepping out and actually looking around, but something held her back. Her old hinky feeling was dancing along her spine, making the hair on the back of her neck stand on end. Jackie always listened to her hinky feelings, so instead of stepping out, she held her breath and listened for any sound that might give away the presence of someone standing nearby in a part of the kitchen she couldn't see.

When she couldn't hold her breath anymore and still hadn't heard anything, Jackie eased the door closed again and took a deep breath as she relocked it. Sighing, she leaned her forehead against the door and silently prayed that she hadn't made a mistake. She'd felt sure that Trevor and Shell could be kept safe if Vincent had them lock the door between his office and the storeroom and then leave via the door leading from his office out into the hall, but now was starting to worry again. Her hinky feeling always meant something was going to happen, and she didn't want it to be that these two people died because of one of her bright ideas.

Jackie sighed unhappily at the prospect, then nearly jumped out of her skin when hands slid around her waist from behind.

"I can feel your worry," Vincent said softly. "Everything will be all right."

Jackie turned to peer up at him and asked in a whisper, "Are you done?"

He nodded, allowing his hands to link around her back. "I wiped their minds, instructed Trevor to lock the door behind me, then take Shell and return to the dance floor via the other door in the office. Everything will be all right."

Jackie released her breath on a slow sigh. "Okay. They should be okay."

"Yes, they should," Vincent agreed, then urged her closer, and brushed his lips gently over hers. "Thank you. Again."

Jackie went still as he kissed her properly. Vincent might be easygoing in nature, but he wasn't when it came to kissing. He showed a masterful side, his hand sliding into her hair and tilting her head where he wanted it while his tongue slid in to lash hers. Jackie gasped and then moaned as her senses were overwhelmed. The man smelled good, felt good, tasted good, and kissed like a dream. She was a trembling, wide-eyed mass when he broke the kiss and hugged her close.

"Damn, Jackie, I don't blame Shell for wanting to lick every inch of you. I'd be happy doing that myself."

She closed her eyes on the erotic images that filled her mind, then forced herself to step away and said weakly, "We should go back to the table."

Turning away before he could convince her otherwise, Jackie opened the door and led him out of the storage room.

* * *

"Would anyone like coffee?" Tiny asked as they entered the house an hour later.

"That sounds nice." Jackie moved up the hall rather than block the entry as Marguerite, Tiny, and Vincent followed her inside. They had gone to a couple more clubs before returning home, and it was late, but she was reluctant to end the evening. Jackie didn't want to be alone. The thoughts waiting to overwhelm her were not happy ones.

"I'm going to go change into something more relaxing," she announced as Vincent paused to lock the door. "I'll check the answering machine on my way back."

"I'll make a pot of coffee and maybe a snack of some sort," Tiny said as he led Marguerite up the hall. He added, "If anyone's interested?"

"I am," Jackie answered promptly.

"Me too," Vincent said as he moved to the security panel to punch in the code to keep the alarm from going off. "I'm going to change as well and check on Stephano, but I shouldn't be long either."

Jackie started upstairs, hurrying to prevent being caught alone with Vincent. If he started to kiss her again . . . She shivered at the very idea, but then closed her mind to the possibility. There were far too many complications involved in any possible relationship between them. For one, it wouldn't be professional while she was working for him. And then there was the whole life mate, turning only one business. None of which she wanted to contemplate at the moment.

Jackie kicked off her shoes as she entered her room, removed her stockings and changed quickly into a black jogging suit, then headed back out. She wondered how Stephano was doing as she passed his door, but didn't stop to look in. Vincent could tell her when he got back down to the kitchen.

She had reached the foot of the stairs when Jackie remembered saying she'd check the answering machine. Neil had been home all night, but anyone wishing to get hold of him would have called on his cell phone. Vincent had told him not to worry about the phone and to let the answering machine get it while they were gone. She'd just check and see if there were any messages before heading to the kitchen, she decided.

On that thought, she turned in the direction of the office. Some part of her mind registered surprise when she saw that the door was closed. It was never closed unless someone was inside. When a cool breeze slid over her feet as she paused in front of the panel of wood, Jackie's hand froze on the knob.

Recalling the night the employee lists had gone missing and the fact that one of the French doors had been left open then, Jackie glanced around to the security panel and saw that it wasn't activated. Vincent had apparently punched in the code to prevent the alarm from going off, but not resecured the system. A soft sound from inside the room drew her attention back and Jackie instinctively thrust the door open. She was just in time to see a dark figure slipping out of the room via the same French door that had been opened last time.

"Hey!" Jackie said and rushed forward.

"There we are," Tiny said, turning on the coffeepot. "Coffee will be ready in a few minutes. In the meantime, I'm going to go change into my joggers. These dress pants are too tight."

A Bite to Remember

"Okay." Vincent said, his head half inside the refrigerator as he perused its contents. He'd changed, then glanced into Stephano's room to find the injured man lying still and pale and Neil nodding off in a chair by the bed. Leaving them in peace, he'd come below, surprised to find that he'd beat Jackie back.

"Can you grab me a bag of blood while you're there, please, Vincent?" his aunt asked.

"Sure." Vincent retrieved a bag and straightened just in time to see Tiny slip from the room, then his glance slid to his aunt. "In a glass, or out of the bag?"

"The bag is fine, thank you," Marguerite murmured.

He carried the bag to her, handed it over, then took a seat at the table and shook his head.

"What is it?" Marguerite asked, catching the action.

"I was just thinking, I've owned this house for almost ten years and had never once used the kitchen until this last week or so, and now we seem to use it all the time."

Marguerite smiled faintly. "That's not the only thing that has changed since Jackie got here."

Vincent nodded in agreement, his gaze moving around the cozy room. It had always seemed somewhat cold and utilitarian to him before Jackie and Tiny had arrived. They'd filled it with sound, warmth, and the delightful smell of cooking food. Somehow, they'd made his house a home.

"Have you tried to read Jackie?" Marguerite asked suddenly.

"Yes, I tried to read her tonight and couldn't," he admitted quietly and then lowered his gaze to his clasped hands on the table top, his mind a muddle.

Vincent liked Jackie and enjoyed her company. He even liked her bossiness with him at times. And then there was tonight as they'd danced . . . Vincent had never felt so at peace in his life. Holding her in his arms, he'd felt like he'd found home.

As for when he'd kissed her . . . God, he hadn't felt such passion in centuries. His heretofore lack of interest in sex had most definitely been revived this evening. In fact, if he were to be honest with himself, he'd admit it had been revived even before tonight. Since the day in his office when he'd slipped into her dreams, Vincent had wasted hours each morning before going to sleep, just lying in bed, imagining stripping her naked, laying her on various flat surfaces, and feasting on every inch of her body.

But it had all seemed to be happening too fast. He'd delayed trying to read Jackie and finding out if she really was his life mate to allow himself time to adjust to the possibility that he had finally found his life mate, as well as to allow her time to get to know him. Immortals knew that when they found the one they couldn't read, they'd found their life mate. They accepted it and went with it easily. For mortals, it was a little different, they generally needed time to adjust. Their desire was there, and the bonding happened, but the logical part of their mind often insisted on a courtship.

Unfortunately, Vincent's delay had lost him any chance with Jackie. He could never turn her now. If he hadn't been such a coward and delayed, if he'd turned her right away—

Vincent shook his head. If he'd done that, Stephano would

now be dead, although he wasn't sure the man might not still die. He frowned to himself as he wondered why the man hadn't yet awoken. They were all starting to become terribly worried.

"Jackie has no family, nothing to hold her to the mortal world," Marguerite said suddenly, drawing his mind back to the topic at hand. "She would do very well as one of us, Vincent. She will be a good life mate to you. She compliments you perfectly."

"We will not be life mates," Vincent said quietly.

"She *is* your life mate, Vincent. Your missing half."

He shifted with irritation and snapped the truth he hadn't wanted to look at too closely before now. "I cannot turn her."

"But I can," she pointed out.

"You—" Vincent paused abruptly and glanced toward the door as it opened, not wanting Jackie to overhear what they were talking about. However, it wasn't Jackie who entered. It wasn't even Tiny. He stared blankly at the man standing in the kitchen doorway. Tall, at least his own height or more, the man had long auburn hair pulled back in a ponytail. He was also dressed all in black and eyeing them with cold, grim eyes.

"Who the hell are you?" Vincent asked, getting to his feet.

The stranger remained silent, his gaze sliding over Marguerite, only switching back to Vincent when he stepped protectively in front of her.

"Well?" Vincent asked.

The man arched one eyebrow, looking vaguely amused at his reaction to his presence as he finally said, "Christian Notte."

"Neil and Stephano's cousin from Europe," Vincent realized and his stance relaxed. Obviously, Jackie had let the man in and sent him to the kitchen. "When did you arrive in California?"

"Today," he admitted. "We called when we landed at the airport. There was no answer.

"We were out earlier making the rounds of the clubs and only got home about fifteen minutes ago. I told Neil not to bother answering the phone," Vincent explained. His gaze slid to the door as he wondered where Jackie was, but he supposed she was still in the office and would be along shortly. He glanced around the kitchen, but was at a complete loss as to what to do or say, finally he sighed and offered, "I'm sorry about Stephano. He's a good man. A friend."

Christian Notte nodded slowly, but he was frowning as he asked, "You were out tonight and just got back?"

"Yes." Vincent's eyebrows drew together at his expression. Concerned the man was offended that they appeared to be out partying so soon after Stephano's attack, he said quickly, "It was necessary. We weren't just out having a laugh." He hesitated, then added, "I have to feed off living donors because of a genetic—"

"Neil explained about that," Christian interrupted. "He said the last donor you fed off of was murdered after Stephano's attack."

"Yes." Vincent nodded. "Well, I've been avoiding going out to feed for the past several days and have been feeding on delivery guys, but Tiny pointed out tonight that the saboteur would soon realize that was what I was doing if I didn't at least look like I was going to the clubs again. The last thing I want is anyone else killed, so we went out, and went quickly from one club to another in the hopes of losing my saboteur long enough for him to think I'd fed while he was trying to catch up to us."

Christian nodded. "It's probably for the best. If he didn't think you were feeding on the delivery people, he would probably assume you were feeding on your detectives and target them."

Vincent felt Marguerite stand behind him, then she touched his back. "Vincent, he might have thought as much when you slipped into the storage room with Jackie tonight. If he was there watching, he might think you were in there feeding on Jackie."

Vincent frowned at the suggestion. It was something he hadn't considered. He didn't want to mark anyone for death by feeding on them, but he definitely didn't want any harm coming to Jackie . . . or Tiny, he added as an afterthought. In truth, Jackie was his main concern.

"I'll have to talk to Jackie about this," he muttered, pushing one hand though his hair and then his gaze focused on Christian. He asked, "Did she go back into the office after she let you in?"

"No one let me in."

Vincent blinked. "What?"

"The panel at the end of the driveway was broken so we couldn't buzz you to open the gate. I left my cousin in the car, came over the wall and up to the house to have you open the gate so he could drive in. That's why I was surprised when you said you'd just got home. There's no way you could have driven past the damaged panel without noticing it. It's smashed and the wires pulled out."

Vincent stiffened at this news and frowned. "What did Jackie say when you told her about it?"

Christian tilted his head and asked, "Jackie is one of the private detectives your brother Bastien sent out from New York to help you with this saboteur?"

Vincent nodded. He'd told Neil everything. He'd felt he owed it to him to be honest about why his brother had been attacked.

"I haven't—" Christian began, then paused as the kitchen door started to swing open again.

They all glanced toward it, waiting to see if Tiny or Jackie entered. Neither mortal did. Instead, another man paused in the doorway. Fair-haired and also dressed all in black, he peered around the people in the kitchen. His gaze moved with disinterest over Vincent, but flickered briefly with what might have been recognition on Marguerite before finally settling on Christian. One eyebrow rose in question.

"I told you to wait in the car, Marcus," Christian said with irritation.

"You were taking a long time," the man said with a shrug. "I came to nose around and found the French doors open, so I came in and followed the voices."

"The French doors are open?" Vincent asked, the hair on the back of his neck beginning to creep.

Marcus nodded.

"That's how I got in," Christian announced. "As I came up to the house I saw the French doors were open. Between that and the broken front panel, I thought there might be a problem, so I came in and followed your voices to the kitchen."

Marguerite turned and clutched at his arm. "Vincent, if the saboteur does think you fed on Jackie tonight and she is a target . . . Jackie was going to check messages in the office."

Vincent felt the blood drain from his face. Jackie would never leave the French doors open.

"I'll go see if Jackie is upstairs changing."

Vincent heard his aunt's words and saw her hurry out of the kitchen, but his mind seemed to be in something of a panic. Everything was moving at super slow speed for him. He gave himself a mental shake, glanced from one man to the other in his kitchen, then slowly followed his aunt's path and walked out of the room. She'd already disappeared upstairs, but Tiny was now coming down and his eyebrows flew up at the sight of the two men who had followed Vincent out of the kitchen. He supposed the man was a bit shocked. He doubted Tiny often saw men his own size and to see two now seemed to startle him.

"She's not in her room!" Marguerite didn't bother to hide her alarm as she reappeared at the top of the stairs.

Tiny glanced from Marguerite to Vincent. "Maybe she's still checking the answering machine."

Turning, Vincent continued up the hall to the office. He thrust the door open, his gaze flying around the empty room as papers flew off his desk, blown off by the wind coming from the still-open French doors.

"It was like this when I entered," Marcus announced, making Vincent aware that all of them had followed.

Vincent stared at the darkness beyond the open doors.

His heart seemed to stop dead in his chest as panic claimed him. Images swam before his eyes of Jackie's pale, broken body lying twisted and drained of blood. He'd made her a target without meaning to. He couldn't lose her now. She was his best hope for happiness in the future. And there was still hope for them.

Vincent wasn't sure if he would allow his aunt to turn her and give up her own hope of turning a life mate if she found one in the future, but it had reminded him that Stephano's mother had always wanted to turn her son. Neil's father was her life mate, she might be willing to turn Jackie for him. But even if she didn't, fifty years or so of bliss with Jackie were better than nothing.

Vincent rushed across the room and into the night, silently praying he'd find her in time.

Jackie's feet were cold. It was late enough that dew had formed on the grass and she was creeping barefoot through the damp blades. She wished she'd at least put slippers on. She also wished she'd called out for help before chasing off after the intruder she'd seen slipping from the house. Running after him had been instinct, but it had been a bad instinct. She was a lone, unarmed mortal tearing through the darkness on the heels of a strong, fast immortal. How stupid was that?

She glanced to the side as she ran around the back of the house. Light was spilling out of the kitchen windows in a wide square onto the tiled patio between the house and pool. In that lit room, Vincent, Tiny, and Marguerite were waiting for her to join them for coffee.

Jackie considered shouting out to them, but decided

against it. The intruder was already far enough ahead of her that she wasn't likely to catch up. Her best hope at this point was to follow him, discover where he'd come onto the property so that they could perhaps prevent his using it again. And maybe to catch a glimpse of the license plate of his vehicle as he drove away.

If she got there in time to even see what he was driving, Jackie thought grimly as the dark figure ahead of her slipped into the trees and hedges that ran the length of the tall fence that separated the lawn from the sandy beach. These immortals were damned fast. Gritting her teeth, she put on a burst of speed and charged for the narrow line of woods bordering the back of the property.

Branches snapped under foot as she crashed into the trees and Jackie winced, knowing the stealth factor had just disappeared if it had ever been there. The saboteur definitely knew he was being pursued now. Although in truth, he had probably known prior to this, she acknowledged. The hearing of immortals was exceptional.

She paused as she reached the high wall that surrounded Vincent's property and glanced along its length both ways. There was no sign of anyone nearby. Either the saboteur had vaulted the fence, or was hiding.

Jackie hesitated, then glanced sharply up at the trees along the fence as a branch snapped. She'd barely glimpsed the figure in the branches overhead before he swung himself out and over the wall. She barely heard the thud as he landed on the other side. She was already climbing the nearest tree.

She would have someone out the next morning to cut the damned things down and to clear away all the hedges along the fence so that there was nowhere to hide, Jackie decided as she climbed. They might look more attractive than the plain wall, but safety was more important than aesthetics.

Unfortunately, Jackie was a city detective. Running up alleys, jogging up stairs, racing through subways . . . All of this she could manage without difficulty. However, there wasn't much call for tree climbing in New York. She managed to get herself up the tree and make her way out on the branch, but that was where her luck gave out. She heard the snap one heartbeat before the branch suddenly collapsed beneath her.

Jackie grabbed wildly at passing branches as she fell, but it was no use. She landed on something hard and only realized it was the intruder when she heard an "Oooomph!" as they both crashed to the ground.

Her panic immediately increased.

Jackie had been trained in martial arts since she was a small child, her father had insisted on it, and still she wouldn't take on an immortal unarmed. One, two, or maybe even three mortals? No problem, but immortals? Nah-uh. Not on her own and without a weapon of some sort to back her up. It wasn't just that they were stronger and faster. They didn't seem to feel pain like mortals either, as if the nanos blocked some of it when necessary to allow them to continue to do battle. And they were damned hard to knock out. As for killing them, forget about it. Unless you had something to take their heads off with, say a sword or grenade, you weren't going to win.

However, having fallen on the intruder, she didn't have

much choice. Jackie was in the battle now and reacted automatically, her body scrabbling to do whatever was necessary to survive. It was a very short, desperate struggle. Realizing that she wasn't going to survive if she persisted, Jackie managed to take the intruder by surprise and roll away and to her feet in one move.

She had barely become conscious of the cold, gritty sand squishing between her toes when she was jerked around by the hair and into a dark embrace. Jackie grunted as her chest slammed against the intruder's chest, then gasped as her head was suddenly jerked back and to the side, then he struck like a snake, his head swooping forward toward the throat he'd exposed.

Suddenly as paralyzed as a cat caught by the scruff of the neck, she moaned at the rending pain as her throat was ripped open by unseen fangs. She then stared blindly at the stars overhead as the scent of blood drifted up around her, and slurping sounds filled her ears, and knew her life was being sucked away.

Jackie didn't know if it was blood loss, or horror, but after several endless moments, the pain and sounds began to fade to nothingness and even the stars overhead began to twinkle out of view.

"Jackie!"

She heard the shout with some faint part of her mind, but didn't understand what it meant until her attacker suddenly stilled, head jerking up away from her throat. Jackie's mind struggled back from the hopelessness and shock that had laid claim to it, the smallest flicker of hope sparking to life within her soul.

"Jackie!" This time she recognized Vincent's voice. She also saw blurry movement beyond her attacker, and immediately understood that it was salvation coming. Then she saw the glint of metal as her attacker suddenly released her. Some part of her mind was terribly alert, blindingly so, and instinct made her grab for the arm swinging the weapon in Vincent's direction, clawing at it with both hands, but she was weak with blood loss and couldn't hold on.

It was desperation and instinct that made Jackie sink her teeth into that arm. If she couldn't keep her attacker from wielding the weapon at Vincent, she would force him to drop the damned weapon. That was her only thought. She had to save Vincent.

Blood gushed into her mouth as Jackie chomped down on the wrist, but she merely swallowed the salty liquid to keep from choking and held on like a bulldog, terror and rage giving her the strength to do so.

A curse reached her ears, then her attacker pressed one hand to her forehead and pushed her off. Jackie felt more blood gush into her mouth as her teeth tore through flesh, then her hold slipped and she was tumbling backward to the sand. She moaned as her back slammed to the ground, then rolled weakly onto her side and lay limp, watching helplessly as her attacker turned on Vincent.

Much to her relief, her efforts had helped after all. Vincent had seen the weapon in the hand she'd been struggling to hold onto and now kicked out at it. She saw the knife go flying off into the darkness as the two began to struggle.

Heart pounding and hands clenching around her bleeding throat, Jackie curled into a ball in the cool sand and watched the shifting shapes in the darkness. It was hard to see anything, however, and she was so weak and weary.

"Argeneau!"

Eyes that Jackie hadn't realized had closed, snapped open at that yell. She didn't recognize the man's voice. However, she did recognize Marguerite and Tiny as they called out to the two of them and relief flowed through her as their shouts drew nearer. She wasn't the only one to hear their calls, Jackie noted as the intruder suddenly gave up his fight with Vincent and made a run for it.

Vincent didn't even hesitate; ignoring the quickly disappearing shape, he hurried to her side.

"Jackie?" His voice was deep with worry as he turned her onto her back to check her over.

"Argeneau?"

Jackie saw two shapes burst through the gate behind Vincent. She blinked and tried to focus on the two men. Both were big enough to be Tiny, but she didn't think either man was. Vincent didn't even glance toward them, his attention was wholly on Jackie as he scooped her into his arms.

"He went that way." Vincent jerked his head in the direction her attacker had run. Leaving the two men to pursue the saboteur, he then strode toward the gate through the wall.

"Vincent?" Marguerite rushed forward with Tiny on her heels as Vincent started across the lawn. "Is she going to be all right? Did you find her in time?"

"I don't know." His voice was terse, Jackie noted as she floated on the edge of consciousness.

"Her throat." Tiny's voice was a weak sound of despair.

"Open the door, Tiny," Vincent growled, sounding terribly upset and her mind, growing delirious, thought that was just the sweetest thing. He really liked her, she thought, then released a little sigh and allowed unconsciousness to claim her.

Thirteen

"*Lay her on the table.*"

Vincent scowled at that order from Christian Notte as the man hurried past him into the kitchen and cleared away the empty cups from earlier in the day. Scooping them off the dining table with quick hands, he shoved them at Tiny to put somewhere, then turned back.

"Why aren't you chasing after her attacker?" Vincent asked with sudden fury.

"Marcus went after him. I stayed to see if I can help," the man answered tersely. "Set her on the table."

Vincent hesitated, then moved to the table and lay Jackie gently on it. He'd rather carry her upstairs and put her in bed, but he supposed they had to clean her up first. There seemed to be an awful lot of blood. He frowned over that as he straightened from setting her down. A lot of blood, he noted numbly, his heart sinking.

"Dear God," Tiny whispered, a catch in his voice and his face paling sickly as Christian gently clasped Jackie's chin and turned her head to examine the wound. It wasn't a bite, it was a tear. Her throat had been ripped open with a vicious intent to kill. Vincent couldn't even guess at the amount of blood she'd lost.

He turned away and moved to the sink to grab one of the new tea towels they'd bought for his kitchen. After dampening it, Vincent hurried back to her side and began to wipe ineffectually at the blood. It was on her neck, down her chest, soaking into the white cotton of the t-shirt she wore under her jogging suit.

The sound of Tiny's deep voice made him glance around. The mortal was speaking into the phone.

"I need an ambulance," he said urgently.

Vincent glanced down at Jackie's injury. An ambulance would never get there in time to save her. "Hang up, Tiny."

The giant glanced his way with surprise. "But she—"

"Look at her. They can't save her," he said grimly.

"What are you doing?" Christian asked sharply as Vincent began to undo the buttons of his sleeve.

"I'm going to turn her," Vincent said calmly and knew from the man's expression that it wasn't the answer he'd expected.

"Vincent?" Tiny said uncertainly, but didn't move to stop him and did hang up the phone. Vincent supposed that was tacit agreement and was glad. He didn't want to argue with the man, nor did he want to take over his mind to keep Tiny out of the way while he did what he had to do to save Jackie.

"Neil said you saved Stephano's life by turning him," Christian said slowly.

Vincent shrugged indifferently. He didn't care about rules or laws. He cared about Jackie.

"The bleeding has slowed to a trickle," Marguerite said, and Vincent turned to find her bent over Jackie, watching her throat as she moaned and shifted on the table.

"Move, Aunt Marguerite. I have to turn her." Vincent began to roll up his sleeve.

Marguerite ignored him, her gaze remained on Jackie's wound for a moment, then shifted to her face and she asked with bewilderment, "Why is her face covered with blood?"

Vincent peered down at Jackie's face, noting the blood around her mouth, but just repeated, "Move, Aunt Marguerite."

"You are not turning her, Vincent," she said harshly. "If anyone does, it will be me. Now . . . why is her mouth full of blood?"

Vincent shifted impatiently. "She tried to help me. She bit him."

Marguerite's gaze became sharp. "She *bit* him?"

Vincent frowned at being bothered with these questions at a time like this. "He had a knife. She bit into his wrist to keep him from using it on me when I first reached them."

They all turned to Jackie as she moaned again, more loudly this time, then she suddenly began to convulse on the table.

"What's happening?" Vincent asked in a panic. He stepped up to the table again, grabbing for Jackie's shoulders to keep her from convulsing right off the table top.

"Could she have got enough blood while biting the killer to be turning?" Christian asked.

"It's possible," Marguerite said slowly. "But I've never seen someone convulse like this during a turning. Not this early on." She frowned. "She's lost a lot of blood, though. That could be why."

"What do we do?" Tiny asked anxiously.

Marguerite hesitated, then ordered, "Grab a bag of blood, Tiny."

The giant rushed to the refrigerator at once, returning with the bag. Marguerite slit it open with a fingernail, then held it over Jackie's mouth. Vincent immediately moved to lift her head so that the liquid would slide down her throat and get to where it needed to be.

"Do you have enough bagged blood here to see her through the turning?"

Vincent frowned and glanced over his shoulder at the question from Christian. It was something he hadn't thought of and he already knew the answer before his aunt said, "No."

Much to his relief, Christian merely nodded and said, "We brought some with us. We had it sent on ahead to the hotel. I'll send Marcus for it when he gets back."

"I'll call Bastien and have him ship more blood out tomorrow to replace it," Marguerite murmured. She added, "We'll need an IV too, if we can find one."

"Why?" Christian asked with surprise.

"We've used it while turning others. It comes in quite handy," Aunt Marguerite explained.

"How many times have you overseen a turning?" Christian asked curiously.

"Four times over the last three years," she said with a shrug.

"Four?" he asked with surprise.

"My children's mates," she explained. "Then there were a couple others in the seven hundred years I've lived," Marguerite added with a shrug. "We can do this, but we need blood and an IV."

"We'll find an IV too," Christian assured her, then fell silent as Marguerite removed the now-empty bag and Vincent eased Jackie back onto the table. They all crowded closer around the table, watching her pale, still face.

"The convulsions have stopped," Tiny said with hope.

Vincent nodded slowly, then glanced from Jackie to his aunt as she moved to the head of the table and used her thumbs to pull Jackie's eyelids up to peer at her pupils. Vincent didn't see anything, but she must have, for she nodded with satisfaction and straightened. "It's beginning. You'd better move her upstairs, Vincent. Do you have any rope?"

"Rope?" he asked with confusion.

"She'll need to be tied down for a bit so she doesn't hurt herself," Marguerite explained.

"We'll get that too. I—" Christian paused as the door leading out to the pool opened and the blond Marcus entered the kitchen, a grim expression on his face. When Christian raised an eyebrow in question, Marcus shook his head.

Vincent knew what that meant. The saboteur had got away. He felt a moment's bitter rage that the attacker had escaped, but then let it go, more concerned with Jackie.

"Take her upstairs, Argeneau," Christian said grimly. He

gestured Marcus closer as he said, "I need you to go get a couple things, Marcus."

Vincent didn't listen to the rest. Instead, he scooped Jackie up into his arms and carried her out of the kitchen. Just before he left the room he saw Tiny try to follow and Marguerite stop him. He heard her begin to murmur low and soothing words to the giant, then Vincent was out of the kitchen and on his way upstairs.

Jackie was completely still in his arms as he carried her and he fretted over whether she really was turning or not. Aunt Marguerite could have made a mistake. She might not have got enough blood from the saboteur to facilitate the turn.

But then Vincent had barely laid Jackie in her bed before she began to moan. Soon after that she began to shift restlessly on the bed. Oddly enough, this reassured him. This is how Marguerite had described the turn to him. It was why Stephano's stillness had so disturbed her. The turning was a painful process, not something they slept through peacefully unless well drugged.

By the time his aunt joined him in the bedroom, Jackie was moaning continuously and loudly and writhing on the bed.

Marguerite frowned as she approached. "This is quick. I wonder if she got more blood from biting the attacker than we thought."

"What does that mean?" Vincent asked anxiously.

"Nothing," Marguerite reassured him, then glanced toward the door with a frown. "I hope Christian is quick."

"Did Christian go with Marcus?" Vincent asked.

"No. He felt it inadvisable to leave us here alone with the

saboteur still out there and Jackie as she is. He's checking the garage for rope."

Vincent frowned, not at all comfortable with the idea of tying Jackie down. He changed his mind several moments later when she began to thrash, her body bending and twisting, arms and legs whipping viciously this way and that as she began to scream in pain. Vincent and Marguerite were struggling to try to hold her still and keep her from hurting herself when Tiny came rushing into the room.

"What's happening?! Why is she screaming?!" Tiny cried with alarm, rushing to the bed.

"It's the change," Marguerite said soothingly, then glanced toward the door with relief as Christian hurried in.

"I found some rope," he announced, which was unnecessary since they could see the rope dangling from his hand as he hurried to the bed.

It took all four of them twenty minutes to get Jackie tied down. Once it was done, Marguerite led Tiny out of the room, murmuring reassurances. Christian followed, silent and grim and Vincent had to wonder if the man had ever seen a turning before. He himself hadn't and hoped never to see it again. Jackie seemed to be in agony. He tried to reassure himself by repeating the mantra that when it finished, she would be immortal like him and they could be true life mates, but it didn't seem to help much. He hated to see her suffer so.

Suddenly weary, Vincent pulled the dressing table chair over to the side of the bed and sat down. There was nothing he could do to ease her way, but he would endure it with her. Jackie was his now. Forever. As long as she agreed to it, he added wryly. She was his true life mate. He just had to make her see it.

Vincent spent the rest of the night and all the next morning trying to figure out a way to do that as he watched over Jackie. Marguerite spent most of that time keeping him company, leaving the room every hour or so to retrieve another bag of blood from the kitchen. They took turns changing the bags until she retired to her own room to take a short nap at midmorning. Vincent was nodding off in the chair when she returned at noon with a fresh bag of blood in hand.

"How is she?" she asked, moving to the bedside to peer down at Jackie.

"Fine. Quiet now," Vincent said as Marguerite removed the empty blood bag in the IV stand beside the bed and replaced it with a fresh, full bag of the red liquid.

Vincent had no idea where Marcus had found the IV stand and didn't care enough to ask. It was enough that he'd found one while fetching the extra blood from the hotel he and Christian had planned to stay in. He supposed the man must have got it from the hospital, or a hospital supply store, but hadn't cared enough to ask.

Vincent hadn't spoken much to either man since Jackie had started to turn. He'd been told they were staying close in case the saboteur returned to finish what he'd started. They seemed to think everyone in the house might now be a target, at least Tiny, Marguerite, and Jackie. It seemed they'd decided his saboteur was determined to hurt him. While Vincent had to admit that was how it looked, he couldn't imagine what he might have done to make anyone hate him so much.

"Thank God she's stopped thrashing and screaming," Marguerite murmured as she finished her work with the IV and threw out the empty blood bag. "I don't think Tiny could handle much more. The poor man is terribly upset. He loves Jackie like a sister and while he's glad she'll live, he's concerned about what all this means and how she'll take that she's turned."

Vincent nodded. "I know. Thank you for keeping him out of here and keeping him busy."

"It was for the best," Marguerite said with a shrug. "He's been cooking up a storm downstairs. He's also eating the food as quickly as he's cooking it. I think he's a comfort eater."

"You're fond of him," Vincent said.

"Yes. Having him around is like having a second daughter."

Vincent blinked at the comment, then gave a short laugh. Six-foot, two-hundred-and-eighty-pound Tiny . . . a second daughter? He shook his head.

Marguerite returned to Jackie's side and frowned as she brushed a finger lightly down her cheek. "She's much more peaceful now. The worst of it must be over."

"We can hope," Vincent said quietly. "How much longer will she be out?"

Marguerite shook her head. "It's hard to say. In my experience, it usually only takes a day or two, but with Stephano it took three."

"Four," Vincent corrected.

"What?" Marguerite peered at him blankly.

"It's been four days and he still isn't awake . . . Is he?" Vincent added as he caught the expression on her face.

"I'm sorry," she said on a sigh. "He woke up shortly after

Jackie was attacked last night. I meant to tell you, but when I got back here Jackie was screaming and thrashing and I forgot."

"He's awake?" Vincent asked, sitting up with amazement. Marguerite nodded.

"Has he said who attacked him?"

She shook her head. "His mind was wiped. He can't recall anything about being stabbed, though there are fragments of the episode in his mind, none of them reveal the intruder. I suspect those fragments are why the saboteur felt it necessary to kill him. He probably feared he might pull the memory together eventually. And he might," she added encouragingly. "He's trying to sort it out now."

Vincent sagged back in his chair, his gaze returning to Jackie. For a brief moment he'd hoped Stephano might be able to tell them who his attacker was and this whole ordeal would be over. He was terribly disappointed that his problem persisted. He was hungry, but didn't dare feed.

"Allen Richmond has finished fixing the panel at the gate," she announced.

Vincent nodded with disinterest. Marguerite had mentioned earlier that Christian had made Tiny call the security company about the broken panel first thing that morning. It seemed it was repaired.

"And I ordered pizza. It's here," she added.

"Why?" Vincent asked with bewilderment. "You said Tiny was cooking up a storm."

"I ordered pizza for you," she explained firmly. "Tiny can toss the pizza for all I care, but I put the delivery man in your office for you."

"I'm not—" Vincent began to deny he was hungry, but it was a lie. His body continued to need blood whether he wanted it or not. "Thank you, Aunt Marguerite, but I . . . I can't. What if the saboteur—"

"I don't think that's a concern, Vincent. It's the middle of the day," she pointed out. "The saboteur will be home asleep and having sweet dreams about what he thinks he's done. This is probably the safest time for you to feed."

Vincent nodded slowly, seeing the sense in what she said. This probably *was* the safest time for him to feed. Sighing, he stood and moved toward the door. "I won't be long."

"I already paid him, but you might want to give him a tip," Marguerite said as he slid out of the room.

Vincent didn't run into anyone on the way to his office. After finishing with the delivery man, he slid a twenty-dollar bill into his pocket, then saw him out of the house. After locking the door behind him, he turned to find Tiny in the hall.

"How's Jackie?" the giant asked with concern. The mortal looked horrible: pale, exhausted, and haggard, with anxiety pulling at his bulldog features.

Vincent forced a smile. "She's stopped thrashing and screaming. She's resting much more peacefully. I think the worst is over. Hopefully she'll wake up soon."

Tiny's shoulders sagged with relief. "Thank you. I've been worried."

Vincent clapped a hand on his shoulder in understanding. "She'll be fine," he assured him and was relieved to be able to say it. For a while there, Vincent hadn't been sure Jackie would survive the turning. She'd lost so much blood

247

in the attack . . . But she'd survived the worst of it and should be fine now. He hoped.

"Can I see her?" he asked. "I wanted to come up earlier, but the Italians wouldn't let me."

"The Italians?" Vincent asked, then realized he meant Christian and Marcus. Marguerite had told him that they were in the kitchen, grilling Tiny about everything that had happened in the hopes of figuring things out and stopping the saboteur before someone else got hurt. He didn't doubt for a minute that retribution was part of it too. Stephano was their cousin after all.

As if drawn by the fact that they were talking about them, the kitchen door suddenly opened and Christian and Marcus strode out. Their footsteps slowed as they spotted Vincent.

"How is she?" Christian asked.

"The worst is over," Vincent admitted. "She'll survive."

"Good." Christian nodded at the news, then asked, "Marguerite said you didn't recognize the attacker?"

"No." Vincent felt his shoulders slump with defeat as he admitted that. It had been so dark and everything had happened so fast . . . Then too, the guy had been dressed all in black and with a half mask over his face from his nose up, leaving only his mouth free to tear into Jackie's throat. "I got a vague impression of size, small and wiry. Other than that . . ."

Christian nodded again as Vincent's voice trailed off. His gaze slid to Tiny and then back before he said, "We've been up all day, we're going to catch a couple of hours sleep. Dante and Tommaso will watch the house until we get up."

"Dante and . . . ?" Vincent's question died as the newly

repaired buzzer sounded, announcing someone at the gate. Eyebrows rising when Christian nodded, Vincent moved to the panel and asked who it was. He wasn't surprised to hear the names Dante and Tommaso. He pushed the button to open the gate, then turned to catch Tiny peering warily at the two immortals. It made him wonder what threat the men had used to keep Tiny downstairs and away from Jackie.

Vincent turned his gaze to Christian and Marcus. "Dante and Tommaso—?"

"My cousins. Twins," Christian explained. "You can trust them."

Since Vincent hadn't determined yet if he trusted Christian, his assurance wasn't worth much, but he let it go.

"Which rooms do you want us to use?" Christian asked.

"The first two on the right are still empty," Vincent announced. "If you're all staying, you'll have to double up."

Christian nodded acceptance, then a knock at the door drew Vincent's attention. Turning, he moved back to open it to reveal a man clad in leather and even larger than Tiny. Vincent managed to hide his startled reaction at his size. Nodding in greeting, he stepped out of the way for him to enter, noting that the second man, his twin, was also large and covered from tip to toe in black leather. Both men had long, black hair.

Vincent closed the door behind them as Christian rattled off a couple of sentences in Italian. He then added in English, "Vincent is in charge until I get up."

Vincent's eyebrows flew up at this announcement, but Christian was already leading Marcus upstairs and the two mountains that were Dante and Tommaso were turning expectantly his way. He didn't have a clue what to say, or what orders to give.

"This is Tiny," he said finally. He asked, "Do you eat?"

They looked young to him. Vincent couldn't say what it was about them that made him think they were young, something about the eyes. He'd gotten good at judging the age of other immortals over the centuries and these two appeared to him to be young enough that they might still eat. Of course, they were big too, like Lucern, and it generally took food as well as blood to keep the muscle mass.

"We eat," Dante said solemnly.

Vincent nodded. "There's pizza in the kitchen."

When the two men simply stared at him, he realized they didn't know where the kitchen was. Turning impatiently, he headed for the kitchen, saying over his shoulder, "Go on up and look in on Jackie if you want, Tiny. Marguerite's there."

Tiny was halfway up the stairs before Vincent finished speaking. He led the twins into the kitchen and then eyed them uncertainly. He didn't know them or their medical status. It was probable they could feed off bagged blood, most immortals could, but just in case he said, "Tiny is mortal. No biting."

Dante and Tommaso exchanged a grimace that suggested they were insulted that he felt he needed to say as much, but both nodded as they moved to sit at the table. Dante dragged the pizza box closer and opened it to inspect the contents. It was still completely intact.

"No anchovies?" Dante asked.

"Sorry," Vincent said, then stared as Tommaso ripped off the lid of the pizza box, lifted out half the pizza, and dropped it on the lid, using it as a makeshift plate. Dante then drew the bottom half of the box fully in front of himself, apparently laying claim to the other half of the pizza.

"Maybe I should order more," Vincent muttered, turning to head out of the kitchen.

"Anchovies on two of them," Dante called after him.

Vincent went into the office to place an order for four pizzas, two with everything, including anchovies. He then walked back up the hall and stuck his head into the kitchen.

"Give me a shout when the pizzas get here and I'll come down and pay for them," he instructed, thinking he might as well get in another bite while he could. "I'll be upstairs if you need me."

Dante and Tommaso both grunted in response, their concentration on the pizza they were stuffing into their mouths.

Shaking his head, Vincent headed back upstairs. He hadn't slept since the attack and was tired, but didn't intend to sleep until he was sure Jackie was out of the woods. Marguerite seemed to think she was, but he wouldn't be sure until she opened her beautiful eyes and spoke.

Jackie felt like hell. It was her first conscious thought and was accompanied by a moan as she shifted in bed. Her body was aching and weak. She'd obviously either been beaten black and blue and left to recover, or she was waking up from one hell of a flu.

She barely had that thought when her memory returned and the events of the night before flashed into her mind, harsh and stark. Sucking in a breath, she reached for her throat, almost expecting to find it still torn open and crusted with blood. She didn't feel either. Her skin felt a little raised, but there was no blood, and surprisingly enough, no bandages or pain.

Her gaze slipped to the side and she peered at the man asleep in the chair by her bed. Vincent. He was a dark outline in the faint light. It was obviously nighttime and her room would have been completely black, but the bathroom light had been left on and the door cracked open to allow some of it out. In that bit of light, she could see that his eyes were closed, his head nodding on his chest.

Jackie watched him sleep, recalling his coming to her rescue on the beach. He'd charged in fearlessly, risking himself for her. She smiled softly at the memory as her fingers played over her throat again. Where was the wound? Troubled by its absence, she pushed the blankets aside and eased to a sitting position, shocked at how difficult it was. She was as weak as a baby.

Shifting her legs off the bed, Jackie managed to push herself to her feet, but her legs trembled as she stood and she swayed a bit. Using the wall as a brace, she made her way to the bathroom, glancing back twice to be sure Vincent hadn't awakened and noticed her absence.

She slipped through the cracked open door, then eased it fully closed and moved to the counter in front of the mirror. Jackie stared at herself in amazement, the wound on her neck briefly forgotten. She looked about as bad as she felt, her complexion pallid, her hair lying in lank chunks around her head, her face almost oily-looking with the damp sweat blanketing it.

A small groan slid from her lips at the thought of Vincent

having watched over her while she looked like this, then Jackie let that go with a sigh and turned her attention to her neck. Her throat was healed. Not fully. It was badly scarred, but it looked like a months-old injury, and Jackie was positive the attack couldn't have taken place months ago. She couldn't have slept here in this room for months. So what had happened?

You were turned, some part of her mind whispered the answer, but Jackie shook her head. No. Impossible. Surely not?

No, she thought more firmly. If that were the case, she'd be svelte and beautiful like Marguerite, but she was her same old self, carrying fifteen or twenty pounds more than was considered beautiful in Hollywood.

Just the thought of her weight made Jackie realize that she was hungry, starved actually, and terribly thirsty. Turning the tap on, she bent over the sink and scooped some of the cold liquid up in her hands, then lifted it to her mouth to slurp up as much as she could before it ran through her fingers. She did that several times, but hardly managed to get any liquid out of it, certainly not enough to satisfy her raging thirst.

Giving up the attempt to drink from the tap, she instead splashed the water on her face and head, then ran her fingers through her hair to try to return it to some sort of order before turning off the tap. She straightened and moved back to the door.

Vincent was still asleep in the chair, Jackie saw with relief as she opened the door. She'd really rather he not see her this way. Too thirsty to waste time on dressing, she decided the large, bulky t-shirt would have to do while she went below and fetched a glass of water . . . or ten. She was parched, her mouth unpleasantly cottony and pasty.

Jackie crossed the room on shaky legs and eased the bedroom door open. Much to her relief, the hall was empty. She made her way slowly to the stairs and started down with determination. That determination pooped out before she'd gone halfway. It left Jackie clinging weakly to the rail, wishing she'd woken Vincent up after all.

Sighing, she rested a moment, then forced herself to continue. Jackie was incredibly relieved when she finally reached the hallway's hardwood floor. At least if her legs gave out on her now she wouldn't fall far.

"Jackie. What are you doing up?" Tiny rushed up the hall from the kitchen and she smiled with relief.

"I was thirsty," Jackie admitted as he reached her.

"And hungry, no doubt," he rumbled, slipping an arm around her to take some of her weight.

Jackie opened her mouth to answer, but instead paused and inhaled deeply as he urged her into his side.

"You smell good," she murmured with surprise.

Tiny glanced at her sharply, obviously as startled by the comment as Jackie was that she'd made it. He frowned. "Are you okay? Your eyes are dilating."

Jackie found herself leaning toward him, inhaling deeply. He smelled so good. Yummy even. She could just bite him.

Startled at the thought, Jackie pulled back and nearly overbalanced. Tiny quickly tightened his hold, keeping her upright, then they both stilled and stared up the hall as the kitchen door opened and a mammoth man stepped out. Fear rippling through her, Jackie immediately stepped closer to Tiny.

"It's okay." Tiny patted her arm. "He's Dante, one of Christian's men."

"Christian?" Jackie asked with bewilderment, then forgot the question as her eyes landed on his throat. With his head turned to look at the big man, Tiny's vein ran taut along his throat and she could actually see it pulsing with warm, life-giving blood.

"Christian is Neil and Stephano's cousin. He's here to help and has brought his men to keep an eye on things and help too," Tiny explained.

It all sounded like "blah, blah, blah blood" to her. Had Tiny said something about blood? Or was that the thought whispering through her own head, Jackie wondered vaguely as she inhaled deeply, breathing in his scent. It was the oddest thing. His scent was making her mouth water as efficiently as the smell of freshly baked pizza. She stared at the pulse beating at the base of his neck, and felt an odd shifting sensation and pressure in her upper jaw.

"Bad!"

Jackie glanced to the side to find the large, dark-haired Dante there. She gasped in surprise when he suddenly scooped her up in his arms and turned toward the kitchen.

"No biting," Dante said firmly as he carried her.

"But I'm hungry," Jackie complained, then blinked in surprise as she realized what she'd said. She *was* hungry, and thirsty as well, but Tiny shouldn't be associated with that. Perhaps it was because he cooked all the time, she reasoned a little fuzzily.

"Blood, Tommaso," Dante said as he carried Jackie into the kitchen with Tiny trailing them.

Jackie stared with amazement at the second man as he lurched to his feet and moved to the refrigerator. He was an exact replica of the one carrying her. Tall, muscular, and handsome in a dark-eyed, dark-haired, Italian way.

"Are you two—?"

"Twins." Dante set her down at the table and Jackie peered into his face as he straightened, her attention narrowing on his eyes. They were not silver-blue like Marguerite and Vincent's. They were black with silver streaks. Definitely vampires then, she decided.

"Open your mouth."

Jackie glanced to the side with a start and found the one called Tommaso standing, patiently waiting with a bag of blood in each hand.

"What are you going to do with that?" she asked warily.

"Open," he insisted, setting one bag on the table.

Jackie hesitated, then opened her mouth.

"Teeth out."

"She won't have control over them yet, Tommaso," Dante pointed out and—much to her amazement—pulled out a pocket knife and used it to jab the end of his own finger. She watched in horrified fascination as a pearl of blood bubbled to the surface, then he ran it back and forth under her nose. Jackie started to shrink away, but paused and inhaled deeply as the tinny scent of blood quivered up her nostrils.

"Oh," Jackie breathed, amazed at how pleasing the scent was, then she blinked in surprise and raised a hand to her closed mouth as she again felt the odd shifting pressure along her upper jaw.

"Open," Tommaso repeated.

Jackie frowned and opened her mouth to ask why, only to find the blood bag suddenly in the way. Worse yet, it appeared to be somehow affixed to her teeth, she realized.

"Just relax. You need this," Tommaso instructed.

Jackie tried to scowl at him over the bag, but was distracted as she realized the bag was shrinking and her aches and cramps had begun to subside. Within moments the bag was empty, and replaced with the second full one. When that too was gone, he took it away and peered at her expectantly. "More?"

Jackie stared, her mind in an uproar as she moved her tongue almost fearfully across her teeth. Something sharp nicked her tongue and she was suddenly off her seat, hurrying toward the only mirrored surface in the room. The toaster.

Jackie stared into the reflective surface and saw silver-green eyes peering back. She blinked, surprised she'd missed that when she'd looked in the mirror upstairs, then reluctantly opened her mouth to reveal her teeth. There they were . . . Her teeth . . . But with a difference. A pair of sharp canines were now protruding on either side of her incisors.

Fourteen

It was a piercing shriek that woke Vincent up. He sat up with confusion in the chair by Jackie's bed, his gaze immediately searching for her. His heart seemed to stop when he saw that the bed was empty. Then he was suddenly wide awake and on his feet.

He was sure the long, drawn-out shriek he was hearing was Jackie's, and it was coming from somewhere downstairs.

Vincent heard doors open behind him as he rushed out into the hall, but didn't bother glancing back. The scream had ended by the time he started down the stairs, but it didn't slow him in the least. He practically flew down the steps, his feet barely touching the treads he sailed over. Then he was pounding up the hall.

Vincent saw Dante and Tomasso standing in the hall, burly arms crossed over their wide chests as they stood shoulder to shoulder in front of the kitchen door, but he didn't really think they would try to stop him from getting to Jackie . . . until he reached them and they didn't move out of his way.

"Move," he growled, trying to squeeze his way past, but there wasn't room to slip between them and they weren't moving.

"Dante? Tomasso? What's happening?" Christian's voice made Vincent glance back to see Marcus and Christian walking up the hall toward them. Apparently the scream had woken them too.

"Tiny and Marguerite are talking to Jackie," Dante answered.

"Marguerite said to keep everyone out," Tomasso added, scowling at Vincent as he tried once again to get past them.

Christian hesitated, then caught Vincent by the shoulder.

"Tell them to move," Vincent turned to snap at the man.

Before Christian could respond, Marguerite opened the kitchen door, peered over the shoulders of the two large men in front of the door and said, "Vincent, go wait in the living room. I'll call you when you can come in."

Vincent opened his mouth to argue, but Marguerite was already closing the door. Scowling, he shifted from one foot to the other, then turned and stomped back up the hall and into the living room, aware that Christian and Marcus were following. Dante and Tomasso apparently stayed at the door like a couple of gargoyles, Vincent realized when they didn't follow.

"What do you think happened?" Marcus asked as the three of them began to pace the living room.

"I think she didn't take well to the idea of being one of us," Christian said dryly.

Vincent frowned at the suggestion. He hadn't thought about how Jackie would take being turned. His main concern had been that she survive the attack, that he couldn't let her die. But he'd forgotten one small fact. Despite how well they'd been getting along the last couple of days, Jackie had hated immortals since her experience with Cassius at nineteen.

"Cassius," Christian murmured and Vincent turned his head sharply to find the man's eyes narrowed on him. He'd been reading his mind. Even as he opened his mouth to tell him to mind his own thoughts, Christian said with surprise, "She hates immortals."

"You don't hate immortals," Tiny said firmly for the third time.

"I do." Jackie scowled at the giant. He was being annoyingly calm and soothing about all this. "How could you let them do this to me?"

"Because I love you and didn't want you dead," Tiny said grimly.

Jackie blinked at the raw expression on his face and suddenly became aware of how haggard and exhausted he looked. It seemed obvious he hadn't slept since the attack.

"And you don't hate immortals, Jackie," Tiny said quietly. "You fear them. There's a difference."

Jackie closed her mouth and sat back as she recognized the truth of that. She'd feared them since Cassius, feared their ability to control her. But she was an immortal now as well. Did that mean she had no reason to fear them anymore?

Tiny rubbed wearily at his eyes and Jackie frowned with concern. "You should go to bed, Tiny. I bet you haven't slept even a couple minutes all night or today."

"No," he acknowledged. "I haven't."

Jackie nodded. "Go to bed."

He hesitated, then peered at her with worry, "Are you going to be all right?"

Jackie grimaced and gave a laugh. "I'm an immortal now, Tiny. I'm perfect."

"I'll sit with her, Tiny," Marguerite murmured quietly, reminding them of her presence. Vincent's aunt had sat so silent and still at the table, Jackie had forgotten all about her being there.

Tiny nodded solemnly, then stood and moved to Jackie's side. Bending at the waist, he gave her a quick, tight hug. "You're my best friend in the world and I thought I'd lost you last night. I'm sorry if you're not happy to be a vampire, but I'm glad you're alive, vampire or not."

Straightening, he turned away and left the room. Jackie watched him go, then sighed and sat back in her seat. She and Marguerite were silent for several minutes, then Jackie asked, "Was it Vincent?"

Marguerite took so long to answer, that Jackie finally turned to meet her gaze. The moment she did, Marguerite asked, "Do you recall biting your attacker? Vincent said you were trying to prevent his being attacked with a knife."

Jackie blinked, remembering the event in question. "I was too weak to hold on with my hands, so I tried biting, hoping to force him to drop the knife."

"You swallowed blood."

"Two mouthfuls at least," she said with a grimace, then blinked. "You mean, that's what turned me?"

Marguerite nodded.

Jackie peered down at her hands, unsure how she felt about that.

"You turned yourself, Jackie," Marguerite said quietly. "And I, for one, am glad. True life mates are rare and wonderful things. Vincent would have been miserable without you."

Jackie raised her head slowly. "Excuse me?"

Marguerite tilted her head and considered her thoughtfully, before asking, "Do you know about true life mates?"

Jackie nodded her head slowly. Immortals had true life mates, a mate that they couldn't read, and couldn't control, but who was meant to be with them. Or so they believed.

Jackie grimaced at that cynical little add-on. She'd met immortals with true life mates and she'd met immortals without. She'd also met immortals who had mated themselves to the wrong person for whatever reason, like Marguerite and her husband Jean Claude. And there was a vast difference between the three sorts of immortals.

Unmated immortals tended to be harsh, arrogant, and usually cold. Sometimes they were even self-destructive. Those mated to the wrong mate tended to be worse: bitter, controlling, and cruel even. Jean Claude Argeneau had been one of those. Her father had once said the man had married Marguerite Argeneau for the wrong reason, that he'd wanted her because she'd reminded him of his previous wife, who had died ages before he'd met Marguerite. Only Marguerite wasn't a proper life mate for Jean Claude. He could read and control her and had become a bitter, cruel tyrant over the centuries.

In comparison, those immortals Jackie had met who had found their true life mates seemed more at peace, softer somehow and eminently happier.

"I'm not—" Jackie began to protest, but Marguerite cut her off.

"He cannot read you, Jackie," Marguerite said firmly. "And I can read his thoughts and feelings for you. You *are* his true life mate."

She shook her head slowly, unable or unwilling to accept this news. Jackie was attracted to Vincent . . . okay, his kiss had sent her up in flames. She also liked and respected the man, but to be a true life mate . . . One fated to be with an immortal . . . It was difficult to accept that.

On the other hand, it was also difficult for her to accept that she was one of them now. She would live hundreds of years, never age, never grow ill, never—

"Hey!" Jackie tilted her head, a frown on her face as she scowled at Marguerite. "Why am I not thin now?"

Marguerite blinked at the change in topic. "What?"

"I thought the nanos made us our perfect, peak condition and all that," she pointed out, then gestured to herself. "I'm still the same size I was before. Shouldn't I be thinner?"

Marguerite bit back a smile, then shook her head. "The nanos *do* see you are at your peak condition. So, if you haven't lost any weight, this size is your peak. It's the healthiest weight for you." She tilted her head. "And you look a perfect weight to me, dear. I'm afraid your belief in what is attractive has been colored by Hollywood's Twiggy-type figures. That isn't a natural weight for most women . . . Including you."

"You're thinner than me," Jackie pointed out.

"Actually, I'm not," Marguerite countered, and shrugged. "I'm afraid you just see yourself as larger than you are."

When Jackie began to shake her head at that possibility, Marguerite moved to sit at the table saying, "According to my daughter Lissianna, most women see themselves as bigger than they are. In one of the psychology courses she took at university, they did a study where they had people, both men and women, look at a chart of bodies in varying sizes and shapes. They were to circle the one they thought best represented themselves. According to the findings, women tended to circle a figure a size or two larger than they truly are, while men tend to circle a figure a size or two smaller than themselves. I'm afraid women have a very poor self image overall. I guess that includes you."

Jackie felt herself relax a bit as what Marguerite had said sank in. If the nanos insured you were at your peak condition and she was the same size she'd been before being turned, then she supposed that did mean that this was her peak condition. That explained why she could never lose those fifteen pounds despite her best efforts.

Sighing, Jackie shook her head. Here she was, suddenly an immortal, with Marguerite claiming Vincent was her true life mate, and what was she fretting over? Her weight. Gad. What was the matter with her?

"Marguerite," Jackie said quietly. "I'm not sure of much right at this moment, but—"

"I know," the older woman interrupted quietly. "And I don't

expect you to go rushing out and vow your undying love for Vincent right this minute. You need time to adjust. I realize that. But after watching my four children and their mates flounder around, I've come to the conclusion that perhaps it's better just to put the matter right out there for you to see. This way you can at least think about it while you come to accept what has happened to you."

Jackie breathed out slowly. "All right. I'll keep it in mind."

Marguerite nodded, apparently satisfied. "The good news is that you know more about us than any of my new daughter-in-laws or son-in-law knew when they were turned, so we won't need to explain that we aren't soulless demons or such."

"No. That isn't necessary," Jackie agreed wryly. She took a deep breath and asked, "What did they do with the saboteur?"

Marguerite was silent so long, Jackie knew the news wasn't good. Still, it came as something of a shock when she sighed and admitted, "He got away."

"Damn," Jackie breathed with disappointment and pondered what that might mean. Would the saboteur return to finish the job? It might not be a bad thing. She could be the bait. The saboteur might not realize she'd been turned. And she was one of them now, so she would be stronger, faster, and safe from being controlled. Or would she?

Jackie didn't know. She'd heard tales of Marguerite's marriage to Jean Claude Argeneau and had heard that he had been able to control her mind and read her thoughts. Perhaps she wasn't as safe as she hoped.

Frowning, Jackie bit her lip, then asked, "My being one of

you doesn't necessarily mean I'm safe from being controlled, does it?"

Marguerite took Jackie's hands in her own and patted them soothingly. "You can't be read and controlled as easily as you could as a human, but yes, until you become stronger and better able to control your thoughts and mind, you're very vulnerable. Even once you learn to use the new skills you'll have, you'll still be vulnerable to older immortals. The really old ones."

"Like you were with your husband," Jackie murmured with a frown and Marguerite stiffened. For a moment, her face was a picture of conflict, then she sat back with a sigh.

"Not quite as bad as that," she said quietly. "My husband liked being able to control me, so he did his best to keep me from meeting others of our kind that might teach me how to protect myself from his abilities. I won't let that happen with you. I'll teach you all I know, Jackie. What it took several hundred years for me to learn, you will know from the start."

"Thank you, Marguerite," Jackie murmured and squeezed her hand.

Marguerite squeezed back, then stood abruptly. "I'd best go let the men back in. The curiosity is probably killing them. Besides, they can help."

"Hold 'em, hold 'em, hold 'em," Dante chanted encouragingly, watching her open mouth closely as Tomasso continued to wave a glass of blood under her nose.

Jackie clenched her fingers, digging them into her palms with determination as she concentrated on fighting the automatic response her body had to the scent of blood. Her teeth wanted to slide out in search of the nourishment her nose could smell, but she forced them back, keeping them in place for what seemed an eternity as Dante and Tomasso shouted encouragement and Marcus watched his wrist watch.

The three men had spent all evening trying to train her to control her teeth. In the meantime, Vincent, Christian, and Marguerite were all helping Tiny with the case she was supposed to be working on. The other four had gone out to interview the people who had worked on the play in New York. Jackie had tried to insist that it was her place to be doing that, but had quickly had it pointed out that they couldn't risk her going out in public until she was able to control her teeth. It could be bad if her fangs decided to pop out while she was talking to one of the humans.

Recognizing the truth behind that, Jackie had given in. She knew Tiny could handle the job and she was sure the presence of the others wouldn't hurt things. She also recognized that they were right about her teeth showing.

"Five minutes!" Marcus announced suddenly, drawing Jackie from her thoughts. "You did it!"

"That-a-girl!" Dante cheered and scooped her from her chair to swing her around the kitchen.

Jackie squealed with surprise, then gasped as Dante passed her to Tomasso, who did the same thing.

"We need to celebrate," Dante announced and Jackie glanced over just in time to see him exchange a glance with his twin, then nod toward the door. She glanced back toward Tomasso and caught his wide, wicked grin just before he whirled toward the door leading out onto the back patio.

"No!" Jackie shrieked and began to struggle, but it was

too late; before she'd finished speaking the word, Dante had thrown the back door open. The siren went off even as Tomasso started through the door. Not that it stopped him. She couldn't hear his laughter over the alarm, but she felt his chest vibrating against her side as he carried her to the pool, then she was sailing through the air.

The water was cold as it closed around her, but it also had the added benefit of briefly muffling the alarms. Jackie let herself sink to the bottom, then pushed against the concrete floor of the pool, catapulting herself back to the surface. Dante, Tomasso, and Marcus stood at the water's edge, laughing.

Making a face at them, she shook her head and struck out for the ladder to get out of the pool. Dante and Tomasso immediately moved to the ladder, to offer her a hand out. Jackie climbed halfway out before reaching with both hands for the men's, then paused abruptly and glanced toward the house when the siren suddenly went silent. Her eyes widened as she spotted Vincent in the door staring out toward the pool, hands on hips and an annoyed expression on his face.

Jackie smiled faintly, then held onto the men's hands as she took another step up the ladder. She paused again then and threw herself backward, tugging on her hands as she did. Taken by surprise, both Dante and Tomasso flew forward, actually sailing over her and into the pool as she allowed herself to fall back into it. They landed in the water behind her.

Jackie surfaced and swiftly reached out for the ladder, then scrambled out as the men surfaced, sputtering and cursing behind her. Laughing at their outrage, she rushed past Marcus, toward the house. The man was so busy laughing at the twins, he wasn't prepared when she reached out and gave him a shove.

Jackie didn't look back, but heard him squawk one moment before he splashed into the water.

Beaming a wide smile now, she rushed to Vincent.

"I did it! I held my teeth in for five minutes," Jackie announced proudly as she skidded up to him.

"Way to go!" Tiny congratulated, drawing her attention into the kitchen where he stood with Marguerite and Christian.

Jackie smiled back briefly before her gaze slid back to Vincent. She frowned at his grim expression. "What's the matter?"

"I was unlocking the front door when the alarm suddenly went off," Vincent said quietly.

Jackie blinked, then said apologetically, "Oh. Yes. Well, Dante and Tomasso thought they should throw me in the pool to celebrate."

"I was afraid something had happened," he explained, then forced a smile. "I'm glad you're okay."

Jackie reached out and slid her hand into his, giving him a squeeze. He really looked quite pale. Obviously the alarm had distressed him.

"Five minutes?" Christian asked as Dante, Tomasso, and Marcus made their way to the house. Water was dripping from their clothes and pooling with every step they took.

Jackie watched them approach with amusement. She was soaking wet too, but while she was in a jogging suit, they were in leather and were now squelching with every step. All three men nodded at Christian's question, not one of them looking nearly as happy as they had after throwing *her* in the pool.

"Thanks for helping me learn to control my teeth, guys." Jackie smiled at them sweetly, then turned to make her way into the house, adding, "I'm off to dry off and change."

Jackie slipped past Christian and the others, then paused at the kitchen door and turned to peer at Tiny. "How did the interviews go?"

Tiny shrugged. "I think we eliminated some more people, but no one screamed guilt."

She nodded. "I shouldn't take long to change and then you can give me a proper rundown."

"I'll make coffee," Tiny announced and Jackie shook her head and smiled as she pushed out of the kitchen. The giant was forever making coffee and baked goods. It was like having her gran around, although then it would have been tea and baked goods.

Jackie was quick to change into dry jogging pants and a t-shirt and the first to return to the kitchen. The moment she arrived, Tiny handed her a cup of coffee, then the five of them settled around the kitchen table while Tiny gave her a rundown of how the interviews had gone. Christian, Marguerite, and Vincent added comments here and there, but Tiny did most of the talking.

Marcus joined them during the debriefing and took the last seat at the table. With no chairs left when the twins joined them, the pair leaned against the wall, arms crossed over their chests as they listened.

To be thorough, Jackie had wanted to include some of the humans in the interviews. Chances were that it was an immortal, but the humans might have seen something useful. However, no one else had agreed with her. The attacks on Stephano and herself pointed to an immortal, as did the onset of "contagious anemia" in the play's cast, so they'd insisted on interviewing only the immortals. They'd apparently changed their minds during the evening and interviewed a couple of mortals along the way. However, their main interest had been to feed Vincent at those stops under the guise of interviewing them and they'd done little in the way of real questioning.

Jackie thought they were wrong to neglect the humans, but, finding herself outvoted, had shrugged and let them do as they saw fit. She'd even hoped they were right and would come back with at least someone looking suspicious. However, that wasn't the case. Marguerite was seven hundred years old and Christian five hundred. Between the two of them, they'd been able to read the minds of the immortals while Tiny and Vincent had distracted them with questions. And still, they hadn't been able to remove half of the immortals from the list. The others had either had better control over their thoughts, or their thoughts had been such a jumble neither Marguerite nor Christian had been able to make sense of them.

"Well," Christian said once the debriefing was over, "if we're done here, the boys and I should get moving. Aunt Elaine and Uncle Roberto are expecting us for dinner."

"The boys mentioned that while you were gone," Jackie commented.

Christian was speaking of Elaine and Roberto Notte. Elaine was Stephano and Neil's mother. Roberto was Neil's father and Stephano's stepfather. The couple had flown to L.A. from Italy the moment they'd returned home from a business trip to hear the news of Stephano's injury and turning. Vincent had invited the couple to stay at his home, but they'd decided there really wasn't room for them all and had checked into a hotel, taking a suite so that Neil and Stephano could stay with them while Stephano completed and adjusted to the turning. Christian and the boys had decided to continue staying at the house.

Christian glanced from Jackie to Vincent and raised an eyebrow. "Now that the boys have taught you to keep your teeth in, maybe while we're gone, Vincent can teach you how to get them out."

"How to get them out?" Jackie asked with surprise. "They come out on their own. Or try to," she added, since she'd now learned to force them back and not extend.

"Only when you're extremely hungry or the scent of blood is around," Christian pointed out. "You want to be able to feed when you need to. You need to be able to bring your teeth out at will so that you can arrange your feeding around your life, rather than arranging your life around your feeding."

"For instance," he said, "you'll wake up hungry, just like mortals, and at those times, probably just the sight of bagged blood will be enough to bring your teeth on. But what if you have a stakeout or something to see to? You'll want to feed before you leave so you don't need to take blood with you. But what if you aren't hungry? At this point, your teeth won't just slide out when you wish them to. Will they?" he asked, then raised an eyebrow. "Try to bring them on for us."

Jackie hesitated, then ran her tongue along her teeth and concentrated on trying to bring them out. Nothing happened, and she frowned. "How do you—?"

"Eventually, you'll be able to bring them out and put them away at will," Marguerite assured her. "As with keeping them from coming out, making them come out is a learned task."

"Until then," Christian said, "there are three things that will bring on your teeth. The sight—or sometimes even just the thought—of blood when you're extremely hungry."

"Like with Tiny when I first came down after the change," Jackie muttered, casting him an embarrassed and apologetic glance.

Christian nodded. "Then there is the scent of blood which works even when you aren't hungry."

"And what's the third thing?" Jackie asked.

"Sex."

"Sex?" she echoed uncertainly.

Christian smiled, stood and rounded the table. Pausing at her side, he held out his hand.

Jackie hesitated, then took it and allowed him to draw her to her feet. Her gaze slid to Vincent as she did. He'd gone stiff, his expression flat as he watched with narrowed eyes. It seemed to her he knew what Christian was going to do and wasn't at all happy about it. Jackie didn't get the chance to analyze any more than that as Christian suddenly tugged her into his arms and kissed her.

Christian was a good kisser, all masterful technique and thrusting tongue. Unfortunately, Jackie was too aware of their audience to appreciate it much. She stood stiff and still in his arms, aware of Vincent's eyes drilling into the back of her head. She even thought she heard a growl from his direction, but then Christian broke the kiss and pulled back, frowning.

"Your teeth aren't coming out," he commented with a frown, and Jackie supposed he'd know. He'd just given her teeth a thorough examination a dentist would be proud of, though he'd done so with his tongue.

"Relax," Christian instructed, his voice soothing, then he kissed her again, this time toying with her lips briefly, nibbling before deepening the kiss. It was well done and Jackie was convinced he was the second best kisser she'd ever met. Unfortunately, Vincent was the best and was sitting just three feet away. She was positive that now constant low sound she was hearing was him growling. It was just too distracting to allow her to relax as Christian had instructed.

"This isn't working." Christian sounded bewildered as he again broke the kiss.

"Perhaps Vincent should try," Marguerite suggested mildly.

Vincent was on his feet and had whirled Jackie out of Christian's arms and into his own so fast, she gasped with shock as her body was suddenly plastered against his. Once again, Vincent proved that while he was pretty laid back about most things, kissing wasn't one of them.

He peered down at her for a moment, his eyes intense. Jackie didn't know what her expression was, probably simple bewilderment, but whatever he saw made him relax and his expression softened. Then, he lowered his head, allowing his lips to drift first over each eye, kissing them closed, then he kissed the tip of her nose lightly before pressing his lips to hers.

His mouth was soft at first, questing, then abruptly became firm as he slid his hand into her hair and tilted her head to the angle he wanted.

Jackie gasped and moaned as he urged her mouth open and plundered its moist depths. This time, she forgot all about having an audience, her mind and body focused on the excitement and want Vincent was engendering in her. Pressing closer into his embrace, she slid her arms around his neck, tugging at him just as demandingly as he was holding her. It wasn't until her own tongue caught on one of her fangs and she jerked in surprise that they were both recalled to the kitchen and the people watching them.

"Are you all right?" Vincent asked with concern as he broke the kiss. He'd obviously tasted the bit of blood drawn by nicking her own tongue.

Jackie was breathing heavily, but nodded.

"Well," Christian said dryly. "It seems Vincent would be the better one to teach this lesson."

Jackie glanced at the man and felt herself flush. She almost wanted to apologize for her teeth not coming out when he kissed her, but managed to keep from doing so.

"It's for the best anyway. We have to go see Elaine," Christian went on, glancing at Marcus and the twins. The three men immediately moved to leave the room and Christian followed, saying, "We'll be back as quickly as we can. Call me on my cell if there are any problems."

Vincent looked annoyed at the man's words, but didn't comment. Jackie knew the four men were staying at the house in the hopes of deterring any further attacks on anyone, or perhaps in the hopes that they were around to catch the saboteur if there were any future attacks. They were all keen to catch the saboteur.

Marguerite was the next person to move. Getting up from the table, she announced, "All the mind reading tonight has left me with a bit of a headache. I think I shall have a lie down and try to get rid of it."

"I'm ready for bed myself," Tiny announced, getting up as well.

Jackie glanced from one person to another with a touch of panic. She was suddenly shy of being alone with Vincent after what had just happened. Taking the coward's way out, she slipped out of Vincent's arms and moved for the door, saying, "I should go give the office a call and see if there's anything needing my attention."

She rushed out of the kitchen ahead of Marguerite and Tiny. It wasn't until Jackie had reached the office that she realized that had been about the stupidest excuse she could have used. It was midnight in California. Only 3 A.M. in New York. The office wouldn't be open yet.

"Coward," Jackie muttered to herself as she stopped at the desk and blew the hair out of her face with an upward blast of air from her lips. And she knew it was true, but dear God she'd been all set to climb Vincent like a dog in heat when her fangs had made their appearance and ruined everything. She'd completely forgotten their audience. And now she found herself embarrassed by her own behavior.

Leaning against the desk, Jackie peered with disinterest at the papers and messages on the wide surface and wondered if Marguerite had mentioned her theory of their being life mates to Vincent. And if so, what did he think of that, she wondered.

The sound of the office door opening interrupted her thoughts and Jackie turned to find Vincent standing in the doorway, a bag of blood in hand.

Fifteen

"I thought you might be hungry," Vincent said as he closed the door.

"I am," Jackie admitted. The boys had said she needed to be able to control her teeth while hungry, that it was the true test of her control and so she hadn't fed all evening. She was now famished, though she'd been so distracted, Jackie hadn't realized it until she turned and saw the bag of blood in Vincent's hand.

"Are you hungry enough that just the sight of it will bring on your teeth? Or do you need some help?" he asked, stopping before her.

Jackie ran her tongue over her teeth. Her fangs had receded during her embarrassment after the kiss, and—despite her hunger—didn't appear to be thrusting themselves out now at the sight of blood. She blushed as she realized she'd need help.

"I'm sorry," she began with embarrassment. "But I think I need help."

A slow smile curved Vincent's lips as he set the bag of blood on the desk, then he slid his arms around her. "Trust me, there is *nothing* to apologize for. Surely, you can tell that I'm quite happy to help with this?"

Jackie blinked as he pressed his lower body against her and she felt the proof of his being happy to help. She obviously wasn't the only one affected by their kisses. However, while her teeth had slid away in the embarrassment that had followed, it seemed his erection hadn't. That knowledge made excitement pool between her legs and she felt the pressure and shifting along her upper jaw. Without even thinking about it, Jackie used the skill she'd just mastered and forced the teeth back. It was a subconscious action, but one her body wholly approved of if it meant she would enjoy more of his kisses.

"More than happy to help," Vincent said softly as his mouth lowered to hers.

There were no tentative kisses to eyes and nose this time, no slow workup to a proper kiss. Vincent claimed her like a victor claiming spoils, his kiss aggressive and hungry. Jackie moaned and found herself arching against him, her arms around his shoulders and hands burying themselves in his hair as she opened to him and did a little demanding of her own.

Until meeting Vincent, no one had been able to compete with Cassius when it came to exciting her. While she knew it had all been mind control and that he'd placed that excitement inside her, still it had felt like true passion and Jackie had decided long ago that real passion would never be able to compete. Yet, Vincent could, and did, and won hands down and she knew he wasn't placing those thoughts or feelings in her head. Her body simply went up in flames at his touch, sending warm juices to her nether regions as if to try to douse the fire, but that simply made it worse.

Jackie was pressing against him, trying to get as close as she could. Every inch of her body ached to feel his against it, but their clothes were in the way. Fortunately, Vincent appeared to feel the same way, for he began to tug at her clothes. Jackie murmured encouragement against his mouth and trembled in his arms as he pushed her t-shirt upward. His fingers spread over the flesh of her stomach, then curved over her breasts through the silk of her bra. It wasn't enough though and she briefly broke their kiss to help him remove the t-shirt altogether.

The moment it was off and flying into a corner of the office, Vincent covered her mouth with his again as he began to work on her bra. Much to her relief, it was gone in seconds. Jackie shuddered and gasped as his warm palms closed over her aching, erect nipples.

She murmured into his mouth, then knotted her hands in his hair, her kisses becoming desperate as he fondled and kneaded her breasts. Within moments, she was breathless and panting, desire shooting through her like lightning. Growing unbearably excited, she let go of his hair and dropped her hands between them to begin working on the buttons of his shirt.

Jackie wanted his naked flesh against her own, she wanted to feel all of him. When she ran into trouble with the buttons,

Vincent left off caressing her to help her, then the shirt was undone and she was able to push it off his shoulders.

"God, Jackie," Vincent gasped against her mouth as they came together again, the scattering of hair on his chest brushing her erect nipples. He kissed her once, hard, then pulled back to work at the knot of the drawstring of her jogging pants, muttering, "You remember how I said that sex was one of the other things I'd grown bored of over the centuries?"

"Uh-huh." Jackie began to work on his belt.

"Well, I'm not finding it boring anymore," Vincent informed her grimly as he finally managed the knot and began to push her joggers down.

"Thank God for that," Jackie breathed.

Vincent got the joggers to her knees, then apparently grew impatient with the task and grabbed her by the waist to set her on the desk. Her bottom had barely settled on the desktop, when he whipped the joggers the rest of the way off and stepped between her legs to kiss her again.

Jackie sighed into his mouth, then bit aggressively at his lower lip as her body plastered itself against his and his hardness pressed against her through his jeans. Her teeth were well out now, but both of them ignored that until Jackie—not used to having fangs—nicked herself again and the tang of blood entered the kiss.

Vincent immediately paused and Jackie almost groaned aloud with disappointment. She didn't want to stop what they were doing. Apparently, neither did Vincent, for he merely reached around to grab the bag of blood, and popped it on her teeth.

"Hold the bag," Vincent instructed and Jackie reached up

to take over holding the bag to her teeth. The moment she did, he scooped her up off the desk and carried her to the couch. By the time he'd set her down on the sofa, the bag was empty. Vincent took it away and tossed it on the table beside the couch as he knelt between her legs.

Jackie's eyes widened incredulously as he caught her under the knees. He used his hold to tug her forward to the edge of the couch, spreading her legs wide as he did, then he began to trail kisses up one thigh. This was so like the erotic dream she'd had in this room the other day, Jackie could hardly believe it. Then she forgot all about the dream and focused firmly on the here and now as Vincent reached the center of her and set to work driving her crazy.

Aware that they weren't alone in the house, Jackie tried to control herself and keep from making too much noise, but in the end, had to grab for one of the throw pillows on the couch. She pressed it against her own mouth to muffle her cries of pleasure as Vincent proved once and for all that true passion really could beat out the false pleasure Cassius had planted in her mind all those years ago. Jackie was writhing and sobbing, gasping and straining, and then she was screaming into the pillow as her body bucked with orgasm.

She was as weak and limp as a damp cloth by the time Vincent rose up between her legs. And while she'd only managed to half undo his pants earlier, they were fully undone and pushed down now. Vincent slid right into her.

For one moment, Jackie felt sure he couldn't raise any interest in her for the main course after such a sating appetizer, but she was wrong. It took only two strokes for her body to revive and regain interest, and then she caught Vincent by the shoulders and held on for dear life as he took her to the peak of pleasure again. This time, he came with her, and they both cried out as one, neither of them thinking to silence the sounds. They then collapsed against the back of the couch.

"Dear God," Vincent breathed after a moment.

"Mmmm," Jackie moaned. Every muscle in her body was trembling and she couldn't seem to find the energy to murmur more than that as agreement.

Vincent started to straighten and Jackie—still wrapped around him like a limpet—went with him. It made him chuckle softly into her hair and he kissed her cheek before lifting and shifting them both so they lay lengthwise on the couch with Jackie half beside and half on top of him. Vincent then reached out to catch the throw off the back of the couch and pull it over them both.

Jackie cuddled against him, her head nestling on his shoulder and a smile curving her lips as she dropped off to sleep in his arms.

She didn't sleep long. Jackie opened her eyes a little while later and found herself staring at Vincent's chest spread out before her eyes. She lay still for several minutes, then found her gaze dropping down over his body, a body that had given her great pleasure earlier. Vincent was an amazing lover, passionate and giving, all a woman could want. The idea of spending eternity—or as close to eternity as immortals got—with him wasn't an unattractive one.

He was charming, handsome, and incredibly sexy. He was also intelligent and amusing and just plain interesting. But he was very different from her in many ways. Jackie tended to take everything terribly seriously, while he appeared to take things much more lightly. And yet she couldn't help thinking it might be a good thing. Perhaps they could balance each other out. Perhaps they would make an excellent team. He could help her enjoy life more and she . . . well, Jackie didn't want to say she could make him enjoy it less, but she could help him see where he needed to be more cautious and more security conscious.

That sounded so dull, Jackie realized unhappily. Her gaze slid over what she could see of his body from where she lay with her head on his chest. The man had given her great pleasure. If nothing else, she wanted to give him back some of that pleasure.

Holding her breath, Jackie eased off the couch, grateful he'd positioned her on the outside, then she shifted to her knees and peered at the length of him. He was long and lean and beautiful to look on. The man had a gorgeous body. Perfection. She could just eat him up, but where to start?

Smiling faintly at her own thoughts, she leaned forward and began to press kisses down his chest and along his stomach. Jackie's smile widened when his stomach muscles rippled under her caress and he murmured sleepily and shifted his legs restlessly. He didn't wake up until her lips reached his hip, then she heard him murmur her name with confusion.

Jackie turned to glance up toward his face and found his head up as he peered down at her.

"What are you—?"

The question died on a groan as she took him into her mouth. Vincent was only half-hard when she did it, but was already growing larger as her lips closed around him. His hips jerked at the intimate caress and a growling hiss slid from his lips, then his hand caught in her hair and he tried to urge her away. Jackie ignored him and continued to move her mouth over his erection, her hands sweeping over his stomach and thighs as she did.

"Oh God," Vincent muttered and she could tell it was through clenched teeth.

Jackie glanced down toward his feet and almost smiled at the sight of his curled toes. That had to be a good sign. She'd barely finished the thought when Vincent suddenly gave up tugging gently at her hair. She thought he was going to let her work undistracted, but instead he rose up on the couch, caught her by the upper arms and dragged her on top of him as he fell back.

"But I wasn't done—" Jackie began to protest, only to be silenced by Vincent dragging her mouth down to his. He held her head in place with one hand, but the other was roaming over her body, smoothing down her back, clasping her buttocks and squeezing briefly before he allowed his hand to drop between her legs and began to caress her. He trailed his fingers over her sensitive flesh as he thrust his tongue into her mouth and Jackie groaned in response, her legs instinctively trying to close around his hand.

Vincent was having none of that, however. Retrieving his hand, he used it to pull her leg to the side until it slid off of him and rested on the couch. He used his other hand to pull her leg over on the other side as well, so that Jackie was straddling him. Vincent then caught her head with one hand to keep her from lifting up, while he slid the other hand between them and began to caress her again.

Jackie groaned into his mouth as his fingers trailed over

her warm, trembling flesh, then bucked into the caress when he parted her damp flesh and slid one finger inside. This wasn't what she'd intended, she'd meant to give him pleasure, but he wasn't cooperating. Reaching between them herself, she took Vincent in hand and began to guide him toward her, but Vincent stopped her again. Moving abruptly, he suddenly shifted, sitting upright and forcing her with him.

Jackie gave up what she'd been trying to do and grabbed at his shoulders to keep from tumbling off as Vincent suddenly stood.

"What?" she asked with bewilderment, her legs instinctively wrapping around his waist. Vincent silenced her again with a kiss as he crossed the room. With one hand under her bottom to hold her up, he opened the door to the office with his other, then carried her out into the hall to the stairs, kissing her the whole way.

It wasn't until they were halfway up that Jackie recalled they weren't alone in the house. At that point, it was too late to worry about it, but she squeezed her eyes closed and prayed that Christian and the boys didn't come home suddenly at this point, or that Marguerite or Tiny didn't come out of their rooms. She was relieved when they made it to Vincent's room undiscovered. He opened the door, stepped inside and pushed it closed with one foot, which left them in complete darkness. It didn't seem to cause Vincent problems, however; he crossed the room in the dark without stumbling into or over anything, then laid her down on the bed and came down on top of her.

"Mmm," Jackie sighed and arched as his mouth closed over one nipple and suckled gently. She then groaned as he began to roll the other nipple between thumb and forefinger. Sliding her hands into his hair, she writhed beneath him in rhythm with his suckling, then spread her legs and raised her knees so that she could push down with her heels, lifting her hips to rub against him.

Vincent immediately groaned, the sound vibrating over her nipple as he pushed back.

"I want you inside me," she whispered. "Please, Vincent. I want you inside me."

Raising up, Vincent silenced her plea with a kiss. He caught her hands in his own and held them on either side of her head as he drove into her.

Jackie cried out into his mouth, wrapped her legs around him, her heels urging him on as he took them to the heights of pleasure again.

Jackie was starving when she woke up. She supposed it shouldn't really be a surprise. Even as a mortal she'd woken up hungry in the mornings and Marguerite had warned her that she would need quite a bit of blood at first, while her body continued to change. It seemed turning wasn't a quick thing and while she now had teeth, everything that was going to change, hadn't yet. According to Marguerite, her night vision would increase over the next while, along with her hearing, physical strength, speed, and many other things.

Wiping the sleep from her eyes, Jackie glanced around. She was still in Vincent's room, in Vincent's bed. They'd both fallen asleep again after he'd carried her up to his room and made love to her a second time. She'd awoken a little later to find him kissing and caressing her. Vincent had made love to her several more times during the last hours of night and well into the morning, until they'd both collapsed in exhaustion.

Her gaze slid to the digital clock on the bedside table and she grimaced. It was after three in the afternoon. Not very late considering what time they'd fallen asleep, but extremely late when compared to the hours she used to keep. Her conscience hadn't caught up to the change in the situation and she felt guilty for sleeping so late. She supposed she'd adjust with time.

Jackie glanced to the man asleep beside her. Vincent had turned the bathroom light at one point last night and left the door cracked open so that it wouldn't be pitch black in the room. She was grateful. The light was enough that she could see his face. He was still asleep and she smiled at how adorable he looked. Vincent's hair was tousled, his chiseled features softened in slumber and his usual smile missing, replaced by a peaceful, but neutral expression.

Jackie found herself reaching out and running a finger lightly down one cheek, wanting to touch him, but not wanting to wake him. He'd had a long night and deserved his rest. Vincent had proven to her last night, repeatedly, that he hadn't been bragging when he'd said he used to be good at sex. If anything, he'd understated his prowess. Vincent was an *amazing* lover. Incredible. Mind blowing. And he was all hers . . . Maybe.

Biting her lip, Jackie pulled her hand back and peered up at the ceiling. They hadn't spoken about much of anything last night, not their status or whether he agreed with Marguerite that they were true life mates now. She had no idea if he accepted, or even wanted her as his life mate. Come to that, Jackie wasn't sure she was ready to accept him as a true life mate either, though last night had urged her a step closer. She hadn't experienced such passion in all her thirty years, but this seemed all to be happening so quickly to her and she feared making a mistake.

A cramp stabbed through her stomach, distracting Jackie from her thoughts and urging her to get up and feed. Moving carefully, she slipped from the bed, then paused, recalling that her clothes were still down in the office where Vincent had helped her remove them.

Pursing her lips, she peered around the dim room and spotted a robe over a chair next to the bed. Jackie picked it up and slid into it, smiling as she was enveloped in Vincent's scent. She found herself repeatedly lifting the lapel and pressing her nose into the soft cotton and inhaling as she left the room and made her way downstairs.

It being mid-afternoon, Jackie expected to find Tiny in the kitchen, but the room was empty. Wondering where he was, she moved to the refrigerator and retrieved a bag of blood, then stared at it blankly as she realized she had a small problem.

Despite Christian's claim that just seeing the blood on awaking might be enough to bring on her teeth, such was not the case. It would appear being close to Tiny the first morning she'd awoken had been enough to raise them because of the blood loss and the change. This afternoon, her hunger wasn't enough to bring them on. She stood for several minutes, staring at the bag of blood in her hand and trying to figure out what to do.

Jackie briefly considered slicing open a bag to bring her teeth on, but didn't think she could stomach actually drinking the liquid out of a glass. It was one thing letting her teeth draw it straight up into her body, but gulping it down like orange juice held absolutely no appeal. In fact, the very idea made her feel nauseous, which meant if she punctured it to get the scent of blood to bring on her teeth, she would be wasting a whole bag of blood, because she wouldn't be able to pop the open bag onto her teeth. All that would accomplish would be to make one hell of a mess, she was sure.

Grimacing, Jackie shifted briefly from one foot to the other, then walked to the knife drawer with a sigh. There seemed little choice but to give the end of her finger a jab as Dante had done to his own finger the first day. That little pearl of blood had been enough to draw her teeth out and should work now. She hoped.

Jackie chose a little paring knife from the selection in the drawer, then pushed it closed with her hip and set the bag of blood on the counter. She then held up her left hand and mentally prepared to jab herself . . . and prepared some more . . . and some more.

"Geez," she muttered. "It's just a little jab. You can do it."

"But why bother when you don't have to?"

Jackie jumped in surprise as Vincent suddenly slid his arms around her from behind. She'd been concentrating so hard on trying to convince herself to accomplish the task, she hadn't heard him enter the kitchen.

"Hi," she sighed as his hands eased their way into her robe.

"Good morning," Vincent murmured. Using his chin to

brush the hair away from her neck, he placed a kiss there. "You don't have to cut yourself. I'll help you bring on your teeth."

"Yeah?" Jackie asked, leaning back into him and allowing her eyes to close as his lips trailed over her neck, and his fingers caressed her breasts.

"Yeah," Vincent let one hand slide away from her breasts and Jackie shuddered as it drifted down across her belly, then moaned and pressed her behind back against him as his hand continued downward. When it slid between her legs, she gasped and tipped her head further back, her body arching. Jackie was sufficiently distracted that she didn't feel her teeth slide out. In fact, she wasn't aware they had until Vincent took his other hand from her breast, grabbed up the bag of blood from the counter and popped it on her teeth for her.

Startled, Jackie almost closed her mouth on the bag in surprise, but then caught herself, and raised her hands to take over holding the bag. The moment she did, Vincent turned her to face him and tugged her robe closed, then tied the belt tightly for her as well. When Jackie raised her eyebrows in surprise, a wry smile crossed his lips and he nodded toward the door. "We have company coming."

The bag still on her teeth, Jackie turned toward the door just as it opened and Tiny walked in.

"Oh, hey. Hello," the giant greeted them with a smile and Jackie found herself smiling around the half-empty bag in her mouth.

"Morning, Tiny," Vincent said for both of them, then turned and gestured toward the almost full coffeepot. "Is the coffee fresh?"

"Yep. I was just coming to see if it was done," he admitted, then glanced to Jackie to add, "I was just on the phone with New York. I thought I'd call and check things out for you. Everything's fine there."

" 'ood, 'anks," Jackie said around the almost-empty bag. It was very difficult to pronounce consonants with a bag in your mouth. Shifting to the side to get out of the way as Tiny joined them at the counter, she watched Vincent fetch cups and set them down for Tiny to pour coffee into. They then each fixed their own coffee, Jackie working one-handed until the blood was done and she could take the bag away and toss it. She did so, then stirred her coffee and carried it to the table. They sat in silence for a moment, just enjoying their coffees, then began to discuss Vincent's saboteur. They were still doing so when Christian entered the kitchen and joined them.

Unlike Vincent, Christian didn't bother with human food or beverages . . . ever. Ignoring the coffeepot, he retrieved a couple of bags of blood from the refrigerator and slapped one on his teeth. Once it was gone, he replaced it with the fresh bag, then tossed both empty bags in the garbage and moved to join them at the table.

"So, today you'll be working on bringing on your teeth," he commented, then glanced toward Tiny before adding, "You should also learn to slip into the thoughts of mortals and control them. You need to be able to do both to feed on one."

"But feeding on mortals is forbidden," Jackie said with confusion. "Only people with medical conditions like Vincent are allowed to feed on living donors."

"And any immortal who finds themselves in an emergency," Christian corrected. "You have to learn how, in case you find yourself in an emergency where your life is threatened if you don't feed."

"I'd rather die than feed off of—" Jackie began.

"You may think that now," Christian said, "but once your life was threatened it would be another story. Besides, it isn't just for our individual good that we have to survive."

Jackie frowned. "What do you mean?"

"Say you were in a car accident," Christian suggested. "You weren't decapitated or anything else that was life threatening, but were injured enough that you've lost a lot of blood and are weak, too weak to get yourself away from the scene without feeding. The driver of the other vehicle is alive and well and uninjured."

Jackie frowned with displeasure, already knowing where he was going with this.

"If you don't feed off the other driver, you will be there when the police and ambulance arrive. The ambulance would pack you up and take you to the hospital and they would take all sorts of tests, and so on that would make you a threat to the rest of us. A threat that could have been easily avoided if you'd just fed off the other driver."

Jackie sighed in defeat, knowing it was true.

"So," Christian continued, "you can practice on Tiny and—"

"Oh, no," Jackie interrupted firmly. "Fine, I see the need to learn how to read thoughts and control people, and I'll even acknowledge that there might come a time when I need to bite a mortal, but I'm not using Tiny that way."

"It's okay, Jackie," Tiny said soothingly. "I don't mind."

"Well, I do," she said grimly. "We've been friends for too

long for me to intrude on your thoughts like that, or use you as a pin cushion."

"Then who would you like to practice on?" Christian asked dryly. "Tiny is the only mortal around. Besides, at least he's given permission for you to read his mind, so you wouldn't be intruding on some unsuspecting person's thoughts."

Jackie frowned at his argument. It was one of the things she disliked most about immortals, when they rudely tried to read someone else's thoughts. But Tiny was giving permission. If she practiced on anyone else, it would probably be without permission.

Sighing unhappily, she gave a brief nod. "Fine, I'll practice reading thoughts and controlling minds and bringing my teeth out, but I'll do it on my own time. Right now we have a saboteur to catch."

"Actually, right now you have a funeral to get ready for," Vincent said. When Jackie turned a blank face his way, he reminded her, "Stephano's fake funeral. You thought it would be a good idea to hold one."

"Oh, yes," Jackie murmured. They had started the preparations with a view to keeping the fact that Stephano had survived a secret until he could wake up and tell them who had attacked him. However, when he'd awoken and not been able to do so, she'd decided it might be good to go through with a fake funeral. She was hoping the saboteur would show up at the funeral and somehow give himself away . . . Or make another attempt on her. It was also necessary to continue to keep him safe. She didn't mind herself being bait, but wouldn't put Stephano in that position.

"Come." Vincent stood and caught her hand to pull her to her feet. "The funeral is at six P.M. We still have a couple hours. You can try my sunken tub. I'll scrub your back."

Jackie smiled despite the blush that colored her cheeks at the offer and allowed him to urge her to the door.

"I folded your clothes and set them on your bed," Tiny announced as they started through the door and Jackie groaned inwardly as the door closed behind them. She'd forgotten about her clothes left scattered around the office. And he'd seen she wasn't in her own bed when he'd taken the clothes up to her room.

"Tiny knows," she whispered with embarrassment.

"Everyone knows. We weren't exactly quiet last night and this morning," Vincent murmured gently, sliding an arm around her as they walked to the stairs. "Do you mind?"

Jackie met his concerned gaze, then shook her head. She was a bit embarrassed, but other than that didn't mind if everyone knew what they were doing. She just wished she knew what they were doing.

Sixteen

"Neil must have closed down the office so everyone could attend," Jackie said as she peered around the crowded interior of the funeral home.

"He did," Vincent acknowledged. "He wanted to be sure the saboteur could attend. He's as hopeful as us that the man will show up and somehow give himself away."

Jackie nodded, but thought the problem now would be that—even if the saboteur came and did do something telling—there were so many people in attendance they might miss it.

"Actually, Neil is *more* hopeful than us," Christian commented. "Stephano's making him crazy. He's feeling fine now and is getting irritable about being stuck in that hotel."

"Irritable isn't the word," Neil commented dryly, making his presence known as he joined them in the corner where they'd taken up position to watch the room. "My brother is as grumpy as hell. He wants to get back to work."

"That's understandable," Vincent commented.

Neil just arched one eyebrow and added, "He also wants pictures."

Jackie blinked. "Pictures?"

"Hmmm." He pursed his lips and grimaced. "He wants to see who attends, and who's upset, and if the funeral is *nice.*"

As the others fought to keep their solemn expressions at this news—one didn't laugh at funerals—Jackie bit her lip and said, "Well, as it happens, Tiny is taking pictures. Stephano can have copies."

Everyone glanced at Tiny then, no doubt in search of a camera.

"Haven't you noticed he's wearing glasses?" she asked with amusement. "They aren't to see through. Tiny has perfect vision. The camera is in the nose piece."

The men were all obviously impressed.

"That's cool," Dante said with surprise.

"I want a pair," Tommaso decided.

Tiny merely smiled. He loved his spy camera.

Boys and their toys, Jackie thought, exchanging an amused glance with Marguerite. Shaking her head, she peered around the room again, her gaze falling on Elaine and Roberto Notte. It was the first time she'd actually seen the couple. Jackie had been in the midst of the change when they'd arrived at Vincent's house.

Her gaze slid over Elaine Notte. She was slender with short blond hair and—guessing by how she measured up to the men standing around her—wasn't much taller than Jackie herself. Roberto Notte was only a couple of inches taller than his wife, with a stout build. Not fat. Immortals simply didn't get fat, but he had the wide, thick body of a laborer. Of course, neither of them looked old enough to have adult children.

"I suppose we should offer our condolences," Marguerite commented.

Jackie nodded. "It would seem odd if we didn't."

"Come," Neil said. "I'll introduce you."

Vincent took her arm and followed as Neil led them across the room. Tiny immediately took Marguerite's arm to escort her, leaving the rest of the men to trail behind. Two people Jackie recognized from V.A. Productions were offering their condolences when they reached the couple. The two men now nodded respectfully to Neil and Vincent, then moved on to view the closed casket. Jackie had no idea how the men had explained the reason for the closed casket, but there had been no other choice. They could hardly expect Stephano to lay silent and still in the coffin for hours while people walked past viewing him.

"Mother, Father, this is Vincent Argeneau, his personal assistant, Jackie Morrisey, his aunt, Marguerite Argeneau, and Tiny McGraw."

"Vincent." Elaine Notte's eyes widened, then glazed over with tears as she clasped his hands. Her voice trembled with emotion as she said, "Thank you for my son's life. You—"

"Mother," Neil said in warning tones, reminding her of the situation, and that Stephano was not supposed to be alive.

Jackie hardly noticed. Her gaze was moving around the

group with surprise. While she'd been unconscious when the couple had come to Vincent's home, he hadn't been, and she'd thought he'd met Stephano's parents.

"Vincent didn't leave your side during the turn," Marguerite whispered by her ear, apparently reading her confusion. "This is the first time he's met them too."

Jackie nodded her understanding, and then forced a smile as Neil's parents turned their attention to greeting her and the others.

"Miss Morrisey," Roberto said with heavily accented English. His Italian ancestry was very obvious. "It's a pleasure to meet you. You will find the man who did this, yes?"

"I'll do my best," Jackie murmured, thinking that the entire cover story was blown all to hell if anyone was near enough to hear.

Vincent murmured something then, a few polite words she missed altogether, then she found herself being urged away.

"I don't think anyone heard," Vincent assured her as he led her across the room.

Jackie nodded, but her thoughts were on the promise she'd just made to Neil's father. She would do her best to catch the saboteur, but didn't seem to have gotten very far yet and it bothered her. Had she been so distracted by her attraction to Vincent that she hadn't been doing all she could to track down the saboteur? Jackie had no clues, no ideas. Usually, when they took on a case there was some sort of trail to follow, or they had some idea of what the motive was, but with this case, she felt as if she was stumbling around blind. Vincent had no idea of anyone who might wish to cause him such grief, and the only trail the saboteur was leaving was becoming a bloody one.

As if reading her thoughts, Vincent squeezed her arm and said firmly, "You're doing everything you can. I know that."

But it wasn't enough, Jackie thought and was grateful for the distraction when Neil and the others rejoined them. She listened absently as the men spoke for a bit, but her gaze was moving around the room, gliding over face after face, searching every expression for something that might stand out. Unfortunately, no one had *killer* or *saboteur* written across their forehead.

Sighing inwardly, Jackie let her gaze drift back to Neil's parents. As if sensing her gaze, Elaine Notte suddenly looked her way. The woman smiled faintly, then her face was blocked by the back of a man's head as someone else stepped up to offer their condolences.

Jackie was about to continue examining the other people in attendance when the man turned his head to speak to Roberto Notte and she caught a glimpse of his profile. Jackie immediately sucked in one quick gasping breath of shock, then shook her head. No. It couldn't be.

"Jackie?" Tiny asked under his breath and she was vaguely aware of his stepping closer to her, but didn't respond. Her attention was wholly focused on the man across the room, waiting for a better look at his face. She seemed to wait forever, then the man turned to glance around the room and she felt a shock of horror slide through her.

"Cassius." The name came out on a shocked expulsion, but Tiny, Vincent, and the others heard it and turned, their eyes all locking on her.

"Cassius?" Tiny echoed on a rumble of displeasure. "Here?"

"Where?" Vincent asked sharply.

Jackie blinked in surprise at the harshness to his voice and peered at him with confusion. She hadn't told him about Cassius, yet his expression was tight and he'd immediately moved closer to her in a protective manner.

Vincent saw the question on her face and hesitated, then sighed and admitted, "I know about him. I read Tiny's mind."

Jackie stilled, anger welling up in her at this news. Before she could respond, Tiny squeezed her arm.

"Don't be angry with him," he rumbled. "I let him read me. I thought he should know about it."

Jackie turned her furious glance toward her partner, her anger immediately transferring to him.

"And I read Vincent," Christian announced, drawing her fire away from Tiny. He added, "Without his permission."

"So did I," Marcus announced.

Jackie was scowling at the two men when Dante said, "We didn't read anyone."

When she glanced at the twins, Tomasso added, "But we overheard the conversation in the kitchen while we were guarding the door and know he hurt you somehow and made you fear immortals."

Jackie's shoulders drooped and she let out a small sigh. It seemed everyone knew, or at least knew Cassius had done something, if not what. Except Neil, she realized as he spoke.

"Is there a problem?" the vice president asked with a frown. "Cassius works for Vincent."

"He what?" Vincent looked shocked at this news, but Jackie was frowning over the information. Vincent had taken her from office to office in search of information on who had worked on the play in New York. She'd thought she'd met everyone.

"We consult him over contract issues on occasion," Neil explained. "He actually works in the legal department of V.A. Incorporated, not the production company itself."

"Not for much longer," Vincent said grimly.

Jackie squeezed his hand. "You can't fire him for something he did years ago."

"The hell I can't. I can fire whomever I want," he said arrogantly. "They're my companies."

"Yes, but we have labor laws," she pointed out. "Besides, why bother?"

"He hurt you," Vincent said simply. "And mortals have labor laws. Immortals don't. I don't want someone of his kind working for me."

"Mr. Notte?"

Jackie glanced around, recognizing the voice of Vincent's secretary, Sharon. She couldn't see her, however, the men were in the way.

"I just wanted to tell you how sorry I am about Stephano. He—oh, Vincent." Sharon blinked at her boss as Neil shifted and Vincent's presence was revealed, then her gaze slid to Jackie and surprise crossed her face. "Jackie."

The woman was obviously startled to see her there. She wasn't the only one. Lily stood beside her, looking just as stunned at her presence.

"Is there something wrong, Sharon?" Jackie asked calmly.

When the secretary simply stared at her wide-eyed, Lily forced a smile to her face and said delicately, "She's just surprised. We didn't think you knew Stephano Notte."

Jackie was silent, considering the two of them. She suspected it was more than that. After all, the last time they'd seen her she was a mortal. One look at her eyes now and they should both be able to tell she'd been turned.

"No," Jackie said finally. "I never had the pleasure of meeting Stephano while he was alive. I'm just here out of respect for Neil and his family."

"Yes, of course," Lily murmured, then glanced toward Sharon as the secretary returned to offering her condolences to the vice president of V.A. Productions.

Once the attention was off her, Jackie glanced back toward Elaine and Roberto Notte. Cassius had moved on and Max Kunstler was now there, speaking solemnly to the couple. Jackie started to peer around in search of Cassius, then sucked in a breath as she saw he was moving in their direction, his eyes fixed on Neil. She had no doubt he was coming to offer his condolences and suddenly wished she was anywhere but there.

Jackie felt Vincent step closer, his arm sliding around her waist. At the same moment, Tiny moved nearer on her other side, then the rest of the men crowded closer as well, puffing up like protective roosters. It seemed they'd been paying attention to what Cassius was doing too. The entire group was suddenly stiff and tense.

You aren't nineteen anymore. The words floated through her mind and Jackie turned her gaze to Marguerite. The woman stood a little to the side, watching the men with

303

amusement. As her gaze shifted to Jackie, Marguerite's expression became solemn and she nodded meaningfully. *And now you're immortal too.*

Straightening her shoulders, Jackie turned back as Cassius paused at Neil's side. She peered at him curiously, noting that he wasn't nearly as attractive as he'd always been in her memory. His hair was blond as she recalled, but when she'd met him at nineteen it had seemed to shine like spun gold and she'd ached to touch it. Now, it just looked dirty blond to her. As for the body of Adonis she'd always recalled him having, he was slender and wiry, and not especially tall. Five foot ten was her guess. Every man around her had at least four to six inches on him.

Jackie turned her attention to his face, inspecting him closely. His lips were a bit thin, his nose straight, his eyes neither large, nor small. He was just average in looks. Only the color of his eyes was not average, at least compared to mortal eyes. His were a shining bronze brown, incredible next to normal, mortal eyes, but not nearly as beautiful as Vincent's silver-blue eyes, or as interesting as the silver-flecked black eyes of the Nottes.

Jackie shook her head with confusion. There was absolutely nothing noteworthy about Cassius. Either her tastes had been vastly different at nineteen, or the man had controlled her from the moment she'd opened the door to him that day a little more than ten years ago. Jackie suspected the latter was the case. Cassius had come to their home intending to seduce her and shame her father. He'd made himself appear beautiful in her mind to do it.

She hadn't had a chance, Jackie realized. For years she'd

felt guilty, thinking that if she hadn't followed her attraction for Cassius and rebelled enough to go on that first date with him, he'd never have been able to get control of her as he had. But she no longer believed that was the case. He'd made her think he was attractive. Perhaps he had even instilled that rebelliousness in her to go against her father's wishes and sneak out to meet him. Cassius had set out to control her from the start. He'd probably even arrived when he knew her father wasn't home just so that he could do so.

Finished with his duty, Cassius glanced expectantly around the group, obviously awaiting introductions. Jackie stiffened as his gaze slid from Sharon, to Lily, to Vincent, then her, but his eyes continued on to Tiny without stopping. His expression was polite and enquiring. He hadn't recognized her.

Neil started his introduction with Christian, Marcus, Dante, and Tomasso. The four Italians stared at Cassius with cold eyes, none of them accepting the hand he offered in greeting. Neil raised a curious eyebrow at their rudeness, then introduced Vincent. "And this is Vincent Argeneau. The V.A. in V.A. Incorporated and V.A. Productions."

Cassius's attitude immediately became annoyingly obsequious. The fact that he behaved so with Vincent and not Neil, said he considered himself an equal to the vice president of V.A. Productions. But then, Jackie supposed, he wouldn't feel threatened by Neil, or as if it was not worth much effort to impress him. Neil was the vice president of V.A. Productions, not V.A. Incorporated, where he worked. Vincent, on the other hand, was the owner of both, and Cassius was suddenly basically brown-nosing, telling him how pleased he was to meet him and how much he admired him.

Vincent stared at the man with open dislike and—as with Christian and the others—didn't accept the hand he was holding out in greeting. Instead, he took over the introductions then, introducing first Tiny, who reacted exactly as Christian and the others had, peering down his nose at the shorter man with cold eyes.

"And this is Jackie Morrisey," Vincent said, but even the name didn't bring any recognition to Cassius's face.

Jackie felt her stomach roll over with disgust. She'd spent the last ten years haunted by this man, agonizing over what he'd done to her, what he could have done . . . and he didn't even recognize her name. It appeared he'd forgotten her as soon as she was out of his life and yet she'd been tortured by his actions all these years. She'd been torturing herself.

Jackie felt Vincent squeeze her side and offered a stiff smile to let him know she was okay. He squeezed her again, then turned back to Cassius. "Her father was Ted Morrisey. You may have met him. He did lots of work for my cousin Bastien in New York. You lived there, didn't you?"

Cassius went stiff and turned slowly back to peer at Jackie. The recognition was there on his face now as his gaze raked over her. The look said that he was recalling what she'd looked like under her clothes all those years ago. A small, leering smile immediately tilted his lips up and his eyes flashed.

Jackie was aware of the way Tiny and Vincent both moved in closer still. Each of them was now pressed up against her sides. She thought she heard a small growl from one of the Italian troop too, but didn't glance around at the angry sound. Her gaze stayed locked on Cassius until he finally noticed her eyes. A slow smile pulled her lips apart as his own eyes widened with the realization that she was now an immortal too.

"Hello, Cassius," she said sweetly, then tilted her head and commented, "you're not nearly as tall as I remembered. You wouldn't have been using some of that immortal mind control on me all those years ago, would you?"

"I . . ." Cassius glanced toward Vincent nervously.

"I bet you did," she commented with feigned amusement. "It makes me wonder what else is smaller."

Jackie heard the snort of amusement that came from the direction of the Italian troop and was aware that the cough that suddenly claimed Tiny was to disguise a laugh. Her attention, however, was focused on Vincent. He wasn't amused. There was tension in every line of his body as he glared at Cassius. Still, he took her completely by surprise when he announced, "Jackie is my life mate, Cassius."

Jackie froze as those words made their way through her brain. She turned abruptly to Vincent and he lowered his gaze to her, the hard anger on his face immediately giving way to a soft smile. He lifted a hand to her cheek, caressing her softly. His eyes radiated reassurance and, she thought, love. She hoped it was love.

Jackie's lips turned up in a smile and she leaned into him, then turned back to Cassius. However, he hadn't got over his own shock at Vincent's announcement quite as quickly as she had, and was still gaping at the man.

As she watched, Cassius seemed to regain himself. He finally turned toward her, his mouth opening, but whatever he would have said died in his throat as she smiled at him, flashing her fangs. She'd finally managed that skill just half an hour before leaving for the funeral and was glad she had.

Cassius snapped his mouth closed, murmured an excuse and quickly moved away to disappear into the crowd. Jackie felt like a chapter of her life had finally closed as she watched him walk away . . . and was grateful to have it so. She relaxed into Vincent's side as he hugged her.

"You didn't tell us you had mastered bringing on your teeth," Christian commented as everyone relaxed. "Well done."

Jackie smiled and nodded to acknowledge his compliment.

"You shall have to tell me what that was all about. I seem to be the only person here who hasn't got a clue what just happened," Neil commented.

"Not the *only* one," Sharon murmured, reminding Jackie of the other women's presence. Sharon and Lily had remained so still and quiet, she'd forgotten they were there.

"We'll explain," Christian said as he glanced toward the front of the room. "But later. Now it appears the service is about to begin."

Christian was right, and they all moved to find seats. Jackie, Vincent, Tiny, and Marguerite settled near the back of the room where they could see everyone. Sharon and Lily settled nearby and Neil and the others made their way to the front of the room, where the family was situated.

The rest of the funeral was uneventful, but Vincent stayed at her side throughout. He also spent most of his time glaring at the back of Cassius's head. He'd said he was going to fire Cassius, but Jackie suspected the man should be grateful if that's all Vincent did. She considered telling Vincent firing him wasn't necessary, but didn't bother. Cassius had brought it on himself, let him reap what he'd sewn so long ago. Perhaps he needed the reminder that every action had a consequence, and that someone weak today may be the strong one later. Even mortals, with their short lives, forgot that lesson.

The service was very similar to human funeral services, but the burial was different. Inside the well-lit funeral home, it had been easy to forget that it was night outside, but at the cemetery this was not possible. Here, night encroached all around them as everyone made their silent way to the graveside. Jackie was slightly surprised that they didn't bother with some form of lighting to illuminate the path to the graveside, but most of the funeral attendees didn't seem to need it. Jackie was reminded that immortals were night hunters by nature and that their silvery eyes were more than just pretty; they were to allow them to see in the dark. There were few people at the funeral who had trouble navigating the path; she had a little trouble, though not much. It appeared her night vision had already improved. Tiny, on the other hand, had a lot of difficulty negotiating the path.

Jackie knew she wasn't seeing as well as the rest of the immortals around her. Marguerite had already explained that her new skills and abilities were still in their infancy, and would increase with the passing of time. Night vision was obviously one of the abilities that would continue to improve, but it was still a little frustrating. She spent her time at the graveside examining the others in attendance, searching expressions for some telltale sign of satisfaction, and wishing that her eyesight was already one hundred percent to do so.

Neil had arranged for a wake at his home to follow the funeral and Jackie wondered if all funerals for immortals were so similar to human burials. Or if it was because Stephano was mortal and had been raised with this culture, but it was Tiny who actually asked the question as they drove to Neil's home.

"Are all immortal funerals like this, or is this because Stephano is mortal?" His voice was a low rumble coming from the darkness of the back seat.

There was a brief silence, then Vincent cleared his throat and said, "I don't know. I've never attended a funeral for an immortal."

Jackie blinked at him in surprise. "Never?"

Vincent nodded, his attention on traffic as he drove.

"But surely you've known others who have died?" she asked with amazement. "What about your mother?"

"She was burned at the stake," he reminded her quietly. "There was nothing left to bury. My father searched the ashes, but there was nothing."

Jackie stared at him blankly, finding it impossible to believe that in medieval times they'd managed a fire so hot it had destroyed even the bones. Surely there should have been something left?

"What about Jean Claude?" Tiny asked and Jackie glanced into the backseat as she waited for Marguerite's answer.

310

"Another fire," Marguerite pointed out. "There was nothing left of Jean Claude to bury either."

"But that's—I mean, it's rare for a fire to burn so hot it could incinerate the bones. Even in cremation there are bits left . . . I think," Jackie added, because she wasn't at all certain this was true.

"Bastien thinks that the nanos somehow feed the fire, making it burn hotter. We are apparently quite flammable," Marguerite said quietly.

"Then how do you know Jean Claude is truly dead?" Tiny asked and Jackie stiffened in surprise. That thought hadn't occurred to her.

"His ring was in the ashes of the fire," Vincent answered.

"And I felt him die," Marguerite said quietly. When Jackie's eyes cut sharply to her, she said simply, "He was my sire. He shared his nanos with me. We were connected. I sensed his death, felt it, and knew it was by fire."

Jackie turned slowly in her seat and glanced at Vincent. He hadn't turned her, but in their excitement while lovemaking they'd bitten each other a time or two and shared their nanos. Would she feel it if he ever died?

As if sensing her solemn gaze and the thoughts behind it, Vincent took one hand from the steering wheel and reached over to take hers and give it a reassuring squeeze.

They were all silent the rest of the way to Neil's home and pretty much remained that way once at the house. Jackie drank wine and listened to the hushed voices around them while she continued to watch everyone closely, but her mind was now pondering what she'd learned about the connection to a sire. She wondered how connected she and Vincent now

311

were. And what exactly caused it? Was it his sharing his blood, his nanos, with her? If it were caused by the sharing of his nanos, it was possible she had some connection to the saboteur now as well. She'd swallowed his blood.

The idea was not an attractive one. She needed to talk to either Marguerite or Vincent about this. Jackie needed to know what else the connection might bring about, how it would affect her . . . and whether Marguerite thought she had enough of the saboteur's blood in her to have a connection.

With all these concerns on her mind, Jackie was more than relieved when Vincent decided it was time to leave. He left them to go speak to Christian and Marcus, then returned, announcing the others were staying a while longer, but would follow later.

"I'm going to call my daughter and make sure everything's all right at home," Marguerite announced as they entered the house several moments later. It seemed obvious that the funeral—sham though it was—had upset her, but then it had upset them all, Jackie suspected. She wasn't terribly surprised when Tiny trudged up the hall to the stairs, saying, "I'm going to bed. Funerals tire me out."

"Well, I guess that leaves you and me," Vincent murmured, sliding his arms around her as they were left alone in the hall.

"Hmmm." Jackie leaned into his embrace and kissed him lightly on the lips, then said, "Your aunt could come out at any minute."

"Uh-uh." Vincent shook his head. "If she were calling Bastien, she might be right back, but calling her daughter,

Lissianna, means she's in the mood for a chat. She'll be a good hour, at least."

"Yeah?" Jackie asked with amusement.

"Yeah," Vincent kissed her on the tip of the nose, then took her hand and headed for the stairs at a run.

Seventeen

"Slow down," Jackie laughed as Vincent charged up the stairs. She had no idea if she was any faster or stronger than she used to be yet, but he was definitely still much faster. She couldn't keep up with him and feared stumbling on the steps in her attempt to do so.

Vincent didn't just slow down, he paused on the steps and turned back to sweep her into his arms.

Jackie managed to bite back a startled gasp. She grabbed for his shoulders and simply held on for dear life as he hurried upstairs and along the hall to his room. Vincent let her feet slip to the floor so that he could open the door, then he herded her forward into his room with the arm still around her waist.

The door had barely closed behind them before Vincent had her in his arms and was kissing her, backing her through the darkness toward the bed as he did. Jackie laughed into his mouth as he urged hers open, then gasped, her laughter dying as one of his hands found her breast.

She didn't know if this was the after-effects of the funeral or what, but Jackie was suddenly desperate to have him inside her, to feel alive. Reaching between them, she undid the belt of his dress pants, then quickly undid the snap and zipper as well. His pants fell open and peeled away with ease to drop to the floor.

Vincent kicked them impatiently away, his own hands already working on removing her clothes as he continued to back her toward the bed. The black dress she'd worn to the funeral came off over her head the moment it was unzipped. Her bra quickly followed. Jackie found herself in only her panties, stockings, and high-heeled shoes when she stumbled back into the bed, then overbalanced onto it with a laugh.

She couldn't see a thing, but it was obvious Vincent didn't have the same problem. He bent to catch one foot and lifted it in the air to set to work on the strap of her high-heeled shoe.

"God, you're the most incredibly sexy woman I've ever seen," he murmured and suddenly stopped trying to undo the shoe. Leaving it on, he bent and caught her panties. With one quick jerking motion, they slid off, then he dropped on top of her, caught her hair in his hand and kissed her again.

This kiss was just as frantic as the first had been, and Jackie responded to it at once. Little moans and gasps slipped from her lips as she arched and shifted beneath him.

"I need you," Vincent muttered, breaking the kiss.

"Yes," Jackie gasped, it was the best she could do at that point. Her mind didn't seem to be capable of long, drawn-out conversations. She needed him inside her, needed to feel alive as only he could make her feel. She needed him. Unable to verbalize all that, she reached between them, caught him in hand and guided him into her.

The moment Vincent realized what she was doing, he took over, thrusting into her with a groan that ended on a sigh.

Jackie shifted beneath him, arching and pushing back into him, urging him on with little moans and murmurs of pleasure. It was only a matter of a few moments before they were both crying out with pleasure. Vincent filled her with one last thrust, then stayed there as he poured himself into her.

Vincent was snoring.

Jackie heard the sound and recognized what it was before she was quite fully awake. Blinking her eyes open, she peered at his profile in the bit of light seeping through the cracked open bathroom door and smiled faintly. She'd never heard him snore before, but good God, it was loud.

They'd made love tonight with an almost desperate edge. It was as if the thought and talk of death brought on by the fake funeral and burial had raised an urge in both of them to reaffirm life. There had been little in the way of foreplay, both of them desperate to be joined, and had ended with their collapsing in a sweaty heap on the bed.

Apparently, however, they'd shifted apart in their sleep. Jackie was now lying next to him on the bed, with her hand on his chest. Vincent was asleep on his back, one arm over his head, the other across his stomach and he was nearly raising the roof with one growling snore after another. It made her smile, then chuckle silently at herself. No doubt in a hundred years or so the sound would annoy the heck out of her, and she'd be nudging him and telling him to turn on his side to silence the sound, but for now it made her smile and want to kiss him.

Easing up on one elbow, Jackie peered down at his sleeping face and brushed a wayward lock of hair off his forehead, then frowned as she noted how pale he was. Vincent's skin was so white, it almost glowed in the dark. Now that she noticed that, Jackie began to notice other things, like the hand across his stomach that was clenched in sleep and moving slightly, as if attempting to rub away pain.

She peered more closely at his face, wishing it was a little lighter in the room so that she could see his expression. From what Jackie could see, it looked to her as if he were grimacing slightly.

It was then she realized that Vincent hadn't yet fed today. They'd got up late this afternoon, he'd joined her in the tub and made love to her, then they'd divided what little time they'd had before going to the funeral between teaching her to bring on her teeth, and trying to eliminate more people from the list of the employees who had worked on the New York play. She'd fed twice, grabbing a bag from the refrigerator and slapping it on her teeth once she'd finally learned to bring them on, then again before leaving for the funeral, but Vincent hadn't fed at all. And she hadn't even noticed, Jackie realized and immediately felt guilty. She now understood what it meant for him to hunger. She'd experienced it and had even experienced mild cramps, but knew right now what Vincent was suffering was much worse than that if the pain disturbed his sleep.

Vincent moaned and shifted on the bed, turning on his side and drawing his legs up so that he was almost in a fetal position. He had to feed, Jackie decided. It would only get worse as more time passed.

Slipping from the bed, she collected her clothes from where they'd landed on the floor and tiptoed to the bathroom. Vincent was still asleep when she slid back out several minutes later. Jackie paused at the bedside to peer at him for a minute, then made her way out of the bedroom and headed downstairs.

She was at the foot of the stairs when she heard the murmur of voices coming from the kitchen. Knowing Marguerite was the only one still up and about, Jackie frowned, then moved to the kitchen door and pushed it open. Her eyebrows rose when she saw Marguerite and Tiny seated at the table.

"I thought you'd gone to bed," Jackie said to Tiny with surprise and he lifted his large shoulders in a shrug.

"I couldn't sleep."

"Oh," she hesitated, then said, "Vincent hasn't eaten yet today. I'm going to order takeout. Are you hungry?"

Tiny considered the question, then nodded. "I could eat something."

"Any preferences?"

He shook his head. "Whatever you're getting. You'll probably be limited to pizza at this hour anyway."

Frowning, Jackie glanced at the clock to see that it was 3 A.M. He was right, their options were limited at this hour. Jackie let the door ease closed and headed for the office. Grabbing the phone book, she settled at the desk to look through the yellow pages in search of a pizzeria that would be open now. She found one she knew delivered more than pizza, but wasn't sure what else was on their menu.

Shrugging, Jackie punched in the number and sat back to wait for them to answer. Pizza would be fine. It was one of Tiny's comfort foods and she suspected he needed comfort food tonight. Funerals were a depressing business.

Finished placing the order, Jackie hung up and sat back in the desk chair, her gaze sliding to the couch. The sight of the large leather sofa reminded her of the first time Vincent had made love to her . . . and it *had* felt like lovemaking. It had felt like he was cherishing her with his body, something she'd never really experienced before Vincent. And tonight, at the funeral home, he'd introduced her to Cassius as his life mate.

"Life mate," Jackie whispered aloud. Her feelings on the matter had fluctuated over the days since she'd awakened to find herself turned. Marguerite had said that after watching her children and their mates flounder around, she'd decided it might serve better simply for her to tell her she was Vincent's life mate so that she could keep it in mind and come to accept it.

Jackie had kept it in mind, all right. The possibility hadn't been far from her mind for more than a moment in all the hours since then. A true life mate, fated to be with him, meant to live the equivalent of several lifetimes as his mate and love and partner. Who wouldn't like to be that? Life mates didn't divorce and Vincent had claimed her as his tonight. Had he meant that? Or had he merely introduced her to Cassius as such to freak him out? Jackie thought he might have meant it, his eyes had certainly appeared to her to be full of love as he'd looked down at her at the time, but he hadn't said anything tonight once they were alone in his room. Vincent hadn't told her he loved her, or even whispered that he'd meant what he'd said.

Jackie had wanted to bring it up and ask him about it, but hadn't had the courage to do so. Then she'd got carried away with their passion and let it slip away. She wished she'd had the courage to ask. She wished she'd had the courage to tell him she loved him, that he was good and smart and funny and the perfect balm for her wounded soul. She loved him.

"Jackie?"

She glanced up with surprise as Tiny slipped into the room.

"You didn't come back and I started to worry," he said as he moved to the desk to peer down at her.

Jackie smiled faintly, then shrugged. "I was just thinking."

"Worrying you mean, about Vincent, and the case, and—" He paused at the flicker of her expression, his eyebrows rising in question. "What's wrong?"

Jackie stared at him for a moment, guilt soaking through her, then admitted, "I wasn't thinking about the case. I should have been. That's why we're here, but instead, I was sitting here thinking that I love Vincent and wondering if he loved me back."

Tiny hesitated, obviously debating which issue to address first, then he settled on the corner of the desk and said, "Yes, he loves you. I knew he was coming to care for you early on, but the night you were attacked it was obvious he loved you. Vincent was so upset, and so determined to save you." He shook his head. "And tonight he introduced you as his life mate. Vincent loves you, Jackie."

Jackie felt a smile pull at her lips. She'd known Tiny for ten years. The man was an excellent judge of people, both mortal and immortal alike. It reassured her that he thought Vincent loved her.

"As for not thinking about the case," Tiny went on, and Jackie felt herself stiffen as she realized how quickly her concern had shifted from guilt over not thinking about work, to relief that Vincent might love her. What was the matter with her?

"I think you should cut yourself some slack there, Jackie," Tiny went on. "You were attacked and nearly died no more than a couple days ago. Your body has been going through major changes since then and still is. And you're falling in love for the first time in your life."

"But Bastien asked me to come here to help catch the saboteur. That is my primary job. These other distractions are just—"

"Your life," Tiny inserted dryly. "We will catch the saboteur, but your life is important too."

Jackie opened her mouth to respond, then paused and glanced toward the door as the buzzer sounded. "That will be the pizza."

Tiny started to get up, but Jackie waved him back to his seat as she stood and moved toward the door. "I'll get it."

Jackie moved to the panel and flipped on the monitor to show who was parked at the gate. When she saw the pizza delivery name on the top of the car, she pressed the button to open the door and said, "Come on up."

She then turned and moved to lean in the office door as she waited for the pizza. "We only have two or three immortals left on the list that we haven't eliminated."

Tiny eyed her solemnly and for a minute she feared he wouldn't go along with the topic change, but in the end he nodded.

Relaxing a little, Jackie sighed and ran her hand through her hair. "I don't think any of them are the saboteur. I'm starting to think stealing the list was just a red herring."

"You mentioned that as a possibility at the time," Tiny murmured and frowned. "But surely the saboteur wouldn't go to all the trouble of stealing it from the office and attacking Stephano just to send us down the wrong path?"

"Wouldn't he?" she asked with a frown. "It's kept us from looking in other directions and had the benefit of upsetting Vincent at the same time."

Tiny looked troubled at the possibility, then they both stilled as a knock sounded at the door. Straightening, Jackie turned and moved to answer it.

Vincent was having a nightmare. He was lying stretched out on the cold tiles beside his pool and ugly little demon things with sharp, sharp teeth were perched on their haunches on his chest. They had ripped open his stomach and were feasting away on his insides. It was a most unpleasant dream and terribly painful, and yet in the dream he wasn't screaming, Jackie was. Vincent could hear her terrified screams, but couldn't see her. He tried to raise his arm to knock off the little creatures on his chest, intending to get up and look for Jackie, but he couldn't move his arm, he couldn't even move a finger.

"Vincent! Vincent!"

Vincent blinked his eyes open and stared at the figure bent over him. Coming from the nightmare he'd just been having, he almost struck out at the figure, but was glad he hadn't when he recognized Tiny's voice.

"Wake up! They took Jackie!"

"What?" He sat up abruptly, fully awake now. His gaze shot automatically to the bed beside him where Jackie should have been, but Vincent could see in the light coming from both the bathroom and bedroom doors that she wasn't there.

"Where is she?" he asked with concern.

"That's what I'm trying to tell you," Tiny growled unhappily. "She ordered a pizza. I think she wanted to feed you. The pizza guy buzzed and she opened the gate, then there was a knock on the door and she went to get it and . . ." Tiny shook his head. "I was sitting on the desk in the office. There was no scream, no warning, nothing. Just silence, but I started getting Jackie's hinky feeling. It was too quiet, I guess.

"I went into the hall to see what was happening, but it was empty. I opened the front door and she was walking to this pizza delivery car. There was a young guy at the wheel, staring straight ahead like he was in a trance and Jackie was walking to the car with a woman."

"A woman?" Vincent shifted the blankets off and got up to start pulling on his clothes. "Why? What did they do once they got to the car? What happened?"

323

Tiny shook his head, his expression upset. "I didn't know what was happening. I didn't *do* anything," he mourned, obviously feeling guilty. "I thought the saboteur was a man. Wasn't it a man who attacked her on the beach the night you had to turn her?"

"Ye—" Vincent paused. Everything had happened so fast that night and he'd been in such a panic . . .

"It could have been a woman," Vincent admitted, feeling like he'd been punched in the stomach. Frowning, he growled, "What happened? You said someone took her?"

"She got in the front passenger seat of the car, but she was walking funny, almost like a robot, stiff and blank-faced. The woman got into the backseat and the pizza guy turned the car and drove off."

"Jesus!" Vincent had his pants on now and snatched up his shirt as he headed out of his room. He tugged it swiftly on as he jogged down the stairs.

Marguerite was in the hall, peering into the office when he reached the bottom of the stairs.

"Have you seen Jackie and Tiny?" she asked as she spotted him. "Jackie went to order pizza and Tiny followed to tell her something and they never came—oh," Marguerite interrupted herself as Tiny reached the top of the stairs and started to hurry down after Vincent. She frowned at their upset expressions. "What's happening?"

"Someone's taken Jackie," Vincent said grimly.

"Who?" Marguerite asked with alarm.

Vincent stilled halfway up the hall and whirled to face Tiny. "What did the woman look like?"

"She was one of the two women who came over just

before Cassius at the funeral," Tiny said. "The little one who looked so young."

Vincent stared at him blankly, then finally said with disbelief, "Lily? The thin, little blonde who looks about fourteen?"

Tiny nodded, then frowned with realization and said, "But Lily had normal eyes at the funeral. They weren't metallic like the rest of you guys. She couldn't have been controlling Jackie and making her get in the car. She couldn't be the attacker."

Confusion covered his face and he added, "But Jackie wouldn't just walk off like that either. Maybe there was someone else in the car too."

"Lily is an immortal," Vincent said on a sigh and moved to his office.

"Why would she have done all this?" Marguerite asked, following him.

"I'm not sure." He grabbed his Rolodex off the desk and began looking for Lily's card with her address on it.

"What are you doing?" Marguerite asked. She pointed out, "She'd hardly take Jackie to her house."

"She might have," Vincent argued and desperately hoped she had. It was the only place he could think to look for her.

"Marguerite's right," Tiny said. "That hasn't been her pattern. She attacked Stephano at the office, killed that one woman in the hills, and attacked Jackie here on the beach. She won't take her back to her house."

Vincent stared at them, feeling completely and utterly helpless. His mind was running in circles, panic stealing his ability to think. Where would Lily take her? Why would Lily do this? Where was Jackie? His mind seemed stuck in stupid, like a hamster running on a wheel and getting nowhere . . . and then his phone rang.

"Maybe that's Jackie," Tiny said hopefully as Vincent pulled the phone from his pocket and flipped it open.

"Vincent?"

His shoulders slumped as he recognized Christian's voice. Vincent's voice was dull when he said, "Yeah."

"We're stopped at the stoplight on the corner two blocks from your house. There's a pizza delivery car stopped on the opposite side and Jackie is in the front seat with some pimple-faced kid driving. What's going on?"

"Is there anyone else in the car?" Vincent asked sharply, moving out of the office and up the hall.

"Yeah. It looks like there's a blonde in the backseat. I can just see her head over the front seat . . . It looks like your production assistant."

Vincent grimaced and his hand tightened on the phone. It wasn't that he hadn't believed Tiny, it was just that it was hard for him to accept that little Lily was the one behind all this madness. She'd worked for him for about six months and hadn't even been on the play in New York. She'd been on vacation then. Still, as Tiny had said, Jackie wouldn't just wander off. Someone had to be controlling her and it appeared Lily was that someone. But was she doing it on her own, or for someone else?

"Do we stop them?" Christian asked.

Vincent hesitated, unsure what to say. If Lily was working with someone else, Jackie might be safe if he had Christian and the boys stop the car somehow. But, if Lily was the saboteur who was out to make his life a misery, stopping the car might get Jackie killed on the spot. He wanted to catch Lily if she was the saboteur, but was more concerned with Jackie being alive than doing so.

"The light's turned green, they're driving past us," Christian announced. "What's happening, Argeneau? What do we do here?"

"Either Lily's the killer, or she's taking Jackie to the killer," Vincent said grimly. "You need to follow them, but not let them spot you."

"Turn around, Marcus!" Christian barked at the other end of the line, then said into the phone, "What are you going to do?"

"We'll follow you," Vincent announced firmly.

"Fine. Call me once you're on the road and I'll tell you where we are," Christian instructed.

Vincent's mouth tightened as the phone went dead in his hand. Flipping it closed, he headed through the kitchen to the door leading into the garage.

"What's happening? What did he say?" Marguerite was hard on his heels as he snatched his keys off the hook by the door and hurried into the garage.

"Christian's going to follow them. We're to call once we're on the road," Vincent announced, leading the way out to his car. He got into the front seat, hit the remote to open his garage door as Marguerite slid into the passenger seat beside him, then handed her his cell phone and started the engine as Tiny got into the backseat. "Call Christian back and see what's happening."

"How do I call him?" Marguerite asked, staring at the phone uncertainly as Vincent steered out of the garage.

"Give it to me, Marguerite. I'll do it," Tiny rumbled from the backseat.

Vincent was aware of his aunt handing the phone back to Tiny, but concentrated on his driving as he raced up the driveway. The gate was closed, and Vincent tapped his fingers impatiently on the steering wheel as he waited for it to open. His gaze shifted to the rearview mirror as Tiny found Christian's number on the received calls page and dialed back.

Tiny put the phone to his ear just as the gate finished opening. Vincent steered through and paused at the street, unsure which way to go.

"Christian?" Tiny's voice rumbled and Vincent shifted sharply to glance in the backseat.

"Ask him which way we should go when we leave the driveway," Vincent ordered.

Tiny nodded and asked the question. He listened briefly, then his head lifted and he barked, "Right."

Vincent turned the steering wheel right and pulled out with a squeal of tires. "Have they caught up to the car yet? They didn't lose her, did they?"

"They're following it now," Tiny answered after a pause during which he listened to Christian speak.

"Tell them not to lose them," Vincent hissed.

"Turn left here," Tiny ordered a moment later and Vincent turned left.

"Christian says they're on the highway," Tiny announced.

Gritting his teeth, Vincent nodded and followed the directions Tiny continued to give. He was speeding and fear was making sweat trickle down his back. He couldn't believe it was Lily: sweet, smiling Lily. He'd kill the little bitch if she hurt Jackie, he thought coldly.

"Vincent?" Tiny asked suddenly and Vincent glanced in the rearview mirror to see the troubled expression on his face. "If Lily is an immortal, why doesn't she have the metallic eyes?"

Eighteen

If Lily was immortal, why did she have hazel eyes?

That question kept running through Jackie's head as they drove along the highway. It was not the most important thing she could ask right then, but it was the one that bugged her the most. The day Sharon and Lily had come to the house with the list and she'd seen Lily's normal, hazel eyes, Jackie had assumed she was mortal. Boy, had she been wrong.

Jackie attempted to shake off the control Lily had over her mind, but wasn't surprised when she was unable to. They had concentrated on teaching her to keep her fangs in, bring her fangs on, and she'd even attempted to read Tiny's mind a time or two, but other than that she hadn't yet learned any of the skills Marguerite wanted to teach her that would have kept her safe tonight. Those had been next on the list of skills to learn. Unfortunately, it looked like the lesson had been left too long. She'd realized that the moment she'd opened the door tonight and felt Lily slip in to take control of her thoughts.

Jackie hadn't even had the opportunity to shout to Tiny or Marguerite for help. She'd opened the front door, blinked in surprise at the sight of Lily, then found herself turned into a puppet. All control of her body had just vanished and she'd found herself walking out of the house, pulling the door quietly closed, and walking calmly to a pizza delivery car in the driveway. Or, at least, it had looked calm on the outside, she was sure. Jackie certainly hadn't been feeling calm on the inside, and still wasn't.

Jackie had tried to fight off the sudden control Lily had taken of her mind, but it had been useless. As far as she could tell, Lily didn't appear to be having any more trouble controlling her than Cassius had when she was nineteen and still mortal, and Jackie promised herself that if she survived this night, she would make darned sure they taught her how to keep from being taken over like this again.

God, she hoped she survived. Jackie didn't want to die. There were a million and one things she still wanted to do before she died. But then, she supposed few people were ready to go when it was their time.

Unable to do anything else, Jackie stared straight ahead, and silently prayed that Tiny had wakened Vincent when he realized something was wrong. She wondered how long it had taken Tiny to realize something *was* wrong. Probably only moments, she guessed. Hopefully, in time to see her getting into the delivery car.

Jackie instinctively tried to turn her eyes to the left to peer at the delivery driver and actually managed it. Lily must have eased her control, she realized. But then, Jackie supposed it must take more effort to control two at once. Vincent had said it did. That might give her half a chance here, she realized, and wondered why Lily would risk having to control two people at once.

A moment later, Jackie recalled the day Sharon and Lily had brought the list to the house. Sharon had said Lily didn't drive. Jackie supposed that meant that she'd had no choice but to involve another person. While she could have forced Jackie to drive her wherever she planned to take her, presumably Jackie wasn't intended to return. Someone had to drive her there, so that she would have someone to drive her back. Had Lily hijacked someone else's mind to take the woman Vincent had fed into the hills, Jackie wondered. If so, she hoped the girl had not been conscious and frightened at the time.

Her gaze slid out the window, and Jackie wasn't sure if it was good news or bad that Lily didn't appear to be taking her into the hills. They were headed in the wrong direction.

"You can speak now."

Jackie turned her head in surprise at Lily's comment, then blinked as she realized she was able to move that as well as her eyes. Lily had eased her control considerably. Jackie tried moving other parts of her body, but it seemed she'd been given back control of her mouth and head only.

"You're an immortal," Jackie said abruptly.

"Wow. I can see why Vincent hired you, your powers of deduction are brilliant," Lily said dryly.

Jackie ignored the sarcasm and said, "Your eyes don't

have the metallic gleam immortals have. I assumed you were mortal."

Lily laughed. It was an unpleasant, mocking laugh. "My eyes are silver-green."

"They're hazel," Jackie said.

"Look at me."

Jackie turned at the order and peered at Lily as she bowed her head and lifted a finger to each eye. She blinked in surprise as Lily removed something, then lifted her head to reveal beautiful sea-green and silver eyes.

"Colored contacts," Jackie breathed, feeling incredibly stupid. One of the secretaries in her own company wore colored contacts. Some days she came in with green eyes, some days with blue. Yet, Jackie had never considered colored contacts. God, for a detective, she was an idiot, but it had never occurred to her to think that an immortal would want to hide their beautiful eyes behind contacts. "Why?"

"Many of us wear them. Having silvered eyes tends to draw attention."

"I've never met another immortal who wore them," Jackie argued.

"Would you know they were immortal without their silvered eyes?" Lily asked archly, then laughed again. "You've probably met many immortals and just not recognized them, because you didn't see silvered or bronzed eyes."

Jackie breathed out slowly, knowing Lily could be right.

"Immortals who don't have to interact a lot with mortals don't tend to bother, but anyone who wants to blend with mortals, does their best to blend."

"I didn't know," Jackie muttered. Bastien had never

mentioned this tendency and her father had never made a note of it. Perhaps her father hadn't known, and perhaps Bastien simply didn't think of it. She was pretty sure Bastien never used contacts. Nor did anyone who worked for him that she knew of, but then Argeneau Enterprises was filled mostly with immortals.

"So much mental effort wasted on my eye color," Lily said with a shake of her head, making it obvious she was reading Jackie's mind. "I would have thought you'd ask me something more important."

"Why did you steal the list of employees on the New York play when you weren't even on it?" Jackie asked, and the question brought another smile to Lily's face.

"No, I wasn't on the list," Lily admitted with amusement. "As it happens, I was on vacation, first in Canada, then in New York."

"The fire at the theater in Canada," Jackie realized. Lily would have had to go there to set it. And then she'd followed Vincent to New York to sabotage that play too.

"Yes," Lily said, having read her thoughts. "I planned it all out ahead of time, and didn't want to risk being under suspicion for the sudden case of anemia that went around in New York. So, I asked for some vacation time. I flew to Canada, caused a little trouble, then flew to New York ahead of Vincent and took a position on the janitorial staff as a young boy named Bob. I put overalls and a baseball cap on and pretty much disappeared for everyone. It was incredibly easy." She smiled faintly. "But to answer your question, I stole the list to lead you down the garden path." Her smile widened. "And you all followed so easily."

Jackie felt her mouth tighten. She'd wondered about that the night the papers had gone missing, but they'd had to look into the names on the list anyway. Of course, there had been reason to do so when the lists had shown up missing from the office as well and Stephano had nearly died.

"It was a lot of effort to get us off the track; removing the list from every office and then attacking Stephano."

"Yes, but it was worth it," Lily assured her, then added, "though I never meant to kill Stephano. Up until then it was all terribly easy. I simply went into work early, while all the mortals were still on shift, and had them erase the computer files while I pulled the hard copies."

"Accounting was the last office," Lily said and pursed her lips. "I'd done all the others. The human day secretary was still there when I arrived, but it was getting late. Meredith, the night girl would be there soon.

"As I'd done with the other offices, I had the day girl erase the computer files, but then I sent her on her way and went into the filing room to retrieve the hard copies myself. I was coming out of the filing room with the files when Stephano Notte walked in."

"And you killed him," Jackie said when she stopped and grimaced at the memory.

"Not right away," Lily countered. "He was in a rush. Apparently, he had some hot date that night, but needed some information from Phillip's files before he went. He asked what I was doing there, of course and I said I'd needed a file for Vincent, but that Meredith had been leaving the office as I arrived and said to feel free to grab it myself. Was there something I could do for him?"

She frowned. "I knew I'd probably have to kill him, but I could hardly do it there in the outer office where anyone passing by might see."

"So you lured him into the inner office," Jackie said.

Lily's mouth tightened with annoyance. "Don't rush me. I'm telling this."

Jackie bit her lip and waited for her to continue.

Annoyed, Lily took her time about it, her eyes drifting to look out the window as she made her wait. Jackie took that opportunity to peer around the front seat of the car herself. She needed a weapon, something to defend herself with when they got to wherever they were going. She had no doubt that Lily intended to finish what she'd started the other night, and while she'd be harder to kill now, she *could* die. Immortal was really a misnomer, she thought as Lily finally continued.

"Anyway, I asked if there was something I could help him with . . . or did he want to wait for the night secretary?" Lily made a face. "He hesitated, but his impatience won out. Men are always impatient, no matter if they are human or immortal," she added in a lecturing tone. "So I sat at the secretary's desk and pretended to look for the file he wanted printed up, but I was really making sure the file I'd asked the day girl to remove had been erased. It had. So then I put one foot against the extension under the desk and used the other to pull the power plug.

"Stephano saw the computer blink off and asked what had happened and I frowned with confusion then said, 'Oh yes, that's why Meredith had stepped out. She'd gone to see Sharon, she mentioned she was having computer problems and wanted to find out who she should call in to deal with it.' I frowned prettily, then brightened and said, 'Phillip's computer should work though. Do you want me to try that, or would you rather wait for Meredith?'

"Once again, his impatience sealed his fate. Stephano turned and led the way into Phillip's office. He walked to the desk, then paused and turned back to gesture me toward the chair to do the grunt work for him."

Lily sneered. "Lord knows the big vice president wouldn't lower himself to doing the grunt work of a secretarial-type job. So, he politely paused and turned back to gesture me forward, only I'd grabbed the letter opener off Meredith's desk in the outer office when he turned to lead the way into the inner office, and the moment he turned back to face me in Phillip's office, I plunged the letter opener into his heart." She smiled. "Lights out."

"I did try to slip in and wipe his memory beforehand," Lily suddenly announced, as if that would make a difference. "As we were walking into the office, I slipped into his thoughts and tried to wipe them, but as I say, he had some ability at blocking us and I wasn't sure it had taken. I couldn't take the chance that it hadn't and he'd recall my being there. You might have put two and two together." She shrugged. "So he had to die."

Jackie managed to keep from showing any emotion at the blasé way the woman said it, as if she were announcing that a fake nail had broken so she'd taken it off. However, it was difficult. In her mind's eye, she was seeing Stephano Notte lying pale and seemingly dead on the floor of the office, and Neil's upset at his brother's state, as well as

Elaine's tear-glazed eyes as she thanked Vincent for saving her son.

Controlling her expression did little good, however, since Lily was inside her head and could read her thoughts. Her face suddenly clouded over with anger. "He's alive!"

Jackie winced as the blonde spat the words. All their efforts to keep Stephano safe had just been thrown out the window.

"I should have cut off his head," she snapped. "If he'd been an immortal I would have, but he was mortal, I thought . . ." She paused suddenly and frowned. "If he's alive, why didn't you come after me the minute he told you who had stabbed him?"

Jackie tried not to think anything at all, but knew she'd failed when Lily suddenly burst out laughing.

"Oh, that's precious," she crowed. "He couldn't remember. The wiping took after all." She laughed softly, then said, "Hmm . . . Maybe I'll let him live then, after all."

Jackie felt her mouth tighten. She glared at the woman who spoke so carelessly about taking the life of a good man, a brother and son, as if it meant nothing. And she supposed it did mean nothing to Lily. None of them meant anything to her; except a means to upset Vincent, but for what? Before she could ask that question, the car began to slow and she glanced around sharply to see where they were.

They were no longer on the highway. Apparently, they'd left it while she'd been distracted listening to Lily. It looked to her as if they'd left the city altogether. Now they were on a road that appeared rarely traveled. There was an occasional house, but mostly there were trees and the occasional glimpse of ocean seen through bald patches in the woods along one side. It was a coastal road, she realized with confusion, and wondered what they were doing there.

Jackie somehow doubted it made any difference that they weren't in the hills. While Lily had killed the woman Vincent had fed on and left her body in the hills, she didn't think for a minute that because they were at the beach rather than the hills, the production assistant had different plans for her. It appeared Lily had decided to change her pattern and kill Jackie on the beach.

Suitable, she supposed, since the first attack had taken place on the beach as well.

Lily had gone quiet. Jackie glanced at her to see that she was concentrating on the side of the road, appearing to look for something. When the woman stiffened and her eyes shot to the back of the driver's head, Jackie turned to peer at the side of the road, her heart sinking when she saw the dirt road they were approaching. Her gaze slid back to the driver now that she could actually look at him, and Jackie peered at his blank face. He was young, perhaps eighteen, with short brown hair and a long face.

"Does he drive you to all your murder scenes?" The dry question had slipped from Jackie's mouth before she realized she was going to ask it.

Lily turned hard eyes her way, then slowly smiled. "No. For the other one I took control of a taxi driver. I'd never seen this young man before tonight when he pulled up to the gate to buzz. I slid into the car while he was waiting for the gate to open."

"How did you know I'd open the door and it wouldn't be Marguerite or Vincent?"

"Because it was your voice that answered over the intercom when he buzzed. Besides, I knew it would be either you or Tiny to open the door. Neither Marguerite nor Vincent would have ordered the pizza."

Jackie supposed that meant Lily hadn't figured out they'd been having Vincent feed off delivery people in an effort to keep from marking anyone else for death. At least, she'd done something right, Jackie thought grimly, then realized she shouldn't be thinking such things. Lily might read them and then go after the delivery people. Fortunately, she seemed to be distracted controlling the driver.

To get these thoughts out of her head, Jackie asked, "And what if Tiny had answered the door?"

"Then it would be him sitting here tonight and I'd have saved you for another time," Lily said easily.

Jackie felt her stomach roll over at this news. Tiny was a target too and if Lily succeeded at killing her tonight, Tiny's days were numbered. If that were the case, there was little hope for him, especially since Lily wasn't on the list of people on the New York play, and they'd been concentrating their efforts that way.

Unless Tiny had seen her getting into the car with Lily, Jackie reminded herself. *If* he'd seen her . . . She frowned to herself with worry. It was possible he hadn't.

"What were you doing in the house the night I caught you in the office?" she asked suddenly.

Lily glanced at her with amusement. "You didn't *catch*

me in the office. You followed me out of it and *fell* on me coming over the fence."

Jackie managed not to wince at the description. It made her sound completely incompetent. When she showed no reaction to her words, Lily shrugged and said, "I'd followed you that night, but lost you after your little rendezvous in the storage room with Vincent." She tilted her head and asked, "Is he a good lover? I presume the two of you snuck in there for hanky panky?"

Jackie started to recite "Itsy Bitsy Spider" in her head. She so wasn't revealing anything that personal . . . or endangering anyone else.

Lily's mouth compressed with displeasure as Jackie apparently managed to block her out, then said, "After I lost you, I went back to the house to wait for you to return. When you pulled in, I tried to follow on foot. I'd snuck Sharon's remote out of her purse that evening and planned to just open the gate and walk up, but the remote didn't work."

"We changed the sensor and code," Jackie said with satisfaction. She added, "But why did you break the panel? It didn't get you in."

"I was annoyed," Lily said with irritation. She frowned and said, "If you hadn't followed me, I never would have attacked you that night. I was just going to slip in and leave a message so that Vincent would know he wasn't as safe as he thought he was. But you came into the office before I could do anything. I tried to get out when I heard you coming, but you were barefoot; by the time I heard you I couldn't get out quick enough."

Jackie suspected she was telling the truth. There was

really no reason for Lily to lie at this stage in the game.

Her thoughts scattered as the driver turned down the road Jackie had noted just a moment ago. The car rattled and bumped over the hard-packed dirt, moving along a path between the trees and Jackie felt her heart sink. It looked like they'd arrived.

Nineteen

"You may as well stop pretending. I know you can see where you're going," Lily said as Jackie stumbled and fell to her knees for the second time on the uneven path.

Jackie ground her teeth together and pushed herself back to her feet. She'd been feigning night blindness since they'd left the car in an effort to slow down their progress and give her a chance to come up with an idea for escape. Unfortunately, Lily was inside her head and knew exactly what she was doing. It was incredibly frustrating. Even if she did come up with an idea, Lily would know it the moment she thought it.

Jackie glanced back in the direction they'd come as she started forward again. They'd left the delivery car and driver at the edge of the woods, just out of sight of the road. Lily had done something to make the young man pass out, and he'd been slumped in his seat when they got out. Jackie had no doubt Lily would undo whatever it was she'd done when she returned to the car. She only hoped she'd let him go after finishing with him. He was just a kid, too young to die.

"It's not much farther now," Lily announced and Jackie became aware of the sound of the ocean. It grew louder with each step they took. It all reminded her of the night she'd turned and was giving her a definite aversion to the beach.

"Why the beach?" Jackie asked to distract herself from what was coming.

"Your death here will be symbolic," Lily announced.

"Symbolic how? Why are you even doing all this? What did Vincent ever do to you?" Jackie asked with frustration.

"Nothing."

The answer made Jackie pause and turn to face the woman. "What?"

Lily laughed at her expression. "Turn and walk under your own power, or I will take full control again."

Jackie hesitated, then turned abruptly and kept walking. It hadn't occurred to her that Lily must have let up on some of her control for her to have been able to stumble and fall a time or two. But then, her thoughts had been a bit distracted, she supposed. The fact that she apparently had control of her body again, made her wonder what Lily would do if she suddenly lunged for the woods.

"I'd take full control of you and that would be the end of your questions," Lily answered as if she'd asked the question aloud, reminding her that she was in her thoughts. "I'm sure you'd like to know why this is happening, wouldn't you? You do want to know why you're going to die?"

"Yes," Jackie muttered with disgust.

The ground underneath their feet began to shift with each step, telling her they'd reached sand. They should be out of the trees soon. Not eager to think about what would happen then, she prompted Lily, "So, what are you going to do to me and why?"

"I'm going to stake you out in the sand and leave you there through the day," Lily announced. "Then I'll come back and behead you at sunset."

Jackie glanced skyward at this announcement. The trees had thinned out the closer they got to the beach and she could now see the sky through the branches. It was no longer full dark, daylight wasn't far away. She'd place the time at somewhere between four and five in the morning. Sunlight would be creeping up the sky in less than an hour or so.

Staked out in the sand for the day, then beheaded, Jackie thought unhappily. It was how the council punished immortals who broke one of their serious laws. From what she'd heard it was a most unpleasant way to go. Her body would dehydrate, the nanos would begin to eat her organs in their desperation for blood . . . she'd suffer horribly before the sun set.

"Why?" she asked, pausing abruptly as they suddenly reached the end of the trees and the beach spread out before them.

"For my William." Lily didn't bother to tell her to move, she simply took back control of her. Jackie found herself moving a good ten feet out of the trees before her body stopped and turned to face Lily.

"William?" Jackie asked, still retaining her ability to speak.

Lily turned her gaze to the ocean, her voice sounding far away as she said, "They killed him, you know. They staked him out in the sun and then beheaded him at sundown."

"Who did?" Jackie asked with a frown.

"Lucian Argeneau, Michael Moreau, and Vincent's father, Victor."

"Okay," Jackie said slowly. "So, Vincent's father and two other men killed your William. Why are you going after Vincent for it? He had nothing to do with it."

"I know." Lily sighed unhappily. "When I decided to seek revenge for William, I went after Michael Moreau first. I stalked him, caught him, then staked him out in the sun and left him there all day long, enjoying his screams from a nice little cave nearby. Then I beheaded him at sunset."

Lily frowned. "I didn't feel any satisfaction at all. I expected to gain some peace from it, but I didn't. Then I realized that he hadn't really suffered as I have. Sure, he went through the same pain as my William, but it was only a day's agony. I've suffered for a hundred years over what happened. I realized then, that to gain true satisfaction, I have to make them suffer as I have. I can't just kill them, I have to torment them by torturing and killing someone they love."

"So, Vincent is to suffer and eventually die so that his father, Victor, suffers for what he did to your William," Jackie said slowly, trying to follow her reasoning. Then she shook her head. "If it's Victor you're trying to make suffer, why are you tormenting Vincent? Why didn't you just stake Vincent out in the sun and behead him?"

"Because his father isn't here," Lily said with irritation. "I thought if I began to sabotage Vincent's work and so on, he'd call Victor in. *He's* on the council and should have been called in to take care of things, especially when I began to harm humans. Instead, the idiot called you in to handle it. The fool has ruined everything."

Jackie raised her eyebrows at her frustration, then said quietly, "From what I understand, Victor has been withdrawn and reclusive since his life mate was burnt at the stake in England. Vincent rarely sees him. I don't think he'll ever call him about this if that's what you're hoping."

Lily's mouth was a firm line of fury as she said, "I'd come to that conclusion myself. So, instead of dying, he'll just have to suffer the loss I did in his father's place. You will die like William did, and he will agonize over it for centuries."

Jackie considered that and wondered if it meant she'd leave Vincent alone and move on after this? Would he and Tiny be safe once she was dead?

"Tiny is a mortal, no more than a friend to Vincent. I won't trouble myself to bother with him," Lily said, obviously reading her thoughts. "But I've been thinking I will try Marguerite next. Lucian Argeneau is said to be very fond of his sister-in-law. Her death this way should be upsetting to him and Vincent both. Of course, I'd prefer a life mate or child in Lucian's case, as well, but he has neither. I will have to settle for Marguerite now and a life mate or child later, if he ever has either. In the meantime, I have you."

"Right," Jackie sighed.

"Obviously, if you were mortal, staking you out would be a waste of time, but it's perfect now that Vincent has turned you."

"He didn't," Jackie said.

"He didn't what?" Lily asked with amusement. "Are you going to try to convince me you aren't immortal now? I have seen your eyes and unlike me, you don't wear contacts. Besides, I can read your mind, Jackie. You *are* an immortal."

"I *am* immortal, but Vincent didn't turn me. You did," Jackie said solemnly.

"You can't think I would believe that nonsense?" Lily asked, but there was uncertainty on her face as she concentrated on Jackie. Apparently disturbed by something she was reading there, she muttered, "I would know if I'd turned you."

"Yes, well, perhaps I should say I turned myself then," Jackie said quietly. "When I bit you, I swallowed a couple of mouthfuls of your blood, enough to start the turn. It's why I didn't bleed out and die before they got me back to the house."

Lily peered down at her own wrist and Jackie saw that it was perfect now. There wasn't a mark on it from the other night, it had completely healed.

"It hurt like the devil at the time," Lily muttered, then laughed. "This is perfect. You turned yourself. I'll have to watch that in the future." She shook her head, then said, "It doesn't matter who turned you. He claimed you as his true life mate."

"Only to piss off Cassius," Jackie assured her. "Cassius and I have a history. Vincent, and the others, knew about it. It's why they were all so cold to him when he came up to us at the service tonight. It's also why Vincent claimed me as life mate. He wanted to put a scare into Cassius."

Lily's eyes narrowed and Jackie let her feelings for Vincent show, along with her fears that he didn't really think of her as a life mate. It was the best she could do with Lily able to read her thoughts, but the woman shook her head. "Nice try, but I have seen him with you. He's been eating since you arrived. He's smiling all the time, laughing—"

"According to the agency files, Vincent is happy-go-lucky and always smiling," Jackie interrupted with surprise. "That's hardly proof of his thinking I'm his true life mate."

Lily snorted. "Only around his family. Around them, he's Mr. Smiley, but the rest of the time . . ." She shrugged. "I don't think he's a very happy vampire. In fact, before you came along, I thought he might be heading toward that terrible self-destructive state that some vampires go through. But then you arrived and he started smiling and laughing. It was like he'd found a new lease on life.

"In fact, I should really thank you. Before you, attacking his business, then the people around him upset him, but not as much as I wanted it to. Then you came and reawakened him and now everything matters to him, but especially you."

Jackie stayed silent, but hoped what Lily said was true. She hoped she'd made Vincent happy, and made him smile and find his pleasure in life again. He'd certainly shown her how to enjoy life, something she seemed to have lost at nineteen. The years since then had seemed somewhat colorless until coming to California and meeting Vincent. But there was still so much she wanted to do with him. Jackie wished she'd told him she loved him last night while she'd had the chance. She wished she could make love to him one more time, that she could take a night swim with him, laugh, cuddle, and kiss him.

Jackie supposed she should be grateful she'd had a chance to know him at all and taste the happiness she could have had with him. But it wasn't enough, she wanted more, and this woman who looked like a child planned to make sure that didn't happen.

Jackie frowned. "Why do you look so young?"

"What?" Lily seemed startled by the question.

"Nanos make you your peak health, strength, speed, etc," she pointed out. "Yet you look like a child, and you're incredibly thin. Being that thin can't be your peak health."

A sudden rage covered Lily's face as she said, "I had no one to look after me once they'd killed my William. No one to teach me. I didn't know what I could and couldn't do. I thought being a vampire meant I couldn't eat anymore, so I stopped eating food. But, with no one to bring me donors to feed from, I nearly starved to death.

"I suffered the debilitating cramps of dehydration every minute of every day for the first twenty years. I never got enough blood then. I didn't know how to hunt. I lived on the streets, gnawing on rats and sometimes children when I got the chance, scurrying from darkness to darkness and cowering out of the sun during the day. I had no idea what I could or couldn't do."

Jackie's eyebrows flew up. It was obvious Lily had been turned before blood banks, but that didn't explain why William hadn't told her she could eat. Had he died right after turning her? None of what she was saying made sense.

"Lily was only twelve at the time of her turning."

Lily and Jackie both turned sharply at those words to find Marguerite standing at the mouth of the path through the trees. She was alone, her expression pitying as she looked on Lily.

Growling, Lily immediately grabbed Jackie, holding her between them as she glared at Marguerite.

"What do you mean?" Jackie asked. "I thought you weren't allowed to turn anyone that young?"

"William was a pedophile," Marguerite said quietly. "He cared little for anyone's laws. He liked his women young. Children really. He turned them as young as ten, kept them as his pet, feeding them only blood, and scantily at that, to ensure they didn't develop properly. You can always tell those not properly fed, it confuses the nanos and they are stunted, thin and young-looking like Lily."

Jackie glanced back at the girl, horrified that someone had deliberately done this to her. Lily looked like a young teenager . . . and apparently, always would.

"He kept them till he tired of them, and then usually killed them and turned another," Marguerite added with disgust.

"Why did no one stop him?" Jackie asked with amazement.

"No one could prove he was doing it," Marguerite said with a shrug. "As I said, he kept them as pets. Until Lily, not one of them saw the light of day after he turned them. He kept them on his family estate in England. They slept in a crypt with him during the day, and remained hidden inside during the night. Then he made a mistake and turned Lily. She was the granddaughter of his housekeeper. The woman

351

had worked for him for fifty years and had seen two children he'd done this to. When he turned Lily, she was enraged enough to approach someone on the European council. They went to look into it, but he got wind they were coming, killed her family, and fled on a boat for America."

"You lie," Lily growled and Jackie could feel the fine tremor of rage in the woman's hand. "He did not kill my family. And I was the first he'd turned so young. He only did it because he loved me so much."

Marguerite peered at her with pity. "He killed your grandmother, your mother, your father and your two younger sisters. He wiped out your whole family before he took you to the boat, Lily. Though I'm not surprised he didn't tell you."

"How would you know?" Lily snapped.

"Lucian," Marguerite said with a shrug. "I overheard him and my husband, Jean Claude, talking about it at the time."

"Well then they lied," Lily said furiously. "They all lied. He wouldn't have done that, and I was the only one he ever turned so young. He loved me."

"You were far from the first he turned so young," a deep voice growled.

Jackie winced as Lily's fingers dug into her arm as she turned them both so that they could keep Marguerite and the second speaker in view.

Christian was standing about ten feet to Marguerite's left, Jackie saw with surprise. He and the rest of the men had still been at Stephano's when Lily had taken her. Or she'd assumed they were, though it had been late enough they may have been back and in their rooms. Were the others here? she wondered.

"I was one of the council members sent to look into the matter," Christian said, drawing Jackie's attention back to the conversation.

"So was I," Marcus announced, appearing suddenly ten feet to Christian's left. He fell silent as Lily scrabbled backward, drawing Jackie with her in an effort to be able to keep an eye on all three people at once. The trio were forming a crescent before them. Lily was getting anxious and panicky.

"We were both there when the bodies were discovered in the crypt," Marcus explained. "There was one large empty coffin that we suspected William shared with you during the day, then four smaller coffins, each holding two or three bodies apiece. All told, there were ten beheaded young girls between the ages of ten and twelve judging by the size of them. If your grandmother had not told on him, you would have been the eleventh body there once he'd tired of you."

"Liar!" Lily yelled.

"Instead, he killed your family and fled to America with you," Christian took up the explanation again. "That was out of our area. We didn't follow, but we did send word to America via another ship, warning the council here of what he'd done and they began to hunt him."

"Hunting him down and killing him probably saved your life," Dante suddenly spoke, making his presence known.

"Lies, all lies!" Lily cried, turning again to include him in her view.

"The tale of what William did is well known in Europe."

Jackie wasn't the least bit surprised when Tommaso spoke up. She'd never seen one twin anywhere without the other. They were now forming almost a complete circle around them. It was impossible for Lily to watch them all at once.

"The two of you were able to hide out here for almost a year before they tracked you down. Isn't that true?" Tommaso asked.

Lily didn't speak, either to deny it, or affirm it. Jackie took that as a yes.

"And yet in that year he never bothered to teach you to feed yourself," Tommaso pointed out. "He kept you dependent on him, fed you himself, kept you away from food when eating it would have allowed you to mature normally, and didn't teach you any of the skills you needed to know to survive."

"He loved me! He took care of me!" Lily protested.

"He kept you completely dependent on him, Lily," Vincent said quietly behind them and Lily turned sharply, dragging Jackie with her. He met Jackie's gaze briefly, sending her a message of reassurance, then returned his gaze to Lily and said, "And he made sure you stayed that way. Look at you. Have you seen another like yourself in the hundred years since you were turned?"

"Shut up," Lily snapped. "You don't know anything about me."

"I do," Vincent countered. "I've known who you were from the day I hired you. I just figured you didn't want to talk about it and it was your business."

When Jackie's gaze turned sharply to him, asking why he hadn't mentioned this bit of history to her when she'd asked who might have something against him, he added, "I never imagined you were walking around hating me and anyone else related to the men who saved you from him."

"Saved me!" Lily snarled with fury. "They killed my sire and left me to fend for myself."

"I was told you fled," Vincent said quietly and Lily snorted.

"Of course I fled," she snarled. "They'd just brutally killed my lover. I had no idea what they would do to me."

"They would have taught you how to fend for yourself," Marguerite said softly, and Jackie glanced over to see that she'd moved closer.

"Sure they would have," Lily said bitterly. "Right after they staked me out in the sun for a day and let me bake too. William told me they would."

Vincent took a step forward and this time Lily seemed to notice. She suddenly whipped a half-sword out from under the back of the thick sweater she wore and held it to Jackie's throat.

Everyone went absolutely still.

"Let her go," Vincent said quietly. "Jackie has done nothing to you."

"No," Lily agreed. "But you love her and it would hurt you if I kill her."

"Kill me instead," Vincent suggested and Jackie scowled at him for the suggestion.

"I don't want to kill you," Lily said. "I want you to suffer like I have, for centuries, your true life mate gone and you left alone to carry on the best you can."

Jackie rolled her eyes at the repeated refrain and snapped, "You're getting boring."

Lily jerked a little with apparent shock, the blade cutting a thin line along Jackie's throat.

"What?" she asked with disbelief.

"You heard me. You're boring," Jackie repeated, uncaring at that point that she had a half-sword to her throat. "All this nonsense over nothing."

"Nothing?" Lily echoed. "They killed my William! I had no one! No one to feed me, no one to—"

"Lily, a hundred years ago they didn't have blood banks. No one fed anyone," Jackie said dryly. "They all had to hunt."

"William used to feed me. He brought men to me and controlled their minds while I fed, he—"

"Then he's the one you should be angry with," Jackie snapped impatiently. "He had a year to teach you how to survive before the council caught up to the two of you. A year! Vincent and the others taught me to take care of myself in days. Your William deliberately left you dependent and helpless. He wanted a child, a helpless dependent child he could control and abuse because he was a sick, twisted pedophile—"

"Shut up! William loved me!"

Lily was in a rage now and Jackie realized she'd gone too far. On the other hand, since she already had, there was little sense in back-pedaling and she was too damned angry to care. She snorted with open derision at her claim, then said, "Grow up. William didn't love you. If he'd loved you he'd have taught you what you needed to know like Vincent taught me. He'd have wanted to be sure you could take care of yourself . . . Vincent doesn't try to control me or make me dependent on him. *That* is love," she repeated and the moment the words were out of her mouth, she knew they were true. Vincent did love her. And she loved him. And dammit, she wasn't going to die here today. She was done being the victim.

Lily was still in her thoughts and caught wind of her intentions at once, but it was already too late. Following instinct more than anything else, Jackie grabbed the blade with her hand, ignoring the way it sliced into her skin as she drew it away from her throat. Her fingers would heal, everything would heal, but decapitation. Aware of that, she held on to the blade firmly and rammed her elbow into Lily's chest.

The little woman stumbled back, but held onto her half-sword. Jackie winced as it cut deeper into her hand before she let it go and leapt back out of the way herself.

The moment she was free, Vincent was at her side, dragging her a safe distance away as Christian and the others converged on Lily. Within seconds they had her disarmed and held firmly between Dante and Tommaso. Lily screamed and struggled furiously, but to no avail.

"What will they do with her?" Jackie asked as she watched the twins drag her toward the path that led through the trees to the street.

"She'll go before the council. They'll decide her fate," Christian answered.

Jackie frowned, knowing that didn't bode well for Lily. On the other hand, the girl was like a rabid dog. She'd killed innocent people and would have killed more. Her time with William had obviously twisted her mind. Besides, she reminded herself, while Lily looked like a girl, she was actually over a hundred years old and had said herself that she'd gnawed on children every chance she'd got.

"Give me your hand."

Jackie glanced to the side with surprise as Tiny appeared with a first-aid kit.

"They made me wait in the woods," he told her with obvious disgust as he began to bind her bleeding hand. "They said I'd be safer there."

Jackie smiled faintly at his disgruntlement and patted his arm soothingly, then glanced at Vincent. He was watching with concern as Tiny worked. Jackie stared at him for a minute, then blurted, "I love you."

Vincent blinked, then breathed, "Thank God." Bending his head, he pressed a kiss gently to her lips, and whispered, "I love you too."

"That should do," Tiny announced, finished with her hand. He lifted his head and eyed her solemnly. "I'm glad you're all right."

"As am I," Marguerite said joining them. She smiled and said, "Welcome to the family, dear."

"Thank you," Jackie murmured shyly.

"Well . . ." Marguerite raised an eyebrow at Vincent. "I guess now you can start up your plays again."

He shrugged. "Stephano and Neil can make that decision, I couldn't care less. I'm not really interested in the theatre anymore. Four hundred years is long enough in one career. I think it's time for a career change."

Jackie raised her eyebrows. "What will you do?"

"Actually," he said slowly, "I find myself rather interested in what you do. Being a private eye seems interesting."

Jackie glanced at him with surprise, but before she could comment, Marguerite agreed, "Me too. I found it challenging, like a puzzle. With Jean Claude gone and the kids all married and starting families, I've been trying to decide on something to do as a career and now I know what it can be." She smiled at Jackie. "I could help Tiny."

"Help Tiny?" Jackie blinked. "Why would Tiny need help?"

"Well, you have a lot to learn in the next little while, dear, survival skills like how to control minds and so on. The faster you learn them, the better. You should concentrate on that," Marguerite pointed out gently. "Besides, if the two of you are going to marry, you'll want to take a honeymoon. It will leave Tiny without a partner. I'd be happy to be his partner and help him run your company. It will give me a purpose."

"Do you do jobs in Europe?" Christian asked suddenly while Jackie was still gaping at Marguerite.

Blinking, she closed her mouth and glanced at him with confusion. "Europe?"

"Yes. If you do, I have a job for you there."

"What sort of job is it?" Marguerite asked curiously.

Christian hesitated and then said, "Finding out who my mother is."

"Your mother?" Jackie echoed blankly. The immortal was over five hundred years old.

Christian nodded.

"Oh, I could do that!" Marguerite looked excited as she glanced to Tiny. She added, "We could, couldn't we, Tiny?"

She didn't wait for him to answer, but slid her arm through Christian's and began to lead him toward the path through the trees.

"You must tell me everything you know," she murmured. She glanced back to say, "Come along, Tiny, you have more experience in this than I. You know better the kinds of questions we should ask."

Tiny hesitated briefly and glanced toward Jackie. When she just shrugged her shoulders helplessly, he sighed and hurried after the pair.

Jackie watched them go and shook her head. "How could anyone solve that mystery? It isn't like they kept good records five hundred years ago. Surely his father could tell him who she was?"

"Julius has refused to speak about it for five hundred years," Marcus announced, then added, "Marguerite is the best person for the job."

"Why?" she asked curiously.

Marcus merely smiled, then turned to follow the others.

Jackie glanced to Vincent in question, but he didn't seem to understand it any more than she.

"I love you," Vincent whispered, distracting her.

Jackie smiled as she leaned into his embrace. "I love you, too."

"So, my true life mate," Vincent slipped his arms around her.

"Are you really sure about this?" Jackie peered up at him uncertainly. She knew how she felt, but was so afraid of making a mistake.

"Aren't you?" he asked quietly.

"Yes," she said solemnly. "I love you more than I ever thought it possible to love another. But," she hesitated, then blurted, "I know Marguerite's story and how horrible it can turn out when you choose the wrong life mate and I would never want you unhappy because of me."

Vincent smiled and brushed a finger lightly across her brow, rubbing away the worry on her forehead. "Jackie, I've been alive for more than four hundred years. I've met millions of women and slept with thousands. I had a long time to discover what kind of woman can make me happy and whom I could spend eternity with." He cupped her face in his hands and peered solemnly into her face as he added, "You're that woman."

Jackie felt tears well in her eyes as her heart gave a pang in her chest. She now understood the phrase to love someone so much it hurt. Leaning up, she pressed her lips to his and kissed him with all the love she felt. Vincent kissed her back, but all too soon pulled away.

"So, the wedding," he said, turning her to follow the others. "I was thinking Vegas."

"Vegas?" she asked with surprise.

"Yeah." He smiled. "An Elvis look-alike minister, me in a rhinestone suit and blue suede shoes. You in—" he paused, eyebrows rising as Jackie began to laugh. "What? You don't have any family and this cuts out the long delay of a big wedding."

"True," she acknowledged with a smile as he urged her to walk again.

"And we can have a big reception afterward up in Canada at Aunt Marguerite's. She already offered her house. We'll fly Tiny and your other friends up," he promised, then smiled and said, "Then we can honeymoon in . . ."

Jackie raised her eyebrows when he hesitated. "Yes?"

"Well, I was thinking maybe Disneyland?" he said hopefully and Jackie could have just kissed him he looked so adorable.

"I've never been to Disney," she said with a grin, then shook her head. "Life is going to be interesting with you, isn't it, my love?"

"Eternity is going to be interesting for both of us," Vincent assured her, and paused to kiss her again.

Why Do Women Love Inappropriate Men?

*Y*ou know who you are, but perhaps you won't admit to it. You're the wild child drawn to the quiet, bookish guy reading *The Economist;* or maybe you're the reserved society lady who secretly loves nothing better than a ride on a Harley clutching a leather clad biker; or perhaps you're human and he's a vampire . . . But any way you look at it, there's no greater thrill or challenge for you than being with someone you know you shouldn't.

Well you're not the only one . . .

In these four upcoming Avon Romance Superleaders, the old adage that opposites attract never rang more true. Enjoy!

Coming May 2006

THE
Care and Feeding
OF
UNMARRIED MEN

By Christie Ridgway

Palm Springs's "Party Girl" Eve Caruso has finally met her match. "The Preacher," aka Nash Cargill, is in town to protect his starlet sister from a stalker, only to realize that he'd rather "stalk" Eve! But can this granddaughter of a notorious mobster be tamed?

The rain was pouring down on the Palm Springs desert in biblical proportions the night he stalked into the spa's small bar. He was a big man, tall, brawny, the harsh planes of his face unsoftened by his wet, dark hair. Clint Eastwood minus forty years and plus forty pounds of pure muscle. Water dripped from the hem of his ankle-length black slicker to puddle on the polished marble floor beside his reptilian-skinned cowboy boots.

She flashed on one of the lessons her father had drilled into her. *A girl as beautiful as you and with a name like yours should always be on guard for the snake in Paradise.*

And as the stranger took another step forward, Eve Caruso heard a distinctive hiss.

The sound had come from her, though, the hiss of a quick, indrawn breath, because the big man put every one of her instincts on alert. But she'd also been taught at the school of Never Showing Fear, so she pressed her damp palms against the thighs of her tight white jeans, then scooted around the bar.

"Can I help you?" she asked, positioning her body between him and the lone figure seated on the eighth and last stool.

The stranger's gaze flicked to Eve.

She'd attended a casual dinner party earlier that evening—escorted by her trusty tape recorder so she wouldn't forget a detail of the meal or the guest list, which would appear in her society column—and hadn't bothered to change before taking on the late shift in the Kona Kai's tiny lounge. Her jeans were topped with a honey-beige silk T-shirt she'd belted at her hips. Around her neck was a tangle of turquoise-and-silver necklaces, some of which she'd owned since junior high. Her cowboy boots were turquoise too, and hand-tooled. Due to pressing financial concerns, she'd recently considered selling them on eBay—and maybe she still would, she thought, as his gaze fell to the pointy tips and her toes flexed into involuntary fetal curls.

He took in her flashy boots, then moved on to her long legs, her demi-bra-ed breasts, her shoulder-blade-length blonde hair and blue eyes. She'd been assessed by a thousand men, assessed, admired, desired, and since she was twelve-and-a-half years old, she'd been unfazed by all of them. Her looks were her gift, her luck, her tool, and tonight, a useful distraction in keeping the dark man from noticing the less showy but more famous face of the younger woman sitting by herself at the bar.

Eve placed a hand on an empty stool and gestured with the other behind her back. *Get out, get away,* she signaled, all the while keeping her gaze on the stranger and letting a slow smile break over her face. "What would you like?" she asked, softly releasing the words one by one into the silence, like lingerie dropping onto plush carpeting.

"Sorry, darlin', I'm not here for you," he said, then he and his Southern drawl brushed past her, leaving only the scent of rain and rejection in their wake.

Eve froze in—shock? dismay? fear? *"I'm not here for you."*

What the hell was up with that?

Coming June 2006

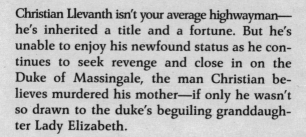

Her Officer and Gentleman

By Karen Hawkins

Christian Llevanth isn't your average highwayman—
he's inherited a title and a fortune. But he's
unable to enjoy his newfound status as he continues to seek revenge and close in on the
Duke of Massingale, the man Christian be-
lieves murdered his mother—if only he wasn't
so drawn to the duke's beguiling granddaughter Lady Elizabeth.

"I have no wish to fall in love." Beth declared.

"Which is exactly why you are so vulnerable to
it."

"Nonsense. That will never happen to me. Beatrice,
you seem to forget that I am far too pragmatic—"

"May I have this dance?" came a deep voice from
behind Beth.

She started to answer, but caught sight of Beatrice's face. Her cousin stood, mouth open, eyes
wide.

Beth turned her head . . . and found herself looking up into the face of the most incredibly handsome man she'd ever seen. He was a full head taller

than her, his shoulders broad, but it was his face that caused her to flush head to toe. Black hair spilled over his forehead, his jaw firm, his mouth masculine and yet sensual. His eyes called the most attention; they were the palest green, thickly lashed, and decidedly masculine.

Her heart thudded, her palms grew damp, and her stomach tightened in the most irksome way. Her entire body felt laden. What on earth was the matter with her? Had she eaten something ill for dinner that evening? Perchance a scallop, for they never failed to make her feel poorly.

Unaware his effect was being explained away on a shellfish, he smiled, his eyes sparkling down at her with wicked humor. "I believe I have forgotten to introduce myself. Allow me." He bowed. "I am Viscount Westerville."

"Ah!" Beatrice said, breaking into movement as if she'd been shoved from behind. "Westerville! One of Rochester's—ah—"

"Yes," the viscount said smoothly. He bowed, his gaze still riveted on Beth.

Before she knew what he was about, he had captured her limp hand and brought it to his lips, pressing a kiss to her fingers, his eyes sparkling at her intimately.

"Well, Lady Elizabeth?" he asked, his breath warm on her hand. "Shall we dance?"

Coming July 2006

♥

A Bite to Remember

By Lynsay Sands ♥

When Vincent Argeneau's production of *Dracula: The Musical* closes, he suspects sabotage and calls in private detective Jackie Morrisey. He quickly sees that she's more than just a tempting neck, but unfortunately, Jackie doesn't have a thing for vampires . . . that is, until she meets Vincent.

♥

Vincent Argeneau forced one eyelid upward and peered around the dark room where he slept. He saw his office, managing to make out the shape of his desk by the light coming from the hallway. Oh yes, he'd fallen asleep on the couch in his office waiting for Bastien to call him back.

"Vincent?"

"Yeah?" He sat up and glanced around for the owner of that voice, then realized it was coming through his answering machine on the desk. Giving his head a shake, he got to his feet and stumbled across the room, snatching up the cordless phone as he dropped into his desk chair. "Bastien?"

"Vincent? Sorry to wake you, cousin. I waited as late as I could before calling."

Vincent grunted and leaned back in the chair, running his free hand over his face. "What time is it?"

"Five p.m. here. I guess that makes it about two there," Bastien said apologetically.

Vincent scrubbed his hand over his face again, then reached out to turn on his desk lamp. Blinking in the increased light, he said, "I'm up. Were you able to get a hold of that private detective company you said was so good?"

"That's why I couldn't call any later than this. They're on their way. In fact, their plane was scheduled to land at LAX fifteen minutes ago."

"Jesus!" Vincent sat up abruptly in his seat. "That was fast."

"Jackie doesn't waste time. I explained the situation to her and she booked a flight right away. Fortunately for you, she'd just finished a big job for me and was able to put off and delegate whatever else she had on the roster."

"Wow," Vincent murmured, then frowned as he realized what Bastien had said. "She? The detective's a woman?"

"Yes, she is, and she's good. Really good. She'll track down your saboteur and have this whole thing cleaned up for you in no time."

"If you say so," Vincent said quietly. "Thanks, Bastien. I appreciate it."

"Okay, I guess I'll let you go wake yourself up before they arrive."

"Yeah, okay. Hey—" Vincent paused and glanced

toward the curtained windows as a knock sounded
at his front door. Frowning, he stood and headed
out of the office, taking the cordless phone with him.
"Hang on. There's someone at the door."

"Is it the blood delivery?" Bastien asked on the
phone.

"Umm . . . no," Vincent said into the phone, but
his mind was taken up with running over the duo
before him. He'd never set his eyes on such an unlikely pair. The woman was blonde, the man a brunette. She was extremely short and curvy, he was a
great behemoth of a man. She was dressed in a black
business suit with a crisp white blouse under it, he
wore casual cords and a sweater in pale cream. They
were a study in contrasts.

"Vincent Argeneau?" the woman asked.

When he nodded, she stuck out her hand. "I'm
Jackie Morrisey and this is Tiny McGraw. I believe
Bastien called you about us?"

Vincent stared at her hand, but rather than take it,
he pushed the door closed and turned away as he
lifted the phone back to his ear. "Bastien she's *mortal!*"

"Did you just slam the door in Jackie's face?" Bastien asked with amazement. "I heard the slam, Vincent. Jesus! Don't be so damned rude."

"Hello!" he said impatiently. "She's *mortal*, Bastien. Bad enough she's female, but I need someone
who knows about our 'special situation' to deal with
this problem. She—"

"Jackie *does* know," Bastien said dryly. "Did you
think I'd send you an uninitiated mortal? Have a
little faith." A sigh traveled down the phone line.
"She has a bit of an attitude when it comes to our

kind, but Jackie's the best in the business and she knows about us. Now open the goddamned door for the woman."

"But she's mortal and . . . a girl," Vincent pointed out, still not happy with the situation.

"I'm hanging up, Vincent." Bastien hung up.

Vincent scowled at the phone and almost dialed him back, but then thought better of it and moved back to the door. He needed help tracking down the saboteur out to ruin him. He'd give Ms. Morrisey and her giant a chance. If they sorted out the mess for him, fine. If not, he could hold it over Bastien's head for centuries.

Grinning at the idea, Vincent reached for the doorknob.

Never A Lady

By Jacquie D'Alessandro

Colin Oliver, Viscount Sutton, is in need of a wife—a demure, proper English paragon to provide him with an heir . . . everything Alexandra Larchmont is not. She's brazen, a fortune-teller and former pickpocket. Clearly they're all wrong for each other . . . Aren't they?

From *The London Times* Society page:

Lord and Lady Malloran's annual soiree promises to be more exciting this year than ever as the entertaining fortune-telling services of the mysterious, much-sought-after Madame Larchmont have been secured. As Madame's provocative predictions have an uncanny knack for accuracy, her presence at any party guarantees its success. Also attending will be the very eligible Viscount Sutton, who recently returned to London after an extended stay at his Cornwall estate and is rumored to be looking for a wife. Wouldn't it be delicious if Madame Larchmont told him whom it is in the cards for him to marry?

Alexandra Larchmont looked up from the tarot cards she'd just shuffled and was about to deal, intending to smile at Lady Malloran, the hostess for the evening's elegant soiree where Alex's fortune-telling services were in high demand. Just as Alex's lips curved upward, however, the crowd of milling party guests separated a bit and her attention was caught by the sight of a tall, dark-haired man. And the smile died on her lips.

Panic rippled along her nerve endings and her muscles tensed, for in spite of the fact that three years had passed since she'd last seen him, she recognized him instantly. Under the best of circumstances, he wouldn't be a man easily forgotten—and the circumstances of their last encounter could never be described as "best." While she didn't know his name, his image was permanently etched in her memory.

She dearly wished that's where he'd remained—not standing a mere dozen feet away. Dear God, if he recognized *her*, everything she'd worked so long and hard for would be destroyed. Did he normally move in these exalted circles? If so, more than her livelihood was at risk—her very existence was threatened.

Her every instinct screamed at her to flee, but she remained frozen in place, unable to look away from him. As if trapped in a horrible, slow-moving nightmare, her gaze wandered down his form. Impeccably dressed in formal black attire, his dark hair gleamed under the glow of the dozens of candles flickering in the overhead chandelier. He held a crystal champagne glass, and she involuntarily shivered, rubbing her damp palms over her upper arms, recalling in vivid detail the strength in those large hands as they'd gripped her, preventing her escape. Out of necessity, she'd learned at a young age how to master her fears, but this man had alarmed and unnerved her as no one else ever had, before or since their single encounter.

The tarot cards had repeatedly warned her about him—the dark-haired stranger with the vivid green eyes who would wreak havoc with her existence—years before she'd ever seen him that first time. The cards had also predicted she'd someday see him again. Unfortunately the cards hadn't prepared her for someday being *now*.

Looking up, she noted with a sickening sense of alarm that his gaze moved slowly over the crowd. In a matter of seconds that gaze would fall upon her.

USA Today Bestselling Author

Jacquie D'Alessandro
Never A Lady

Alex can't believe her ears. Two men are discussing murder as if they were contemplating a day at the races! Then the only thing that could be worse happens—she runs into Colin Oliver. She had hoped that he'd have forgotten their little run in five years ago, but no such luck. And he's now accusing her of something underhanded. Of all the nerve! But she's going to need some help if she's to save this unknown victim from death, and unfortunately for Colin, he's just the man to help her. If he can stop looking at her as a scrumptious dessert, ready to be devoured. Because they're all wrong for each other. Aren't they?

PROWL THE NIGHT WITH
RACHEL MORGAN AND

KIM HARRISON

DEAD WITCH WALKING

0-06-057296-5 • $7.99 US/$10.99 Can

When the creatures of the night gather, whether to
hide, to hunt, or to feed, it's Rachel Morgan's job to keep
things civilized. A bounty hunter and witch with serious
sex appeal and attitude, she'll bring them back alive,
dead . . . or undead.

THE GOOD, THE BAD, AND THE UNDEAD

0-06-057297-3 • $7.99 US/$10.99 Can

Rachel Morgan can handle the leather-clad vamps and
even tangle with a cunning demon or two. But a serial
killer who feeds on the experts in the most dangerous
kind of black magic is definitely pressing the limits.

EVERY WHICH WAY BUT DEAD

0-06-057299-X • $7.99 US/$10.99 Can

Rachel must take a stand in the raging war to control
Cincinnati's underworld because the demon who helped
her put away its former vampire kingpin is coming to
collect his due.

A FISTFUL OF CHARMS

0-06-078819-4 • $7.99 US/$10.99 Can

A mortal lover who abandoned Rachel has returned,
haunted by his secret past. And there are those willing to
destroy the Hollows to get what Nick possesses.

www.kimharrison.net